MW01089401

WHAT
WILL
PEOPLE
THINK

WHAT WILL PEOPLE THINK

?

A NOVEL

Sara Hamdan

Henry Holt and Company
New York

Henry Holt and Company
Publishers since 1866
120 Broadway
New York, New York 10271
www.henryholt.com

Henry Holt® and 🅗® are registered trademarks of Macmillan
Publishing Group, LLC.

Library of Congress Cataloging-in-Publication Data

Names: Hamdan, Sara, author.
Title: What will people think? : a novel / Sara Hamdan.
Description: First edition. | New York : Henry Holt and
    Company, 2025.
Identifiers: LCCN 2024023663 | ISBN 9781250329813
    (hardcover) | ISBN 9781250329820 (ebook)
Subjects: LCGFT: Novels.
Classification: LCC PS3608.A54996 W47 2025 |
    DDC 813/.6—dc23/eng/20240812
LC record available at https://lccn.loc.gov/2024023663

Our books may be purchased in bulk for promotional, educational,
or business use. Please contact your local bookseller or the
Macmillan Corporate and Premium Sales Department at
(800) 221-7945, extension 5442, or by e-mail at
MacmillanSpecialMarkets@macmillan.com.

First Edition 2025

Designed by Meryl Sussman Levavi

Printed in the United States of America

1   3   5   7   9   10   8   6   4   2

This is a work of fiction. All of the characters, organizations, and
events portrayed in this novel either are products of the author's
imagination or are used fictitiously.

For my family,
with all my love

When you read something beautiful, you find co-existence; it breaks down walls.

—Mahmoud Darwish, Palestinian poet

If you're creating anything at all, it's really dangerous to care about what people think.

—Kristen Wiig, American comedian and actress

CHAPTER

1

"You're on in five," said the man with the goatee.

In the darkness backstage, I switched off my phone. I needed to stop endlessly scrolling through Jackson's social media posts instead of rehearsing my opening. A private, airless ritual. By actively telling myself not to think about him, that was all I did.

Breathing in slowly, with my eyes closed, I listened to the emcee tell the audience about the exits, toilets, and absolutely-no-recording rule.

My mind wandered back to Jackson, picturing him in the audience having come straight from work, with a loosened collar and a navy blazer flung on the chair next to him. A slow smile spread over my face, imagining the shock light up his eyes at seeing me work the stage. Maybe one day, when I was ready, I'd have the courage to invite him to a show.

I'll obsess over him later with a tub of ice cream, I thought, shaking nervous energy off my hands. *Right now, it's time to shine.*

I peered through the curtain. Although it was the early crowd, it was a full house. I was seconds away from the spotlight. My stomach flip-flopped.

"Put your hands together for . . . Miaaaa!" boomed Mr. Goatee.

I licked my lips, stepped up to the microphone, and greeted the silhouettes through the glare of the light.

"I know, I'm surprised I made it on time, too. I was almost late, because I'm Arab and we had to prepare a meal for twenty people at home . . . because *one* family friend said she *might* come by and say hello," I began. "That's how my people roll. Like, literally *roll*, because we overfeed each other to show respect. Then we work it off by shouting at each other about very important things like politics, marriage, and DJ Khaled."

I paused, reveling in the ice-breaking chuckles, as elbows thudded on tables and people leaned forward to rest faces on cupped hands. My eyes adjusted to the brightness of the spotlight, and the silhouettes became more defined. I could see wet rings already forming on tables from cold beer mugs.

"We're a little too comfortable around a dining table. We'll happily stay seated until it's time for the next meal. Want to know where Arabs are *least* comfortable?" I paused. "Passport control," I whispered loudly into the microphone.

Heads bobbed in agreement.

It was a good thing this venue strictly prohibited recordings. It was about to get heated. I smiled in anticipation.

"What's worse than being asked to step aside to the 'brown people waiting room'? I have a story for you, New York." I smiled again, raising my finger in the air. "See, I'm nearly twenty-five, but I look young for my age when I don't have all this going on."

I gestured to my black high heels, then to my made-up eyes and red-lipped pout. With an exaggerated wave, I traced my curves in the air and then let my hand rest on my protruding hip. Catcalls ensued. My cheeks felt warm. I did a little curtsy.

"The last time a passport control officer winked at me, when

I stepped away and flipped the pages, I discovered his wink had come with . . . a Winnie. The Pooh. Stamp. Give me a 'random' security check any day over that!" I pretended to put on a glove and imitated a TSA agent with a George W. Bush accent. "Ma'am, believe me, this is for your own protection."

I shielded my eyes from the spotlight, smiling as if I had a hammock stuck in my mouth as laughter washed over me. It felt holy.

"It's not all bad. To be honest, people often mistake me for Brazilian, Italian, Kardashian—basically, anything off-white-ian," I continued, giving a thumbs-up. "I have to confess that sometimes I do fake an accent, you know. It helps get me into the cool places. Definitely not an Arabic accent, though. I want to get in, not get blacklisted."

With a lower, breathy voice, I leaned so close to the microphone I could smell the metal. My real life felt so far away right then, belonging to some other woman in another time. Cradling the microphone in both hands, I drawled: *"Hola,* I am Valeria, I come from Colombia for one week for *festival de la salsa!* I come in, please? *Muchas gracias, papi . . ."*

I winked at a man in the front row.

"You bet there's no ID needed there!" I said. "Better than an Arab telling the bouncer 'I hear za barty here iz blowing ub! Let me come inside—I set za roof on fire for you.'"

They were right there with me, celebrating my naked imperfections as I stood on that dinky stage and stripped my soul bare. It was somehow easier to be so openly myself from up there, bathed in the spotlight and silliness, with my voice raised onstage and speaking to a room full of strangers, than at a restaurant trying to blend in with friends.

"Such a naughty audience, laughing away at an Arab," I added in a thick, grandmotherly accent, wagging my finger at the dark faces in the crowd. "Thank you for laughing with me, so I don't bomb onstage. No, no, relax, I didn't say there *is* a bomb onstage! I'm just saying that I killed it tonight. Killed the set—*the set!*"

I pointed at a blond guy in a sky-blue T-shirt: "Just thought I'd clarify for Jim Bob here, who looks like he joined us from a cornfield in Kentucky."

Applause burst throughout the room like confetti. From within the sunny spotlight, I saw people standing and clapping. One woman was wiping tears from her eyes, her shoulders shaking with laughter.

"That's my time—thank you for being such a fantastic audience," I shouted with a wave of my hand. "My name is Mia. And you won't find me on social media easily because I'm busy hiding . . . No, not from the cops . . . From my nosy relatives!"

I shimmied in a spirited belly dance off the stage to the beat of the applause. Back in the greenroom, I dissolved into a happy dance in a rush of euphoria.

Patrick Ryan, an Irish up-and-comer working the same amateur comedy circuit, high-fived me as he took his turn in the spotlight. I smiled, listening to the opening that we had sharpened together over the past few weeks, hidden backstage before shows, breathlessly repeating the lines until they sounded unrehearsed and spontaneous.

That was the beauty of my friendship with Patrick and the other comedians: we just talked about punch lines and sets, our conversations punctuated by unscripted laughter. There was no room to discuss our lives outside the comedy club. No quiet pauses, no heads cocked to the side with concern, no pitying looks. None of that in this happy bubble.

There were two new faces backstage. I nodded hello, basking in their praise and pats on the shoulder.

A blue packet of Chips Ahoy! lay open on a rickety table in the greenroom, next to bottles of room-temperature water for the "talent." I reached for an open pack of wet wipes. Back at the makeup mirror in the corner, flanked by parallel columns of light bulbs, I looked myself square in the eyes. With a sigh, I rubbed the red lips, mascara, and glitter off my face.

I took my bag out from underneath the vanity desk, swapping the black stiletto heels for demure gray ballet flats. One by one, I fastened the buttons of a black cardigan over my tank top, despite my post-show sweat. I held my gaze in the mirror, turning my face left and right, thinking my tousled hair looked like wild laughter. My heartbeat slowly returned to normal as I weaved strands of my rebellious curls into a tight braid. I winked at my prim reflection: *Welcome back, Mia Almas.*

She returned a half-assed smile. After taking off my chunky gold hoop earrings, the transformation was complete. I missed her already, the free spirit onstage who wasn't afraid to shine brighter than the spotlight. I just needed to find a way to make her better friends with the other Mia: the responsible one who always turned assignments in on time no matter what life threw at her, who helped her grandmother in the kitchen even though she hated cooking, the version of Mia who had become an expert at hiding grief and pride behind the sweetest of smiles.

Mr. Goatee came up to me with a smile and a piece of paper.

"Good work, Mia. I think this is from a talent scout," he said, handing me the paper. "Dude in a suit. One of those big agencies or TV stations. I hope that's an audition invite in there."

I unfolded the paper and found a few words in scratchy writing.

Mia—

Nice delivery. Animated. Needs depth. This is all sur-face. Dig deeper, make the pain funny. I hope to see you again—and really bring it next time.

Got my eye on you.

—C.B.

There was no name. Just initials.

I reread it a few times, hoping for missed clues, then folded the paper. I felt it burn in my back pocket as I made my way toward the exit. No gaze trailed me as I walked right by the audience, who were laughing at Patrick's jokes. I continued straight out the front entrance of the Greenwich Village Comedy Club, unable to smother the pride that blossomed inside me at getting noticed up onstage.

A small smile tugged at my lips. This person, C.B., wouldn't have bothered with feedback if they hadn't spotted real talent. Right?

Dig deeper, though? When it's already hard enough being me? I thought, walking up the black steps. *And anyway, what is the point . . . ?*

Two people coming in late held the double doors open for me. The air was a few degrees cooler than the underground bar, and I was grateful for the warmth of my cardigan. MacDougal Street was full of chatter. I loved this part of Greenwich Village—this street alone was a medley of falafel stalls, a chess club, and ice cream parlors. Voices rose high above the din of blaring horns and music spilling out from a sports bar nearby as people weaved their way toward the hot spots dotted along the street. It was a wonder any cars could get through at all.

I sidestepped around a small crowd outside the Comedy Cellar, a few doors down, likely waiting for someone famous to perform that night. The last time Jackson had scored tickets for all of us from work, Aziz Ansari was the surprise guest.

Maybe my name could be on the Comedy Cellar's secret roster one day, I thought, sending a little prayer up toward the club's colorful block-letter sign. My father used to always say that comedians are the true philosophers of our time. I smiled to myself as I walked past three women making repeated O shapes with scarlet lips, blowing smoke rings into the cool night air. They looked like fish in an aquarium.

But probably not, I told myself.

As I walked past them, I took the folded note out of my back pocket, crumpled it, and threw it in a nearby trash can.

The version of Mia who had just performed onstage, who had nonchalantly passed by those girls blowing smoke rings and holding drinks with pink umbrellas, was already disappearing. She was regressing to a different kind of normal, one that resided inside a completely different kind of bubble.

Mia Almas had to come back now in full force, which always made me feel a little sad. I thought of my grandmother, most likely sitting in the dim kitchen with a single lamp on, table already set for dinner, prayer beads in hand. My grandfather noisily flipping pages of a newspaper, grunting and mumbling to himself.

Just a little longer, I thought, breathing in the crisp autumn air and watching people laugh as they sauntered into bars. Past the string of comedy clubs, I paused at the busy intersection on MacDougal and West Third Street. I wanted to lose myself in the crisscross of streets in this zigzag neighborhood, with names that sounded like they came out of a British spy novel.

I loved the faded red and orange brick buildings on Bleecker Street, Carmine Street, and Winston Churchill Square, sprinkled with loud bars and bright sushi joints. They felt a world away from the orderly grid system of my neighborhood in Morningside Heights, where each street was tame, a number with no name, a straight or perpendicular line.

Tonight had been a huge success. I deserved to hold on to that feeling. I walked a little farther along West Third, closing my eyes for a moment beneath the flapping indigo flag of the Blue Note Jazz Club. Above the street noises, I could hear the thump of a faraway bass and the trill of a piano of a band rehearsing for the night ahead. I breathed in the fall air, fragrant with the scent of cheesy pizza from the place with the really good marinara sauce on the corner.

"Hey! What's a girl like you doing in a place like this?" came a playful, familiar voice. "No, seriously, what are you doing here?"

Katie.

CHAPTER

2

"Do my eyes deceive me?" Katie went on, batting her eyelashes and putting a hand on my arm in false concern. "Are you—dare I say—here to have some fun? Or did an article drag you out to the bars of Greenwich Village, you workaholic?"

I didn't like lying to Katie. I looked into her warm, earthy eyes. We were more than just classmates turned colleagues. During college, she was once a keeper of late-night secrets; we'd shared tears in bathroom stalls and laughing fits in department stores over frilly dresses. I just wasn't ready to let her—or anyone else—in on my little stage-time secret yet.

"Yep, you got me," I lied, putting my hands up like I was speaking to the police. "A Love Unfiltered column takes place right where we are standing. I needed to see if you could really hear the sounds of the band from the street."

"God, you're thorough." She sighed, peering through the window at the band practicing onstage at the Blue Note. "Ever heard of this thing called Google? Maybe I would be thorough, too, if

I had your job instead of fact-checking cushions and curtains for *Designing Interiors*. Drink to numb my pain?"

I checked my watch and nodded. I let her guide me while she chatted about the horror of someone at work using the micro-wave to heat up fish. Other than teasing me about my crush on Jackson, she liked to talk about herself and books and theorize on modern relationships. The spotlight was always trained on her.

And that worked for me.

After my father died when I was fifteen, I shielded myself from the world, hiding out in libraries and befriending characters from books instead of actual people. School hallways full of chatter would dull to a respectful hush when I walked by with my heavy backpack slung over one shoulder. Teachers would ask if I needed extra time to turn in papers. That boy from the grade above who used to smile at me would keep giving me puppy dog eyes.

I was an eggshell they passed around carefully with soft words. Until the cracks formed.

My grief had been part of a larger, citywide mourning for the city of New York after 9/11. Soon after that black day, Robbie the Class Clown took a big piece of orange fabric in art class and put a makeshift hijab around my curls. The class had filled with snickers.

It was the first time I realized that I was the only Arab girl in my grade.

When the fabric fell to the floor, I found a yellow Post-it in the center with the words "Mia + Bin Laden" in a heart.

"Oh, come on, it's just a joke," Robbie had said as the teacher looked up from her desk at the hooting and laughter. "Lighten up."

Next was the note tucked in my locker that read "Terrorist Hotline," along with my phone number. It was only after the third incident—when someone put raw bacon on my desk first thing in the morning—that the school decided to issue a warning against bullying.

But it was too late. As I remained in the shadow of mourning my father, my social existence was chipped away with each small act.

After that, I retreated fully into my books. Each day, I felt as if I was wearing a school uniform beaded with gray grief and shame, even when I made an effort to talk about normal things like boys and makeup with girls I had known for years. I stopped getting invited to birthday parties and sleepovers anyway. I wondered what they talked about when I wasn't there.

Poor Mia, losing her mother as a baby and now her father. It's just too much.

Do you think her parents were foreign spies or something?

Should we invite her over for a Sunday roast, or will seeing us as a normal family make her feel worse?

Over time, even small kindnesses introduced a layer of pain I didn't know how to deal with.

So I didn't.

I skipped prom, hiding from their prying eyes, only to get a little wild when I finally got to college. Even though I still lived with my grandparents to save money, there was a delicious sense of reinvention in the elegant corridors of Columbia. Nobody knew me, so I could re-create myself. I could be whomever I wanted to be.

When Katie and I met in English Lit 101, we became fast friends, with matching winged black eyeliner a la Amy Winehouse. While I stayed sober, I learned that loud music was a blissful escape from my mind . . . from myself. Katie brought a much-needed dose of mischief and helped me let loose. Implicitly, she understood that with my fun, partying side came the Dark Days, when I shut out the world, playing old videos and reading chats saved on an old BlackBerry, in a room with the curtains drawn.

Most nights, we partied together in museums across Manhattan at raves that took place after-hours. My grandparents praised me for "studying" in libraries all night. I would come home before dawn, creep into the laundry room in the basement of our building, and wash my clothes to rid them of the scent of cigarettes, sweat, and traces of makeup. I would sit on top of the humming washing machine with a book and a smile until it beeped.

"Which bar? Do you care?" Katie asked now as we surveyed our options on West Third Street.

How many nights had she and I spent perusing dive bars on busy streets like these during college, sidestepping loud groups as laughter filled the air? She pointed at the neon blue sign of the Fat Black Pussycat bar across the street from the jazz club. The sky was darkening, and soft streetlights came on outside. We crossed to the other side of the street after a yellow taxi whizzed past, angrily beeping at pedestrians who were in the way.

"I've only got ten minutes," I warned her. "Can't stay out late."

"I'll take what I can get," she said with a wink. "Leave you wanting more of me."

I studied her for a moment, wondering how she would react if I told her I had just performed onstage wearing more makeup than she had at the company Christmas party. I knew she would be happy for me, intrigued and excited even, but I still wasn't ready to unmask that part of myself yet.

I had discovered that thinking about comedy, planning my sets, performing—all of it—relieved me a little of the heavy shadows in my life. As if my stand-up were a secret affair, I wanted to stay in this happy, private space with it.

And with an audience that is prohibited from recording any video or posting on social media . . .

Holding my elbow, she steered me past the NYU kids inside the Fat Black Pussycat. Comedians often hung out here after sets at the Comedy Cellar. I scanned the place for familiar faces as I followed her. I watched guys turn their heads to check her out as she walked past.

Katie chose a booth near the red pool table, her face aglow from the light of a neon sign above a colorful row of bottles. I took my phone out to take a photo of the pool table to send to Jackson. We had a "suggestion box" email at work that went straight to his inbox, and I had gotten into the habit of making outlandish "suggestions" just to make him smile. Nobody else seemed to send in suggestions, and sometimes he and I would end up writing back and forth for hours . . .

Fuzzy, faux-fur pink pool table in the lounge to help boost employee motivation? I wrote, and sent the email.

Within seconds, Jackson texted me a screenshot of the email, followed by a photo of himself laughing.

How do you come up with this stuff? he wrote.

~~*You inspire me.*~~

~~*I like to see you laugh.*~~

~~*You're softer than fuzzy faux fur.*~~

Too much TV growing up? I answered lamely.

He responded with a smiley face.

"What are you smiling about?" Katie asked.

"Just . . . happy I bumped into you," I said, slipping my phone into my pocket. "Don't have much time, but it really is nice to hang out with you outside the office for a change."

"Yay! Just like old times," Katie said. Then she put one hand up and the other over her heart. "Ten minutes is more than enough time for me to tell you all about this new guy. Promise."

CHAPTER

3

In the leather banquette, my back to the room, I watched Katie fluff her black pixie-cut hair. She looked like Tinker Bell's naughty older sister. When she shook her arms out of her dark biker jacket and placed it next to her, the tattoo on her bare shoulder caught the blue light: *K* for Katie. A reminder to put herself first, no matter the circumstances.

"So, he's a lawyer and an amateur photographer," she began, after ordering a gin and tonic. "I think there might be something there."

"Wow, that's great . . . and fast!" I said. Eight minutes left. "Do you think you—"

"Except that his sister called twice while we were together," she said, cutting me off and dropping her voice. "Is that weird?"

I shrugged and laughed as she began to describe how he had answered his sister's calls while she was half-undressed. I doubted this man would help her get over Pablo, the Colombian chef she had lived with for two years, who would send homemade golden cheese empanadas for the office to enjoy every once in a while.

When Pablo lost his job, there were no more empanadas at work, just a very frustrated Katie, who picked up extra shifts as a bartender in Queens in the evenings to make ends meet rather than deign to ask her parents for financial support and admit "failure." The relationship didn't last, and eventually Pablo moved in with cousins in Florida.

"So, I told Kevin—that's my lawyer-slash-photographer guy— that I'm a fact-checker for a living and I swear he went a little pale." She laughed. "It's like I said I was a police detective. Now I really need to stalk this guy online a little to see why my job made him feel edgy."

"Better do it sooner rather than later if you're starting to like him," I said. A few more minutes and I would have to leave to catch the 1 train home. I kept my head down when the bartender came by with Katie's order, waving my hand to let him know I didn't need anything.

"Maybe that wasn't his sister calling at all . . . Maybe he's married!" she continued, her brown eyes wide, irises like two cups of coffee. "Now why does that turn me on . . . ?"

We laughed, and I swatted her arm. Sometimes I thought Katie would have made a fantastic eagle-eyed corporate lawyer. Aside from the fact that her petite frame was perfectly suited for sharp pencil skirts—to match her wit—she definitely would have made a lot more money than our meager fact-checker salary.

Alas, while in grad school together, we had both fallen under the romantic spell of Vibe Media, a place for serious journalism.

Jackson is an unexpected bonus. I smiled to myself.

It was already warm in the bar, and a small crowd had formed around the pool table next to us. A girl with a waterfall of dark, wavy hair leaned over it, aiming her cue at a yellow ball, when a guy came up behind her to fix her aim by a few degrees. I watched his fingers graze her bare arm and wondered if her smile widened because his breath had tickled her ear. When she caught my eye, she winked.

My phone buzzed in my pocket.

Another text from Jackson. *Fun night out?*

As I was crafting a witty response, a notification from Facebook popped up. The beautiful Adriana had tagged him in a post. After another selfless evening of volunteering together at the Big Brothers Big Sisters of NYC program, Jackson and Adriana had taken their mentees to a café to indulge in fat slices of chocolate cake. She had checked them in online at a place called Ziggy. A zing of jealousy traveled up my spine.

It was bad enough that Adriana had glorious sleek dark hair. The fact that she was kind and shared Jackson's Latin heritage made me feel small in comparison. Especially when his warm family values and love of volunteer work contributed to the butterflies in my stomach.

Just trying to keep up with you. Hope you and Adriana are having a good night, I wrote back, and instantly regretted it. My heart was racing, wondering if I sounded petty and stalkerish. Was I misreading a flirty vibe or was he just being friendly with me? Or was this thing with Adriana so casual that it was normal for him to text another girl while on a night out?

Frustrated with myself, I put on a bland expression and looked back up at Katie, who was still talking about Kevin.

"Hey, all okay?" she asked. Her eyes searched my face, and her hand moved across the sticky table to cover mine. She knew how to read a shift in my mood within seconds. I wanted to talk to her openly, tell her about how free I felt onstage, how caged I felt by Adriana's post tagging Jackson, how things might have turned out differently if I had just let him kiss me in the elevator that time when his face came so close to mine, instead of turning away . . . But then she tilted her head slightly to the side, just like teachers and friends used to do in high school, and something in me hardened. I refused to spiral into an evening of pity.

"Yeah, no, just hope he's a good guy and you're having fun," I answered lightly, putting the strap of my bag on my shoulder. I moved to the edge of the banquette, ready to leave. "Don't let this guy get you down, okay? I need our upbeat morning coffee dates. They keep me going."

I looked over at the couple flirting at the red pool table and sighed. It reminded me of the night Katie and I had visited her parents' house for a fundraiser: her Upper East Side home full of coiffed blond women wearing strings of pearls; starched, stiff napkin swans on plates; and white-haired men in suits talking about skiing in Chamonix. Katie and I kept escaping to hang out with the caterers in the kitchen, with me standing guard to warn them to put out their cigarettes by the fire escape whenever I saw her mom approaching.

Katie was pouty and quiet that night after her parents had announced to their friends—with a clink of pink champagne flutes—that their daughter was going to intern at Bloomberg over the summer . . . without consulting her. Katie, who dated moody artists instead of bankers, preferred Cheetos to caviar, wore flats instead of Manolos. So, when dinner ended, we followed the catering crew to a dive bar that had a giant red pool table in the center, just like this one. Katie sat in a prim, structured black dress in the corner, slowly removing bobby pins and running a hand through her short hair. I kept fiddling with the oversize bow on the tailored maroon dress that she had insisted I borrow for the evening.

After a few rounds of pool and a handful of songs on the jukebox, someone brought out a microphone. An impromptu karaoke party began. Each person took their turn standing on the red pool table, swaying and singing off-key to Frank Sinatra and Alicia Keys, even rapping to Eminem. Katie, who normally lapped up attention as if it were her right, stayed in the corner sipping a cold beer, absently watching the performances. I had nudged her, winked, and walked up to the pool table.

"No way," she said, her face breaking out into a smile. "You're going to sing?"

I shook my head. I took the microphone and stood up on the pool table, smiling into the crowd.

"A bunch of you are caterers, so here are some food jokes for you," I remember saying, ducking to avoid hitting the swinging lamp above my head. "My grandma is a cook, too. Like most relatives, she's very nosy. She has no problem getting *jalapeño* business!"

It was corny, but it worked. I launched into my first ever stand-up comedy routine that night, using bits and pieces I had rehearsed with my father over the years.

My grandma's fave dish to serve at home is karma. She judges us and we just get what we deserve!

The drunk caterers in the small dive bar were the perfect audience, slapping their legs and nudging each other amid bursts of genuine laughter. By the end, Katie had forgotten all about her parents, the fundraising dinner, and the expectations of the world. When they all stood and clapped for me, Katie hooting and cheering, I'd known I'd have to do it again.

That was in 2006. Five years ago. And comedy had been a lifeline for me ever since.

I looked at Katie now and smiled affectionately. The next morning, she had called Bloomberg's HR team and declined the internship in favor of the lesser-paid job at Vibe Media with me. Her parents were furious, calling from their yacht somewhere in the South of France a few weeks later. It had been a big night for her, but she had no idea what that night had meant to me, too, or how I had kept up with my comedy years later. Not just for her. For me, for my dad. For that delicious combination of laughter and applause that buoyed me for days afterward.

"I don't let any man or woman get me down," she was saying, eyebrows raised. "Unlike you ... with a certain stud whose name rhymes with Shmackson."

A warmth settled into my stomach at the thought of him. Of course she knew that I was thinking about him. That's how great friendships work. Sometimes you don't need to speak a feeling for the other to feel it, too.

Are he and Adriana laughing and chatting away, moving on to a bar to spend time alone, somewhere in the city, at this very minute? I wondered sadly. *Or worse, cuddling while shooting pool?*

"Please, Katie, Jackson is my boss. I just ... respect his ... opinion," I said, standing.

"Oh, is *that* what we're calling it now?" she said, her laughter rising above the chatter at the bar. I could see in my periphery heads turn toward us and felt a blush rising to my cheeks.

"First, you didn't encourage him because you work together. Now you won't entertain him because he just started seeing someone else," she said, ticking points off on her fingers. "Classic, textbook interest in unavailable men. Even though he totally flirts with you all the time and we all know it. You're just afraid of getting hurt. You know what that spells? A-L-O-N-E."

She empathetically reminded me about a serious crush she'd had on one of our professors at Columbia. As she reminisced about her fantasies of running her fingers through his salt-and-pepper beard, I mulled over her YouTube-inspired theories on my attraction to unavailable men. I had to admit that I approached romance with more caution than most of my friends. Despite raising me in Manhattan, my grandparents had acted like we lived in a conservative Arab society circa the 1950s. *Your reputation is like a glass vase—every scratch shows.* I could hear my grandmother's voice in my head. *Don't give people a chance to say bad things about you.*

They don't care about your US passport. You are an Arab woman at heart. They will wait for you to slip up and make it a big deal. You have to hold yourself to higher standards, my grandfather would lecture. *Always.*

After a lifetime of being told that sex was the single greatest mortal sin, I could never bring myself to let things progress past heated kisses. Even my wildest college nights—the ones that ended with some of us laughing with our arms around each other while half the group decided to go streaking through Central Park during a full moon—never got ... wild enough.

Katie had moved on to the rumors swirling at work about a new reporter position opening up, but I was busy daydreaming about Jackson's eyelashes.

"Hello? Are you listening to me or planning a wedding in your head?" she asked, waving her arms in front of my eyes. "Do you think I should go for this job or what?"

"Don't ask, don't get ... You may as well apply, right?" I said, sitting next to her on her side of the booth. "I totally think you've earned a promotion ... though Kevin's secret wife probably disagrees."

I watched her throw her head back in full laughter and took it as a perfect cue to leave. I had missed Katie's carefree laugh, but not enough to stay longer.

I gave her a side hug and stood up again. The bar was getting crowded now, with students filing in from nearby NYU classes ... and my grandparents would start to worry about my unusual delay from "work."

"How lucky that we bumped into each other," Katie said, adjusting the straps on her top. "My big date is at a bar a few streets down."

"Ah, so you are meeting Mr. Kevin," I said. "Will you score?"

"Okay, nobody says 'score' like that anymore," she said, putting a few bills down on the table and standing up next to me. "He has a car. Last time we got a little creative in the back seat. Do you know how sexy it is for someone to lick your eyeball?"

"The thought of that makes me queasy," I said.

As usual, Katie was oversharing about her sex life. It felt like God was trying to maintain sexual balance in the world by giving Katie too much activity and me . . . none whatsoever.

And I bet Jackson can sense that, I thought with a sigh. *God, please don't let me die a virgin.*

When Jackson began seeing dainty Adriana a few months ago, I was jealous because of everything they had in common . . . but I also didn't have to worry about possible repercussions anymore. Whatever it was between us—the electricity when our hands reached for the same elevator button, catching him looking at me during editorial meetings, the chocolates left on my desk—could now clearly be only in my head. I could just pine after him in private. Suffering was romantic. Like in my grandmother's favorite telenovelas.

I anxiously walked past the growing crowd in the bar, keeping my eyes lowered. *I'm trying to work up the courage to imagine undressing in front of someone and she's licking eyeballs,* I thought, resisting a headshake.

"Don't knock it 'til you've tried it," she said once we were back out on the sidewalk. The temperature had dropped a few degrees, and the sky was a slightly darker blue. There were throngs of people now, some wearing T-shirts, with their hands jammed in pants pockets to keep warm, others already in the black peacoats that dominated the streets come winter.

"Besides, the night is yet young," she said. "Although I feel like a cougar with all these college kids around here."

A man in a beanie offered to sell us weed. I declined and Katie accepted. She took a quick selfie of the two of us, smiling side by side, with an ATM in the background, and sent it to me.

She called it proof that I had a life outside home and the office for a change.

CHAPTER

4

The air felt wonderfully cool against my cheeks after the mugginess of the crowded bar. I speed walked a few extra blocks to find the 1 train. Passing a man dressed in a bright red Elmo costume for no apparent reason, I resisted the urge to send Jackson another photo for the "suggestion box." He was probably busy with Adriana and her long, glossy dark hair. I cringed.

Was Katie right about me? I wondered, passing a couple kissing on the corner, leaning against a doorframe.

My attraction to Jackson had been instant, but it only deepened when I found out about his serious passion for introducing diversity to newsrooms and his volunteer work with his Little Brother, Michael. I had grown up watching cheesy Christmas movies with big families shouting at one another over a giant turkey, wondering what it would be like to sit at a table like that, when my family life had always been so small and relatively quiet. And here was Jackson, offering a young person that exact taste of a picture-perfect snow globe of a world, without asking for anything in return. His kindness almost matched the beauty of his long eyelashes.

In truth, I had always told myself that I was holding myself back from Jackson out of respect for office decorum. Dating wasn't prohibited at Vibe, but it was definitely frowned upon. What was worse: a one-night stand that wouldn't end up anywhere anyway or a real, fully fledged relationship? The idea of an uncomfortable chat with HR about where he and I stood sounded like a terrible way to spend an afternoon.

And nothing compared to the prospect of sitting my grandparents down to explain to them the concept of a boyfriend. A young man who doesn't meet the family first, state clear intentions to get married, or welcome chaperoned meetings and phone conversations? It would be over before it ever started. My only other option was to fan the flames between us secretly, blanket our relationship in layers of fake meetings in neighborhoods where nobody would recognize us. But I didn't have the strength to spin a spiderweb of lies every time I wanted to be with him. Thoughts of him alone made me melt. What would happen if we were physically alone together . . . ?

Who could blame me for my restraint, after seeing my father raise me as a single dad who refused to remarry? After watching the courteous way my grandparents behaved around each other, rarely kissing or holding hands, though always kind? I had grown up with subdued models of romance. Was it that strange that I found it inappropriate to flirt with my boss, especially when he was dating someone else?

I rounded the corner past a buzzing Irish bar.

"Hey, hot stuff, come join us," a blond man shouted out the wooden window, waving me over with one hand, holding a brimming beer mug in the other. I rolled my eyes and smiled.

"Thanks, have fun." I waved as he and his friends booed my decision.

My mind raced back to the last time my friends and I had done a pub crawl on this street and landed here to celebrate someone's job promotion. Around this time last year.

I shuddered. Gathering my scarf tighter around my throat, I picked up my pace.

That night, I had sipped on my sparkling water, watching collars and chatter loosen up around me. I picked at the lemon in my glass with a toothpick. I envied the pink-faced freedom, the lowered inhibitions, the complete disregard for tomorrow's headache of the rest of the group. I was like a ladybug at a loud picnic. There but not there . . . but there.

We ended up meeting a group of NYU law students and, soon enough, the "where are you *really* from" questions started. The discussion turned to Arabs in America. And then . . . the inevitable. I became the evening's unofficial spokesperson on all Middle Eastern affairs.

Oh, your family is from Palestine originally? I don't know much about Pakistan. I have Indian friends. Anyone up for curry after this?

Organized religion is crazy. Is your family really religious? Is that why you aren't drinking? I know a Mormon guy who . . .

What is your expert opinion on Iran or Iraq or [insert Muslim country currently making headlines in the news] . . .

Is it weird for you living here after 9/11? Or are you one of those conspiracy theorists?

All I could think about was that I didn't want to be connected to the tragedy of 9/11. I shouldn't have to be. Almost a decade later, thinking of that day still made me feel sick and helpless, emotional beyond the scar that every New Yorker carries. A personal loss.

I had offered bland responses in the moment, wanting to avoid every outing turning into a political debate. I knew I'd come up with cleverer responses to their questions on the subway home or much later in the shower. In fact, many of those responses had ended up flavoring my stand-up comedy sets . . .

Arabs love spicy food. Know what we like to put in our tacos? Allah-peños!

Later that evening, the handsome one with the dimples and dark wavy hair had offered to walk me to my subway stop. Katie winked a goodbye at me. We ended up in the dark tree-lined children's playground on the corner down the street, his hot breath on my neck.

I had tried to pretend he was Jackson, wondering what his lips would feel like instead, telling myself this was a rehearsal, and trying to moan encouragingly in all the right moments. I leaned back against the cold slide. Instead of ripples of pleasure, I felt pure disgust at the stale stench of Tanqueray on his lips.

Dimples told me his grandmother was Lebanese and that he loved attending protests at embassies. He pulled on one of my curls like it was a spring when I told him I prefer to keep a low profile. A chilly breeze rustled the leaves above our heads.

"Oh, so you're a good little Arab girl?" he asked, leaving a wet constellation of kisses on my neck. "We can do it from the back if you want to keep your virginity. I'm down with that."

I tried to push him away then, and he got really aggressive, roughly putting his hand up my shirt. His fingers pawed at the clasp of my bra. He only stopped when a dirty alley cat shrieked nearby and surprised him.

I ran.

"Cock tease," I heard him yell as I hailed a passing taxi. "I just felt sorry for you, you know."

Memories of childhood taunts rose up like bile. During the entire ride home, I couldn't see the road ahead clearly, because my eyes were brimming with tears that I kept blinking back.

I told Katie about it at work the next morning, hands shaking as I spoke. She didn't see the offensive severity of it. Her focus was on the fact that it was a mild incident that turned out okay, like those of so many women we knew. That this wasn't an uncommon occurrence alarmed me even more. I wanted her to put her arms around me, punch the air in solidarity and frustration, stalk the guy on Facebook and send him a strongly worded message educating him about sexual harassment, while threatening to tell his employer, family, and friends about his words and his uninvited touch. Instead, Katie just nodded kindly and said: "Yeah, it happens. Sucks. I'm surprised it's your first time dealing with an idiot like that. But a stray cat saving the day? That kind of thing only happens to you, I swear."

Staying in and reading novels became much more appealing than facing more nights like that. I went out with Katie a lot less after the stray cat incident. At the time, she was conveniently busy moving in with her boyfriend, Pablo, so she didn't notice how often I declined evenings out.

It was fine by me, because we still had each other all day at work.

Lately, I just found people to be tiresome. I would arrive home from occasional outings absolutely drained, standing still in the shower with a steady, hot stream running over my face and body until my skin turned a splotchy pink. I would turn it off only when my grandfather gently rapped on the bathroom door, complaining about me using up all the hot water.

I steadied my breath now, walking down the steps to the subway platform. I always enjoyed the anonymity of the crowded space, feeling my hair rustle around me whenever a train whooshed past. I put my headphones on and pulled up Jordan B. Brown's comedy sketch recap video. When my train finally arrived, I took a seat and rubbed wet wipes on my face and neck, removing any lingering traces of cigarette smoke, alcohol, and fun from my body.

CHAPTER

5

I found my grandparents deep in a heated conversation in the living room. They jumped when I opened the door, Teta breathing a sigh of relief when she saw it was only me.

"Who else would it be?" I joked. "Obama?"

"Did you know there was a shooting at the convenience store on 113th and Broadway?" my grandfather said in English, his face a dark scowl. "Do you know what this means? You and your jokey-wokey comments?"

I set my bag down softly in the kitchen, hoping to avoid my grandfather's rising temper. My grandmother began squeezing lemon onto a salad, plates already laid out on the table.

"*Khalas*, let's just eat yesterday's food. He will feel better after eating," Teta whispered to me. She was already reheating the okra and meat stew, the aroma of bubbling tomato sauce filling the small kitchen.

"Now extra police will be all over the area," he grumbled, sitting at the table, his head in his hands. He switched to his accented

English again. "Every time someone do something very bad, they find the brown man and ask him all the questions. Guilty until proven innocent, isn't it!"

Teta placed a full dish in front of him, which he began to devour, grumbling to himself the entire time.

At one point, we heard people speaking in the corridor outside the front door and froze, exchanging glances, irrationally wondering if a SWAT team was in fact planning to break the door down. We waited for the voices to recede, and then my grandfather went back to attacking his plate.

"It's too hot," Jeddo said, opening his mouth wide to air out chewed stew. "Did you buy this meat from the new Egyptian butcher on Amsterdam Avenue? He tried to overcharge you last time, Mia. Don't let him take advantage like that. All Egyptians are thieves."

I loved playing the "stereotype generalization" game with my grandfather. *Let's see how quickly I can make him contradict himself this time*, I thought to myself.

"Should we watch that Omar Sharif film that came out years ago? The French one where the actors won a bunch of awards?" I asked, scooping rice onto my plate. "I never got a chance to see it. I just love his movies."

"It's not a surprise. They are the best entertainers, best judges of character," he said instantly, arching his thick gray eyebrows. "We like to watch those Egyptian classics on TV, don't we, Amal? All Egyptians are extraordinarily talented and they are just born funny."

I lived for these little wins. I was still warming him up to the idea of being politically correct in front of others.

"My favorite one is—"

Three sharp knocks at the front door interrupted my grandfather. Nobody ever interrupts him—much less an unwanted guest at dinnertime. My breath caught in my throat. What if it was Katie? Or, in my wildest fantasies, it would be Jackson at my front door with a giant stuffed teddy bear, coming to sweep me off my feet. But that would never happen.

Your life is not a Love Unfiltered story, Mia, I reminded myself. *Jackson and I, even in my fantasies, can't exist together in this space.*

He can't see that this is how I live.

Only the building's residents and owner knew that the "superintendent's office" was actually this basement apartment. The elegant Upper West Side building was leased by Juilliard to provide subsidized housing for scholarship students, guest lecturers, and tenured professors. My grandfather's job for the past few decades had been limited to the inner workings of this building: carrying his wrench to fix a shower head, bringing a plunger to unclog a toilet, or gently unscrewing an AC unit to clean off sheets of dust that had built up inside.

My grandmother did occasional cooking and laundry for the tenants: all musicians-in-residence with dainty hands and odd hours. We had become a sort of patchwork family.

My grandparents were homebodies, preferring me to use my "perfect American accent" to deal with the outside world. That way, they didn't have to face the question marks in people's expressions. Like the sharp, nervous glances when I read an Arabic book on the subway. The eyebrows that shot up when my grandmother kissed my forehead and uttered *Allah yehmeeki,* or God protect you, when I helped her unload date cakes to sell at the local farmer's market. The lips that smile politely when I say I'm American, then ask where I'm *from* from.

With their wages—and now mine—my grandparents and I had cobbled together a good life. Minus the overpriced meat from the Egyptian butcher. A narrow but decent life.

And yet we couldn't help but jump every time there was a knock on the door.

"Ignore," Jeddo said in Arabic. A command, not a question.

The fan near the sink whirred dutifully in the background, ruf-fling my hair each time it faced me.

I offered him the red bread basket. He tutted at me, fingering the pita bread in the center where it hadn't properly defrosted. My grandmother stood to spoon salad onto his plate. No comments. She smiled and winked when passing the salad bowl to me.

"How was work?" he asked me. "Did you check all the facts, Miss Vibe Media? You were later than usual today. I was about to start calling you."

"Yes, Jeddo, you'll see a good story about the annual earnings report of Bank of America tomorrow," I said, scrolling on my phone to show him the convenient photo of me and Katie in front of the ATM. I hadn't even planned that.

It was only half a lie. I hadn't worked on that particular piece myself, but there would be an actual story about Bank of America in *Money Talks* tomorrow. I'd read it online at midnight and be prepared to answer his questions about it in the morning before the paper dropped at our front door. My grandparents had sacri-ficed so much for me to achieve a measure of greatness, to reach that ever-dangling carrot of an American Dream, which comes with earned respect. They felt I was on my way in my job fact-checking articles about people in positions of power, those in charge of where the money flowed. Jeddo got a thrill out of know-ing that my work was important, and he read every article by Vibe Media, proudly showing me typos our proofreaders didn't catch. I knew he interrogated me out of love, to show me he was interested in my work, but I couldn't bear the thought of what he would do if he knew what I really did: regularly fact-checked Love Unfiltered columns about fairy-tale love stories, not the respect-able financial pages.

Or worse, that I secretly performed comedy on stages all across town. Part of the issue was the typical struggle every musician, artist, and writer can empathize with: the sheer terror of admitting to their traditional family members that they are "wasting time"—precious hours that could be devoted to work or family or spirituality—with their chosen art form. The other issue with comedy was the performance element, when living a quiet, respectable life is a key value in our family. Getting onstage in a full face of makeup to crack raunchy jokes about sex and poke fun at our culture was akin to blasphemy. And instead of it being a phase that I would eventually get out of my system, I was now doing comedy once a week—twice if I could . . .

Jeddo had dealt with a lot of disappointment in his life. I didn't want to add to the list.

"Good, Katie is a lovely girl," Jeddo said. "She seems so hardworking. I respect this."

"It's nice you two saw each other outside the office," Teta chimed in. "You used to have so much fun together in university. Now so serious. Work, work, work, and no play."

Teta had met Katie only a few times, but she really liked her. Once, on my father's birthday, Katie had ridden the subway home early with me, and we shared headphones while I played a video of Dad reading aloud from a book.

His blond curls framed a tanned face with a crooked smile. He held the red book open with one hand, fully cracked spine, and gesticulated exaggeratedly with the other. With a deep voice, he recited a Shakespearean poem I had been assigned to analyze for a class, but he had turned it into a rap. My giggles could be heard off to the side. When he looked straight into the camera, his eyes were impossibly sea blue.

"I know it's totally inappropriate to say, but your dad is really hot," Katie had whispered, popping open a blue bag of my favorite Salt & Vinegar Lays. She had bought them for us while we waited for the train. There was no pat on the shoulder, no suggestion that it was okay to cry, no request to wait until we had reached my house to avoid making a scene.

I had burst into real laughter; her offbeat response was exactly what I needed. She then went on to describe a recent heated night with a waiter after one of her parents' stiff dinners.

And when we arrived back at my apartment, Teta was happy to see that I was relatively okay. I was smiling.

Another two swift knocks broke my reverie. Sharper this time. Spoons suspended in midair, the three of us fired questions at one another with our eyes.

Maybe it wasn't Jackson, but it could possibly be the suave gentleman who just moved into apartment 5. Divine intervention, to reward me for having my best set ever earlier? I imagined him with a crisp white collar and a blazer, holding a bouquet of daisies.

Terribly sorry to interrupt at dinnertime, he would say with some sort of posh international accent. *I held the elevator door open earlier for a striking woman with angelic curly hair who pressed the down button. Does she live here? By the way, I am a wealthy doctor of Arab descent.*

This was what happened to my brain when my job was to read Love Unfiltered columns all day. *Note to self: those are other people's true fairy tales, not mine.*

I picked up my spoon. Tomato sauce dripped onto the starched white tablecloth.

Another knock. With a huff and a clatter of his spoon as it fell, my grandfather heaved himself up. His wooden chair sounded angry at being pushed back. Teta dipped her napkin into her ice water and rubbed my spreading tomato stain, then poured salt on it to absorb the oil. I stood up, but my grandfather waved me off.

"It's probably the Dominicans next door whose washing machine I fixed for free," he said. "Dominicans have no practical sense. They just want to dance salsa all day long."

My grandmother rolled her eyes. I looked down into my lap. Here I am, battling stereotypes onstage every day . . . and in my own home.

"Yes? We are having dinner," Jeddo bellowed from the living room in his heavily accented English.

I could picture him speaking to the closed wooden door, hands clasped behind his back, not dignifying the unwanted visitor with a look through the peephole. He hadn't even bothered to turn on one of the five lamps in our living room. His usual excuses were saving the planet, not wasting electricity money, avoiding vanity. If it were up to me, all the lamps would be on to welcome warmth into our basement apartment.

I held my breath so I could listen out for Mr. Apartment 5's voice. Or Jackson's, by some strange cosmic design . . . ?

"It's a woman, Teta," I said to my grandmother, hiding my disappointment by dabbing at the stain. "One of the tenants? Apartment three clogging the toilet with her tampons again?"

"Right. I should get your grandfather's plunger ready," Teta replied in Arabic, getting up. "Maybe he can't be nice to people, but he can get the job done. He needs to, or we move out."

She had been saying this since I was a toddler. They had lived here for decades before I was even born. Shortly after my mother died, my father moved back in with Teta and Jeddo to better cope and to care for me. I'd be twenty-five soon and had known no other home.

"We need to think about the future," Teta said.

The closer we got to my birthday, the more she had been using this phrase. I wanted to talk to her about it, what she meant, what kind of future she saw for me. I thought about how she would react if I dared to bring up Jackson. How many times had I tried to tell her about how my insides would turn into something warm and fiery every time I thought about him? And every time, the sugary sentiment would get caught in my throat and melt before I could vocalize it—because I needed to be really sure of how I felt at first, of how he felt later, and now, with Adriana in the picture, if we would ever realistically have a shot at something real. Again,

I imagined him standing at the door, his eyes crinkling at the corners, holding a bouquet of flowers . . . A blush rose to my cheeks.

Stop acting like an extra in Sweet Valley High, I chided myself.

We heard the clang of a metallic chain and a creak as Jeddo opened the front door, thankfully interrupting my thoughts. Manhattan's wail of sirens blared louder. Jeddo switched a lamp on in the living room. My grandmother turned in her seat, placing a hand on the back of her mismatched kitchen chair.

When I looked down at the table, I noticed that Jeddo had left the newspaper open, dozens of phrases underlined in red.

"Doesn't it annoy you when he marks up the pages like that? It would drive me crazy," I said, warming up. "Dad used to do that, too. Remember?"

My grandmother looked up to see if Jeddo was out of earshot, then touched the chignon at the nape of her neck. It was already perfect, with nary a hair out of place. That was her nervous tell.

After all these years, we still rarely talked about my father. My mother even less so, because she passed away during childbirth. But my father, my Teta's golden only son, the fallen hero . . . Grief was forever present, like a quiet tenant in an empty apartment. It never got easier to talk about him. I could only blame my out-of-the-ordinary request to reminisce on the note that Mr. Goatee had handed me earlier. *Dig deeper.*

"Yousef loved to read," she said simply, her voice just above a whisper. She only talked about him when Jeddo couldn't hear her. "In his bag, always a bottle of water, a book, and headphones."

A memory surfaced of us sharing cheap black headphones, the kind that break easily after a few weeks of use. He was playing a classic Eddie Murphy stand-up clip, Eddie wearing the red leather suit onstage. My normally mellow father had roared with laughter, coming to life in a way that happened only when he was watching comedy.

The effects lingered; he was the one who'd shown me how to tilt my desk lamp so a circle of light shone on the exposed brick wall in my bedroom. We would pretend I was a famous comedian with a makeshift spotlight until darkness came.

And then he would grow serious again. Especially in the mornings, when he went off to work in his security guard uniform. His metallic name tag bore the anglicized version of his name, Joseph, to make it easier for people to pronounce. He would come home in the evenings and stay locked in his room for half an hour or so to decompress after a long day of nodding at people, unseen as they rushed to catch elevators and make it on time to their important meetings.

I would often be studying at the kitchen table, while Teta finished preparing dinner, when he would emerge with a big smile on his face, eyes crinkled at the corners, to show me a funny video on his phone.

"See how he makes consistent eye contact with the audience and uses his eyebrows to express emotion?" he would say, pointing to a Robin Williams stand-up comedy clip we had seen a hundred times. "He is a total master of his craft."

We would then recite the familiar lines of the set together and dissolve into fresh laughter, wiggling our eyebrows at each other. In another life, I believed that my father, with his golden curls, could have become a famous actor.

"Losing him was . . . losing all," Teta said softly. "At least we have you, *habibti*, my love."

I looked over at her, also lost in memories. We smiled at each other, and she stood up, looking toward the living room, wondering why Jeddo was taking so long.

I watched her wash dishes in the sink. Katie's musings on romance earlier that evening had hit a nerve. My father had never fallen in love with another woman after he lost my mother, but I knew little of my grandmother's ideas about romance. I just assumed her and Jeddo's nice, traditional marriage had been arranged by well-meaning family members.

But Teta rarely spoke about her past at all. Gathering crumbs of information over the years, I knew she had had a big fight with her only sister and they'd never spoken again after she left Palestine in the late 1940s. The Great Sister Feud.

And that was it.

The problem was that Teta shut me down every time I tried to find out a little more about my heritage.

I'd always wondered if her reluctance to talk was about not wanting to bring up painful memories—or was it something else?

What is she hiding from me? I thought, studying her slim figure as she scrubbed a pot.

I turned to look up toward the window. It was the biggest one in our basement apartment and ran the length of the wall, right below the ceiling. We had grown used to seeing people's feet as they walked by and the occasional dog lifting a leg to pee.

"Did you need something?" Jeddo's voice continued, losing a little of its edge. I heard a woman's laugh. I looked at Teta, who raised an eyebrow and turned off the faucet. I turned back to the window.

It was completely dark out now. We could see only moving legs and long streetlight shadows.

"Amal, come," Jeddo boomed. "Never mind, we're coming to you, *habibti.*"

My grandmother's eyes narrowed as she returned to her seat at the table. *Habibti?* My love? Who was he trying to impress?

We heard the clack of high heels and smelled expensive perfume before a beautiful woman followed my grandfather into our tiny kitchen.

CHAPTER

6

"Don't just stand there," Jeddo said. "Hello? Where are your manners?"

First of all, we weren't standing. But we jumped up when he spoke, as if someone had spilled cold water down our backs. All that was missing was a salute. But he was right—we had forgotten our manners because we were too busy staring.

The woman who stood in our kitchen sparkled like a disco ball. I had never seen so many sequins outside of an eighties movie. The light from the single lamp over our kitchen table turned into hundreds of twinkling stars on her top, tucked into dark high-waisted jeans. As she walked closer, the light inched its way up around her chest and the curve of her neck, to reveal full lips and dark blond hair set in Hollywood waves.

"I said, this is our new tenant in the penthouse, apartment twelve," he continued. "Just flew in from Dubai and ready to take on Manhattan, hey?"

All the flashing sequins were making me dizzy. Plus, my grandfather almost sounded like he was flirting. Outside, someone threw a beer bottle, and it hit the basement window, making us jump again.

The woman looked familiar.

"Welcome, dear," Teta said in Arabic, with a clap of her hands. "Lovely top. Let us know if your apartment needs any maintenance. I can also take care of some laundry and cooking if you like. Try some okra stew?"

"Good evening, all. Auntie, that's a lovely purple top you're wearing, too," replied the woman in Arabic.

"Vantage," my grandmother answered in English.

"Vintage," I corrected with a smile.

"That's what I said, vantage," Teta said. Clearly, she had been watching too much reality TV while doing the ironing. With a wave of her hand, she invited the woman to join us at the table.

The woman walked closer, her heels like little hammers in our small kitchen. I had never heard the sound of high heels in our apartment. The few times I had worn them to secretly perform or to a college party, I would sneak them in to hide behind a loose brick in my bedroom wall.

"Hello, I'm Mia, the granddaughter," I said with a smile. "I can help if you have questions about the neighborhood."

"Mia, your braided hair is so on trend," she answered. "I'm Phaedra. And no, it's not a stage name, which is how I suppose all this happened."

She motioned to her outfit with a laugh. I let my eyes roam again over her sequin top, red lips, dark denim jeans, and metallic pumps.

Of course she would be named after a mythological Greek princess.

She looked nice but a little too manicured. I wanted to wipe the makeup off her face to see her features more clearly, to tone down the sequins and the high-wattage smile, and dial down the overly friendly showiness of this woman in our simple basement apartment.

Instead, I stood up to give her my chair and pulled a wooden stool out from beneath the table. I sat facing her beneath the glow of the kitchen light. Her eyes were the color of extra virgin olive oil.

While I was busy staring into Phaedra's eyes, my grandmother had sourced a plate and cutlery for her. Phaedra thanked her but remained standing.

"It smells delicious, but I don't want to interrupt your dinner," said Phaedra. "I just came down to introduce myself. I'm a performer and a new guest lecturer at Juilliard."

Polite nods and smiles greeted her in return. My grandparents were used to musicians passing through in the building. I was jealous of her stage time.

The air in the room was warm and stuffy. I wished we could open the window and breathe.

"And I'm embarrassed to say I dropped one of my favorite necklaces down the drain while washing my hands in the kitchen earlier," she admitted. "I would love help retrieving it when you can. I couldn't do it myself."

I looked at Teta, who gently placed her fork down and clasped her hands.

"I'll go at once," my grandfather said, hopping up as if he was a surgeon being called to the operating room.

"No need, really. My show starts in half an hour and I'll be out for hours," she said. "Why not come by tomorrow evening? I still haven't unpacked properly. That Dubai flight is really long. Have you been to Dubai, by the way? I recognize your last name, Almas. Are you related to the big Almas family in Dubai by any chance?"

My ears perked up. As in, extended family in Dubai? Teta never talked about the Great Sister Feud, and I had often wondered if her estranged sister was still alive. Any attempts to learn more had been met with the same stone wall of silence.

I looked at my grandparents, who remained uncharacteristically quiet in front of our guest. They seemed to be smiling and frowning simultaneously.

I glanced up at Phaedra, wondering what she might be able to tell me. What was her story, anyway? She looked to be in her early thirties. I tried to picture her in her new home, the airy penthouse in our building.

The fact-checker in me couldn't wait . . . I casually held my phone under the table and quickly found her on YouTube. My eyes watered at the millions of views on snippets of performances around the world. I planned to cyberstalk her properly later, with Katie's help.

I looked back up at her, putting my phone away. Phaedra's outfit and makeup seemed fit for a photoshoot. Had a designer loaned her this top in exchange for a social media post? Was this really how she went out for a casual evening show? Or was she always this . . . extra?

Maybe people pay to get in line for a chance to stare at her? I wondered.

Self-consciously, I tucked a stray curl behind my ear and fiddled with my braid.

"Enjoy your evening," my grandmother said finally. "Take some okra stew to go. You can have it for lunch tomorrow."

Phaedra smiled gratefully and stretched out a hand for the Tupperware. Lipstick fell out of her bag, and I bent to pick it up. The label read: *Va-Va-Voom.* I resisted the urge to roll my eyes in front of her.

"You know, I could just bring the Tupperware to you tomorrow, since you're on your way out now," I said, ready to see her leave. "Maybe when I come home from work?"

I was curious to see what she looked like in the daytime, how she had made the penthouse space her own. Was she messy? Were makeup brushes and nail polish bottles strewn about everywhere?

Had she painted the grand piano in the penthouse in rainbow shades, just for kicks?

"Very nice of you," she said. "I look forward to it. Okay, wish me luck! Or to break a leg, rather. Good night, and lovely meeting you all."

I felt a fresh pang of jealousy that she was about to go on a stage, while I had to stay home. How nice it must be for her to be the same person onstage and offstage, sparkling with her sequins everywhere. I wondered if I would ever be able to achieve that level of harmony. Thinking about myself onstage a mere hour ago, I imagined Teta's reaction and blushed furiously into my lap.

"By the way, could you tell me which stops I need to take to get to Smokey's?" she asked. "And is there any extra storage down here? I have a lot of shoes and dresses . . ."

"Mia can show you," Jeddo said. "She works at Vibe Media and we are so proud of her."

I smiled.

"Why don't you come out with me?" Phaedra asked. "I'm new to all this, and my family back home are still convinced that New York City is a dangerous place for a woman."

"Where did you grow up?" I asked her. "Did you live in Dubai your whole life?"

"I'm Palestinian American but grew up in Beirut, London, Brussels, Dubai . . . you name it. Diplomat dad."

I half smiled, a joke forming in my mind about how people coming from former war zones in the Middle East now viewed America as an unsafe place.

"She can't this evening, unfortunately," my grandfather answered for me. "Perhaps another time. She can show you the extra storage unit down the hall, though, for your things?"

I smiled politely. Smokey's was an atmospheric little blues bar a couple of subway stops away. But in Jeddo's mind? A cigar lounge with flowing alcohol and scantily clad women? Men with the dark desires of night? There was no way he would have given me his blessing to join her there. I often thought Teta might have had an inkling about the fun mischief Katie and I got up to in college, but I had made extra efforts to shield my conservative grandfather from any details.

I took a key from Jeddo's key ring and guided Phaedra toward the dimly lit corridor outside our apartment. She said goodbye to my grandparents, and Teta proceeded to sing the *Friends* theme song to let Phaedra know we were there for her. My grandmother turned everything into songs. I shepherded Phaedra to the front door.

I downloaded a popular subway app to her phone as we walked, and she thanked me. Her phone kept buzzing to life with social media notifications.

"Let me know the next time you have a show," I said, trying to make conversation when we were alone in the hallway. "I would love to come and support."

I was onstage myself a few hours ago! was what I really wanted to scream. I took a left, and we faced a windowless row of doors. I opened door C as instructed, jiggling the handle a little.

I switched on the light and did jazz hands to show her the small space. There were two rows of bare shelves on one side and a rail, with a single coat hanger, on the other. I hoped it was big enough for all her dresses, shoes, diamonds, and tiaras.

"Glad to hear it," she said, her voice echoing as she stepped into the tiny room. "I usually perform classical concerts at Juilliard or blues in smoky little bars, so let me know which is more your vibe. When I'm not running around at events, that is. Either way, I could use a friendly face in the audience."

Stage? Lights? Yes, and yes. I just had to leave out the "smoky bar" part when I pitched this outing to Jeddo. I was about to turn out the light when I noticed a dusty gray box in the far corner.

Dreading a mouse or something with a pungent scent, I opened the shoebox an inch to find thick books inside. *Traditional Palestinian Dishes* read the dusty title in Arabic. I shifted it to find another cookbook beneath it, this one a faded red color that read: *Simple Home-Cooked Meals to Impress Your Family.* The books looked like they hadn't been touched in years. I picked up the box, turned off the light, and shut the door on the empty room.

I looked over at Phaedra, her heels clacking in the hallway. Back erect, shiny hair bouncing like we were shooting a shampoo commercial. Perhaps this is why she had 3.4 million devoted subscribers on YouTube. And counting.

Ever since she had uttered my family name, I had waited for the right moment to nonchalantly bring it up again.

It was quiet in the dim hallway. We paused outside my front door. This was my chance to ask her the burning questions I had about the Almases in Dubai.

Phaedra spoke first. "Well, see you tomorrow. I want that Tupperware of okra stew! Gotta go, left a cute guy waiting too long. I'm always late."

Maybe tomorrow, I told my disappointed heart.

I watched her walk away, feeling slightly irritated at the pep in her step and the extra-nice words she used. It was like talking to Barbie.

I walked back inside, my mind elsewhere. I placed the shoebox on the kitchen counter, then retook my seat at the dinner table. Phaedra's perfume lingered in the air as we finished dinner.

"Would you like coffee or tea?" I asked Jeddo afterward.

"Coffee. That Dominican stuff you got was excellent," he said, heading to the bathroom to wash up. "They have the best coffee in the world, the Dominicans. They are the loveliest people."

After performing the *Isha* evening prayer, he sat in his armchair in the living room to practice his evening sport: shouting abuse at the TV. Maybe one day I'd break it to him that they couldn't actually hear him.

This was a good opportunity. His cup of coffee was half-full. The TV volume was loud. And I had Teta alone in the kitchen.

"So Phaedra, huh," I said, clearing dishes from the table. "Not a name you hear every day. She was . . . a little extra. Trying too hard, don't you think?"

"She seems like a nice girl. Maybe she can be your friend," Teta said, clearing the table with me. "You spend too much time alone in your room. Work and home, work and home. Not healthy. It's good for you to go out and have friends. You are young."

"I'm . . . fine," I said, surprised. If anything, Phaedra was the one who needed to tone it down. It was fine as an act onstage, but real life was not a sequin-dusted Broadway musical. I tightened my braid, trying to imagine Stage Mia sitting at the kitchen table, curls bouncing wildly, lips rose red, talking about fantasizing about Jackson's upper lip. I shuddered and focused on Teta.

"Look at me—I have my book club and my farmer's market. It's good to be around people, Mia," Teta went on. "And Phaedra is an Arab girl like you. Meet her for a coffee. I don't want you to be like Diego, in his room alone."

She tutted, rehashing the episode of our favorite telenovela, in which Diego's mother discovered his excessive drinking to get over the fact that Marcela didn't love him. He refused to leave his room for days on end, strumming tuneless songs on his guitar. I knew it had been a mistake to introduce Teta to the guilty pleasures of telenovelas.

She wrapped an apron around her slender frame and tucked her hair behind her ears, ready to wash the dishes. Her eyes landed on the dusty shoebox, out of place on the kitchen counter.

"Oh, yeah, I found this shoebox full of your cookbooks or something," I said to her back. "Wasn't sure if you wanted me to just throw it out or . . ."

Her hands remained frozen in midair as she took in a sharp breath, but she didn't utter a word. Then she gave me a small smile and turned on the faucet. Maybe she was annoyed at me for dragging dust into her clean, lemon-scented kitchen.

"What was Phaedra, uh, saying? About the Almas family in Dubai?" I asked, taking my opportunity. "Do you know anyone there?"

Teta said nothing and began scrubbing dishes loudly. I usually would have given up, but today, I continued. "Since you won't talk, can I ask Phaedra for details?"

Teta waved her hand at me as if shooing away a fly. I pressed on.

"I deserve to know. By the way, I hear Dubai is like Vegas—"

"Enough ... *enough*," Teta snapped, her voice like a knife. "Don't fill your head with silly ideas. We are *not* going to bring up the past. I told you, it hurts. We can't change what happened. So I won't waste my breath."

Her sharp reaction took me by surprise.

Normally, I would retreat. We were used to tiptoeing around the subject of family, simply because, for us, family was synonymous with loss. We were blessed to have one another, my grandparents and I, like survivors in a makeshift lifeboat navigating our way . . .

But today, after the note from C.B. at the comedy club and then hearing Phaedra talk about extended family links in Dubai, I needed more. An image blossomed in my mind of a handful of cousins with my hair and Teta's smile. Could it be? A second chance for the bigger family I had always craved?

What am I missing, Teta? I silently asked her.

For once, I pressed on, my heart racing: "How can you hold a grudge your entire life? Why don't we speak to any other family members? It's bad enough you never want to talk about Dad. I have a right to know. I'm going to be twenty-five soon! Besides, we're . . ."

My voice tapered off as I studied her movements to understand her mood. She put down the rag in her hands and took a
few deep breaths while we waited to see if my grandfather was
going to ask us what the fuss was about. When he didn't, she quietly said in English: "Let sleeping cats lie."

"Sleeping *dogs*," I corrected. "Will you ever tell me what really
happened? It's my family, too, not just yours."

Her back was to me. The water in the sink was running, splash-
ing on plates. Teta's hands gripped the edge. She stared at a spot
on the wall before turning to me. Her eyes were moist.

"Just go to bed," she said, her voice breaking. "Another day, we
will talk. I just can't now."

Her hands were shaking. My heart was beating wildly in my
chest. I carefully made hot drinks and set my grandfather's fresh
espresso cup down next to him, along with a medjool date. Teta
didn't turn to face me as I passed by her in the kitchen, her hands
sloshing in the sudsy sink.

Resigned, I took a cup of chamomile tea to my room and shut
the door. I half-heartedly checked my phone. Jackson had actually
responded to my last text, saying he had to head back into the
office. I responded with a smiley face and told him to dig into my
snack drawer if he needed it. I felt champagne bubbles rising up
inside me, hoping this meant he wasn't spending the night locking
lips with Adriana. Katie had posted the photo of the two of us
with a heart on Facebook, which I "liked."

Frustrated by the ups and downs of the day, I propped open
my laptop in bed. I tried to google "Almas family Dubai" and
"Almas UAE," but nothing concrete came up . . . as usual. "Almas"
in Arabic means diamond, so all I found were listings of jewelry
stores. Defeated, I spent time scrolling through Phaedra's You-
Tube videos and sneaking glances at Jackson's Facebook posts.

When I could no longer hear my grandfather's TV program

blaring from the living room or any activity in the kitchen, I stood up. Teta must be at her friend Ghada's place nearby.

I locked my door, angled my desk lamp toward the brick wall behind my bed, and let my hair down. Time to test some new material. I cleared my throat and smiled at my imaginary audience.

"Why did the Arab chicken cross the road? Because her family was trying to arrange a marriage for her, but they didn't know she was already skewered . . ."

CHAPTER

7

The next morning, the elevator doors slid open, and I nodded hello to Ivory as I walked into work. As always, the sleek receptionist had a perfect middle part in her hair and dark skin that she set off beautifully with bright dresses and studded headbands. She was wearing a magenta dress with sunny yellow flowers on it today. I made my way past desks stacked with back issues of different magazines and walls with colorful printouts pinned up.

Jackson wasn't in his glass office yet.

He must have pulled a late night here. A quick social media check displayed a post about having midnight snacks at his desk with the hashtag #PigOfMediaStreet. I "liked" it.

Then I saw his latest Facebook post. It featured Adriana, long hair cascading over one shoulder, seated on his desk, with the hashtag #BurningTheMidnightOil. I remembered she worked on Wall Street, so she must be used to those kind of hours. Her maroon leather pencil skirt looked painted on.

They spent hours together last night with their Little Brother and

Little Sister . . . then she brings him snacks at the office like a good girl-friend? I thought. *That can't be good.*

I didn't "like" that one. With a huff, I ripped a page off my Word of the Day 2011 desk calendar. I crumpled it without reading it.

"It's official, there's a new reporter opening and I'm totally going for it," Katie said, pointing to her email inbox as I set my bag down and switched on my monitor. "Jackson sent the email out to everyone this morning. Your coffee is on your desk, by the way."

I smiled in thanks, swiveling in my seat to listen to her suggest writing samples to submit. A reporter job would mean better pay and interviews with important people. Although I was happy as a fact-checker and great at it, I could imagine Jeddo's eyes lighting up with pride if I got the new role. I drummed my fingers on my coffee cup. Should I consider going for it, too?

Katie had moved on to her saucy adventures with Kevin the night before. That was when Jackson strode in and waved to us on his way to his glass office.

I felt a swirl inside me, as if I had just jumped into cold water and my body was trying to find equilibrium again. I pulled out a berry-tinted lip gloss and applied it, my eyes trained on him.

He had been wearing the same patterned blue tie the first time Katie and I had met him, when he visited our ethics class at Columbia to give a recruitment speech to journalism students. I had been riveted, drinking in his passionate distaste for foodie phrases used to describe people of color in the press: caramel skin, almond eyes, honey-toned hair. He had used himself as an example: an Afro-Latino who doesn't feel he belongs with the Latin, Black, or American communities most times.

Afterward, I had lingered along with a handful of students to get his card, Katie and I extending our hands with smiles and polite introductions . . . and his eyes had singled me out. Misfits recognized each other.

The conversation had flowed as we walked side by side to the café on the ground floor of the journalism school, where I had joked that my skin was the color of fried chicken and his bellowing laugh had made me feel instantly warm inside. We had spent over an hour in the school's café unraveling our cultural-identity crises, talking over each other in excitement.

Him: *My mom's a descendent of Ethiopian Jews! I didn't even know that was an actual community and—*

Me: *My father was the whitest Palestinian you'll ever meet. I sometimes wish I had inherited his blue eyes and curly blond hair because—*

Him: *I get it, life in America is easier when you look white and—*

I had felt guilty wondering what his skin might taste like if I licked it.

He's even more of an outsider than me, I'd thought as my heart had swelled. When I shared a piece I had written for class about the complexities faced by Arab American journalists in a post-9/11 world, he had pitched it to Vibe Media's *The Culturalist* and scored me my first—and only—major byline. He had given me a big break, then hired me and Katie to join his team as fact-checkers after we had graduated.

Isn't that true love? I wondered now, my hand reaching for my phone to instinctively stalk him on social media.

"So, are you going to go for the reporter opening, too? Is this going to be a Hunger Games thing between us?" asked Katie, pretending to shoot me with an imaginary bow and arrow.

"I mean . . . more money would be nice," I admitted. "I'm thinking about it. But I just love being a fact-checker and I know nobody gets it."

The truth was that I had Jackson to thank for my job. I was a decent writer and had assumed I would get an internship at a news agency or website after grad school, but he sold me on the idea of being a fact-checker. I had always loved writing and reading, but the idea of analyzing text in forensic detail gave me a thrill that most people never understood.

If a journalist mentioned traffic on Broadway, my job was to confirm whether that stretch was one-way. If a writer described eating a mushroom-and-anchovy pizza at Ray's, I would look up the menu to confirm that was a real offering. It was the tiny details that made a story pop—and probably helped make my comedy sketches good. And I had to admit, I liked the sense of control . . . when I didn't seem to have it anywhere else in my life.

Not to mention the warm, fuzzy thrill of seeing Jackson every day. Gazing at his absurdly long eyelashes. Smiling at his penchant for dropping big words into casual conversation and then wiggling his eyebrows . . .

As he passed our desks, he dropped a chocolate bar on my desk and caught my eye, holding my gaze for a full two seconds before winking with a small smile. There was something so sweet and cheeky about the way he consistently made an effort to keep my snack drawer replenished with my favorite candy bars. I had shut the door on any hint of an office romance, and now he had Adriana, but these chocolate bars still kept appearing on my desk. I hid a smile, taking a sip of coffee, taking this as solid proof that he still thought about me as much as I thought about him. And that made me glow a little inside.

"Aaaand I've lost you," Katie said, nodding slowly. "If you do talk to him later, put in a good word for me, too, will you?"

I did want to steal time to talk to him. I was curious—and slightly nauseous—over how his night with Adriana had ended. I also wondered if his Little Brother, Michael, a self-proclaimed bookworm like me, had enjoyed the next Harry Potter book, which I had scoured secondhand bookshops to find.

It was wonderfully kind of Jackson to be part of the Big Brother program—and a nice surprise that his Little Brother had turned out to be a quiet booklover with whom I had formed a secondary connection. I liked being his distant book fairy, supplying stories that his school's library in the Bronx sometimes couldn't stock. I knew all about how it felt to escape the mad world by losing yourself in the pages of a novel. And the fact that my book-swapping endeavor made Jackson smile was a happy by-product.

Adriana might have bought him chocolate cake last night, but nothing beats magic and wizardry, I thought.

I knew Jackson had a team meeting at nine a.m., but maybe I could catch him alone after that. *For Katie,* I lied to myself.

CHAPTER

8

It was almost 9:45 a.m., and I could see that the management team meeting was still in full swing in the boardroom. Jackson had his back to me. I kept rereading the same lines in the latest Love Unfiltered column, but my brain wouldn't absorb the information, much less check all the facts accurately.

Love Unfiltered

"It's in the Tea Leaves"

BY HARUKI KATSUHIKO

I didn't expect to feel love at first sight when I met Aiko. We were introduced during a stiff afternoon tea in her family's home in the heart of Astoria's Japanese community. No one verbalized it, but the two families had come together to see if Aiko and I would be open to an arranged marriage after the modern way had failed us.

But love is exactly what happened: in a lightning-bolt instant, in all its complex simplicity, in a cheesy flash. All my misgivings about my mother choosing a wife for me melted away when I looked into Aiko's mischievous eyes, the steam rising from a cup of green tea between us. This was infinitely better than a match on eHarmony—a shot in the dark. But when Aiko's family chose a wealthier man for her, I . . .

I made notes to check details about the Japanese community in Astoria, the ages of Aiko and Haruki, and whether green tea was commonly served in their households, and to get consent from their families to publish this personal story.

Then I gave up.

I watched the managers stand up and nod at graphs projected on a big screen before filing out. Jackson caught my eye and smiled, then made his way to the reception desk.

My leg was thumping like a rabbit's foot beneath my desk, and I kept clicking a pen as if doing so was the solution to all my problems. Katie raised an eyebrow at me. This was my chance.

Smiling at her and putting my pen down, I picked up my lukewarm cup of coffee and a tin can of Caprice chocolate sticks. I walked toward the elevator, slipping my phone into my back pocket. I went all the way to the highest floor and took the extra flight of stairs to the roof, pushing the heavy door open to be greeted by a gust of cold air. I breathed it in, my eyes scanning the empty area until they landed on the exact spot where I knew Jackson would be.

I stared at his silhouette, his sunken shoulders and bowed head against the backdrop of a jungle of skyscrapers. It was all I could do not to fling my coffee cup and chocolates to the ground, run my fingers through his curls, and tell him it was all going to be okay.

"Thought I would find you here," I said softly, coming to stand next to him. The air was crisp, but I could feel the warmth of his body as he shifted his weight to lean toward me. We stood together quietly for a few beats, shoulder to shoulder, hip to hip, him lost in thought, me trying to hear my thoughts over my thudding heartbeat.

"How is Michael?" I asked, knowing he loved talking about him.

"Not my thing, but I gotta say he really loved the latest Harry Potter book you gave him. Says they just keep getting better." He smiled at me. "You're so good at finding books with the craziest notes written in them."

The sun was in his eyes, and I forgot for a moment that normal conversation meant I should respond to his last statement. Instead, I found myself lost in the gold threads branching out like little sun rays as his eyes held mine for a few beats longer than necessary. I broke our gaze first, then looked up again to find him still smiling, his eyes slowly roaming over my face. Our time together was full of these tiny, intimate moments that I would dissect later, replaying them endlessly, trying to derive special meaning.

"That's why I love those secondhand bookshops," I said finally, as he took out his phone to show me a close-up photo of Michael openly laughing, his finger pointing at a handwritten note on the first page:

To Florence,

When the world gets you down, go for a walk outside near trees and then eat some pasta and you will feel good again.

Love,

Your Aunt Who Loves You More Than Your Other Aunt

P.S. Chocolate works, too.

"I mean, that's pretty solid advice." I chuckled, proud of my find.

"Yeah, he needs it. Kids in his class have been picking on him again," he said, his voice dropping. A shiver ran up my spine as memories of my own childhood taunts rose up before me like heavy fog.

"Kids can be so mean," we said in unison, then smiled down at our hands. His hands were so much bigger than mine, and I resisted the urge to ask him to touch palm to palm, to laugh at the difference in size. In my fantasy, we would then recite those lines from *Romeo and Juliet* about a holy palmers' kiss and then he would lean in and this time—*this time*—I wouldn't turn my face away . . .

Instead, I asked him if he planned to do anything about Michael's bullies.

"Well, I got four company tickets to a big hockey game at Madison Square Garden next month—and guess who has lived in New York his entire life and never been there?" he said, and winked. "So now his greedy little classmates are kissing his butt trying to get one of two invites to the box to join us. He's excited and feeling popular."

I felt bubbles of emotion rising up in me. A kind word alone would have made all the difference to me when high school was a black time of turned backs, grief over my father, and whispers in hallways. Jackson's gesture was another level. I couldn't speak for a minute, trying to bring myself back to the present, restraining myself from throwing my arms around him in a bear hug.

Far below us, Manhattan's sirens blared and throngs of people crossed intersections, dodging errant taxis, but it was all a blur. I could, however, accurately count every single one of Jackson's eyelashes if asked.

"Those board meetings are long, man." He sighed, switching

gears. "Keep up your good work and you'll be stuck in there with us managers soon. You ain't in grad school, anymore, Dorothy."

He seemed tired. I looked at the sharp frown line that had formed between his eyes and resisted the urge to trace it with my finger. I smiled and nudged him.

"Katie is really keen on that new reporter job, and I'm thinking of going for it, too. But, hey, maybe Katie and I will both impress you with viral stories next week, and you'll have to create an extra reporter opening," I said. "Pshh, you'll be answering to us soon."

He chuckled and took the can of Caprice sticks from my hand. I felt a zing of electricity when his fingers brushed against mine. I had a ridiculous image of him putting one chocolate stick in his mouth like a cigarette, with me biting the other end until our lips met.

He offered me one, and I took it, both of us blowing on them like they were cigars before crunching into them.

"Don't forget me when you're a big shot, then," he said, tapping my nose with his chocolate stick. "Remember, I knew you back when you were just a pretty student."

The phrase *pretty student* hung in the air between us like fairy lights. I could feel a warm blush rising to my cheeks. He smiled and dusted off a few chocolate flakes that had fallen on the collar of my coat.

"You think I'm pretty?" I heard my voice rise from somewhere deep down. I couldn't look at him. My eyes were trained on the city spread out beneath us. I looked up at the audience of windows and tall buildings. My breath was growing shallower. Could they all tell how I was feeling?

Is he going to kiss me?

"Pretty? Stop it. You're gorgeous, Mia, and you know it," he said, nudging me. "Sweet and smart, too. Kinda girl you bring home to mama."

I will go anywhere with you right now, I wanted to shout. I tilted my face toward him as another cold breeze picked up, teasing a few curls loose from my tight braid. His lips parted, and I was so close I could feel the warmth of his breath on my face.

Oh, God, please let this happen, I thought. *I'll give to charity. I'll pray five times a day.*

I wanted to give in to the moment, to pretend we were just two lovers on an island made of skyscrapers, to ride this wave and let myself be taken out to the wild sea ... but thoughts of Adriana and our colleagues buzzing about the newsroom downstairs began to cloud my mind. He must have sensed the way I stiffened ever so slightly. He pulled on one of my curls playfully and cleared his throat.

"It's funny, this New York City life, isn't it?" he said, taking a slight step back. "It's fast, I'm always hustling. And now we have to hustle back downstairs. Because I'm freezing my butt off and you're supposed to become the next Joan Didion. Lots of competition for this new reporter opening, by the way, if you and Katie are seriously interested."

"Yeah, Katie is really interested," I said loyally. "She would be great at it. And I think I'll give it a shot."

"You both would be great at it," he said warmly, motioning for us to walk back toward the door. My heart dropped.

He took the empty tin Caprice can and put a hand on my back, leading me to the door. I wanted to stay here, work out all these beautiful things he'd said to me, forget that we worked together for a moment. Just a man and a woman alone on a rooftop with cigarettes made of chocolate. Why couldn't I let myself relax into him? All those years of study, of hard work to achieve, of consistency, to reward the sacrifices my grandparents had made for me, of utmost respect at work so I could do better ... all of that was on the line every time my body responded to Jackson's nearness. But would a kiss really be so bad?

I sighed deeply, acutely aware of the sound of his steps behind me as we made our way toward the stairs and the elevator.

With each step down, he grew more professional. Boss Man Jackson was back.

"I told Divya—you know, that new lawyer—that we need to up our content strategy game, especially on social channels," he was saying. I wondered if there were cameras and if he was afraid it would look like we were playing hooky. Or hooking up.

Wait, we're not done! I wanted to say. *Let's stay here and hash this out. With our lips!*

I found myself nodding, not really contributing to the conversation, until he brought Divya up again.

"She's great, I have to say," he said, holding the elevator door open for me. "We stayed up working until nearly one a.m. last night, preparing for this crazy week."

"Oh, right. Yeah, you said you came here last night," I said dumbly. "So she, uh, Divya met Adriana, too, then?"

I looked at his face in the harsh elevator light. A quizzical smile played on his lips when I uttered Adriana's name. He didn't respond for a beat, and I wondered if he called Divya and Adriana pretty and gorgeous, too. And were they as childish as I was, hungrily lapping up his words like they had never heard them before?

"Yeah, they actually met last night when she dropped by the office . . ." His voice trailed off.

Are things getting more serious between you two? I wanted to ask, standing idly next to him, watching the floor numbers drop as we descended.

Introducing her to his colleagues? Oh God, please don't invite me on an outing to get to know her, too. I don't think I could handle it.

The elevator took us back down to our office floor. Then he gave my shoulder a quick squeeze and wished me luck. I told him to enjoy the hockey game and let Michael know the next Harry Potter book, complete with a funny note, would be coming right up. I missed Jackson's hand when it left my shoulder. He turned to walk toward his glass office, and my eyes trailed his back until my breath returned to normal.

I felt like the cold cup of coffee that I realized I had forgotten up on the roof.

CHAPTER

9

"Thank you for coming after work," said Phaedra, opening the door wide that evening. "Please come right in."

I had always loved this apartment. As a young girl, I used to tag along with my grandfather on weekends when he needed to fix things. He would busy himself mumbling to a leaky toilet or a faulty sink, while I had strict orders to sit still on the couch, read a book, and not touch anything. My grandfather went ahead to the kitchen sink to retrieve Phaedra's necklace, and, as if on autopilot, I went straight to my usual spot on the sofa and sat down.

Every time I came here, I would sit on my hands and look around at the floor-to-ceiling windows that flooded the entire apartment with light. Birds always perched on the external AC units outside the windows, near the fire escape. If I sat up really tall, I could see the Hudson River stretching to the right, hugged by trees in Riverside Park.

Then I would sink into the cream sofa and just stare at the grand piano in the center of the living room. It was painted baby blue, and I had never seen anything like it. I used to picture myself as a grown woman sprawled on top of it, wearing a suggestive, sparkling red dress with a matching shade of lipstick and singing a jazzy show tune. Elton John would play the piano in a sequin blazer and matching top hat, occasionally swatting at my errant curls.

I stood up and walked to the window to the left, stretching out my arms. I could see students carrying backpacks heading toward Columbia's black wrought-iron gates for evening lectures. Even at this busy hour, our street was so tame compared to the buzz of the West Village.

Evenly spaced trees lined the gray sidewalk on a much calmer version of Broadway. Even the eating establishments sounded mellow by comparison: Sweetgreen, Blue Bottle Coffee, Mondel Chocolates. The most activity we got in this area was from the tourists who excitedly took photos near Tom's, the diner made famous on *Seinfeld*, a few blocks away on the corner of West 112th Street.

But I had to admit that this building had its own magic. During spring and autumn, when the weather was just right, the tenants would often leave their windows wide open and let their music spill out onto the street. Listening to the Ukrainian violinist in apartment 6 or Jason, the pink-haired drummer from Utah, in apartment 9 never failed to make me smile.

I turned when I heard footsteps coming back toward the living room area.

Were those a man's black shoes near the piano? Was someone else here, hiding near the fire escape?

"I just love the view, too," Phaedra's voice came from behind me. She sat down on the couch next to me, and I extended the Tupperware toward her. She smiled and thanked me for remembering to bring it.

"When I was told housing came with the Juilliard guest lecturer program, I didn't realize it would be *this* nice," she said. "People always talk about shoebox-size apartments in Manhattan in the movies. This is huge."

Unless you're part of the top 2 percent, that's pretty true, I thought.

"You lucked out. It's the nicest one in the building," I confirmed. "Hey, how was your show last night?"

She sat up and touched my hand as she recounted the drama of arriving one minute before she was meant to be onstage. In the daylight, her skin looked like it was photoshopped, and her eyes shone like little pools of water.

She was dressed in a white T-shirt and jeans, but she still had an elegance about her movements, as if we were filming a reality show, with cameras in the corners. She sat with her back straight, like her spine was a flagpole, and she crossed her legs regally at the ankles. There was something so constructed and studied about her appearance, I had to restrain myself from telling her to just chill out.

Would school have been easier on me when I was younger if I looked more like her? I wondered, admiring her feline green eyes and wavy blond hair. I had grown up reading Sweet Valley High and Baby-Sitters Club books. Phaedra would have easily fit right into their worlds.

Arab, but not Arab. There, but not there.

I was used to that.

Maybe Teta was right, I thought. *Maybe I shouldn't be so judgy and should just ask her to grab coffee.*

While studying her, I realized I hadn't listened to a word she had said about her show. I kept imagining the mystery man Phaedra was potentially hiding in the apartment. Those were definitely a man's shoes. There were manly-looking sunglasses on the table, too.

"So, you mentioned another show this Friday?" I said, hoping she hadn't noticed how fidgety I had become. "I would really love to see you perform."

"Leave it to me," she said, leaning in conspiratorially. "I'm a master at this stuff."

How could someone who was so openly herself, not hiding her heels and her sequins and her makeup, be a master of deception? I thought about what it would feel like to have Jackson's shoes nonchalantly strewn in my living room.

I self-consciously put a hand to my braid and licked my bare lips. I didn't know if I could fully trust her yet.

"You, uh, mentioned you met some people with the same last name as me in Dubai?" I asked her. "I've always wondered if we had extended family abroad. My grandparents kind of cut ties with everyone when they left the Arab world, I think."

"I don't know them personally, but the Almas family is known to own a string of jewelry stores," she said. "Nice stuff. More popular than Tiffany over there. But maybe it's a different family, just the same name or something? You know, like Smith over here?"

My eyebrows shot up. Perhaps I had misread the Google searches of my own last name. Could my extended family be behind Almas Inc., the chain of diamond stores I read about online? Why had Teta never mentioned this, even in passing? She had never been materialistic, so I couldn't imagine money being the reason for the split in the family. What had actually caused the chasm? And how big was this extended, well-known family?

"You're all set. Here's your necklace, and I tightened the faucet for you, too," my grandfather said in Arabic, walking into the room and handing Phaedra a gold chain. "We are so happy to have you here, and we are at your service. Just call me if you need anything."

He explained to her that, as the superintendent of the building, he could take care of any maintenance needs. Teta was handy at washing and folding laundry, as well as providing meals for a fee. All so Phaedra could focus on her craft: making beautiful music.

I turned to face the window while he spoke, my mind racing. I mulled over a potential big family rift over money, or ownership of stores. I needed to get to my laptop to do a little digging . . . If the Dubai Almas family was prominent enough, there must be information about them online that I had missed. And did they know about my father's death? Could an old family divide be resolved by the newer generation of lonely misfits, like me?

Cousins, are you somewhere out there?

"This is all so wonderful. Thank you for the hospitality," Phaedra said, getting up with a warm smile. "And I just love practicing on this piano. Makes me feel like a real artist in New York."

"You are. I'm sure the universe conspired to bring your talent here," my grandfather said in the teddy bear tone he used when speaking to anyone outside his own family for some reason. "I'm a fan of Chopin myself."

I had never heard him mention Chopin before. But my mind was still on the Almas jewelry business.

"Oh, he's my favorite," said Phaedra, moving toward the piano and playing a few bars. "I would love for Mia to come on Friday to one of my shows. I could use a friendly face in the audience."

"I . . . Maybe," Jeddo said, speaking for me.

"Thank you," I said, mystified at how Phaedra had avoided getting a straight no from him. Had the mix of faint perfume, the light in the apartment, her olive oil eyes, and that melancholy melody on the piano intoxicated him?

My grandfather and I left in a trance, riding the elevator down in thoughtful silence. Heading back to our apartment to get ready for dinner, I couldn't get Phaedra's speculation about Almas Inc. out of my mind. I had to find out more from Teta.

Tonight.

CHAPTER
10

Would there ever be a good time? I wondered as I helped Teta clear the plates after dinner.

I could see her nerves were still shot from the nearby shooting and from my unexpected tirade of questions about the family yesterday. She moved gracefully around the kitchen, putting on yellow gloves to start the dishes, but avoided my eyes. I was desperate to learn more about the past, but I felt a pang of guilt whenever we did exchange glances.

"Are you okay?" I asked her when my grandfather got up to pray. I stood next to her at the sink, taking each wet dish from her to dry.

She plunged her hands into the soapy water and nodded.

"Does this . . . Do you think it would help if . . . I mean, Phaedra told me the Almas family is kind of a big deal in Dubai and—"

"Mia, stop. I don't want to talk about family or Dubai or anything now," she said, her voice thin. "You will understand soon, I promise."

Today, this wasn't enough. I really needed more.

"I'm not asking you to tell me everything right this minute," I said gently, moving closer to her. "It's just that she mentioned Dubai, so I just want to know if we have family living there and—"

"Mia, *khalas*! Stop! Do you want me to have a heart attack? Do you care about me?" Teta hissed. "I told you, I will tell you when the time is right."

The plaintive emotion in her voice shook me. I didn't understand why she couldn't share her pain with me, so we could soothe each other. I felt as if we were two sandcastles being hit over and over by greedy waves. Wouldn't we be stronger together?

"What about when I want to know? This isn't just about you, Teta, please," I appealed, surprised at the tremor that crept into my voice.

"If you care, you stop asking these questions. Your family is here—it's me and Jeddo. That's it." She looked me square in the eyes. "I told you, *enough*."

The melodrama may have been borrowed from our favorite Mexican telenovela, but the sentiment was all her own. I'd have to try another day, maybe when she was in a better mood. Perhaps I'd have to give it some time.

Dejected, I went back to my room. My desk lamp was still in position, aimed at the brick wall, but I didn't feel like practicing my comedy material just yet. I needed to decompress first. I lay down on the bed.

I miss you, Dad, I said to the ceiling. *Always, but a lot right now. I could use some help sorting out my life.*

I had never gotten to know my mother. Her parents wanted nothing to do with me after she—their only daughter—had chosen to marry a Muslim man and then died giving me life. I often fantasized about what it would be like to have a sweet, beautiful mother; this used to happen more often when I was younger, like when I got my first period or had my first crush on a boy. My mother's name was Jessica, and I had inherited her dark Sicilian hair and eyes. She had grown up in a small town in Indiana before coming to New York City, working as a seamstress on costumes for a small theater in the Garment District before meeting my dad.

As I grew older and my efforts to get to know my mother's family repeatedly hit dead ends, I leaned completely into the warmth of my paternal grandparents and my dad. He was my mother and my father while he was alive.

What should I have asked you, Dad? I thought, trying not to let myself fall into the ever-present darkness of loss. *Do we have more family out there I should know about?*

I wondered if he'd known anything more about the Almas family, if he had shared any details with my mother during their brief marriage. Or had he been as clueless as I was?

Can you help me, Dad? I asked, looking up at the ceiling.

A soft rap on the door broke my reverie.

Teta entered, her white frilly apron still on. She was carrying the dusty shoebox, the one from the storage room that I had opened for Phaedra.

I sat up.

She cleared her throat.

"It was always going to be hard for me to talk about this," she said, her voice uncharacteristically thick with emotion as she played with the fraying cardboard edge. "This . . . strange family situation we have."

"I don't know, Teta. We spend all that time watching telenovelas, and it seems like our family drama might be even spicier," I said, trying to lighten the mood, encouraged by the fact that she had come in to talk to me. I wanted to avoid another blowup, her shutting me down again. Or worse: silence.

It worked. She chuckled, breaking into a small smile.

"Yes, it really is like a bad play," she said, shaking her head and throwing her hand up in the air. "All these years later, still so hard for me to bring it up. Makes it more real if I talk about it."

"Then . . . what about writing about it?" I prodded very gently, scared she might scamper off. "I always see you writing bits of poetry and insanely long letters to your friends on their birthdays. We can write a screenplay and sell it as a TV show! Show Marcela some real drama."

"No! No TV, no fame, no thank you, nobody else needs to know nothing," she said, pinching my cheek. "But funny you should mention writing . . . I have something for you."

She came toward the edge of my bed, holding out her palm. I placed mine in hers, and she traced small circles on the back of my hand with her thumb. I looked up into her eyes, into a face I'd memorized over the years, seeing new expressions.

"Because, you are right," she carried on, still standing. "You are going to be twenty-five . . . and this made me realize I am going to be an old lady soon . . . Even though I don't feel like one, I am. And you deserve . . . to know."

She dropped my hand and sat on the bed, the shoebox on her lap. She opened it absentmindedly, obviously still feeling raw.

Inside, there were the two cookbooks with faded edges and dog-eared pages I'd seen before. She put those aside and reached for a thick blue journal at the bottom. Sitting on the bed next to me, she flipped through it.

"I really was going to tell you everything soon—I was planning to gift this to you on your birthday next month," she said. "Funny how life doesn't go along with your timetables. The universe always has its own plan. It's not finished . . . but I guess you can start. And maybe I'll have an ending to share by the time you are done."

The journal was filled with writing. Some pages had been torn out of something else and glued onto the journal's blue-lined paper; other pages had been written on directly. All of it was in my grandmother's Arabic handwriting, just like the grocery lists she put up on the fridge. There was a sketch of what looked like a big lemon or orange tree on one page.

Was this a diary? Scrapbook? There were notes in the margins, too.

"I may not be able to talk about it so easily, but you can read about it," she said. "I know your Arabic is not perfect, but that's what Googles is for."

"Google," I corrected, my voice a whisper. I was in awe that she was ready to draw the curtain back a little on this dark corner of our lives.

"Yes," she said. "Just read it all and then . . . we talk."

We locked eyes properly for the first time since she'd entered my room. Her eyes were brimming with tears as she ran a hand gingerly over the faded blue cover of the journal.

"Phaedra, she surprised me. It was a shock to hear her bring up the Almas family," she said, handing the journal over to me. "I thought about it all night and decided it's better I tell you what I know. In case, so you don't get surprised like me. I was just trying to protect you. Protect us."

Phaedra had surprised me, too, with her high heels and her strong perfume.

I wondered what secret Teta had felt she needed to hide from me. Was there a moment that passed between her and Phaedra that I hadn't noticed, when Phaedra brought up the Almas family name? What more could she know about the family?

"And I just see you are a little sad, keeping to yourself," Teta said, eyes cast down. "Afraid to open up to people. When I was young and beautiful, all I cared about were suitors. Maybe this is my fault. Maybe reading this will make you see how powerful love can be, even when you think you've lost everything."

Powerful love? Was this the story of how she met my grand-father, then?

My mind raced to the rooftop with Jackson, the sun in his eyes and the lust in mine. I wanted to figure out if I felt strongly enough about him to finally make something happen. I looked down at the journal, nervous and excited.

"I am a big believer in love. I just don't know if it will happen for me," I said, my voice small. I traced random shapes on the cover of the faded blue journal, thinking how it might feel to talk to her about my crush on Jackson. Maybe if she believed love could be a priority, she might be open to the idea of Jackson, of a boyfriend, of her granddaughter working on modern love columns . . .

"Love isn't what you think it is," she said resolutely. "It's even better."

She pointed to the journal and winked. I opened my mouth, willing words to come out about my life, but then I wondered if it was better not to push my luck and bring everything up all at once. She had opened the heavy iron door a crack. Maybe the next time we talked, I could take her cue and invite her to take a few steps into my real world.

With a soft smile, she clapped her hands once and did a half wave. She seemed resigned but relieved somehow, walking briskly to the door. She let her hand linger on the doorknob for a moment. I held my breath and clutched the journal, worried she was going to change her mind.

Then she opened the door, nodded with finality at me, and shut it on her way out.

I sat back, opening Google Translate on my laptop as instructed. The lilting Arabic writing held promise. There was still so much I wanted to learn about my family, and maybe the universe was finally going to give me some context about love—even if Teta couldn't talk to me directly.

Maybe I'd finally get names or answers to heavy questions that I'd carried around my whole life like pebbles in my shoe. I opened the journal to find the first few pages glued on, written in unfamiliar, sharp Arabic handwriting.

Thanks, Dad, I thought, sending a kiss up to the ceiling.

Then I began to read.

CHAPTER

11.

Zeina and Layla
Teenieh, a small village outside Jaffa, Palestine
Late 1946

Zeina was not a classic beauty. She had, however, mastered how to smile so that her dimples showed, tilt her head to expose inches more of her milk-white bare neck, despite the cold, and laugh heartily at mild jokes in a way that had bewitched most of the men in the towns surrounding Jaffa.

The town was accustomed to seeing men from neighboring villages, after an evening spent playing cards and music at the houses of relatives, dawdle the following morning in front of the Almas house hoping to catch a glimpse of Zeina on their way to work.

Many were often surprised to learn she had an older sister who didn't have light eyes like hers. Layla, always in the background, with her birdlike nose and persistent scowl.

Zeina didn't like to let her admirers down. While black-haired Layla always helped their mother cook and clean, Zeina floated in and out of chores without threat of punishment. Every morning, without fail, she framed herself in the window directly facing the street, sewing quietly and smiling in the general direction of her admirers from behind white lace curtains.

She knew her beauty held a certain power, but was it enough to help her achieve her dream?

Was there a way for her to avoid the expected path into a monotonous life, like that of Maryam down the street, with her five children and constant sweeping of her front doorstep? Or that of Umm Mohamed—mother of Mohamed—whose entire life revolved around running the little grocery store on the corner and complaining that her son never visited? Even her own mother's life consisted mainly of plotting the marriages of her daughters to the wealthiest men—the highest bidders!—she could find to ensure the family's prosperity and reputation.

That was not very romantic.

Zeina wanted something more. She craved foreign, unfamiliar cities and passionate love. She wanted the life she'd read about in French stories—the ones from the American University of Beirut's library that her uncle snuck to her when he visited. The books helped her improve much more than her French language skills.

Zeina's father, a proud Palestinian schoolteacher, vowed to never leave the village where he was born, the rolling green hills he had inherited, the faded stone house his great-grandfather had built. But his own brother, Zeina's uncle Saeed, who taught literature at the university, had a thirst for other worlds and cultures that thrilled her. He often sent the family postcards from his travels to Paris, London, and other tidy, tree-lined cities she had read about in books. She kept every single one and used them as bookmarks.

There wasn't a man in the village who could offer her—or any woman—a life of true excitement and freedom.

But recently Zeina thought she had found a real possibility. Not just to leave the village or experience a different, more exciting life. A chance for the sweeping kind of love that existed in storybooks.

In these snapshot moments by the window, she was not wearing her older sister Layla's hand-me-down dresses made of rough material. The lines in her hands were not visible as she daintily held a needle. Her graceful neck stole attention from the way her plain blue dress hung awkwardly on her slender body. So charmed were these men by her air that they did not see how unruly her black hair was as she perched before them like a bird on the windowsill.

Every once in a while, she would put down the pillow she was pretending to embroider with a fine needle, leaning over to see the men sauntering past her house, nodding ever so slightly when they managed to catch her eye.

Waiting for him to pass by.

The Almas sisters had seen Richard walking along their street nearly every day, running a hand through his golden hair and glancing at the house.

Layla hovered just out of sight as he passed by the Almases' stone house that morning. She saw him smile when his eyes settled on Zeina and noticed her sister's sewing grow more urgent as she hid a smile in her lap. Then Zeina actually looked straight into his eyes, right in front of Layla, and smiled back, nodding in the direction of the lemon tree. Richard nodded back once.

Layla bet he hadn't even noticed her standing behind Zeina.

When Richard had first been stationed in the town, with his khaki fatigues and holstered gun, all the young women would scurry past him or cross the street when he approached.

The growing number of British soldiers flooding into Palestine meant that tensions were rising. In the bigger towns, like Jaffa, there were tens of thousands of them, and nobody felt safer. Yet after a year of watching his little kindnesses in their tiny village—carrying the grocery bags from the *dukkan* for elderly Tante Maryam and showing little Fadi how to play that silly game with rocks in his front yard—Zeina had seen how the formalities had melted between him and the townspeople.

The events erupting in other parts of the country—small villages decimated and entire families displaced—seemed to be happening in a different world, and the young women often forgot why he and the other British army men had come to their safe, leafy little corner of Palestine.

Soon the young women were regularly trading stories about the soldier's crooked smile, how he tipped his hat politely when they passed, and how funny and foreign Arabic words sounded coming from his thin lips. How tanned his skin had gotten, even in the weak spring sun. A cigarette always hung listlessly from his fingers as he walked. (How jealous some of them felt of those cigarettes for touching his lips again and again!)

When families had gathered at Fatima's house for Friday lunch the previous week, Zeina had sat in her bedroom with the ladies while the men played cards in the living room. The British soldier was the main focus of conversation, each girl trying to glean information from the rest, asking if male cousins had interacted with him, what brand of cigarettes he smoked.

Zeina had shrugged and stayed quiet.

Despite all this interest, the young women were never allowed to consort with the soldiers. They weren't free from the eyes of society, not like the beautiful Jewish girls who held dances for soldiers in Jaffa. Their neighbor's daughter, Sabiha, had seen them once when visiting relatives in the main town.

She told the Almas sisters about the women's painted lips and loose, long hair, arms linked on their way to a music-filled dance hall. The Arab girls seemed to have eyes monitoring their every move, every breath, as if they were canaries in a cage.

And nobody had dared talk to him.

Except for Zeina.

This morning, after her show of sewing by the window, Zeina stood up to start her day. She didn't think her sister suspected anything when Zeina insisted on coming to the market to buy fruit, even though it wasn't her turn and the random act of sweetness must seem so unlike her. The sisters walked out the door carrying woven baskets, laughing together at the tear in their father's pants on their short walk to Umm Mohamed's *dukkan*.

The air was perfumed along the way with the scent of orange blossoms in full bloom. Everyone loved this season except for Layla. She preferred the salty sea air, breathing it in deeply even in freshly washed sheets hung out to dry. On very quiet days, in the early morning hours before the *Fajr* call to prayer, Layla could almost hear the waves from their house on the outskirts of Jaffa. But today, the air was sickly sweet. Zeina plucked a white blossom and placed it behind her ear.

They passed the small white mosque, starkly empty between prayer times. Chatting quietly, they took a right at the end of their street at the sandy school playground surrounded by purple flowers of wild thyme. When they reached Umm Mohamed's *dukkan*, they split the list of items to buy.

While Layla busied herself feeling for bruises in the fruit, Zeina slipped through the back door leading into the alley behind the *dukkan*.

Richard was already waiting for her. He greeted her with warm breath, brushing his lips against hers. Then another, slower, softer kiss on her rosebud lips. Then a third, his pink tongue parting Zeina's soft smile as her hands clasped the nape of his neck, drawing him closer.

Zeina's entire body buzzed with new electricity. No one else, aside from this foreign man, had dared defy convention and break boundaries in the name of love in this way. Their kisses opened the door to a life of wild fantasy; visions danced before her with each touch of their hungry lips—of eloping to start a fresh life where nobody knew anyone, of a small cottage in the green English countryside, a desk stacked with novels where she could try her hand at writing one of her own, of children with her eyes and his lopsided smile. Of dances and trains and long cigarette holders. Of freedom from the shackles of women's limited expectations in her suffocating village.

Growing up in a small town with everyone interested in her every move, Zeina felt this man like a breath of fresh air. It helped that his eyes were the color of a cloudless sky.

He was handsome, yes, but he must have recognized the same mischievous spark that she saw in his eyes the first time they met. It was the only reason he could have been bold enough to say hello directly to her instead of politely keeping his gaze down like other men did. An Arab man would never have dared to speak to her so openly and risk word getting back to her father!

As their kisses grew more urgent, the flower behind Zeina's ear floated to the ground.

The two of them didn't notice Layla when she came searching for Zeina behind the store. Layla froze, watching Richard lean in and trail kisses down her sister's neck.

That was when Layla ducked back inside, wild-eyed and short of breath at her sister's brazen behavior, as if she herself was the one who had crossed the line.

Layla couldn't believe the audacity of her younger, more

beautiful sister, passionately kissing the handsome soldier without a care in the world. As usual, acting like she could have anyone and anything her heart desired. Did she know the true meaning of pining, of deeply wanting anything, when life constantly handed her gifts for free?

How could Zeina do this without concern for the Almas family honor, for anyone who might see them? It was one thing for the ladies to gossip about the handsome soldier . . . but kissing him? In public in broad daylight? What if someone else had walked in on them? How could Zeina risk this? For what? Layla would never understand.

Zeina is beautiful enough to have her pick of suitors in the village. Why him, like this? Layla's heart drummed. She's so selfish not to realize how this puts the entire family's reputation at risk . . . Who will want to ask for my hand in marriage if this gossip gets around town?

She realized that the orange she held in one hand now had five deep fingernail marks on its thick skin. She released her grip and watched it roll lazily across the floor.

Would the handsome soldier have ever even looked twice at me? she wondered bitterly. *I bet he doesn't know I exist.*

Layla caught her breath after a minute or so. She stood with her hand listlessly resting on a crate of oranges, staring off into the distance without seeing anything.

She felt a confusing mix of anger, jealousy, and uncertainty bubbling up within her, greeting the familiar fear of her prettier, younger sister getting married before her.

The ultimate humiliation.

Zeina came back into the store, cheeks flushed and eyes so green they looked like fish that jumped out at you from the sea. Her lips looked a little swollen, but her expression was even.

"Ready to go, Layla?" she asked her sister merrily, before

turning to the elderly woman behind the cash register. "Umm Mohamed, you look radiant today! Is your son, Mohamed, enjoying his studies?"

"Yes, yes, but he never calls or visits! He is. . . ."

They chatted away and joked with each other as if Layla wasn't even there, something about a little boy who ran around the store yesterday with his pants off shouting "Farfour!" and wiggling his willy. Umm Mohamed nodded goodbye to Layla as she trailed like a dark shadow behind her charming younger sister.

Layla couldn't sleep that night. As the house grew quiet, she could hear Zeina tossing and turning. Feigning sleep, Layla watched her sister get up and sneak out of the room in the glow of the full moonlight that trickled through the window.

Layla sat up in bed, staring out at the moon, wondering why God had made her plainer than her sister when her own desires were just as strong. She was so tired of constantly being overlooked, cast aside, for a sister who didn't even earn her worth. Why did Zeina's green eyes and white skin add so much value in everyone's eyes? That was when she saw Zeina digging in the ground in the front lawn like a cat, burying something beneath the big lemon tree. She placed a rock over her work.

With a start, Layla remembered that her sister had nodded toward the lemon tree when exchanging glances with the handsome solider that morning.

When Zeina stood up, Layla quickly lay back down in bed and closed her eyes. She heard the water run in the bathroom and wondered if Zeina had managed to rinse all the dirt from beneath her fingernails.

Long after Zeina had crept back into bed, Layla lay still. She tried to imagine what it would be like to have a man's lips on hers, his fingers grazing the exposed skin on her neck, his arms pulling her in tight at the waist. She felt a wet fire between her legs that kept her awake all night.

The next morning, Zeina looked like she had slept for twelve hours, woken by the kiss of a handsome prince, while Layla felt like a widow with dark circles beneath her eyes. Over breakfast, Layla watched Zeina, and Zeina kept her eyes on the tree. When she caught her sister's eye, she simply smiled and turned to make conversation with their oblivious parents.

Later, Layla got to work cleaning the house while Zeina sat near the window overlooking the lemon tree, pretending to sew. Hadn't their mother noticed that she had been working on that same pillowcase for over a week? She must be waiting for him again. For Richard. Either to pass by or to take whatever she buried in the dirt for him.

She watched Zeina as she swept, back and forth, in the hallway.

Why did Layla feel like the dust on the ground?

CHAPTER
12

What the heck was that?

I reread the pages over and over until I fell asleep, dreaming of a forest of wild lemon trees and fingernails caked with dirt. When I awoke, I sat up in bed in a daze, shaking my head at the open journal on my nightstand.

Wet fire? I shuddered. I got ready with my mind on my grandmother. The words were beautiful, but was it a work of fiction or loosely based on her life? A series of short stories mirroring her life as a young girl in Palestine?

Could Teta be Layla or Zeina? Because Richard, the British soldier, was very clearly not my grandfather . . . and Teta's name was Amal.

I wished I could devour the entire story in one sitting, but it took an unexpectedly long time to write Arabic words into Google Translate for a little help. A lot of help. My Arabic was rusty. Just like my knowledge of my family's history—and even of Palestine.

I spent a full hour reading the British National Army Museum's historical timeline of the rising tensions in that region.

Teta never held grudges for very long. I knew she would be back to her pleasant self at breakfast, because she firmly believed that holding on to anger darkens the soul. Teta is someone who has learned to forgive with grace, to let go with peace, to treat each day with gratitude as if it is brand new and fresh, simply because she has dealt with so much loss and grief in her life.

She had asked me to complete the entire journal before discussing it with her, but I needed some clarity now. Who exactly was this story about and could the ending make me feel better about myself, about who I was and where I came from? I recognized so many of the emotions that washed over Zeina when she was around the British soldier. Perhaps there was a way to pull a little more information out of her—I was a journalist, after all.

Teta, how do you feel about men in uniform?

"Teta, can I help you with that?" I asked her instead. I still couldn't get the phrase "wet fire" out of my mind, watching her walk around the kitchen. My grandfather had eaten before us, up at sunrise like a rooster. He was no longer within earshot, engrossed in reading every inch of a magazine in the living room.

"All done," she said, picking mint leaves and tossing them into her tea. She still wasn't looking me in the eye. Her hair was a honey brown, framing her face. Her necklace lay on the table, waiting for her to start her day.

Journalism Lesson #1: Put your subject at ease.

"One day, we will have breakfast on the terrace of a big house facing the sea," I said, sitting down. "Like Marcela in the telenovela."

The most recent episode was about a monstrous mother-in-law living with newlyweds. Teta always laughed, and my grandfather would repeatedly ask how we tolerated such garbage while peering over our shoulders and constantly asking questions.

Teta clapped her hands delightedly.

"Yes! And someone to fan me with a palm tree leaf," she said. "I want a sea view and lots of trees. I like greenery."

My grandfather shouted good morning from the living room, asking us what we were cackling like chickens about.

Journalism Lesson #2: Win the subject's trust so they confide in you.

"Nothing. Teta is just telling me about someone who used coriander instead of parsley when trying to make tabbouleh," I answered.

Teta gave me a thumbs-up for my quick wit.

"When you are finished, please come in here so I can see which story you worked on," he said. "These are all excellent articles, just excellent. You're just as good a writer as all these white people, you know. I am so proud of you, Mia."

I had succeeded in buying myself a few more minutes alone with my grandmother. I played her favorite singer, Fairuz, on YouTube on my phone at a respectably low volume to ensure he wouldn't hear the rest of our conversation. Teta sang along, adding harmonies.

Journalism Lesson #3: Ask open, leading questions.

"What kind of trees?" I asked casually. "We could sit together and drink tea and gossip about that loud woman who visits the hair salon next door."

She dipped warm pita bread into a plate of thyme mixed with olive oil and sesame seeds.

"We used to have a big, beautiful lemon tree outside our house growing up near Jaffa," she said wistfully. "My sister and I spent hours around it. I haven't thought about it in so long."

My ears pricked up. I had read about the lemon tree just last night. Did I dare bring it up? Should I ask her about Zeina and Layla?

Could one of them be linked to the extended Almas family in Dubai?

"I started reading, Teta, and who—"

"Mia, *yalla*, you're running late," my grandfather's voice cut in from the next room. "Don't forget to pass by the grocery store on your way home. And if there are police everywhere, just pretend you are Latina. Mia Lopez!"

I looked over at my grandmother, her eyes a misty color between green olives and wet sand.

"We talk when you finish," she whispered. "You will understand by the end. About me, about you. About everything. But you need to finish it."

I kissed Teta on the cheek.

"Hasta la vista, baby," she said, giving me a hug.

"Whispering prayers in her ear? She will need more than that to deal with the chill in the air this morning," Jeddo said, walking into the kitchen to place an empty cup of tea in the sink. "Need anything while I'm out, Amal?"

"All is okay. I have everything I need to do the cooking for all the apartments," she said, taking an exaggerated bow. "Just need to remember that Mr. Apartment Number Five is vegetarian. The doctor. So not even chicken stock can be used, right?"

I nodded, momentarily distracted by thoughts of the handsome vegetarian. So, he was a doctor.

There was still so much I wanted to learn about my family. I wished I could call in sick for the day, add spices to the onion and garlic to make broth with Teta, while learning about our dysfunctional little family. I thought of the blue journal. While showering this morning, I had safely hidden it from view behind the few loose bricks in the wall behind my bed, just in case. Now it was nestled in my bag, ready to accompany me to work.

I waved goodbye to Teta and walked with my grandfather up

the stairs to the lobby. I dutifully answered his questions about a story in *Money Talks* on a bank's earnings report. I had made sure to read every detail when the story went live last night. I wished we could talk about the Love Unfiltered column I had fact-checked instead. Or about our family.

Jeddo, what do you know? I wondered, looking at his bushy gray eyebrows and kind smile. *Who are we?*

CHAPTER

13

Richard

Teenieh, a small village outside Jaffa, Palestine

Early 1947

Everything the British soldier thought he knew about purpose and heroism and glory had burned and shriveled, like the rolled cigarette he held in his hand, the moment he had to use his full body weight to keep a man's head submerged in a dirty bathtub full of water. After the oil refinery was intentionally set ablaze in Haifa, it burned for three weeks straight, forcing the Arabs to flee. When curfews and normal measures ceased to bring order in neighboring towns, the soldiers had to resort to new tactics, often under the official radar. The shock of the realities on the ground—not black and white but a tangled mess of yarn, a sinking ship full of holes—were taking a toll on Richard. He looked at his pruney fingers, thinking about the times when wetness was a good thing: the sea lapping at his feet back home in Brighton; the rain pecking his upturned face in a surprise summer shower in Palestine; the Jewish secretary, Tally, getting warm and excited when his hand had traveled up her thigh.

He wiped the single teardrop off his face with his bad hand before shoving it deep into his pocket. The boys back home had always teased him about the deformed finger on his right hand, which may or may not have been due to a father who liked a drink and a mother who liked a smoke. He had hated the way the girls fawned over his older brother at school when he took to the guitar in the music room, showing off more complicated songs than Richard could ever play.

And then it got worse; the teasing stopped when he was about fifteen, and nobody looked at him or talked to him at all. Books became his friends. So, when he heard that boys in his town were voluntarily enlisting in the army, and he was told, no, you can't hold a gun and, no, men with disabilities are not allowed, he felt doomed to a life on the sidelines as virtually all his friends in town went off to become heroes. But more and more men were called to fight in countries he had read about in the papers, and he was eventually given the chance to join and to reinvent himself. Books in tow.

Many soldiers had tried to bribe their way out of a post in Palestine with packets of cigarettes and liquor, but he didn't understand the big deal. When he arrived, Palestine paraded promises and goods he hadn't seen after a decade of dark winters, empty pockets, and leaky roofs back home. Here, food grew all year round in the temperate climate, his fellow soldiers patted him on the back like they were brothers, and the girls were beautiful. For the first time in his life, there had been real beauty, forgotten as he was in his post in the tiny village of Teenieh, on the outskirts of Jaffa's busy port.

During his first week in the land of sunshine, a dance was

held in a town square in Jaffa, and he met Tally, who traced her face with his bad hand and then kissed it. She didn't even slap him when he rested his hand on her bum as he walked her home that night. Instead, she gave him a lingering goodnight kiss.

At the start, he made an effort to see her every once in a while, when he visited Jaffa from Teenieh, where he had been sent to ensure there was no suspicious activity. But as he grew more and more attached to the tiny town of Teenieh, with Zeina at its lovely core, the outside world seemed to dim in her sunny presence. He hadn't expected to fall so deeply in love. And with an Arab girl.

The rumbling tensions, the fight for land that had ripped families apart, seemed like a distant problem, far removed from the bubble of happiness he had found with Zeina over the past few months. In snatched conversations and in eloquent letters, they spoke at length about the fact that Suleiman's father—Zeina's grandfather—had been a writer and poet, and that Zeina had diligently read everything he had written. Zeina's uncle Saeed had fueled Zeina's natural love of the written word, always bringing texts back for her during his visits home. He was the one who had taught her how to read in English and even a little French. He had even taken her to see her grandfather's best published works, kept in a little public library in Jaffa.

Richard had surprised her once, after a trip to Jaffa, by bringing her a volume of her grandfather's poetry that she hadn't known existed. He listened with delight as she translated the lyrical Arabic words for him.

This was one of the many things they talked about during those fleeting, timed meetings that had been happening more and more frequently behind Umm Mohammed's *dukkan* and in those letters they hid in Zeina's yard. They both wanted

more out of life than the hands they had been dealt . . . and
they felt they had found the answer in each other. The more
Richard had fed her mind, the more she had hungered for him.
Her command of the English language impressed him, and his
pronunciation of Arabic words made them both laugh.

To Richard, she was more than just a beautiful rose. Her
mind was a garden.

Now, though, the rising tensions had become impossible for
him to ignore. He worried about Zeina, about her future, about
any possibility that they could share one. In his initial months
in Teenieh, he hadn't seen any of the problems that the British
army had encountered in other parts of Palestine, where families were being torn apart and homes destroyed.

The truth was that Palestine was bloated. Even during
decades under Ottoman rule, harmony had existed between
Arab Jews, Christians, Muslims, and atheists, working and living together, borrowing flour and raising children—but times
were changing. Britain had made promises to different sides
that it couldn't keep. Now there were estimates of one hundred
thousand British army men currently on the ground, trying to
patch the flimsy peace between the local population and the
droves of European refugees being shipped into Palestine's
ports. The swollen population was clearly evident in the bigger
cities, but smaller villages like Teenieh still felt relatively safe
and isolated from the chaos.

For now.

He had spent his time monitoring the village, learning the
names of the Arab dwellers and the comforting routines of
lives that had existed in this way for thousands of years,
since before the time of the prophets. He frequently sent for
knafeh from Umm Mohamed's *dukkan* and drank coffee at Abu
Fouad's café, smiling at the men playing *tawleh*.

But like the scent of rain before a storm, heavy changes

were on the horizon, even in the forgotten village of Teenieh, with its elegant sand-colored stone houses and rows of almond, fig, and lemon trees. Abu Fouad's café had been closed for over a week to mourn the violent death of a relative in a neighboring fallen village. Dr. Abraham, the respected Jewish doctor from across the Ouja river, who treated the village's sick, hadn't been able to visit in eight days.

Farther afield, there were rumors of entire villages—just like this one—being abandoned as families fled, seeking safety. The tensions had inched closer and closer to Teenieh, tightening around it like a noose, until this terrible night, when he had been forced to take a truly active part for the first time since his arrival. Now, as the darkness faded around him, he tried desperately to hold on to his initial impression of Palestine's beauty.

In this moment, he could find that beauty in only two things. One was the cigarette in his good hand, with hashish better than the wood-chip grass back home, glowing fiery red with hope every time it touched his lips. His shoulders relaxed, and he could even feel a smile warming up his face like a sunrise.

Very soon, he would see the other beauty. He took his usual stance a few meters away from the lemon tree in front of the stately Almas house. When the darkness completely abandoned the streets and the sky turned silky shades of soft pink, she would take her post by the window and he would step forward. She might signal that something new was waiting for him, buried near the lemon tree. The *Fajr* call to prayer from the nearby mosque would fill the air, the muezzin's voice accompanying birdsong. Then he would look into Zeina's eyes, memorizing the way her eyelashes curved up toward her dark eyebrows like dozens of hands in prayer.

When Zeina came out, Palestine would be beautiful again.

CHAPTER

14

"So, are you going to go for it?" Katie asked, wearing sunglasses at eight a.m. We stood in line for mediocre coffee in the sunlit lobby of Vibe Media, hoping to mingle with famous columnists. In the years I'd been there, it hadn't yet happened.

Where do they get their coffee? I wondered.

"The new entry-level reporter opening?" I asked, knowing full well that was the only thing on her mind. "I think I'll try. I just need to figure out what to write about."

She had been talking about it for ten minutes straight while we stood in the line. My mind kept wandering to my grandmother's secret journal. I had read another entry on the subway instead of watching recaps of my usual *The Jordan B. Brown Show*, nearly missing my stop.

I felt for the blue journal in my messenger bag, feeling a thrill when the rough edges greeted my fingertips. The writing was lyrical and raw, but the unfolding story was really exciting to me, because I was finally allowed to peek into Teta's private past. Was my grandmother Zeina, who loved a British soldier? Or was she the bitter sister, Layla? What had happened to tear them apart? Was the distance I felt with people around me something to do with these loose ends?

I sighed, feeling like my day was a distraction from where I really needed to be: at my laptop, with the blue journal and Google Translate. I wished my Arabic was strong enough for me to power through the entire thing in a day, but my grandparents—even my dad, if I was honest—insisted on speaking English at home. They wanted my accent to be perfect, American, faultlessly clear. That was one of the reasons we had all watched so much TV when I was growing up.

The Price Is Right. Wheel of Fortune. Family Feud. Most game shows had become a family tradition.

Katie was still in full monologue mode about the new job opening, so I let my mind wander freely, half listening to her and nodding in the right places.

I tried to picture a young Arab woman in a gossipy, tiny village, shamelessly kissing a soldier in a side street. I thought of the awful night with Tanqueray Man and many other near misses with immature, drunk frat boys in college. My mind drifted to Jackson and our rooftop chats. He was handsome, brainy, older.

Called me pretty. . . .

Did I have it in me to surprise him with a kiss next time, to show him I had courage and fire in me? I wondered if I was like Zeina, ready to seize what came my way from life, or more like Layla, sitting on the sidelines, frustrated about what I felt life owed me. Maybe that's what Teta was hinting at: that I needed to be more open and take risks when it came to my relationships with people . . .

Will I forever fact-check other people's love stories . . . or have a powerful, all-encompassing one of my own that others want to write about?

Although it was cloudy, sunlight streamed through glass panels into the airy lobby. The scent of pumpkin spice latte was in the air, and women around us were now wearing colorful coats in red, brown, and tan—our own little ode to autumn.

"Ugh, can't you just bat your eyelashes and talk Jackson into giving both of us the job, please?" Katie's mention of his name broke into my daydreams.

I thought of his latest Facebook post. That morning, I had the unhappy surprise of discovering Adriana had updated her status to "In a relationship." Jackson's status remained blank, but I knew they were dating. Was he going to update his feed today, too? My stomach tied itself in a knot, and I shook my head, as if willing the words out of my mind.

"I feel like I need to prove I'm ambitious, too," I admitted after ordering my latte. "But, also, why does everything have to change?"

Why do people need to update their newsfeeds and break hearts?

Jackson and Adriana must be taking their relationship to the next level. I sighed dejectedly into my coffee cup. Had I completely missed my chance at an exciting romance with him? Was it my fault for avoiding him in the name of adhering to office romance rules and respect for my grandparents? What would Zeina have done? I thought of how she felt kissing the soldier and knew that similar fiery feelings would easily come into play with Jackson. I felt a buzz just from standing next to him and from making Michael happy with a new book.

And now, thanks to Facebook's little relationship announcement, I was certain that the idea of anything ever happening between us was moving further and further away.

If it was meant to be, it would have happened, I told myself. He's into Adriana now. Maybe I need to let this go.

If Jackson was out of the equation, would I still be happy at Vibe Media? I thought so. After all, the magazines in Vibe

Media's portfolio had been my passport to understanding the world around me, long before Jackson entered the picture. My grandparents had subscribed to nearly every one of Vibe's titles for me; I grew up thumbing through *Money Talks* while eating breakfast, killing time with *The Book Review* after school in my bedroom, even perusing *Designing Interiors* while on the toilet. In the pages of *The Culturalist*, I had read profiles of Tina Fey and Ellen DeGeneres . . . and fallen deeper in love with comedy.

"Yeah, well, I have zero leads on someone artsy to profile," Katie said, pouting, a note of irritation in her voice. "That's what they need for *The Culturalist*. The next Lady Gaga before she's big-time Lady Gaga. Any ideas?"

"Not really. You go out way more than me," I said as we thanked the barista. "Hey, I'm supposed to see Phaedra perform on Friday. That musician who moved into my building? Want to join me to see her show? Maybe there's something there?"

Katie shrugged, her head down. It was much warmer now than when I had left the apartment this morning. We exited the revolving glass doors, arms linked, holding steaming coffee cups in our free hands. We joined the throng of angry New Yorkers shoving one another on the sidewalk to get slightly ahead.

"I don't know, that sounds like your lead," she said. "She literally lives in your building. So, we're in for a little healthy, friendly competition."

"You're okay with me going for it, too, right?" I asked. "I wouldn't want a job to come between us."

"If you get it, I will be there with celebratory cupcakes," she said, swatting my shoulder. "Question is, can you top that if I get the job?"

I laughed, making a mental note to get her a pair of earrings from the guy who sold the ones made of real feathers in Union Square on weekends. She loved them.

A few blocks away, Times Square was likely already filling up with tourists hoping to get a perfect shot against the flashing neon signs before the afternoon rush. On my morning commute, two groups armed with tripods and expensive-looking cameras had already been on the subway. As predicted, they had gotten off at my stop at Forty-Second Street and walked briskly toward the bright chaos, the women in high heels and frilly dresses. Our office, a nondescript building a block away from the *New York Times* tower, was quiet, beige, and surrounded by scaffolding.

Katie and I stood for a moment outside the local 7-Eleven and watched a couple struggle with two giant suitcases as they left the Port Authority Bus Terminal around the corner.

"Boston?" Katie guessed, aiming her coffee cup in their direction.

"Niagara Falls," I said, pointing to a large sticker on the woman's bag as they rolled past us.

"So, I'm going to ask everyone to go for drinks after work tonight," she said, raising her voice above the noise of a beeping taxi at the busy intersection. "Boost morale, but also see if I can get a better idea of what kind of stories they're looking for, details on who else applied for the job. Want to join? Kevin's friend works at a fun bar in the West Village. Maybe we'll run into Lady Gaga herself and I'll be set."

I shook my head with a smile, and she nodded. She'd anticipated my answer.

The scent of warm bread wafted toward us from the pizzeria across the street. The liquor store sign next door glowed to life.

"How is everyone else living in New York City on these wages *and* paying off student loans?" Katie asked as we stood up to begin our workday. "Or is it just me? Do you think Christiane Amanpour or Joan Didion felt this way? How do you get ahead in NYC?"

"Joan worked her way up at *Vogue*, don't forget," I said with a shrug. "I like *The Culturalist* even better. For what it's worth, I think you would be a fab reporter for that title."

"Maybe," said Katie, sipping her coffee. "Just need a killer story idea. I am so sick of fact-checking pieces about cushions and wall paint for *Designing Interiors*. And I really could use the money. I just refuse to let my parents think they were right about my career choices. But our jobs don't seem like they are going to last in the long run, right? Like, magazines are shutting down left and right. Are we safe as fact-checkers? I don't know."

Maybe we're both on our way out. I nodded silently, thinking of the way Jackson had encouraged me to go for the new job opening.

I just didn't have a game plan. Between Phaedra moving in and my grandmother's diary, my mind was scattered.

Katie and I took turns through the revolving door into our building. She offered to keep me posted about drinks after work in case I changed my mind.

"Doubtful," I said. "What are you up to tomorrow? Sure you won't come see Phaedra with me?"

"I made plans with Kevin the Eyeball Licker," Katie said, her mind still on work. "Maybe there's a story there? Deviant sexual preferences of millennials. What kind of a name is Phaedra, anyway? Are her parents unicorns?"

I loved Katie for always telling it like it was, no holds barred. Then I thought of all the stuff I said onstage to strangers and wondered if she would be bold enough to speak like *me*. I smiled into my coffee cup. I pulled out my phone to check the time to make sure we weren't late.

"I know. I saw Adriana's status update, too. But you gotta stop checking your phone to stalk Jackson online," she ordered as we walked into the building. "Let's go. Time for the editorial meeting. Move it."

We pressed the elevator button and waited with a group of people busily typing into their phones.

I found a message from Mr. Goatee at the comedy club about an opening for a six p.m. slot because one of his regulars had backed out. I smiled and responded yes, then sent a text to my grandmother to let her know I would be delayed at work.

Please, not too late. You know how Jeddo worries, habibti, she wrote back. *And wear your jacket. It's getting colder in the night.*

I looked over at Katie and found her engrossed in her phone, too, so I pulled up Jackson's Facebook again as we rode the elevator up to the third floor. Adriana had tagged him in a photo out with a group of friends for drinks.

I zoomed in to inspect the new photo. She was smiling up at him, wearing bright pink lipstick to match her tank top, his arm casually around her bare shoulders while he talked to a guy in a fedora to his right. Her beautiful, long, shiny, stick-straight hair looked like it had been ironed and encased in glass.

While Jackson and I were only children—and he had been raised by a single mother—Adriana had a loud Latin family, with four sisters and a handful of cousins. My extensive Facebook research had revealed that her parents had even hosted one of the Big Brothers Big Sisters events in their garden in Queens, with Jackson and Michael manning the barbeque. Add to that Adriana's natural beauty and her Wall Street career—complete with sexy pencil skirts—and it felt a little hard for me to compete with my secondhand Harry Potter books.

I felt my insides twist as I was unable to resist imagining myself in her place instead. Would Jackson and I fit together? In a photo of us, would we both be smiling at each other? Adriana looked carefree, with warmth in her eyes to match her smile. We might have been friends if we had met separately.

I hated her a little.

I scrolled on. In Jackson's latest post, he said he would be stuck in board meetings most of the day. I doubted he would have time for a rooftop interlude this morning.

When Katie and I got to our desks, I found a new chocolate bar waiting for me. I looked into the boardroom, where a management meeting was in full swing. Jackson smiled when I caught his eye.

Chocolate fountain in the pantry, I emailed to the "suggestion box" address, instead of a bland thank-you text. I watched him glance at his phone while Isabel motioned to a graph behind her. His full lips curled into a smile, and he gave me a knowing look. He typed a few words into his phone and put it away to focus on the presentation.

I'll bring the pineapple slices. Enjoy the chocolate, he'd written back.

So even though he was seeing someone else, the chocolate had still appeared on my desk. And I liked it. My eyes swept around the busy newsroom. He didn't leave chocolate for Katie or anyone else, as far as I knew. I stared at the email again for a minute before checking his profile to see if he had updated his relationship status to match Adriana's public declaration. Had she met his mom yet?

I sighed. I wondered if yesterday's cup of coffee was still sitting on the rooftop alone.

CHAPTER

15

"What is that, a handwritten Love Unfiltered column?" Isabel, our editorial director, said. I had lost myself in Teta's story and blinked up at her, as if realizing for the first time that I was in the office, at my desk, in New York. Not in Palestine circa the late 1940s, reading about a young woman's illicit romance with a British soldier.

"Oh, yes, isn't that, uh, different?" I lied, mortified that I'd been caught not doing my job. "I was just translating some of the Arabic. I need to see if we can use this or not."

"Nice work. Which reporter brought this to you?" she asked.

Before I had to find an answer, one of the other managers, Davie, called out to her. She smiled at me, then turned, heels clacking as she walked away. Saved. I quickly shut the blue journal and put it into my bag. At least I hadn't been shopping online or wasting time on social media. Still, I didn't want to get fired for not paying attention at work.

"Wow, you're on fire," Katie whispered, an edge to her voice.

"That's pretty creative, a handwritten Love Unfiltered column. Why didn't you tell me?"

"No, no, this is my grandmother's journal," I whispered back. "I was just translating stuff for her, nothing to do with Vibe . . . Don't tell on me! How's everything going for you?"

She shrugged, motioning to her computer.

"I feel like the real stories are out there, not here at my desk," she said, swiveling in her seat. "Kevin said he would introduce me to a photographer friend who sold work to George Clooney. Maybe there's something story-worthy there."

I smiled at her and gave her a thumbs-up. Before getting back to work, I couldn't resist rereading what I had translated from the blue journal. I saved it in a folder titled "Taxes" in case anyone decided to snoop. It was riveting.

Zeina
Teenieh, a small village outside Jaffa, Palestine
Late March 1947

"If you keep resting your face on your fist like that, your cheek will hollow out like an old woman's," Zeina's mother said to her as she passed by the window. "Is that what you so ungratefully want to do with your gift of beauty?"

Zeina wished her mother would leave her alone to sew. Richard was supposed to pass by at any minute, and she hadn't seen him in a full week. She couldn't help it—she just wanted to see his hair falling over his eyes in that Richard way.

"Men like to see healthy women with big rosy cheeks," Fayza continued. "Now, you know he's coming for lunch today, so for Allah's sake put on a nice dress and come help me in the kitchen. We need this to go right."

Zeina looked down at her lap, wishing with all her heart that her mother meant Richard. Of course, she didn't. At the mere thought of the real person in question, the repulsive Haytham Ramle, a wave of nausea rolled through her.

For the past few weeks, the talk on the street had been that Haytham Ramle had grown bored of his first wife, Ismat. She had fulfilled her duty and given him her body and four strong boys, all now in their early twenties. One of them even had a wife of his own. Haytham was ready for a new chapter in his life, without Ismat. More important, he was wealthy enough to openly hunt for something new. That desire had put him onto the trail of Zeina, out of all the girls in the villages surrounding Jaffa, which pleased Fayza.

Haytham's interest was a happy distraction that brought out the competitive spirit in the mothers of all the eligible girls in town. A potential union with a very wealthy man was a way to secure a financially stable future amid the growing uncertainty and rumbles of impending war in Palestine. The mothers all agreed that this peace of mind took precedence over emotional happiness. Fairy-tale love stories were bound to fizzle out. After all, hadn't Haytham fallen in love and married a beautiful young Ismat decades ago, only to hunt for someone half his age now?

And yet, every day since he had expressed interest in her, Zeina was still unable to convince herself of the benefits of being his wife.

His second wife.

It meant giving up on her dreams of a more exciting life with Richard, of experiencing any path other than the traditional one that had been prescribed for her.

"Oh, look, Dr. Abraham is back," her mother said happily, waving to him and asking after his wife.

Dr. Abraham, the kind young Jewish doctor, had come from across the Ouja river to treat the fever that had befallen little Fawzi, whose family lived just down the street. It was so reassuring to see Dr. Abraham walk streets he used to frequent daily, after he hadn't been around in weeks. He had been sorely missed by everyone.

Zeina knew his absence had been connected to the whispers of horrible things happening in the country, which she and Layla didn't fully understand. Of poisoned wells, of children wrenched from the arms of their mothers, of young men meeting in dark rooms to talk about dark plans. Zeina held on to the hope that Dr. Abraham's return visits, albeit sporadic, were a good sign. The Palestinians would still give sugar and coffee to those on the other side of the Ouja river when needed.

Zeina had heard her father and his friends talking heatedly about rising political issues, but she wasn't sure who was responsible for what. A far cry from the days when as a child she had accompanied her family for hours upon hours of walking to other villages to meet relatives or retrieve water from the wells of Ras al-Ain, she and her sister were now being told repeatedly not to venture outside their home or, when buying groceries, far from Umm Mohamed's *dukkan* down the street.

She just knew that she felt safe and happy with Richard; he was all that consumed her mind. Propping an elbow up on the window and leaning her face back on her closed fist, Zeina watched Dr. Abraham's back and his bouncing black medical bag as he grew smaller and smaller in the distance. Then she caught sight of him and sat up: finally, Richard was walking down the street.

There were so many more British soldiers around these days, but this particular one was *her* soldier. As he got closer, Zeina could see that his khaki uniform made the blue in his eyes shine like water against sand. She felt the hairs rise on the back of her neck as his eyes sought hers, intimately tracing his glance down to her lips, her chest, ending with a smile.

"Zeina, *yalla*, get up and change," came her mother's steely voice. She grumbled under her breath about safety in the streets for young women, not knowing the dangerous territory that Zeina's mind had already entered.

With a meaningful glance at Richard as he passed their house, Zeina got up and went to her closet, absently fingering dresses. Layla was watching her, pretending to sweep as usual, so she shut the door.

Her older sister was *always* watching her.

Zeina chose a plain blue dress, borrowed from a relative who came from the big town and had gained too much weight to wear it herself. It brought out the color of her eyes, but it was modest.

She shrugged off her house dress and pulled the blue one over her shoulders. She blinked back tears, which surfaced so easily lately, sighing deeply. How differently she would feel if Richard were coming to meet her family! She could picture him wearing a suit instead of khaki army fatigues, maybe holding a bouquet of flowers, ready to whisk her away to an exciting life in Europe—he made it sound so vast and green—instead of a bigger version of this tiny village, with its lemon trees and dirt roads. How excited she would be! She would wear a little of the rouge she'd stolen from Cousin Fatima's house and put on big, dangly earrings, even if her mother would chide her later. She always forgave her anyway.

While she busied her hands putting in simple studs, her mind—the traitor—ran back to the first time she had laid eyes on Richard, many months ago. Incidentally, it was the very same day she had first seen Haytham Ramle.

She and Layla had walked together to Umm Mohamed's *dukkan*, and her sister was babbling about Zeina not doing her chores.

The note had appeared in her bag when she was about to place her purchases in it. When did he have time to sneak it in there, and how quickly did he write it?

Miss Zeina, beautiful as always. Can I write to you? RD was all the note said.

He had seen her before! He even knew her name! He must have heard the shopkeeper or her sister calling out to her on one of her walks.

Layla had asked Zeina why she was smiling as they walked home. That was when a strong smell of mint and cigars had engulfed them. Haytham Ramle was there at the café right next door to the *dukkan*, and the girls couldn't help but peek at this outsider as they hurried past.

He had a big, sagging body, not unlike their father's, and was seated as if he were a king on a throne as people came up to greet him. He had a large mustache and a head with no hair. The imbalance was comical, yet Zeina had heard the women in the village fervently insist that he was handsome . . . when the truth was that his money looked good.

The villagers were already calling him by the nickname Abu Shanab, good old "father of the mustache," but never to his face.

Zeina had forgotten all about Abu Shanab by the time they reached home, instead focused on Richard's note in her grocery bag. She took it out and hid it in the pages of one of her books. She was always reading, so she knew nobody would notice. That's when their little note-in-a-book exchange began . . .

Zeina knew Richard was musical because of the guitar he sometimes carried around, so his melodic words didn't surprise her. She imagined he could play lively tunes, even with a slightly smaller finger on his right hand. It was his boldness that continued to surprise her, however, with sweetheart words and arrangements to purposefully run into each other at the *dukkan*. She loved every thrill.

She put on a necklace and was about to pull out one of her favorite notes from him from the back of a drawer when her bedroom door burst open.

"Hello? I still need help in the kitchen," her mother said. "Put a towel over your head so your hair won't smell like the food."

When Fayza Almas had first heard a few weeks ago that Abu Shanab was on the lookout for a beautiful new bride, she saw not just an opportunity for Zeina, but also a way to navigate the tense and worrying future. Her cousin's family in the north of Palestine had already fled to safety in Lebanon, and she hoped that matching Zeina with a prominent businessman could shield her family from similar losses. These stories were increasingly prevalent. Fayza had walked slowly past cafés, catching words in midair as they swung from mouth to mouth above the din of clinking glasses, bubbling hookahs, and the rise and fall of men's voices heatedly discussing politics.

She began assessing the competition and devised a strategy to win Abu Shanab over. Unlike the other eager mothers in the village, Zeina's mother, Fayza, didn't take her daughters to the social gatherings where Abu Shanab had confirmed attendance. During these outings, he was seated at the head of a table or the center of a picnic, as mothers pushed their daughters into his line of sight. But Fayza knew that men, no matter how rich or poor or handsome or ugly or smart or simple, liked to feel that they had won a prize. They wanted to warm a woman's heart with effort. No matter how pretty the girl, what was underneath the skirt was all the same. So, what would stand out to a man was the story of how it all came to be.

At the last village gathering following Friday prayers, she had watched Abu Shanab smile politely as the eldest daughter of the Shawwi family, wearing too much rouge and emotion on her face, struggled while pouring him a glass of ice water. The water went everywhere but into the glass as the nineteen-year-old girl shook under her mother's wrathful gaze. She shrank away as she heard whispers of her name spreading from ear to ear, and she reappeared sometime later with a dish towel and eyes red with hot tears and shame.

Fayza Almas could barely hold back her smile when eighty-three-year-old Umm Mohamed told Abu Shanab in the bold way with which only elders can speak: "These girls aren't worth *fils*. No wonder you haven't found what you're looking for—you haven't met Zanzoun yet." To which he replied: "Zanzoun? Are you referring to the same Zeina Almas I keep hearing about over and over? Where can I find her?"

With effort, Umm Mohamed lifted a hand from her wooden cane, pointed a bony finger right at Fayza, and said: "Her mother and father are right there. Ask them yourself. What . . . do you think I work for you?"

After exchanging smiles with two women nearby at Umm Mohamed's inappropriateness, Abu Shanab walked over to sit beside Fayza and her husband, Suleiman. He asked about their family, Suleiman's work, and their life in the village of Teenieh.

Fayza felt the solar system in the picnic area shift. The eyes of the other women gradually centered on her lips, their ears turned toward her to catch her words as they fell, and heads leaned forward as the women inched closer. Basking in the sunlight she had generated, she made sure everyone heard her invite Abu Shanab over the next Friday for lunch following prayers to meet the family and talk more privately.

Fayza spent the week saving up and planning the ideal menu for their esteemed guest.

There would be stuffed squash and *wara enab*, a mix of rice and spices wrapped in grapevine leaves, made as small as possible to show the effort put into the dish. The Shawwis' *wara enab* looked like giant green fingers, and that would just not do for the likes of Abu Shanab, no. Fayza also planned to make *makloubeh*, a rice and honeyed eggplant dish in a pot that would be dramatically turned upside down and served like a cake on a big platter. And she would serve grilled halloumi cheese with tomatoes, tabbouleh parsley salad, and *fattoush*, a salad with fried bread thrown into the mix.

She hoped Abu Shanab wouldn't notice the lack of meat or chicken, which had been too expensive for them to afford ever since the rising tensions had raised prices in the past year. She put her confidence in the delicious flavors of the grand meal and began cooking days in advance.

Now the day was finally here, and she needed her daughters alert and ready to shine. Abu Shanab would be here any minute.

Zeina's life was about to change.

CHAPTER

16

"Don't worry, I still get nervous before every show, too," said a fellow amateur comedian backstage. He had a name tag that read: *Don't call me Joey.*

I gave him a thin-lipped smile and adjusted my black eyeliner in the mirror. I wasn't nervous. My mind was on my grandmother's story. I had always assumed that the sadness she carried around with her was from losing her only son, but did it also have to do with missing out on a true love? She must have been Zeina, doing what everyone else thought was right, rather than following her heart.

This was my first time performing at the club on a Thursday night. I usually stuck to shows earlier in the week, when the crowds were smaller and full of tourists, to avoid being recognized by New Yorkers. Although it was the same early six p.m. slot, I could hear the murmur of the full audience already. Someone was talking loudly about a pop-up art gallery nearby that exclusively showcased glow-in-the-dark paintings with all the lights switched off. I knew I needed to crank it up a notch tonight and leave right after my set to avoid any angst from my grandparents.

I peeked through the curtain as Mr. Goatee took to the stage to announce the lineup. I hid my face in my hands to calm my mind, then remembered I was wearing makeup and went over to the mirror to make sure I hadn't ruined my work.

The woman who looked back at me was fierce. Since this was a last-minute gig, I needed to make up for my plain outfit of ballet flats paired with a black long-sleeve top and jeans. I had done a fabulous Amy Winehouse cat-eye based on a YouTube tutorial and had borrowed glitter from a girl who was performing after me. My curls were damp after I wet my hair in the bathroom sink, giving my reflection a caught-in-the-rain wildness. I had pasted little stars at the corners and outer edges of my eyes for an other-worldly look.

The adrenaline pulsed through me, as it did before every show. I still got the same thrill before getting onstage every time, riding the mix of excitement and nerves like a wave. Backstage, the flickering lights cast erratic patterns, creating shadows that fluttered like nervous butterflies on the walls. The air crackled with an electric charge as I took in deep breaths, willing my heartbeat to keep steady. I wished my father could see me now.

My fellow female performer sprayed herself with a cloud of perfume, then gave me a spritz that filled the backstage area with the heady scent of bergamot and vanilla. She offered me red lipstick, and I gratefully applied it in slow, rhythmic circles, waiting for my name to be called. I drew a small red heart on my cheek with the creamy lipstick.

Something about the mixed signals from Jackson, coupled with the poignant Zeina story and the stress at work, had left me on edge all day. I couldn't wait to get up onstage and let loose.

Is this how normal people feel when they go to the gym? I wondered.

I took another deep breath and let it out slowly.

"This might help," said Don't Call Me Joey. He offered me a cup of water.

I smiled gratefully and took a large swig.

I coughed in surprise, and my eyes welled up. My chest burned.

"Easy there, tiger," he said, and laughed.

What was that? Tequila? Vodka? Liquid fire? I never drank. My nerves were moving into panic-attack territory now. I dabbed at my mouth with a tissue, marking it with traces of red lipstick. In the hushed moment before my name was called, the air hung heavy with anticipation. I felt like I was standing on the edge of a precipice, ready to jump.

"Everybody, please give a loud Greenwich Village Comedy Club welcome to the wonderful Miaaaa," boomed Mr. Goatee onstage.

Exhilarated, my senses heightened to a razor-sharp edge, I felt a warm energy travel through me, and a smile spread over my face. I walked into the light, looking at the expectant crowd and winking in the direction of a wolf whistle. I stepped up to the microphone amid applause. I turned my face toward the spotlight, my eyes closed for a brief moment as if I was on summer vacation, basking in the sun.

"Hi, guys! I'm Mia: Arab American and still learning how to be Arab and American at the same time," I began when the applause dwindled. "I can't even remember to check my Instagram *and* Twitter accounts. How am I supposed to have time for two cultural identities?"

I was about to start with my usual bit about passport control when I spotted a familiar face in the audience. Was that Katie? And Devon from accounting? Mail Room Andy?!

My breath caught in my throat when I spotted Jackson in the row behind them.

What are they doing here?

Ten seconds frozen onstage can feel like an era. The room was so quiet, I could hear someone clearing their throat in the back row. I heard someone to my right cough. A few audience members in the front row began to clap to encourage me to go on.

"You can do it, you got this," hissed Don't Call Me Joey from backstage. I looked around, my hands clasped, shrinking into myself, wondering if there was any way to salvage the situation.

"Uh, is she okay?" I heard a woman say.

New, unplanned words spilled out of my mouth.

"So, uh, I'm gonna be twenty-five soon. Single. Not great at mingling. You know what's the hardest time in a young Arab woman's life? When a single—male—Arab—doctor moves into the neighborhood . . . My family has already started planning a winter wedding, has a baby registry at Macy's, and has put our unborn children on waitlists at the best elementary schools," I said as the room bubbled with laughter. "Sorry, I thought I spotted him in the audience and freaked out. But we're good. This just isn't what I had in mind for our first meeting."

Katie was leaning forward with one hand over her mouth. There was a guy next to her who looked familiar. Then I remembered Kevin the Eyeball Licker worked in the West Village, at a studio nearby. He must have suggested this spot for her postwork drinks. Just my luck.

"My family is so into my business that if I have sex, I think they're the ones who will orgasm," I continued, the words taking on a life of their own.

Katie was staring at me and shaking her head slowly, her hand now over her heart. But she was laughing. It felt nice to shock her for once, instead of the other way around.

I couldn't bring myself to look at Jackson.

"I think my work wife over in row three is about to experience cardiac arrest at the sight of me like this," I said as everyone turned to look in her direction. "That's right, Katie, the Mia you know from the office is gone. I gagged her and left her backstage. Say hello to Mia-aowww!"

I clawed at the air like a cat as fresh applause erupted around the room.

"You are on fire!" Katie called out.

The shot I had taken earlier—my first ever, on an empty stomach—was making me lightheaded. The performer in me was going where she had never gone before . . . and I really liked it. Apparently, the crowd did, too.

"It's really confusing, you know, my life, because I'm different to different people," I said, walking around with the microphone. "Here, I'm hot, and at home, I'm a hot mess."

A fresh wave of laughter washed over me, lifting me higher.

"I'm fighting stereotypes every day, a one-woman soldier," I said. "Mia, the warrior princess of the West Village. When I say 'Arab woman,' I know what you're thinking . . ."

I put on a heavy Arabic accent and held my hair back in a loose ponytail with one hand.

"Yes, I cooked for three hours in the kitchen, where I belong," I said, looking at my feet. "Such a stereotype. I've actually lived in New York my entire life. I have an Ivy League master's degree and a great job. But there's still something about admitting to people here that I have an Arab background that I imagine feels like coming out of the closet."

I pretended to hold a handbag close to me and tucked my hair behind my ears shyly.

"We've been friends for a while now and there's something I want to tell you about me, but I hope you realize I'm still the same 'me' and this won't affect our friendship. I'm . . . Arab," I said, opening my eyes wide.

"We can still do 'normal people' things and hang out! Promise! I'll always give you the bacon on my plate at brunch, and you can have my mimosa, too," I said with an exaggerated shrug. "We can even double date: you bring your sexy Latino boyfriend and I'll bring my Arab doctor fiancé. I just need to meet him first—minor detail. In all likelihood, he and I are probably related, because that's how my community works. That way, you get to meet my future husband and family all at once!"

An audience had never laughed at my jokes this much before. Or was it the alcohol? I couldn't tell, but I felt really, really warm and happy. Katie was wiping tears from her eyes.

I looked over at the seat where I had first spotted Jackson. It was empty.

Did he just leave in the middle of my set?!

I felt like a flimsy paper airplane, flying dizzily toward the ground. My heart was cracking into pieces in public. I looked away from the crowd and saw an acoustic guitar to my right. The microphone near my lips made my shallow breathing sound like rumbling thunder. I thought of Phaedra, carefree, up on stages doing her thing, and Zeina, kissing a soldier in public.

Might as well go out with a bang.

I walked over to the guitar and picked it up.

"With the two chords that I know, I'm going to sing you a little song now, because you've been so good to me," I said. "It's dedicated to my five-minute fiancé. Oh, that's how long it will take for us to get engaged, not how long he lasts in bed. I hope . . ."

Hooting and applause followed as I placed the guitar strap over my head and nestled it into position.

"Only in Ramadan
Do we have a date every night
When you check out my falafels.
I know you want a bite.

But wait, habibi! *clap clap*

The only way you'll get it
Is to meet my entire family
Get married before we kiss
Then pop out a kid or three.

Everybody! *clap, clap*

You just want
My falafel.
Yes, I can tell.
You just want my falafel,
You naughty infidel!"

They were singing and clapping along with me. I was having the time of my life. I wondered if there was any way to keep this Mia alive forever. Let her out to play in real life.

"Thank you, Manhattan, I'm Mia-aowww ... and that's my time!"

Just as I wrapped up, I thought I saw someone in the back recording me on their phone. A warning siren blared in my mind, and I froze. My hands shook as I pulled the strap over my head and put the guitar back in its place.

"Get off the stage, you dirty Muslim." A deep male voice cut through the dwindling applause like a butcher knife.

The room grew still. I squinted into the crowd. I had never been directly heckled before and certainly not like this. I kept my head down and tried to hurry off stage, but the man stood up and spoke again. He had a red cap on and was very tall.

"Go back to where you came from," he shouted.

I could see a security guard move in his direction.

Don't engage, Mia, I heard my grandfather's voice warning in my head. *Don't give him ammunition.*

But I was so tired of keeping quiet. His words triggered

something deep inside me, a kaleidoscope of taunts from Robbie the Class Clown, Tanqueray Man, and everyone else in between. Keeping quiet, with my head down, hadn't served me very well all these years.

What would Zeina do?

My set had gone so well, and this man had ruined it. I caught Katie's eye, who smiled sympathetically, half standing as if to offer some assistance.

The seat behind her was still empty.

The room held its collective breath. I walked slowly back to the microphone stand, shielded my eyes from the spotlight, and looked right at the man with the red cap.

"Well, where I come from is the Upper West Side. And by the way, my father was a security guard at the World Trade Center. He lost his life going back in to save others in 9/11," I said quietly into the microphone to a room that was now silent and still. "He's a goddamn American hero. And I have as much right to be here as you do. Maybe more. My dad pulled people out of a collapsing building to save them. Your dad should have just pulled out . . . to save *us* from having to listen to *you.*"

Total silence followed for three long beats. Then the room burst into unexpected, rowdy applause. Tears stung my eyes, and a headache was starting to form from the stress and the spotlight. I turned my back to the audience and walked slowly behind the curtain. I was shaking.

Did I really just say that?

In the dark sanctuary of the backstage area, people patted me on the back as I grabbed my things and ran out. I didn't even pause to wipe my makeup off. I would have to do that on the subway ride home.

I could hear the crowd chanting my name and making meowing noises.

Don't speak up. You won't change anyone's mind—you will just end up hurting yourself. My grandmother's voice echoed in my mind.

Was this God's way of punishing me for drinking alcohol? It wasn't even on purpose.

And I'm still reeling from the anniversary of his death. Ten years. Ten long, long years. I was so young . . . Dad didn't get a chance to know the woman I am now.

My phone was buzzing in my purse. I was sure Katie was trying to get a hold of me. But the last thing I needed right now was a pity party. Why did they have to show up tonight of all nights?

I took the back exit and stood in an alley next to a large dumpster, light rain falling on my face. Grateful for the cool air and a moment alone, I let the tears stream down my cheeks.

I set my bag down and leaned my head back, listening to the laughter on the other side of the brick wall as if I was underwater. The alcohol-fueled buzz that had lifted me up backstage had evaporated the instant I had seen the phone held up, facing me. That bothered me more than the bigot.

Recording is strictly prohibited here, my mind screamed. *Where the hell was security?*

It was going to be okay. One recording sent to a few friends would not bring my life crashing down. I thought about how hard we worked to get our articles seen online at Vibe.

Normally, I would use this time to bring myself back down to earth from a post-show high, wiping makeup off my face and replacing my heels with sensible flats. Right now I felt scattered. It was a great set, but it had ended with quite an unexpected lightning strike. I had finally spoken up for myself, and I felt . . . good and bad at the same time. And Jackson . . .

What I was really disappointed about was Jackson. Not the idiot heckler, not the camera . . . How could he leave in the middle of my set?

It started raining a little more steadily. I tilted my head upward, facing the gray clouds, my head heavy against the black backstage door. I took a breath and began to walk toward the busy side street. I felt like a dirty alley cat.

The backstage door opened behind me with a clang. I looked over my shoulder.

"Mia, are you okay?"

There, in the rain, stood Jackson.

CHAPTER

17

I heard a squeal and saw Katie, saucer-eyed, standing in the doorway. She held a bouquet of five-dollar yellow tulips that she must have purchased from the flower stall across the street.

Katie knocked one over as she pushed past Jackson, folding me into a hug, the bouquet of flowers getting tangled in my hair. A comedian awaiting his turn onstage came through the back door, did two quick jumping jacks in the alley, then went back inside. The metal door clanged shut behind him.

Jackson's really here, I thought numbly.

"Who . . . who are you?" Katie asked, hands on my shoulders. "That was astoundingly good. So that little show you did in that dive bar years ago wasn't a one-off? You're, like, Kevin Hart good! My Mia is back!"

I couldn't find my voice. I had left it onstage, along with any confidence and sass. I tugged at the hem of my top, breathing in with embarrassment at my made-up face. My identities were colliding outside the safety of the stage, and I wasn't handling it all too well. I could no longer hide myself in plain sight.

And they heard the ugly words that man said to me in front of everyone.

"Security is really lackluster here. How did they let you two back here like this?" I asked shyly. "What are you doing here?"

"Drinks after work? Remember, I told you Kevin works in this area? Oh, my goodness, is *this* what you were doing when I bumped into you earlier this week?!" she said, her sentences racing one another to spill out of her mouth. "So, you seriously do comedy? Like, it's your hobby and everything?"

Jackson was just staring at me. He held my gaze, neither of us looking away or speaking for a beat as he drank me in. His eyes lingered on the heart I had drawn on my cheek. A small smile spread across his face. It felt like the sun peeking out from behind skyscrapers. He said: "You're full of surprises, Miss Almas. Let's get out of here," and gave me a thumbs-up. Clutching Katie's flowers, I trailed after my friends.

What is he thinking right now? My heart thudded with every step. *Did he hate the set? Did I really just sing about falafel in front of Jackson?*

We left the alleyway, with its mixed scents of dampness and trash, and walked past the drag night at the bar next door, before stopping short on the sidewalk. The rain was light and playful. A guy in a beanie, presumably Kevin, gave Katie a kiss on the cheek and congratulated me on a "bitchin' set." Then Katie and Jackson both put their arms around me and began to talk at once.

"I never expected you to—"

"—when's the Apollo Theater special—"

"—and no censor! It's like—"

"—move over, Ellen DeGeneres—"

It went on like this for about two minutes as I sheepishly traced shapes in the ground with my wet ballet flats. The rain was pick-ing up, and we huddled closer to one another, surveying the bars nearby for options.

"What's going on? Why aren't you ecstatic right now?" Katie asked, linking her arm through mine.

Jackson was facing me, his dark brown eyes taking in my lined eyes, shaking his head. He lifted his hand to cover an incredulous smile.

"Just . . . epic, Mia," he said. "That was incredible. Mad talent. What's the matter?"

"I'm in shock that you're all here," I admitted. "Plus, that heckler . . ."

"Oh, screw that guy," said Katie, waving her hand. "I *loved* see-ing you come out of your shell tonight! Reminded me of our col-lege days, babe!"

I looked at her kind eyes, Jackson's encouraging nod, the blur of people around us who had no idea who I was or why I was so worried. My friends were looking at me like I was still bathed in the spotlight, beautiful and confident and at home onstage.

Basically, the opposite of how I felt right now.

"It's . . . I . . . It's just kind of personal," I said. "Comedy was a thing for me and my dad . . . It makes me feel like he's still close. It's not like I expect to make it big. I'm not Seinfeld."

"Right," Katie said slowly. "You're Mia Almas. Comedienne extraordinaire."

They furrowed their eyebrows in confusion as a group of drunk girls bumped into us, laughing their way into a gray phone booth that opened into a secret bar.

"What I saw up there was an absolute superstar," Katie said, her hand over mine. "Don't pay attention to that idiot heckler. Look, I've got to run, but I am so proud of you. Jackson, take care of our girl?"

She winked at me, and I wondered if this was her obvious attempt at giving us alone time. I watched her fluff up her pixie cut and then cross the busy street with Kevin.

I didn't know how to talk to Jackson in this state. How did you string words together again?

"I thought you left," I said dumbly, staring at my feet.

"I went closer to the stage to see if it was really you, then to the back to take it all in . . . You didn't see me? To the left? Hey, I'm sorry about your dad," Jackson said gently, his hand finding its way to my shoulder. "I think you—"

"My bag!" I said with a start. "I think I left it in that alley behind the comedy club."

We hustled a few steps back to the same spot, away from the crowd on MacDougal Street. The rain was picking up now, but it was calmer in the alley. My senses felt so alive, as if Jackson generated his own electricity. I was aware of his breathing as he looked around the dim alleyway.

My time was running out. I thought of my grandparents waiting for me at home, Teta setting the table and Jeddo, his glasses on, reading in his leather armchair. *Your reputation is like a pristine white dress,* Teta's voice said in my mind. *Any tiny flaw will stain it forever, like red wine.*

I started bartering with God in my head.

If you let him kiss me, I won't skip a single prayer this month.

Now that the sun was setting, Jackson used his phone as a light source until we spotted my discarded bag near the heavy black backstage door. His phone pinged to life with a text I could see was from Adriana. He read it and put his phone away without responding. I felt a ball of anxiety forming in my stomach. I breathed in the scent of his aftershave.

If you let it happen tonight, I'll fast all of Ramadan.

I was hyperaware of the touch of his fingers as he handed my bag to me. He adjusted the strap of the tote bag on my shoulder, and his hand lingered. Our eyes locked, and I held his gaze. I didn't want to turn away this time.

If you let him be good to me, I won't do this again for a long, long time. I promise.

He moved closer to me, until there wasn't much space left between us. I tilted my head up, held in a trance by his eyes on mine, buoyed by the natural, calm feeling of his closeness. The rhythm of our breathing was the only sound that rose above the noises of the street.

I want the fairy tale, too, I thought as the rain began to dance all around us, imagining Zeina and her soldier.

I just couldn't help myself anymore.

I dropped the bag and the flowers, put my arms around Jackson's neck, and pulled his body closer to mine. He stumbled for a minute before wrapping his hands around my waist. I leaned against the wet wall behind me, reveling in the feeling of my fingers tracing shapes at the back of his neck. His breath was warm on my nose.

This time, he didn't hesitate and I didn't look away. With a deep hunger, my lips found his, and I lost all sense of myself.

CHAPTER

18

The Almas House

Teenieh, a small village outside Jaffa, Palestine

Late March 1947

Zeina walked behind her mother, her legs feeling as if they belonged to someone else, and surveyed the prepared meal already set on the table. Instead of napping, she had wasted time daydreaming about Richard, and now Abu Shanab was due to arrive any minute. She began to place plates, forks, and knives at each setting, her hands shaking, as she listened to her parents bicker as usual.

"What's ready, Fayza, what can I taste for you?"

"Get out of the kitchen, Suleiman. We're trying to finish and your belly is getting in the way. You can't be full when he arrives. You have to eat with him. Now, you know today is important, so go change your shoes. I hate these brown ones."

"You know I can eat twice. What's the matter with you? I'm

hungry now, and he will think I'm classy if I don't eat like a poor man. I can make better conversation when my mind's not on my stomach."

"Fine, Suleiman, just take some *wara enab* from the top of the pot, but only the broken ones where the rice burst out of the grapevine wrap. Leave the nicely wrapped ones for him."

"So this is what being rich gets you, eh? Beautiful women and the good *wara enab*. Not bad."

"Suleiman, really, go change your shoes."

"I can only think about food right now."

Zeina told herself to focus on Abu Shanab's good qualities. It was the only way to cope with all this. Her heart was breaking over Richard, but she needed to find a way to smile. Women weren't meant to marry for love. They married to secure their families, and society expected no different from Zeina, especially during these troubled times.

Abu Shanab was a good man who could offer financial stability to Zeina's entire family, which may even spill over to others in the village, at a time when they needed it most. He owned hundreds of acres of orange trees in Jaffa. Zeina loved oranges. Wasn't that a beautiful thing?

Oh, but the feeling of Richard's lips on hers was divine . . . She had seen in his eyes, tasted in his lips, read in his love notes a different way to live that made every cell in her body feel alive. Was there anything she could possibly do to hold on to that feeling? She didn't know if she had it in her to throw away the carefully planned life her mother had arranged. She imagined putting a few of her most special belongings in a small suitcase, giving Richard a signal to wait for her by the tree at midnight, running away into the night together beneath a full moon. Find their way to—

"Zeina, you look like death. Why didn't you nap earlier like I told you? Go back and lie down again until he arrives. Sleep is the best way to stay beautiful," her mother said, her voice sharp like fingers snapping. "Do you have diarrhea? Let's not talk about it surrounded by all this food. *Yalla*, go. Layla and I will finish the rest."

Zeina didn't protest. She felt like she had lost her voice. She retreated to her room, shut the door, and reread letters from Richard until a strange rumbling sound grew closer and closer.

She tucked the notes beneath her bed as Layla came in. They exchanged confused glances, moving over to the window to look outside.

The sound grew louder and louder as neighbors opened their doors and began to gather on the street.

"It's not an earthquake, is it? Is that a bomb? I'm so . . ."

". . . Oh no, I just rebuilt one wall of our house . . ."

"Bombs don't rumble like this. Don't be afraid . . ."

". . . no, not the floor moving . . ."

"Look, what is that coming in this . . . ?"

". . . . can't find little Fawzi. Where is he? Fawzi! Faw—"

". . . Abu Shanab is supposed to have lunch there . . ."

". . . for Zeina? Ahhh, will she . . . ?"

The talk ceased as everyone's gaze fixated on the violent thing moving toward the Almases' house, kicking up a fury of dust as it came closer, leaving bold marks in its wake. Abu Shanab's new black car was so large it dwarfed the dirt street, and so loud that it drowned out the sounds people were used to hearing in the village—of the bubbling Ouja river in the distance, of birds, of families chatting on front lawns outside their stone houses, of Umm Mohamed's shrill voice in the *dukkan* down the street.

Mothers held on to their children, and men ventured out a few paces to get a better look as the car slowed in front of the Almas house. Layla and Zeina instinctively shrank away from the window. Abu Shanab parked close to the shade of the lemon tree. One front tire was right next to the rock where her latest letter from Richard was likely buried.

Abu Shanab opened the car door and stuck out a grand wooden cane. Then he swung two fat legs over the seat, holding on to the cane for a moment like it was a scepter, before sinking it deeply into the grass as he heaved himself into a standing position. As he walked toward the house, children ran toward the car, running their hands over its gleaming body and patting the tires and squealing. Eventually the men followed suit, eyebrows raised, trying to figure out how to interact with the car, before poking it and marveling with one another just like their children.

Abu Shanab's knock on the door was not loud and booming, as they would have expected of a man of that size. It was a single, soft rap with one finger, before he rested both hands on his cane, the buttons of his blazer straining to stay together over his round belly.

Layla and Zeina ran to the kitchen so they could peek from behind the door as their father welcomed him. Abu Shanab's large frame filled the little living room. Zeina could tell her father was excited. His leg was bouncing up and down like a child's. Her mother, Fayza, walked past with a tray holding a jug of water and glasses, instructing the sisters to wait until the Moment.

Zeina sank into a kitchen chair and stared at the wall.

Layla could tell that her younger sister had barely noticed she was standing next to her. Trying to keep her own feelings from erupting, she turned her back on Zeina and steadied herself at the sink. Her worst nightmare was coming true.

Her younger sister had a wealthy suitor . . . and she had experienced passionate love. Layla had neither. The townswomen were probably already calling Layla a spinster behind her back. She let a single tear roll down her cheek silently, before casually wiping it away with a rag, putting on a neutral face, and taking a seat near the kitchen door to catch snippets of conversation from the living room.

She looked back at Zeina, who looked desolate and resigned.

"Mr. Ramle, you've honored us with your presence. Here is some water. We will bring some tea; then we can begin lunch. I hope the journey to our humble house didn't tire you much," she heard their mother say softly. Through a crack in the kitchen door, Layla could see a measured smile on her lips as the rehearsed words all fell seamlessly into place, like notes on sheet music.

"Of course, yes, water!" came Suleiman's voice, off-key and high-pitched, accompanied by a chuckle. Fayza shot him a look that instantly sobered him, then excused herself and headed back into the kitchen.

Suleiman was playing his role well, yet couldn't conceal the boyish curiosity about the majestic car that was parked in his driveway. It was like a massive whale that had suddenly washed ashore. He was sure to be the talk of the town for the next year for this. Suleiman, a simple teacher with a humble family, was getting his first taste of celebrity, and he really, really liked it. His own parents had thought of his brother, Saeed, as the golden child—a literature lecturer at the American University of Beirut who raised the good name of the Almas family. Suleiman was usually a kind afterthought, but not today.

This car, this day, this moment would give the whole village something to talk about for weeks. It became increasingly hard for Suleiman to conceal his excitement. This burst of feeling, all before any meaningful words were exchanged—imagine if the Great Haytham Ramle became a part of his family! If there were more fanciful things like this car to be introduced into his life and, indeed, into the lives of all of those in the village! If only he would be allowed to drive the car just once!

His leg shook up and down furiously as he asked questions about learning how to drive (man's second nature), how many other cars there were like this one in Jaffa (only one other), if it was comfortable (more so than an embrace), if he had ever fallen asleep in it (no, but perhaps worth a try?). Beads of sweat began to form on Suleiman's temples as question after question ricocheted around his mind. He didn't stop asking questions long enough to absorb any answers. Fayza, watching from the kitchen with her daughters, decided to make a bold move and walk in before Suleiman could make any mistakes with their important guest.

Soon it was officially Zeina's turn to come in. Layla stayed seated in the kitchen, trying hard to maintain an even expression. In the past, each time that Layla, with her frizzy black hair and raven eyes, was overlooked, she better learned to keep a trained smile on her lips and laugh dutifully with her sister about a suitor's ugly shirt or unibrow—but her insides were always bruised with envy. She sat in the kitchen now, simmering like a pot on the stove about to overflow.

Zeina opened the kitchen door, balancing tea and dates on a tray. She felt like she was an actress in a play, her heart and mind on Richard, imagining the pain he would feel if he knew her future lay with someone other than him. How was she going to break the news to him? If she told him in time, could they find a way to escape and be together, or was this really her destiny?

When Zeina walked into the room, movement and noise dwindled. Abu Shanab looked up to meet eyes that were impossibly bright, that teased him by hiding behind a curtain of thick, black eyelashes as they remained trained on the floor. With her grass-green eyes cast politely down, he was able to take in the provocative rosy pout, the delicate nose, the skin that was made of cream, and the long black hair that moved like water. When she began to pour the tea, steam rose from the teapot and swirled around her face, reddening her cheeks. Her eyes lifted once more, like a sunrise commanding all attention, and Abu Shanab's lips parted in excitement.

"Thank you, dear," he said, his voice barely a whisper as his eyes roamed over her hungrily.

"Would you like sugar, sir?" asked Zeina, her voice melodious and light.

"I have no doubt it is sweet as is," he said. "Thank you, Zeina."

Fayza triumphantly watched the scene before her unfold as if she were the director of a play with an obvious ending.

Zeina moved away from him to pour tea for the rest of the family. Abu Shanab began to talk and ask questions, directing many of them at Zeina. She allowed her parents to respectfully answer for her and only graced him once with a smile and a nod of the head before she retreated back to the kitchen. Layla hadn't moved from her chair and couldn't bring herself to ask her sister what had gone on in the other room.

Before the kitchen door had fully closed, Zeina heard Abu Shanab's rich voice asking her father for her hand in marriage.

CHAPTER
19

On the subway, I rubbed my face with wet wipes, over and over again, my entire body fizzing like a champagne bottle after Jackson's kisses. But when I reached my building, I couldn't bring myself to walk in. I felt like my lust was written all over my face, like Teta would instantly know what I had done, why my lips were puffy. How could I explain to her why my hair and clothes were so wet? That I had taken the story of Zeina a little too literally and kissed a man I shouldn't have kissed in an alley?

And that it felt like all the stars aligned in that divine moment, I thought.

Along with the fresh, delicious feelings, I felt the heavy weight of guilt. Adriana had done nothing to me to deserve this. Was the power of my crush on Jackson enough to justify what I had just done to her, to them? Was it okay for me to focus on how good it felt to kiss Jackson—in the rain!—instead? For the two of us to finally give in to the feelings that had been brewing for years in the form of office glances, rooftop heart-to-hearts, and chocolate bars on desks?

I stood there listlessly in the drizzle, trying to figure out my next step, when Phaedra walked up and asked if I was okay. She was coming home from a lecture at Juilliard. Confused, I found myself taking the elevator all the way up to the penthouse along with her, accepting an invitation for a quick cup of tea. I messaged Teta to say that the subway had faced a delay, buying myself fifteen extra minutes. She was livid.

Are you almost home? pinged my phone. *What's taking so long?*

Ten minutes, I answered.

"You're shaking," Phaedra said, rushing to hand me a fuzzy blue throw from her sofa.

She walked me to her bedroom. I took a seat facing the mirror behind her cluttered vanity desk. She handed me a hair dryer and offered to make me tea. My soaking black jacket was drying on the rim of her bathtub and my wet ballet flats were outside her apartment door.

She didn't ask questions at first, which I appreciated. I blow-dried my hair, watching her in the mirror as she moved around her bedroom. I needed to recalibrate, bring my breathing back to normal, and get dry.

Phaedra disappeared into the bathroom to get me a towel. When she returned, she pulled her loose blond hair into a bun.

Her phone beeped.

"Go ahead, pick that up if you want," I said, turning off the hair dryer.

"No, no, I've just almost missed the call to prayer," she said, jumping up. "Let me do this quickly and then we can chat. Did you pray already?"

I gave a noncommittal shake of the head, motioning with my hand for her to go ahead. My grandmother never missed a prayer and my grandfather fasted every single day of Ramadan, but my attitude toward religion had cooled after I lost my father. I still believed in God and found myself talking to him deeply in my heart about what was troubling my mind, but every time I saw a mosque or a prayer mat, it reminded me too much of my father. And the pain of losing him was forever fresh. Evergreen.

My hair was nearly dry. Phaedra motioned for me to switch the hair dryer back on. I nodded with a smile as she walked to the bathroom. She stepped up to the sink with the door wide open.

Nudging the tap on, she cupped her hands and rinsed her red-painted mouth, careful not to smudge her lips. She drizzled water on her hair and placed the blue throw from the living room over it loosely, without stifling its volume. She smiled at me as she caught my eye in the mirror. She looked like a polished, confident version of that famous photo of the Afghani girl with the colored eyes.

"I figure it's better to do it this way than not at all," she sing-songed above the din of the hair dryer, running wet hands over her feet quickly.

The prayer mat was already stretched out, a pair of pink stilettos discarded next to it as if kicked off and forgotten about at the end of the previous night.

I watched her throw on a pair of gray sweatpants over her red dress. It reminded me of when we'd visited St. Patrick's Cathedral on a school field trip when I was eight, and we were asked to cover our bare shoulders and legs out of respect. I had pulled my crumpled PE sweatpants over my denim shorts, thinking how alike religions can be. When I lit a candle in the cathedral, whispering my own prayers in Arabic to Allah while looking up at the stained glass, it felt divine and warm.

Satisfied with my dry curls, I switched the hair dryer off. I ran a hand admiringly over the assortment of perfumes and creams on Phaedra's vanity. I began to braid my hair, eyeing Phaedra in the mirror as she prayed behind me.

The familiar chants were on her lips like little kisses, and her catlike green eyes stayed fixated on the wall ahead of her. I watched her bend. Kneel. Her forehead grazed the prayer mat. She did this three more times as rebellious blond tendrils kept escaping the loose throw.

A look to the right, another glance to the left, then she was done. She turned to smile at me with a thumbs-up. In seconds, her sweatpants were kicked off, and the blue throw lassoed onto the bed.

"I'll deal with this mess later," she said with a laugh, waving her hands around her room.

She rolled the prayer mat and tucked it into the corner, all the while looking over her appearance in the full-length mirror in her bedroom.

"Let's sit in the living room," she said, motioning for me to follow her. "Want to tell me what happened?"

She offered me a cigarette and a glass of wine, which I declined.

"Everything in moderation, right?" She winked at me, lighting a cigarette and leaning back.

Then, softly, I told her everything. It all came out in a torrent of sniffles and smiles and almost-shed tears. The show, my father, 9/11, the heckler, Jackson. Adriana. Jackson. Kissing in the rain. Jackson, Jackson, Jackson.

She let me gracefully come down from the high of the show and the kisses. Performer to performer, she got it.

I breathed deeply, thinking I had made a good decision in coming here first. My only good decision tonight, perhaps. Despite the harsh, superficial way I had judged her when we first met, I felt myself thawing now at her understanding warmth.

Mia Almas was coming back, in a tidy, button-up purple cardigan, crumpled from an evening spent in my bag. I put a hand to my puffy lips, letting my fingers play lazily with my curls. It felt like the performer in me was refusing to step down so easily this time.

I hate lying to Teta, I thought guiltily. I put a hand to my tender lips and took another sip of the soothing chamomile tea. *I wish I could tell her everything. Jackson, comedy, all of me. But will she accept the parts of me she doesn't understand?*

"Mia, listen to me," Phaedra said softly. "Tonight was a good night. It sounds like you had a great set, aside from that stupid heckler, and you finally know how you really feel about Jackson."

I felt like sunshine in a musical. Those ten minutes in the rain—limbs intertwined, heart rate rising, mingled hot breath—had given me the same high I usually felt onstage.

"I finally know what all those cheesy love songs are about now," I admitted. "But I'm nervous. What next? What if he gives me the cold shoulder at work tomorrow morning? What if he doesn't acknowledge what happened and posts a love tribute to Adriana on Facebook? Or worse . . . what if he wants to take the next step with me? I just feel . . . inadequate. And guilty no matter which way I look at it."

I shuddered again, and Phaedra offered me a shawl to place on top of the blanket around my shoulders. Beads of sweat were starting to form on my temples from sheer nerves, but I took it. It felt like a hug.

"It's normal to have these feelings—you're human!" she said. "It's normal to enjoy kissing someone you like. Why are you so hard on yourself?"

She didn't mention Adriana. I couldn't bring myself to talk about her now. They had only been dating a few months, but I felt terrible. Even more so because I was still glad the kiss had finally happened.

I waved my hand around in front of my face to show I was feeling all over the place. Phaedra came up and gave me a hug.

I put a hand over hers and whispered a thank-you. I was moved by her kindness.

"You know, the Almas family in Dubai owns jewelry stores, and a theater, I think," she said, changing the subject with a smile. "There were rumors about this one lady—she seems about your grandmother's age—she used to host these wild cabaret nights. Can't remember her name . . . Zara? Zahra? Zeina Almas? I think it started with a Z."

Hearing the name was like being stabbed by a dagger. Zeina. Could she be the same Zeina in Teta's journal? I had felt certain that Teta was Zeina.

But Teta's name is Amal, I thought, my mind cloudy.

I cocked my head to one side, listening as Phaedra told me about this woman who shared my last name, whose life had once been full of pink champagne, sequins, and dancing in her youth. She hadn't been seen in years, decades even, but theater folk still occasionally talked about her. Rumor had it that she didn't want people to see her ugly and shriveled and old, preferring to be remembered as a young, powerful woman.

"Never met her, but she is said to have had this larger-than-life personality and a husky laugh," Phaedra said. "There, I succeeded in getting your mind off your guilty little kiss, right?"

My mind was racing. Zeina Almas. Could it be?

CHAPTER
20

I couldn't go straight on the offense. I needed to study my grandmother's mood first.

I mixed lemon juice and olive oil into the salad, tossing some fried bread and zesty sumac spice to complete the *fattoush*. When Jeddo went to open the front door, I quickly grabbed my grandmother's elbow and whispered in her ear.

"I'm sorry I was late. It was a really long day at the office and then there was an issue with the subway," I said quietly.

"Jeddo just worries about you," she said. "Just try to come home on time tomorrow. I can't handle him pacing in the living room until you're back."

"I—I bumped into Phaedra, too," I admitted, curiosity getting the best of me. "She told me more about the Almas family in Dubai. Diamond stores and everything. Please, just tell me, is Zeina Almas your sister? Why are you angry with her? Is it, like, a money thing?"

Silence greeted me.

I could hear my grandfather speaking to someone at the door, a man's voice.

"Jeddo's leg is acting up again and he had that new doctor, apartment number five, take a look at it," she said, lifting the lid off the pot on the stove and breathing in the scent of honeyed rice and eggplant.

"You're ignoring my question," I said resolutely, switching on the fan. It was stiflingly warm in the kitchen. "Tell me about Zeina Almas. Please. I'm going to find out anyway from your journal."

"He treated your grandfather free of charge," she went on in Arabic. "Saved us a trip to a clinic. Prescribed arthritis pills. Very handy having him in the building. Better than that pharmacist who keeps selling him useless creams."

The secrets in me were bursting to come out tonight. I wanted to sit her down and talk to her about the drug-like magic in Richard's and Jackson's kisses, the mixed sense of euphoria and shame that attaches itself to physical expressions of love, and the way I tried to make sense of all my contradictions through humor onstage. I wanted us to cuddle, with blankets and tea, letting soft words about lost love and my gentle dad carry us late into the night.

"I want the full story, Teta," I said, refusing to back down. "Look, can we have an hour together, just me and you? You have to fill me in on all this. It's time I learn details about our family. And I really want to share some stuff with you, too. Tonight, I did something that was so unlike me and—"

The man's voice grew louder and louder, coming closer. He was inside our apartment. I looked to my grandmother to see if she was also confused, but she averted her eyes and quickly unwrapped the cellophane covering a bowl of hummus. My heart leaped into my throat. This couldn't be good.

"Please, come in, come in," Jeddo said in Arabic. "We insist on thanking you for helping me today. I already feel better. Dinner is the least we could do."

And there stood Mr. Apartment 5 holding a bouquet of tulips. Bigger than the one from Katie that I had left in the alley behind the comedy club.

My legs almost gave way.

"You know my wife, Amal, and this is our granddaughter, Mia," he said.

"Hello, I'm Hadi. It smells wonderful in here. I wanted to thank you for the wonderful vegetarian dinners you've sent up," he said to Teta. "Mia, I've seen you around. It is wonderful to meet you."

Wonderful. It was all wonderful. He even had a soft British accent that hinted at a life of private school, foreign travel, and country clubs.

"Mia, did you forget how to speak? She's being modest—she works for Vibe Media," said my grandfather, puffing out his chest. "She went to Columbia and graduated top of her class, too. Full academic scholarship. And she helped with the cooking tonight."

Wait a minute. Now he was reeling off my skill set . . .

"Wonderful traits," said Mr. Apartment 5. "I'm looking forward to learning more. I moved into the building very recently."

"So what's your vice, then? A doctor, and you must be a musician if you live in this building. Well done to your parents on raising you. Sorry, I didn't mean actual vice, obviously," I rambled. "I meant—"

"He doesn't need your advices, he is a man," Jeddo said.

Hadi laughed and held up a hand.

"I understand. I transferred from the UK, where I do shifts in the emergency room, and I am here for three months to train at Juilliard on new developments in music therapy," he said. "I took violin lessons growing up, but I am no professional. I do think the music therapy approach will be useful for some of my stroke and dementia patients. Living in this wonderful musicians-in-residence accommodation is the cherry on top. And meeting you. All of you, I mean."

My brain was still stuck on the doctor bit. Arab doctor, violinist, accent? Flowers, too? Yes, this was real.

This must be the universe laughing at me, I thought.

I felt a fresh pang of guilt when I thought of Jackson. I tried to picture him here, in my home, and I just couldn't see it. I could imagine he was talking to Adriana right now; maybe he was admitting that the coworker he's had feelings for had kissed him in the rain, like something out of a movie. Did I dare check my phone to see if he'd messaged me yet?

Was this how Zeina felt? My heart drummed in my chest. *And Haruki in today's Love Unfiltered column? Am I being set up right now?*

A hardness settled in me like an olive pit.

"Hadi's family is also sponsoring scholarships for four Juilliard students of limited means," my grandfather was saying in Arabic.

"Yes, it's wonderful," said Hadi.

So the man needed to learn another adjective, but he was otherwise eerily perfect. I smiled politely. I just needed to get through this dinner, and we could go our separate ways. I put a finger to my lips, feeling the receding puffiness. I began to wonder if I had hallucinated the kiss in the alley.

We sat at the kitchen table to eat. Hadi complimented the food and talked about his work. He had smoke-colored eyes and a way of scratching his face when he was giving a thoughtful answer that I found endearing. He had slim glasses set against thick eyebrows that furrowed as he listened to my grandfather.

This was what my grandparents had always wanted for me. After losing my parents, this was the type of stability they understood, one with a clearly defined road map: marriage to a doctor, a solid career as a financial journalist. Was this what Zeina thought when serving tea to Haytham Ramle, her mind and her heart craving Richard? Making choices between the firm ground and the heady clouds? Earth and heaven?

"And there is another new tenant, correct?" Hadi asked as tea was served with a pineapple upside-down cake. "I saw a young woman hauling a big bag from Bed Bath and Beyond into the elevator the other day."

"Ah, yes, Phaedra," Jeddo said. "She's the other Arab in the building. The rest are from all over the world. We will have a meet-and-greet soon so you can all get to know each other. Perhaps you have run into her at Juilliard? She plays the piano."

"Not likely, with my hours and us studying different things," said Hadi. "She sounds wonderful."

"Mia is going to one of Phaedra's shows tomorrow night, I believe. Why don't you go along and chaperone?" my grandfather said. "I would feel better knowing someone is looking out for them. New York is not always safe."

Jeddo was already making plans for us. I squirmed in my seat.

"It would be my absolute pleasure," said Hadi. "Consider it done."

I should have known my grandfather had a plan all along when Phaedra invited me to her show. I was nearly twenty-five; it was about time the family began lining up the suitors. How hadn't I seen this coming?

Just wonderful.

CHAPTER

21

Teta and I washed the dishes, side by side, while Jeddo lingered over tea and soccer in the living room. Hadi had left, confirming it was a "wonderful" evening and double-checking my grandfather's knee, but I could still feel his presence in our little kitchen. The extra mismatched chair was still there, and there were more dishes to wash than usual.

I rinsed out the salad bowl, and Teta plunged it into the sudsy sink.

"I would have appreciated a heads-up that I was being set up," I said to my grandmother. My tone sounded angrier than I'd intended, especially knowing they'd meant well by introducing me formally to the handsome doctor-violinist. They had no idea what I had been up to mere hours ago. "I mean, he seems nice and all, but let's just say I would have worn a different outfit."

"The red dress maybe," she mused, taking a plate from me. "We invited him to dinner as a thank-you for helping Jeddo. Then you were so late coming back from work, I kept texting you to rush home. Anyway, it isn't a big deal. I don't even know if it was a "setup" like you say, but it is a nice opportunity to meet a decent young man. If you like him, great. If not, *bye, bye, bye*."

"Well, not really *bye, bye, bye*, because I have to run into him in the building every day," I answered in English. "Elevator rides are awkward enough even if you're not the subject of an arranged marriage."

She smiled. I loved the lines around her kind eyes.

"Take your time," she said. "No rush. But it would be good for you to learn how to handle yourself around a suitor now."

I'm at that magical age, I thought again. I'd completed my studies with top marks, had a nice, respectable job, and now the Arab community wanted me to transition from *never-had-a-real-boyfriend* to *when-is-the-wedding*. There seemed to be something cursed about turning twenty-five when you were an Arab woman. I shuddered to think what happened at thirty.

I felt a wave of sympathy looking over at Teta. She and my grandfather were in their late seventies, and lately I had overheard them chatting in hushed tones in the evenings about their hope that I would find a life partner before they were gone. They always worried about me. Maybe it was time for me to try a softer approach to love with her.

"Speaking of suitors, I'm sorry I sounded pushy earlier. I am just excited to talk to you about what I've read so far," I said, handing her a stack of knives. She paused for a minute before plunging them into the suds. "I'll read it all, I promise. It's so beautifully written. Thank you for trusting me with your story. You know I love you no matter what. Zeina, Layla, or Amal."

She froze, and I heard her inhale sharply. She rinsed her hands and then placed them on the edge of the sink to steady herself.

"I just . . . It's scary that you're actually reading it now," she said, her voice quivering. "But it's time. Almost done, then?"

I put a hand over hers, glancing over my shoulder at the sound of my grandfather shouting at the TV. I shook my head.

"Few pages to go," I said. "What's the matter?"

"Our family story was never easy to talk about, you know that," she said, washing the final dish. "Just . . . tell me when you've read the whole thing."

She hadn't exploded at me this time. At least there was no shutdown, no "go to your room," no mention of raising her blood pressure with my questions. Just an icy quiet.

I almost missed the shouting.

"Finish it," she said, her shoulders dropping, her mouth stiff. "And then it will be easier for me to tell you everything."

I put down the rag I had used to dry the dishes and studied her profile. She busied herself scrubbing the stubborn grease in the casserole dish. She looked older tonight, sadder maybe. I couldn't put my finger on it. I wanted to share what had happened at work today, my stress over competing with Katie for a reporter job, my confusing feelings for Jackson, my comedy . . . but I couldn't bring myself to add to her burdens. Would there ever be a right time?

She remained silent. She picked up a towel, dried her hands, and began to snap shut Tupperware containers filled with leftovers to place in the fridge.

"I need to know what happened in our family so that I make sure nothing ever hurts you, harms us, in any way," I went on, stepping closer to her and touching her arm. "Let me help you?"

She gave a small nod. It was the saddest little nod in the world.

"I trust you," she said. "And I've kept you sheltered for so long, encouraged you to always do the right thing and be the top of your class, never make mistakes. I have not been easy on you. And you're right, you deserve to know. But don't publish my story on your company's website so that suddenly the whole world knows our dirty laundry. Oof, I can just imagine Ghada in my book club giving me the side-eye and I don't like it."

She had even made a joke! This was the most progress I had ever made with her when talking about the past. I tried to look into her eyes. They remained downcast.

It was the second time in my life I had seen her so burdened.

The first was the day she got the phone call from the fire department, with a soft-spoken woman telling her that my father didn't make it out after the second tower fell. I would never forget the grieving howls, the sobbing, and the hours of silence that followed. How had she remained kind and soft, when life had dealt her such heavy blows? What kind of inner strength did she possess to have shown me a life of nothing but love and light despite her own struggles? I looked at her with new eyes, in awe, with empathy, with love.

This wasn't the time to open up to her about Jackson, about what I had done, about Adriana. I needed to see how her story ended so that I could make up my mind about my own.

"I'll get to it right now," I said gently. "I love you forever. You raised me."

I made myself a chamomile tea, and she came and hugged me from behind. I gave her a kiss on the cheek, carried my warm drink to my room, and checked my phone. Nothing from Jackson. No social media updates either.

Silence and confusion. What a wonderful way to sum up the strangest evening I had had in a long time. Thank goodness I had a distraction.

I took a deep breath . . . and began to translate.

CHAPTER

22

The Almas House
Teenieh, a small village near Jaffa, Palestine
April 1947

Zeina was the saddest bride Layla had ever seen. Today, on her wedding day, she looked paler than usual, and her mind seemed somewhere else. Maybe she was heartbroken over Richard, but really, Layla thought having two men who desperately desired you this much must be a nice problem to have.

Layla watched Zeina sit with glassy eyes in front of the mirror in their bedroom, rhythmically brushing her dark hair. Her mother had prescribed one hundred strokes to boost shine. Zeina had stuck to this soothing routine today when there was really no time for it at all. It was nearly noon, and her groom was due to arrive in his grand car in one hour for the *katb ktab* signing ceremony, when she would officially become his wife.

The day hadn't fully started yet, and Zeina already looked

like she needed to rest. She had kept Layla up, tossing and turning all night, until the sisters rose before dawn broke to join the family in morning prayers to bless Zeina's prospective marriage and this auspicious day. In addition to the standard *Fajr* prayer at dawn that involved kneeling down twice, Layla heard Zeina add two extra *rakaat*, kneeling down a total of four times in a special *istikhara* prayer. She did this to ask Allah to let everything go smoothly if this marriage was the best path for her life, if marrying Abu Shanab was indeed her destiny.

Had Layla also heard her whispering Richard's name after chanting the familiar prayer lines, or was just that her imagination?

The rest of the morning had passed by in a blur of half-eaten breakfasts and preparatory rituals. Zeina had rubbed drops of olive oil into her hair and skin to soften them to the touch. She applied honey and lemon masks to bring out the freshness of her skin. After she rinsed her face, Layla helped lace her into a traditional robe of white satin with gold embroidery, wondering if it would ever be her turn. It should have been her turn first.

After the signing ceremony, Zeina would be able to change into the altered wedding dress that had belonged to their mother, with its colorful, geometric embroidery sewn by their grandmother. While the white robe was conservatively cut, the wedding dress had a lovely sweetheart neckline and would showcase Zeina's delicate white shoulders, with her black hair flowing freely around her face.

"You look beautiful," Layla told her. "You're so lucky. More than you realize."

"Do you want to take my place?" Zeina may have meant it as a joke, but her tone had an edge to it.

Before Layla could respond, their mother walked in carrying a bowl with floating orange blossoms in it. Zeina dabbed the fragrant water behind her ears, into her décolletage, and onto her wrists to replenish her skin. Her mother whisked her away to apply rouge to her cheeks . . . and that's when Layla finally had her chance to reread the letter she had found.

Yesterday, she had noticed a book on Zeina's bed—she was always reading—and Layla had swiped it with a plan to misplace it somewhere random, just to annoy Zeina a little. She was surprised to see a letter flutter out of it. Now, finally with a sacred moment alone, Layla shut the bedroom door and began to read slowly, her finger trailing beneath each word. She couldn't read as well as her younger sister . . . because the letter was in English.

> Zeina, ya Zeina,
>
> I find myself searching for words with the letter Z to slip into random conversations. At the dukkan the other day, I let Umm Mohamed talk for a quarter of an hour about za'atar and zeit zaytoon and zanjabil, reveling in the loveliness of that letter and all the images that come with it. I zigzag in a daze through the zoo that is our zany village every day, zealously hoping to catch your gaze . . .
>
> I am jealous of your sister for being blessed with the sight of your beautiful face first thing every morning, jealous of your mother for having breakfast with you, jealous of the bread warmed by your hands, the ground that your feet tread on, the tree in your garden that you lean on, and the sun that finds new motivation to rise every dawn just to kiss your cheeks.
>
> You're avoiding me. You've stopped answering my letters, and when you do, the response is short and cold. What happened?
>
> Please meet me in our special place tomorrow, even

if it is just for five minutes while we cross paths on the road. Without a glance or a smile or a touch of the hand, without Zeina in my life, I am shriveled and colorless and cold.

Bring me the warmth of your smile, the green gardens of your eyes, and the sunlight that always surrounds you. You used to feel the same way—do you still?

I want to ask you what to say to your father when I come to ask for your hand—what will differentiate me from the droves of men who speak with the same honeyed words, hoping to win him over? Are you worried that I am not Arab? Not wealthy? What is it, my darling?

I may not have mountains of gold or a mansion, but, if things go as I can only dream, I will make you a queen and give you whatever you desire.

We have to act quickly. I have heard whispers that British troops may be pulling out of Palestine entirely by next month. My deployment could come to an end in a matter of days or weeks.

I'll be waiting for you at high noon at our spot with another gift for you. My heart will be drumming in my chest until your arrival . . .

Yours forever,

Richard D.

Layla was taken aback at the suggestion of multiple interactions, mutual feelings, scheduled meetings. The kiss Layla saw had obviously been one of many regular encounters.

Was Zeina playing a game with his feelings? Or had she just resigned herself to being the wife of Haytham Ramle and not had the courage to break the news to her secret lover?

A familiar rumbling sound grew closer and closer.

"It's time," their mother said with a clap of her hands as she walked past the bedroom. Layla stuffed Zeina's illicit love note back in its place within the pages of Zeina's book. Fayza's voice made her aware of the men banging on drums and the women of the neighborhood calling out well-wishes to spread cheer outside her house. Layla walked into the kitchen, where several women from the village had popped in to tell Zeina that her eyes had never shone as brightly as they did today, especially lined with kohl like a princess's.

With Teenieh trembling as stories arose of neighboring villages becoming ghost towns overnight, the families had decided to forgo the traditional seven nights of festivities, including the henna night and the big wedding reception. Instead, the Almas family would host the *katb ktab* signing ceremony at the bride's house after a *jaha*, where the groom would come to take her from her childhood home. A festive dinner would follow, as a reception in her new home in Jaffa for whoever could travel there.

Zeina was actually relieved to avoid these duties, where all eyes would have been on her and Abu Shanab at each event, night after night. She adjusted her white wedding veil as the women were shooed out of the little kitchen. Zeina rose to her feet as her mother came into the room.

Fayza placed a small mirror on the kitchen table and stood behind Zeina.

"*Mash'Allah*, he is really lucky to have you," Fayza told her warmly. "He should look up at the sky every night and thank Allah for sending him a woman who is as intelligent as she is beautiful, as warm as she is . . . full of surprises?"

Zeina exchanged a confused glance with Layla.

"You have done well to preserve your beauty and give it the value that it deserves," said Fayza, her eyes gazing meaningfully into her daughter's innocent ones. "With the same effort you have put into restraint, let yourself unleash it all tonight with him. Enjoy your new role as a wife."

Layla could see the shock, clear in Zeina's eyes and parted lips, but there was no time to linger as the drums and voices grew louder and coaxed them all toward the kitchen door, behind which they could hear men talking in the living room. Too overcome with excitement, her father, Suleiman, opened the door a crack for about ten seconds to smile and wave at them, before Fayza sternly shut it to adhere to etiquette.

In those few seconds, Layla caught sight of about twenty men stacked against one another like slices of bread in the cramped living room. The temperature through the door felt five degrees warmer than in the bedroom and kitchen. The men wore solemn expressions and their Friday best. Through the crack in the door, Layla saw the bearded imam seated between Abu Shanab and her father in the center of the room.

Would it ever be her turn? What a horrible twist of fate that Zeina was getting a celebration in her honor. Even if she loved Richard deep down, she should be grateful that life had handed her a clear path.

The rest of the men were relatives and close friends of Abu Shanab, there to support him and show Zeina's family that she would be in good hands should anything happen to him. Outside the house, there were probably more men grouped in a grand show of Abu Shanab's respect to the Almas family.

So, it was finally here. Zeina's sacred wedding day. The sisters had never attended a *katb ktab* ceremony before, but they knew the protocol: the imam would make a speech about how the Prophet Muhammad had honored his wives and women in general, and then the men would make their statements. Customarily, women were not included, with the father signing the marital contract on his daughter's behalf. Umm Mohamed always joked: "My father married my groom. I wasn't even in the room!"

Fayza's ear was pressed to the kitchen door, and she relayed information to Zeina and Layla in whispers.

"Abu Shanab is talking now . . . 'honorable family, with humility I ask for the hand of your daughter, Zeina' . . . *W'Allah*, I still can't believe this is really happening! . . . Okay, okay wait . . . The imam just asked Baba to speak . . . Baba's been practicing—he sounds like an excited poet!"

Her father had rehearsed his lines all week—in front of the bathroom mirror while shaving, while putting on his shoes, while drinking his tea after a meal. "With the grace of Allah, may they live a—no, wait—with the mercy of Allah, may they treat one another with respect and . . ."

Their mother held up her hand to ask them to be quiet. The sisters hadn't spoken, and Zeina had barely moved, her eyes trained on the floor.

"He's saying . . . Abu Shanab is saying he wants to give the *mahr* gift directly to the bride. He's asked Baba and the imam to let Zeina go in . . . Is that normal? Zeina, do you—"

The door opened a crack again, bringing with it another gust of warm air. Eyes glistening with excitement, their father asked Fayza if Zeina would be allowed to come in to accept her groom's present.

"It's not how we do it here, but since we aren't doing the wedding reception in our village, maybe it's best . . . A nice way for her to say goodbye to everybody," said Suleiman. "Maybe our groom's gift is too big for me alone to carry."

His whispered joke was met with a silencing look from Fayza.

Layla stayed in the kitchen near Fayza, both peeking through the door, as Zeina held her father's hand and stood in front of the imam and her future husband. Suleiman resumed his seat. Someone's stomach rumbled loudly in the room. A few men cleared their throats. Zeina kept her eyes trained on the ground, while all others in the room were now centered on her.

"*Bnayti*, your father, Suleiman Almas, has given his blessing to this union," said the imam to her. "With your consent to this marriage, Anisa Zeina, may the groom present you with his *mahr*?"

"Yes," Zeina whispered.

Abu Shanab stood and offered Zeina a navy blue box. Inside was a large gold coin and, next to it, a diamond ring with a gleaming solitaire stone. Layla had never seen a diamond before. She watched Zeina's eyes light up with surprise at its beauty. It was her first genuine smile all day.

"All witness that the bride has received the *mahr* in her hand," boomed the imam's sonorous voice. "And what is the *mahr mu'akhar* in case the couple does not remain together?"

"One quarter of the dunam of my land and an annual ten percent share in revenue from my exporting business," said Abu Shanab as the room filled with gasps and murmurs at sums the men couldn't fathom. What they did know was that in the event of death or divorce, Zeina and her family would have no financial concerns at all—for life. Suleiman, unable to contain his excitement, noisily sped through the prayer beads in his hand and rocked gently back and forth in his chair.

Layla thought that Haytham Ramle may not be a young, handsome prince, but he seemed caring and kind. The diamond was the most beautiful object she had ever seen.

Zeina always gets all the luck, Layla thought bitterly.

Zeina was ushered out of the room as Abu Shanab and Suleiman signed the legal documents, along with two witnesses: Uncle Shadi and Abu Shanab's brother. Their uncle Saeed wasn't present because he thought travel into Palestine was too risky.

She retreated to her bedroom, where aunties had gathered to help dress her in her white sweetheart-neckline gown.

She felt as if the woman in the mirror were someone else, as if she was watching an actress play the role of the happy bride. The shattered dreams of a life with Richard were tearing her up inside.

When she was dressed, Zeina dutifully stood in the doorway, looking as if she were an elegant rose. There were tears in the eyes of Abla Nisreen, who had been their teacher when the girls were little. Little Fawzi broke free from his mother's grasp in the crowd, running up to give her a flower. The fanfare waiting outside her stone home brought a little color to her cheeks, but her smile still felt forced.

"*Aweeehaaaaa*, our princess has today become a queen!" came Umm Mohamed's shrill call from somewhere in the crowd. The women voiced their happiness with ululations of "*Yolololololololoeleeeeee!*"

"*Aweeeehaaaaa*, may he give her jewels that glow like the emeralds of her eyes!" yodeled Auntie Farida.

"*Yolololololololeeeeee!*"

"*Aweeeehaaa*, the kohl on your eyes, I clapped for it, it sang!" ululated Auntie Nada.

"*Yolololololoeleeeee!*"

Fayza and Layla kissed Zeina on the cheek; then she got into the car where Abu Shanab was waiting with his hands on the steering wheel.

Zeina was married on paper now, and Abu Shanab—her husband!—was going to drive her around the village, beeping his horn in celebration and waving to the crowds. Zeina let the tears flow down her cheeks, which her new husband found endearing. He would never know they were the result of a broken heart over another man.

Zeina left the village in a flurry of dust and noise, leaving behind Richard's letter.

Layla would no longer share her bedroom with her sister, the newly married Zeina Almas Ramle. She felt a twinge of sadness, which surprised her. But with the crowd still waving goodbye to her sister, Layla turned to scour Zeina's little library of books. The last thing she wanted was to mill about with the townspeople, their eyes full of pity, telling her they hoped she would be next.

That's when she saw him. He was leaning against the lemon tree, holding the rock that normally marked the spot of their hidden letters.

Layla could see the tears fill Richard's eyes as he watched the car drive away.

CHAPTER
23

I looked around my bedroom. Yes, this was my bed. That was my Eddie Murphy poster on the wall. There was my laptop, with my grandmother's blue journal peeking out of a tote bag. That was the brick wall and the broomstick I pretended was a microphone when practicing my sets.

But am I still the same Mia?

The memories of the night before crashed over me like an ocean wave. Teta's story of leaving behind a true love. The standing ovation at the show. The heckler. I sighed. The kiss in the alleyway . . . I punched the air, then put a pillow over my face to suppress a silent scream. With the whirlwind after the show and then Hadi at dinner, I hadn't had a minute to myself to reflect on a magical moment.

I felt optimistic after a good night's sleep. Jackson's kisses had been softer than I had imagined at first, as if he was treading carefully. I could feel his abandon as his kisses grew more and more urgent, his hands getting tangled in my curls before making their way down to my waist again. He wanted me, I could feel it, he wasn't faking it. Maybe I had misread his feelings for Adriana. A thorough analysis of her social media proved that she was the one who posted photos of them, not him. Was it actually possible that a door between Jackson and I had opened a crack?

And the kiss was all the more romantic because of the rain. A proper New York in autumn, *Breakfast at Tiffany's*, Ross-and-Rachel, Carrie-and-Big moment.

Fairy tales do exist. I smiled to myself. *This is how Zeina must have felt with the soldier. How heartbreaking to read about that sad wedding day. Is this what Teta wanted me to understand? That life is short, that she missed her chance for adventure? That romance should prevail?*

I sat up, excited to see Jackson at work again, but partly wishing I could call in sick and deal with the first meeting post-kiss another day. My stomach was in knots worrying about how the day would go. I doubted I could manage any breakfast. After Jackson's kisses and the intensity of Teta's unfolding story, I didn't know if I could face her this morning, either.

Wow, read a message from Jackson. *See you at work . . .*

A bubble of nerves rose in my stomach. I tried to stop my mind from overanalyzing his words. "Wow" was good. Mentioning work felt less good. A morning message was thoughtful.

Wow indeed, I wrote back with a smiley face.

I got up to shower, full of renewed hope, replaying the evening in my mind. Jackson had offered to order a taxi for me after what felt like hours kissing in the rain. We were out there for only five minutes, actually, I thought. At least the nervous comedian hadn't come back outside to interrupt us with another set of jumping jacks.

Instead, I had insisted on taking the subway home, to give myself time to recalibrate, to bring myself back down to earth a little. I usually plugged in my headphones and enjoyed Jordan B.

Brown's latest recap, watching the faces drifting in and out of the subway car at each stop. But this particular ride home, I hugged my bag the entire time, sitting numbly in a corner and staring into space with a small smile, or reading and rereading lines from Teta's story, before finally resurfacing at the 116th Street station. I had walked up the grimy stairs, stepping aside for a loud group of Columbia freshmen rushing past me in matching baby blue T-shirts, chatting about a pizza night at Ray's. I had lifted my face up to the rain, falling lightly, as the streetlamps glowed to life in the tidy Upper West Side. I had crossed the street toward my building and, luckily, bumped into Phaedra.

Tonight was her show. At least I would get a chance to recip-rocate her kindness.

I weaved my hair into my usual tight braid, but added a little lip gloss and mascara.

What's it going to be like when we lock eyes across the office today? I wondered with a nervous flutter. *And what should I wear today?*

I found a warm *zaatar manakish* with thyme and olive oil on the kitchen table for me with a note from Teta, who had gone early to the farmer's market. Probably to avoid facing more of my questions. Jeddo must have been fixing something for one of the tenants. I breathed a sigh of relief. The apartment was peacefully empty.

I was a block away from work when I realized that I had left my phone at home. I walked up to the receptionist to ask her to call my grandmother's phone to let her know. Ivory, normally an ice queen, broke into a wide smile.

"Mia! When can I see your next show?" she asked.

Mail Room Andy came up to high-five me and spent five min-utes telling me about his own comedy ambitions. He had been writing a script about an office sitcom based on a lonely mail room guy who knows everybody's business. He wanted my opinion on the opening pages and some of the punch lines. Apparently I had established myself as a comedy expert overnight.

What the hell is going on? I wondered as more people gathered around to ask about my show. *Had Mail Room Andy, Katie, and Jackson talked about my set in front of everyone already? Were there more people from the office in the audience whom I hadn't noticed?*

I wanted to walk into the newsroom toward my desk, but people kept standing up and walking over to congratulate me. I was being held hostage by admirers full of inquisitive questions at reception. Even Isabel was making her way out of her office toward me with a smile. Had it been her alone, I would have assumed Jackson had mentioned something to her, but soon a small semicircle had formed near the reception desk as I stood awkwardly holding my latte.

I turned around, and there, on Ivory's computer screen, I saw it. An article titled "A Rising Stand-Up Act: 9/11 Security Guard's Arab American Daughter Puts Heckler in His Place."

There was a photo of me onstage the previous night, with my fierce black eyeliner and glitter. And a short video of me addressing the heckler, with a big play button in the center.

And a byline . . . by Katie Gromley.

CHAPTER

24

I waded through the small crowd in a daze. There was no chocolate bar on my desk this morning. That felt like a bad sign, but I pushed Jackson to the back of my mind. I grabbed my laptop and headed toward an empty glass-walled conference room in the back. I put on "fuck off" headphones to give me the privacy needed to read Katie's article in depth. She wasn't in yet, and I had rushed too quickly past Jackson's office to see if he was there.

One crisis at a time.

> Mia Almas, an emerging stand-up comedian set to take Manhattan's comedy scene by storm, put a heckler in his place after he shouted racial slurs during her set at Greenwich Village Comedy Club. The daughter of a security guard who lost his life saving others during 9/11, the talented Arab American displayed grace and . . .

Although her piece was full of praise for my set, my bravery, and even my eyeliner, I still felt deeply betrayed.

The first time she sees me in a show, and she decides it's her choice to broadcast my art to the world? my mind raged. *Without my consent, let alone my awareness? She, of all people, knows about my father and family situation.*

My eyes glossed over the video, my mouse hovering over the play button. That's when I saw Jackson's name credited beneath the video. So, he had recorded me—violating the club's no-recording policy—and published it along with this article.

He hadn't just known all along . . . he was an accomplice.

I took deep breaths. This was not how I had envisioned the morning after finally kissing Jackson. I had imagined meeting Katie in the lobby, sipping coffee on our sunlit bench, and analyzing every second that had passed during my kissing-in-the-rain evening. Let her assuage my guilt and tell me I was wittier and more beautiful than Adriana.

I looked toward the busy newsroom, buzzing along like nothing had changed. To the right, I saw Katie stride in and set down her bag at her desk. She switched on her monitor and chatted to Mail Room Andy. She had a half smile on her face as she turned her attention to her phone. A few seconds later, my laptop pinged to life with a text from her.

I have a surprise for you, beautiful! Are you in yet? Dying to hear how your night ended . . .

This was followed up by an animated GIF of two people kissing and falling off a couch together.

I couldn't bring myself to respond. She didn't even realize there had been a transgression. Eyeing the fire escape outside the window, I scrambled to think of ways to avoid her, when she looked up and caught my eye. She clapped her hands excitedly and made her way toward me with a big smile on her face, before slowing her steps as a small frown began to form. She had registered my cold look. My heartbeat was thudding in my ears.

All that was left between us was the glass door of the conference room. I made no move to stand up or welcome her in. After a beat, she smiled and mouthed: "Are you okay?" She motioned her fingers to let me know she was coming in.

"What, you didn't love it? You're in *The Culturalist*! We're gonna make you a big star! Don't worry, I won't take a finder's fee," she said, pulling out a swivel chair to sit down. "Just don't forget me when you're more famous than Britney Spears."

I couldn't find my voice.

"Mia, what's going on? Did something happen with Jackson?" she asked more quietly after she had taken a seat. She had swept her eyes with a neon pink eyeliner today. Her earrings were made out of a fuzzy blue material. Normally, I loved her eclectic sense of style and the way her pixie cut brought an edge to any outfit. Today, I thought she looked ridiculous.

K *for Katie indeed,* I thought, glancing at the tattoo on her bare shoulder beneath the strap of her gray cami. *Always looking out for yourself.*

"What were you thinking?" I said, my voice cracking.

Show strength, Mia, I counseled myself. *She meant well, but it wasn't right. Just tell her and keep it short.*

"The article? If there's something you don't like, I can . . . I can take it out?" she said, angling her chair to take a look at my screen. She extended her hand toward my laptop and I shoved it away. "Mia, I was just so happy to see you doing your thing, just like college! You were so fierce!"

That was the moment Jackson chose to knock on the door. I tried to put on a smile, but my insides felt like they were in a washing machine.

"I came to congratulate you for—Mia, are you okay? You look pale," Jackson said.

Jackson was wearing a navy suit that set off the warm tones in his eyes. Why did he have to be so handsome?

I tore my eyes away from him, feeling intensely betrayed. Was it really less than twenty-four hours ago that we had shared a kiss, years in the making? And did he take that kiss to mean consent for publishing a video of me onstage? How could he, when I had kept my comedy a private affair from my own friends?

A quick glance outside the conference room showed life going on as usual, undeterred by the drama about to unfold in this room. Jackson's hand found its way to its familiar spot on my shoulder. I saw him exchange a concerned glance with Katie, who shrugged and stood up to fetch me a glass of water.

"Mia, it's a great piece, and we would never publish anything that would hurt you," Jackson began. "Is there anything that—"

"You published a story about me without telling me," I interrupted him, addressing Katie. Her hand froze in midair, the ice she had placed in the glass of water rattling, the only sound in the room. They waited for me to continue, and she gingerly took a seat. When I didn't speak, she started to answer, but I spoke again before she could start.

"And you of all people know why I keep a low profile. The reason I hold myself back has less to do with being shy or having a conservative background . . . and everything to do with my grandparents," I said slowly. "They are undocumented, Katie. Do you know what that means? They aren't meant to be living in America, even though they've lived here for decades."

My breath was growing shallower, my eyes fixated on Katie. She met my gaze but didn't speak. I repeated the word "undocumented" syllable by syllable, daggers in my voice.

"Un. Doc. U. Men. Ted.

"They overstayed a visitor visa when they first came to New York, and then when my mom died . . . then my father years later . . . and just . . . Lawyers haven't been able to help, when we could afford one, that is," I rambled, waving my hands around. "If you had asked me if I was okay with the article, I would have said a hard no. Because if immigration finds out about their status, they risk deportation . . . to a home that no longer exists. And I'm complicit. And potentially homeless."

I looked at her stunned face. Was it really a surprise to her? Of all my friends, she had actually met my grandparents twice. Seen where we lived, how we lived, the small life we lived. Sentences from her article must be swimming around in her mind, just like they were in mine.

> Miss Almas resides on the Upper West Side with her grandparents. Her grandfather, Maher, is a superintendent in the building where he and his wife have resided for over sixty years, while her grandmother, Amal, tends to the tenants' meals. They both came to this country decades ago in search of the American dream. Today, they have much more than that in Mia Almas. They have a rising star.

It was hard to put into simple words how their illegal status had affected our day-to-day lives—forgoing necessary doctor visits, missing school plays—and the bigger moments. I would never forget how a kindhearted nurse had snuck my grandparents into a private corner of the crowded hospital after 9/11 so they could say goodbye to their only son. They had wept and wailed while I had stared numbly, in shock, at his chart, at the address of a family friend listed on it because we could never put down our actual apartment for fear of immigration knocking on our door. A lifetime of looking over our shoulders . . . and I had blown it by trying to be funny onstage. I felt selfish, exposed, and dizzy.

I worked up the courage to look at Jackson, a confusing mix of emotions simmering inside me, threatening to spill over. Part of me wanted him to envelop me in a reassuring hug, to brush my cheek against the soft merino wool of his sweater, to breathe in the scent of his fruity shampoo.

I was furious that they hadn't run this by me first. Especially after my little tryst with Jackson the previous night. This was Vibe Media, not a school paper, for goodness' sake. How could he be part of this humiliation?

Do their careers matter more than their relationships? I fumed. I felt disgusted by them both.

"You're right, she should have given you a heads-up. We are just proud of you and thought this was a good piece to showcase your talent. Katie wrote about you like we would any other performer on a public stage; we thought you'd be excited," he explained gently, placing a hand over mine. "Do you want us to take the article down until you decide how to proceed?"

I moved my hand from underneath his and clasped both hands in my lap, eyes trained on the floor.

"I don't know if that will help—it's already going viral," Katie said, showing us the screen on her phone. My Twitter follower count had reached the tens of thousands—and was climbing. I never used Twitter. I was scared to check my Facebook account now.

What had she done?

"Let me amend the last paragraph, take out the mention of your grandparents," she said quickly, standing up. "Maybe nobody will—"

"I think you've done enough and shouldn't make decisions about a story about me anymore," I said, my voice as sharp as a paper cut. "You should have asked me. Just asked. I know you're worried about getting the new reporter job, but . . . you're a bad journalist. And a worse friend."

Out of everyone, Katie knew how much I missed my father, how much comedy meant to him and now to me, how delicate my family situation was with my grandparents. Undocumented status aside, how would she have felt if I wrote an article about her wealthy, detached parents without asking her? Why did everything always seem to fall apart whenever I let my guard down?

I needed to get out of this stuffy room. I couldn't bring myself to meet Jackson's eye and no longer wanted to breathe the same air as Katie, until my mind settled a little. I needed a game plan, a backup strategy, a way to ensure my family would not be harmed. Oh God, would Jeddo see this? I stood up, my hands clammy.

"I'm going to call PR and legal to get on this, because my concern is that people will blow this out of proportion," Jackson said, standing up. "Let me do damage control, and we'll plan the next steps together. Mia, don't worry. I got you."

You got me, all right, I thought. *Should have had my back before this was published at all. Did you personally green light this piece, Jackson? How could you have recorded a video? How can I trust you now?*

I looked up at his eyes, wide with warm concern, and felt a blush rise to my cheeks at the memory of his hands tangled up in my hair. He gave me a small smile. There was just so much between us we had to talk about. I wanted to believe him, in his ability to take control and smooth everything over, but I couldn't bring myself to smile back.

Jackson and I had finally, *finally* come together in one beautiful, perfect moment, only to collide and crack. Was this a sign that we shouldn't go down this path? Why was I being bathed in his light, only to scuttle back into the darkness?

My legs wouldn't stop shaking, and I had a sinking feeling in my stomach.

"I'm taking a personal day, going to check in on my grandparents," I said, my voice sounding more even than I felt. "I need to talk to them about this."

And so much more, I thought.

"I'm . . . I'm so sorry," Katie said in a small voice to my back.

"What, for putting your job first?" I said with a bite. "I think you're just sorry your plan to get ahead backfired. Frankly, Katie, maybe you should stick to fact-checking drapes and cushions, because you suck at this."

Pain made me cruel. We had never spoken like this to each other before. With that, I turned around, picked up my belongings while avoiding curious glances, and walked out of the office.

CHAPTER
25

Ismat Ramle, first wife

Haytham Ramle's bayara in Jaffa, Palestine

April 1947

"I am Mr. Ramle's wife. First wife," Ismat whispered to herself. "I am Ismat. Ismat Ramle, first wife. Old wife? Former wife? His wife."

She couldn't bring herself to say courteous phrases like "Welcome to our home." She wanted to scream, shout, bark away at this young woman who was joining the family. Zeina, a sixteen-year-old.

Her husband's new wife.

Ismat felt dizzy with heartache and anger.

She stood by the fountain in an embroidered maroon *thob*, seething to the point that she was sure the others could feel the heat emanating from her body. Her hands were loosely clasped in front of her, and she wore a carefully practiced, neutral facial expression to ensure that the servants wouldn't have anything to talk about.

But the few who had been around long enough would recognize that she was making a bold statement with the choice of this particular *thob*, to wear it today of all days. It was slightly frayed at the back, and even old Umm Suheil's expert sewing could not conceal the worn and discolored ends. But Ismat was proud that it fit her slender figure as well as it had the night of her henna party so many years ago.

She had worn this very *thob* the day she was brought in front of this very fountain and introduced to the house staff as Mrs. Haytham Ramle twenty years ago. Ismat was proud of the way the rich maroon color still played off the cherry red of her lips and the auburn hue of her hair. She had put great effort into maintaining her lustrous locks over the years and just didn't care what others might say anymore.

That an older woman should cut her hair.

That she was trying too hard to act half her age.

Her hair now tumbled down her back in half-moon shapes, framing her face like a fire surrounding a wheat field. It had remained so thick and dark after delivering four boys thanks to her careful, daily application of henna and olive oil.

What is taking him so long? she wondered, her eyes scanning the familiar tree-lined horizon.

Perhaps he had taken his new young bride on an ego-filled tour of his grand *bayarat*: hundreds of acres of fertile groves that were responsible for his growing riches. She imagined him driving past an endless sea full of leafy orange trees first, the scent of blossoms sweetly thick in the air, before taking a detour toward the smaller *bayarat* filled with almond trees, olive trees, fig trees, and grapevine leaves that curled up like hands waving in greeting.

Was he driving her slowly past the grand fleet of dusty

trucks, their backs heavy with wooden crates brimming with oranges on their way to the port in Jaffa? Was he regaling her with stories of how those oranges made their way to Paris, to London, to Athens, to cities that looked so glamorous in Egyptian films? Had he accepted an orange from a field hand whom they met on the road, peeled away its dimpled skin, and offered her a taste . . . like he had with her years ago?

Ismat felt sick.

Her ears pricked up when she heard the rumbling of Haytham's car. She cleared her throat, as if ready to make a speech, and watched two yard boys scramble to open the iron gate to prepare for the arrival of Haytham and his young bride. Green eyes, they said, that jumped out at you like fish in the sea. A river of black hair, they said, and a complexion made of cream. Sixteen years old, they said.

Sixteen.

Ismat looked up at the sky to ward off the unwanted tears that had sprung to her eyes. She had been mentally preparing for this moment for weeks, but, now that it was here, her emotions were threatening not to cooperate. She stood in the courtyard, feeling numb, thinking of how everyone must have run around just like this for her so many years earlier. It made her feel tired and cast aside, like day-old bread at a bakery when everyone is waiting for a fresh cake to come out of the oven.

She and Haytham had lived in separate wings of the main house for nearly a decade now, and the arrangement had been . . . pleasant. Didn't all marriages get stale? Wasn't that part of the journey? Although they were no longer daily companions, hands and legs intertwined while talking all night like in their early days together, they were civil. He had stopped coming to her bedroom at night years and years ago, but she never thought he was unhappy. Just content with the marching of time, like she was. She would not be out on the street or shamed with divorce. She would be taken care of for the rest of her life. She had done her duty, given him four wonderful children, and created a home out of this house. She thought Haytham felt the same way, that it was enough for him, too.

Apparently not.

The first blow had come when women in the center of town told her of his quest for a new bride over coffee one morning. They had heard him asking families about their beautiful daughters.

Romance, at this age? She laughed them off as they studied her face, changing the subject when they saw how genuinely unaffected she was. He was a very wealthy man, prone to being the topic of gossip, and she would have none of it. Over the years—particularly over the past few months—she had heard similar rumors of him transferring large sums of money to other countries, or of his business coming under threat, or whispers of him moving abroad, and none of it had come true. Imagine if it was her, asking around town for a young stallion of a man to bring home now that Haytham's figure and stamina resembled that of a friendly fat cow. Ridiculous. He was *her* cow, and the thought of him still brought an affectionate smile to her face.

The second blow came when he returned home a few weeks later to tell her that he was planning to marry a girl from a tiny village nearby. She hadn't expected to be blindsided by an emotional explosion that burst her heart into a million pieces. She thought they were secure, cocooned, sheltered from the world. Had the escalating threats in Jaffa gone to his head? Families she personally knew were fleeing to stay with friends and family in neighboring countries, but she thought they were safe, nestled in the rich green acres of Haytham's *bayarat*. He was the wealthiest man in town, and she thought she had nothing to worry about.

She was wrong.

The third blow came soon after: she was to move out of the main house, the home where she had raised her children, held dinners for family, and cared for Haytham's mother in her final years. Instead, she would live in a small, stately villa on the grounds that was beautifully redecorated. She knew it had belonged to one of Haytham's father's wives, the eldest one, who had passed away a decade ago. Two of his father's other wives still lived on the property: private lives in private villas in private sections of the grounds she rarely ventured to. She would see the women at occasional events—a birth, a death in the family—but they weren't a part of the daily fabric of her life. What did they do in their villas all day? she wondered. What was she going to do in her own villa, alone in a house full of servants and no love, every single day?

She would want for nothing, Haytham had assured her. She would have her own kitchen staff, a banquet room with high ceilings to entertain ladies who would keep her company and sew with her, play instruments for her. There were extra bedrooms for visits from her sons or grandchildren. He had thought of everything to make the change comfortable for her, except how to tend to a heart that had been discarded.

And now here she was, standing in front of the home they had shared for decades, waiting defiantly to welcome him and the new woman who was to replace her.

She didn't really need to be here. She actually shouldn't be here at all. But everyone else from the house was outside, and she wasn't about to watch from a window like a forgotten pet. She wanted to lock eyes with Haytham as soon as he drove up. She wanted him to see her, perhaps clearly for the first time in years.

As the car approached the driveway and slowed to a grumble, the staff assembled behind her. She could hear the kitchen maids giggling together behind her, the main cook, Sawsan, scolding them for having taken too long to peel potatoes in the morning. Field hands, dozens of them, were chatting to her right in restrained voices used to shouting across fields, while dusting off their clothes and clasping dirt-stained hands behind their sun-kissed backs. Several blond guards in uniform, one of them new, stood slightly behind the assembled group near the main door. Haytham must have paid for extra protection from the British army as the situation in Jaffa grew more precarious.

Ismat sighed, exchanging glances with her main maid, Jumana, who waddled over and asked Ismat if she needed anything before giving her hand a pat and standing next to her.

Then, there they were. The car's tinted windshield framed a scene of Haytham handing Zeina a piece of paper as they smiled at each other. Then he rested one hand on her heart-shaped face as the other casually grasped the steering wheel. Though their laughter was contained in the car, Ismat could feel it washing over her like hot liquid, causing her ears to sting and stomach acid to rise into her throat. The entire staff, huddled together outside, facing the car like an audience at a play, had grown so still and silent that even birdsong sounded intrusive. Ismat's heart pounded against her chest, asking to jump out and choke the girl.

She thought about leaving, saving herself from humiliation, but her legs refused to move.

And so she stood dead center in her worn bridal *thob*, ready to face her husband and his new wife.

CHAPTER

26

"Wha—why are you home now? Are you sick?" Teta abandoned the simmering pots on the stove when she saw me walk into the kitchen. Jeddo must have been somewhere in the building, tending to someone's maintenance needs. I pulled out a chair, and Teta did the same, concerned.

"What's the matter?" she asked softly, putting a warm hand to my cheek. "Did something happen at work?"

It was stuffy in the kitchen, the scent of garlic and coriander heavy in the air. Teta liked to get her lunchtime cooking done in the morning, so she could have everyone's meals ready early, with ample time to wash the garlicky aroma out of her hair. I switched the stove off, took a deep breath, and faced her.

"Do you remember how Dad and I, we used to always watch those comedy shows together?" I began. "How much we laughed?"

"Ah, yes, the Eddie Murphys and Robin Williamses," she said, smiling wistfully. "I think your father could have been a great actor, you know. Always handsome, even from a young age. Remember when he tried out for a Broadway play?"

"Yeah, he couldn't really sing, though," I chuckled nervously. "So, uh, the truth is that every once in a while, I like to do these . . . comedy shows . . . onstage . . . in front of people and everything," I said carefully, before my resolve could weaken. "I'm actually quite good and get asked back often. I didn't tell you about my own comedy stuff because I know you want our family to keep a low profile. And I can't imagine your face if you heard me say a dirty joke—mildly dirty, but still . . ."

"Long time?" she asked, eyebrows furrowed, processing.

"A few, uh, years," I said, trying to downplay it.

I did a half laugh, hoping to lighten the mood. Teta was holding her breath, hands clasped to her chest, waiting for more.

She sat quietly. When she didn't speak, I continued.

"Well, someone really liked my last set . . . and wrote an article about it," I said, a quiver creeping into my voice. "It seems to have made quite an impact online. And I'm just worried how this might affect you and Jeddo. Living here and . . . I don't know, maybe I'm getting ahead of myself . . ."

Teta nodded slowly. I watched understanding seep into her warm eyes. If I saw her eyes well up, I would cry, too. Panic rose in me like bile. How could I have done this to her? What would Jeddo say? My own selfishness, my easy ability to put my selfless grandparents at risk after all they had done for me, felt heavier than a fallen tree trunk.

I only realized the tears were forming rivers on my face when Teta reached out and hugged me close, my nose nuzzled in her hair. She stroked my curls and murmured soft words in Arabic that she had used since I was a little girl, like the time I had left my favorite doll at the park. I was surprised to feel her comforting me when I should have been the one reassuring her.

She leaned back and peered into my eyes. I could barely meet hers, but she lifted my chin up.

She studied me for a few seconds before speaking to me in Arabic.

"I hate that you felt you had to hide this from us, *habibti*," she said. "Do I like the idea of you making naughty jokes in public? No. But I know you are graceful and lovely and would never do anything to intentionally hurt us. Living here like this, no papers, it is our choice. We take the risk. Not you."

Her concern for me, for my quality of life, was so kind, at a time when she should be worried about herself.

"If something were to happen, if this gets bigger and they find out about you and Jeddo, I would—"

"We deal with that if it comes," she said plainly. "Our priority was to be here for you after your father passed. But you are older now and working. Even if we had to leave, I know you will be fine. You are strong and wonderful. Everything works out the way it should. Allah is there."

I tried to picture my grandparents moving back to the Middle East. Palestine was not an option anymore, but perhaps a Gulf country. Dubai? A family reconciliation? They would be foreigners in their own homeland.

"Would you even know how to start over after so long in America?" I asked, dabbing my face with tissue.

"Probably not," she said with a laugh. "No Zabar's. What kind of life is that? But I have been through worse. Much worse. I don't think it will happen. But just know that if it does, I'm okay. We're okay. You are the young one with a bright future ahead of you."

I took in the sweetness of her smile, the lines near her eyes. Close up, I could see her eyes had strands of sea green in them.

"Anyway, I knew you were up to something with all those delays at work," she said, whacking me playfully with a dish towel. "The subway can't break down that often."

I laughed, looking at my lap, wondering if she had thought I was running around with a man. She seemed to be in a good mood: warm, open to talk. I hoped this was a good time to bring up our family issues, finally.

"Almost missed my stop while reading the entry about Ismat," I admitted. "It's such a crazy story. You're an amazing writer, Teta."

I could feel the lingering heat of Ismat's burning rage in those pages. It was a timely entry to read after discovering Katie's betrayal this morning. I felt that furious dignity deep in my core through my own perspective. Was this a story about redemption, about women finding a way to band together against the odds? Or about yet another woman who seemed to want Zeina to move out of the way, just like her sister, Layla?

Or perhaps I was looking at it all wrong . . . and it was actually about the way men don't behave as you expect they should. Like Jackson, reeling me in with a trail of kisses along my neck . . . only to betray me by recording—and publishing—a video without my consent.

Teta withdrew her hand from mine and ran it along her perfect chignon. Then she stood up, opened a kitchen cabinet absentmindedly, shut it. She nodded slowly, her back to me.

The openness she'd had moments ago had evaporated. She refused to meet my eye, switching the stove back on. "Ah, Ismat. So strange to hear that woman's name coming from your mouth."

I felt like I had been running without pause, without processing everything. I felt sure that the universe had sent my grandmother's story about the past at this time in my life in order to tell me something important about my present. About my relationships with those around me, about the meaning of love, and about what to do when life lets you down.

I thought of the blue journal in my bag, that it might contain the clarity I so desperately craved. I looked at Teta, busy on the stove, waiting for her to share more about Ismat. Maybe this was all she could manage today. I felt a wave of fatigue and decided to lie down and try again with her later, but when I walked to my room, my phone glowed to life with messages. Katie, Ivory, even Mail Room Andy.

Four missed calls from Jackson.

I threw the phone aside in frustration. I was simply too furious to speak to anyone today.

Then I picked it up again to text Phaedra, thanking her for the night before and confirming our plans for her upcoming show. I was too drained to try putting into words what had happened this morning, even to my new friend. Perhaps this was an opportunity to officially ask if she would like to be interviewed for *The Culturalist* . . . Maybe showcasing Phaedra's talent would take some attention away from me.

Without another word, I grabbed my laptop and Teta's blue journal and escaped into the next entry.

CHAPTER

27

Zeina

Haytham Ramle's bayara in Jaffa, Palestine

April 1947

Time took no notice of Ismat's pain. Haytham Ramle got out of the car as Zeina struggled with the door handle on her side. Her sparkling laugh filled the air as the door burst open with his help. She stepped out with a smile, shading her eyes with one hand and holding her white dress with the other, before noticing all the people standing in greeting to her. In surprise, she shrank behind Haytham, who brazenly held her hand, kissed it, and pushed her forward.

"Everyone, please greet Zeina with kindness and open arms," Haytham said grandly. "Zeina, welcome to our family."

Zeina stood, a sea of blinking eyes preying on her dress, skin, and delicate hands for the second time that day. She kept her own cast down and clasped her hands in front of her. She didn't know whether to say something, or curtsy, or run back to the car and hide.

She looked up at the large mansion, smiling at the sand-colored stone that reminded her of her own, smaller family home in the village. She breathed in the heady scent of olive trees mixed with the freshness of the nearby sea. The saltiness of the sea air was more powerful here.

She cleared her throat to speak when, suddenly, a chicken ran squawking into the space that divided the couple from the crowd in the dirt driveway, heading straight for the bubbling fountain behind them. A young field hand ran after it until someone else caught it and handed it to him. The crowd broke into laughter and applause.

"In Teenieh, they say that's a good omen," said Zeina, looking up at Abu Shanab. She reminded herself that she must remember to address him as Haytham Ramle, not by that nickname.

This entire day felt so surreal to her. It was as if she was about to wake up from a nap any minute to discover it had all been a strange dream. She would rise from her childhood bed at home, greet her parents, and run to the lemon tree to see if Richard had left her another sweet note.

Her former life was already starting to feel like a fantasy she had conjured. She looked up at her new husband, still in shock that she had a new life to lead, a new role to play in this giant new house.

Haytham squeezed her hand and began to lead her inside as the crowd parted. She smiled kindly as she locked eyes with the different people. Pretty young kitchen maids with flour on their aprons waved shyly, while better-dressed housemaids in white linen uniforms shouted out in welcome to her. She looked to the right and saw a red-haired older woman in an elegant maroon *thob*—the only unsmiling face in the crowd. The woman stood still, and although her expression was neutral, her cheeks were flushed and her dark eyes were blazing. Zeina nodded to her with a warmth that went unreturned, before letting her eyes roll over the men in blue coveralls with olive and orange stains on their clothes. She reached the grand wooden door, which was flanked by men in khaki army uniforms.

Then she saw him. Or was she imagining it?

Richard?

She had nearly reached the front entrance when her legs almost gave way. The servants smiled, blaming it on the heat and her delicate nature. Someone handed her a glass of water, and she took a seat in a chair in the spacious entryway, her mind racing too quickly to take in the polished marble floors, the cream-colored chaise longue, the chandelier that cast dappled light on vases filled with fresh flowers. She breathed slowly, putting a hand to her warm cheek, and looked around the space as servants spread out, going back to their tasks.

She leaned over, craning her neck slightly to look outside the wooden door, left slightly ajar.

Was Richard really standing among those guards in uniform?

She could hear men outside talking and clapping one another on the back, ready to return into the field while the sun was still out. Her eyes found their way to Richard again, like he was a snag in clothing, because he was watching her so intently, not joining in the banter. He stood straight as a rake in his khaki army uniform, hands clasped behind his back. Unmoving, with the exception of his eyes that followed her.

Richard.

Here.

What was he doing here? Had he followed her?

Zeina leaned back, her hand on her forehead. Without realizing it, she smiled as she took a sip of cool water. *Richard came to find me.*

In the few seconds that they'd held each other's gaze, she'd seen a show reel in her mind. There was the first time that she and Richard had seen each other near Umm Mohamed's *dukkan*, the tune she would sing just for him when he passed by her house, the first time they had held hands while pretending to shop for oranges, love-laden words whispered in passing, notes hidden under trees, the kisses nobody knew about that had led to fantasies of a life shared between the two of them after eloping to Europe, a home of their own with a lemon tree filled with love letters, the wrinkles that would eventually line their faces in old age together.

Was it possible that dream was still alive, a tiny, flickering flame that could rage into a fire?

She felt a hand on her back, pushing her forward into the house. She looked up into Abu Shanab's face, taking in the comical mustache and bald head from her seated angle. She had a frozen half smile on her face. Her eyes glazed over the elegant marble in the entrance, the floor-to-ceiling windows that opened up onto private gardens on the other side, the staff that whisked away her few belongings somewhere deep inside the cavernous house. She made no comments to the man standing next to her.

"Why don't you get some rest and freshen up before dinner this evening?" Abu Shanab said to her. "Your personal maid, Hiba, will take you to your bedroom."

He nodded vaguely in the direction of a young brunette about her age, who welcomed her to the house. Hiba wore a white uniform with a simple apron, like the other maids. She was wiry, walking ahead of Zeina with purpose, guiding her through a maze of corridors until they reached a white wooden

CHAPTER

28

Phaedra's penthouse apartment was so familiar, yet unfamiliar with traces of her everywhere. I tripped over a pair of gold, strappy heels in the hallway when I walked in. The ashtray had a few new cigarette stubs and had found a new home on top of the baby blue piano. She had left the windows open to let the fresh fall air into the apartment, or perhaps to let the scent of cigarette smoke float away.

I was happy to have Phaedra as a distraction. I had successfully avoided Katie and Jackson all day, even curbing my dirty habit of stalking him online as I read Teta's story. I was mostly worried about my grandparents, although there had been no urgent knocks on the apartment door, no sign that the article had caused disaster. Terrified of his reaction, I hadn't talked to Jeddo yet, instead praying that this would blow over and he would never have to know. Telling Teta had been hard enough.

I sat primly on the cream-colored sofa, working up the courage to ask Phaedra if I could interview her for an article in *The Cul-*

door. Hiba ushered her inside, helped her out of her white dress, and invited her to lie down in a bed that could have easily fit four people.

Zeina sank into four plush pillows as Hiba spread an airy duvet over her. Everything in the bedroom was white: the blanket, pillows, curtains, even the fresh flowers by the vanity desk. Then Hiba drew the curtains and left, whispering a goodbye, closing the door quietly behind her. Zeina was alone for the first time all day. The tears came, dampening her white blanket where they fell, until she sank into a dreamless sleep.

In a smaller villa nearby on the grounds, Ismat lay her head down in her own unfamiliar new bedroom, darkening the blue of her blanket with her tears.

turalist. Munching on chocolate cookies, I asked her feeler questions, which she answered while flitting from the kitchen to the bedroom to rummage through her wardrobe for a very necessary beret.

"Yes, I performed in that theater in Dubai that I told you about, but there's a certain cachet that comes with performing onstage in New York City," she called out. "I've done gigs around the Arab world, from Egypt to Saudi to Jordan. Residencies in Paris and London. New York seemed like the natural next step."

She popped into the living room with a towel wrapped around her head to offer me a glass of water.

"I do write my own songs, but I got a huge social media following from singing cover songs. I love Britney Spears!" She started singing "Oops! . . . I Did It Again," before plugging in a hair dryer.

I watched her run her fingers through her damp hair, moving the blow-dryer in slow circles around her head with her eyes closed. She was wearing a summery floral red dress with thin spaghetti straps. She had glitter on her bare shoulders.

"My ex in Beirut met Coldplay's drummer and I got a chance to open for them in Dubai. That's where I heard about the Juilliard adjunct lecturer program, and the rest is history," she said when she switched off the hair dryer, placing it haphazardly on the coffee table. I made a mental note, planning to research that gig as soon as I got to my desk at work. That could be a great opener for my article.

"So, listen, as you know, I work at Vibe Media, and there's a reporter opening at *The Culturalist*, where they profile rising artists in New York," I began as she came to sit next to me on the sofa. "They covered people like Alicia Keys and Rihanna before they made it big. How would you feel about a profile?"

I was starting to get excited about the possibility of writing about her. Throwing myself into this could be the perfect way to avoid all the drama at work and at home.

Admittedly, the fact-checker in me was more interested in the details I couldn't publish, rather than what would ultimately make it into the piece. Like ... the man's shoes in the living room the other day. The ex-boyfriend she mentioned in Beirut. Yes, the fact that she opened for a rock band in Dubai was promising, but there was a lot more color to her story than I had expected.

"Can I think about it?" she said, fastening a gold hoop earring. "I can already tell my audience about myself on social media. I don't know if I'm ready for press here yet. Maybe after I get my first big gig?"

I nodded. I'd been hoping she would jump at the chance, but I was relieved it wasn't a straight no. Maybe she would change her mind by the end of the evening. She reached for a makeup bag and spilled its contents out. A clatter of compacts, brushes, and palettes spread out on the coffee table before us.

"Whatever happened to that boyfriend you mentioned you had, in Beirut?" I asked, wondering if he had been supportive of her blossoming music career. "Do you still talk?"

She stopped fiddling with her makeup and looked at me, leaning back on the sofa.

"Off the record?" She smiled.

I nodded, hands clasped in my lap.

"He was my first boyfriend years ago. We met in university and I couldn't bring myself to sleep with him for the two years we were together," she said, her voice soft. "Our family doctor, in Lebanon at the time, lauded my strong sense of virtue. My doctor in London said it was a medical condition called vaginismus. Fear of sex. Isn't that the funniest and saddest thing you've ever heard?"

I listened to her, enraptured. She fiddled with a blond tendril as she spoke, lost in memory. She told me how much she enjoyed kissing, even foreplay, but when the Big Bang Moment arrived, her muscles tightened up and she may as well have been wearing undies made of barbed wire.

She looks like a total white girl on the outside, I thought, *but she's like me on the inside.*

"I mean, I had grown up watching *Sex and the City* and *Friends* on TV, I looked like these women and related to them more than some of my conservative aunties, but when it came to the bedroom . . . Let's just say the light wouldn't switch on," she continued. "Even though I really, really loved the guy. It took another year for me to shed that deeply ingrained sense of shame, to feel okay about having natural sexual instincts. We. Are. Human!"

The tea was growing cold in my hand. I set the mug down on the coffee table, shaking my head. She tossed me a book with a purple cover. It was an anthology of erotic stories written by Arab women, some dating as far back as the seventeenth century, some published this year. I riffled through the pages as she spoke, thinking of my grandmother's story. Of the phrase she had used: "wet fire." Of the man Zeina had loved standing by as another man asked to marry her. Our collective, unfulfilled stories. Perhaps, one day, I could add my own . . . and maybe even get love and lust right. Out in the open.

"The sad part is that your own reputation isn't even about you at all." Phaedra waved her hands in the air as her voice rose. "Every choice an Arab woman makes reflects on every cousin, aunt, uncle, grandparent, neighbor, friend, and pet."

She went on, talking about how the weight of the entire family's honor seemed to rest on an Arab woman's shoulders like a dead animal. For a man, sex meant a native hunger, a physical need, a healthy release. A sign of virility. A man was an animal in his own right.

"It shouldn't just be a woman's duty to stay quiet, glance away, avoid sparking a fire," she said, her voice a little calmer now. "What about the fire in me? I swear, just talking about it, I still feel so frustrated. Women have needs, too."

Phaedra had a lyrical, poetic way of expressing herself. I wondered if it was the artist in her, or if these were words and feelings that regularly circulated in her head, over and over, seeking some resolution.

"Well, sounds like he loved you, too," I said, by way of consolation. "He waited for you to feel ready."

"Yep. After all those years of patiently waiting . . . we finally did it. You know. *It*," she said, her fingers playing with the hem of her dress. "And the next morning, I could feel a shift, like a cold spell. In the weeks that followed, he stopped saying he loved me, ignored my calls, texted hours later. When I finally confronted him, he said I was damaged. Notice: not 'we' are damaged—just me. After that one night together. It broke me. It took me a long time to rebuild my confidence. And find someone new, someone who made me feel good about myself again."

I felt heartbroken for her. I understood. Her ex's taking her virginity and then throwing her away was enough to shatter her faith and sense of self completely.

Her story wasn't even unique; I had heard my grandmother's friends gossiping about similar horrors during their book club gatherings. My mind drifted to random encounters in college that had almost led to the frenzy of sweaty kisses and clothes coming off before I'd reeled myself in. Then to Tanqueray Man . . . and to Jackson.

I watched Phaedra apply cream to her hair. She seemed to have moved on, anyway. She had hinted about a new man in her life. Perhaps the one who had left his shoes in the apartment the other day?

"What about you?" she asked. "How is Mr. Jackson?"

I felt embarrassed. The flood of feelings after our kiss had made it easy for me to open up to Phaedra about him, but now, after what felt like a selfish career move on his part, I felt self-conscious again. I hadn't fully processed what was happening to me, because I was still in the midst of the chaos. Despite being on silent, my phone had been regularly lighting up with a steady stream of text messages from Katie and Jackson. I would have to talk to them both eventually, but I still felt too emotional to address everything calmly.

If I did bring it all up to Phaedra now, I imagined we would end up stalking Jackson and Adriana on social media, looking for hints of change. I desperately wanted to stay away from anywhere I might see Katie's article mentioned. And I didn't want to risk Phaedra seeing that either, for now. I wanted to keep the focus on her and her show tonight. At least she had proven kind and trustworthy, despite the fact that I had admitted to kissing someone who had a girlfriend. I was *that* girl. And she hadn't been judgmental—quite the opposite, in fact.

"It's . . . complicated," I said, my heart thudding at the mention of his name. "Kind of, uh, awkward at work today."

When I was ready to talk, I might find my way to her warm, untidy apartment again.

Hair done, she picked up her compact and checked her eyeliner in the round mirror.

"I need to do this right, because *he* will pass by later tonight and he doesn't usually come out on a weekend because of . . . her," she muttered to herself, snapping the compact shut. Her hair was tousled in loose blond beach waves, lightly scented with shea butter. The soft fragrance filled the air every time she moved.

A sound came from her phone.

"Is that . . . Is he calling you?" I asked. Was she empathetic toward my problem because she had experience being "the other woman"? Who was . . . "her"?

"No, no, it's just my alarm; I didn't want to be late for this show," she said, jumping up. "Okay, prayer, hair, and makeup done. Let's head out. I'll deal with this mess later."

She grabbed a black leather jacket, then handed me a red scarf in case it got colder. I nodded in thanks. We had arranged to meet

Hadi at Smokey's at eight p.m., and if we didn't leave now, we would be late.

We were ready.

As we walked toward the subway, past the neat rows of trees and the small church on Broadway, men eyed us with a mixture of attraction and curiosity. I imagined Phaedra was used to this, with her wild dirty-blond hair, sea-green eyes, and tanned skin. Amid the standard catcalls, the men wondered where she was from.

"Yeah, you're American, but originally? Like, your parents?"

This was then followed up by a variation of:

"No way, but you don't look Arab at all!"

"Guess I can't buy you a drink then, eh?"

Phaedra rolled her eyes, linking her arm through mine as we walked down the stairs into the subway.

"There's really no way to win at these questions, is there?" she asked me.

We talked about how, as Palestinian Americans, our mere existence seemed to be a form of protest or a political statement. In reality, we were third-generation, third-culture kids whose lives were an evolving identity crisis. More so for Phaedra, who had grown up in Lebanon and lived in cities all over the world as an adult.

"We pray a little and we play a little," she said with a laugh. "We're often confused a lot."

Confused was right. I wouldn't mind kissing Jackson a little more. I thought back to our movie moment in the rain, the two of us sharing the same warm breath, the way his lips sent an electric current through me that made every cell in my body come alive. It was like being onstage, in the spotlight, showered with applause and praise. How delicious to have met someone who could make me feel this charged with a look or a touch . . . I sighed, burying any lingering thoughts of Jackson. I had switched my phone off to avoid dealing with everyone and everything outside this bubble tonight.

I hadn't expected to have a detailed talk about cultural identity on our way to Phaedra's gig. I had never had a friend like her, with experiences so familiar yet so foreign to my own.

I was already nervous about meeting Hadi at Smokey's. We could have walked there, but the air had an icy quality to it, and I was feeling spent. A quick, warm subway ride appealed to Phaedra because of her choice of shoes: black leather over-the-knee boots. When I'd seen her sexy outfit, I had been tempted to ask to borrow the strappy gold heels I had seen discarded in her hallway. Instead, I stuck with my usual ballet flats for this first meeting with Hadi.

Is it possible to feel alone on a crowded subway, with someone else's warmth so close that you feel like you share an armpit? Manhattan doesn't stop moving—it never stops hiding you and putting you in the spotlight all at once.

Am I the only twentysomething virgin left in New York City? I wondered, glancing over at Phaedra's long legs in the suggestive thigh-high boots, elegantly crossed at the ankles. Along with her black leather jacket, they offered the perfect contrast to her summery red dress.

"This is us, right?" Phaedra asked when we reached our stop. Hadi would be waiting for us in front of the bar. I nodded, and we walked out into the cool night.

CHAPTER

29

To anyone watching, it was the perfect date. Handsome man, beautiful woman, standing close enough for arms to nearly touch, passionately discussing music. Eyes scanning for an empty table in a busy bar, with jazz blaring in a way that made you instantly smile, sway your shoulders, and clink glasses. Faces lit up by candles on tables. A classic New York City autumn evening.

With me trailing behind.

At first, Hadi and I made pleasant conversation in the dimly lit bar as we waited for Phaedra to join us after she checked in with the stage manager. She walked down the steps near the stage to greet us, now wearing the burnt-orange beret. Her lipstick had large speckles of glitter that caught the light when she spoke. Chain necklaces hung around her neck. On anyone else, this ensemble would have looked ridiculous. On her, it made me wonder in desperation why these exact items were missing from my closet.

"It's an olive tree branch," she was saying as she walked down the steps, motioning to the delicate tattoo on her left collarbone. "Peace in the Middle East, yo."

I looked down at my basic jeans and ballet flats, wishing I had at least chosen bolder earrings than simple gold hoops. I felt like a nerd on a rare night out with the popular girl.

I was practically invisible as she and Hadi chatted about music in a highbrow way: "Schubert is so underrated," and "I actually get excited when I see strange time signatures." Then Hadi talked about his "wonderful" work for a long, long time, and Phaedra linked her arm with mine in a show of camaraderie. I felt like a third wheel. He had behaved so differently around my grandparents, had seemed interested in me. I had been hoping for a distraction tonight, a little ego boost after the mess with Jackson. What had happened?

Matters didn't improve when we took a seat near the front in the smoky bar. There were a dozen small round tables with chairs facing the stage, each lit by a flickering candle. We walked through the jungle of plants and heat and men to find seats near the center.

Phaedra squeezed my shoulder and waved, making her way to the stage. The men's eyes trailed her back. She took a seat at the piano, her milky skin bathed in the spotlight.

This would be great color for my piece, I told myself, trying not to feel disheartened as Hadi checked his phone next to me. He had yet to engage me properly in conversation.

"Hey, thanks again for helping my grandfather," I opened, playing with a coaster on the table. "He would have refused to go to see a doctor until things got real. I really appreciate you sorting him out."

He smiled and went back to his phone. I turned to admire the stage. I sighed, thinking of my last show and how much I still loved the idea of being bathed in the spotlight onstage, making people laugh. The heckler—and Katie's story—couldn't take that love away from me.

"Give it up for Color Me Blue," said the emcee to introduce the band. "Shakira may be the queen of pop, but guest singer Phaedra Younan is the Arabian princess of our stage. Let's give her a warm welcome, everybody. Take it away!"

Phaedra was now framed in a bluish light, seated at the brown upright piano next to a cellist and a trumpet player. A drummer began a subtle beat and a hush fell over the crowd, our faces aglow from the candles. The huskiness of Phaedra's voice surprised me as she began to sing and play a Britney Spears song in bluesy tones that elevated the melody to a new level of artistry. Her green eyes shone like gemstones in the spotlight.

The rest of the evening was a blur of frozen smiles on my part and slightly excessive clapping after every song on Hadi's. He occasionally talked about himself during breaks, including something about a beekeeping hobby when he was in university. He didn't ask me once about what I did for a living or even about my family. I found myself aching to browse social media out of boredom.

At one point, he got into a lengthy chat with the waiter, so I caved and switched my phone on to check the time beneath the table. I wasn't surprised to see a string of messages from coworkers.

Please call me, Mia, came one from Katie.

We're going to have to talk eventually. When you're ready, chocolate and I are here, read the latest one from Jackson.

A small, soothing balm of hope eased its way onto my cracked heart. Part of me had expected him to stop trying to reach me, for me to fall into a well of despair when I checked my phone to be greeted by silence instead or—worse—by images of him having a grand old time with Adriana as if no tectonic shift had occurred in our lives. Our kiss was transcendental. I was avoiding him, out of immaturity and a need to protect myself, but I had to admit that his consistent attempts to connect made me feel the tiniest bit better. I wasn't ready to talk, but I would be soon. And he promised to be there . . . with chocolate.

I sighed heavily and looked over at Hadi, who was totally absorbed in talking to the waiter. What was I even doing here with Hadi? I knew settling down with a man like him would make my life plan clearer for my grandparents, but maybe it was high time we were all honest with one another. Hadi seemed to have no interest in me anyway. I really needed to sort myself out. I left the messages as "read," planning to answer later, in my bedroom, quietly, thoughtfully, alone. I turned the phone back off as Phaedra started another song.

Soon after, Phaedra played the final notes, which melted into applause, and the show ended. We gave her congratulatory hugs when she got offstage and joined us. I recognized that post-show, euphoric glow in the flush of her cheeks and the vibrancy of her eyes. These would be great details for a profile of her.

I'm so jealous, I thought, looking over at the now-empty stage. *I just want this whole drama to subside so I can go back to my private stage time.*

"This place is amazing," Hadi said, offering Phaedra a glass of water. "You are outrageously talented! I was thinking of sticking around a little longer, unless you two prefer we head back home?"

Phaedra gave him a smile and told him to stay and enjoy the music. She linked her arm through mine as we walked out into the cool air toward the subway station. She put her leather jacket on to ward off the cold.

"Hey, thanks for coming to support," she said, taking off the beret and putting her hair up into a bun as we walked down the steps to the subway platform. "What strange, small hands Hadi has, with long fingers. Did you notice? Did you have an okay time?"

I studied her, this confident, beautiful woman who was looking at me with uncertainty. The train whooshed past, drowning out our voices, then stopped for us to get on. We sat in the scratchy orange seats, angling our bodies so we could look at each other.

"You were really amazing," I said. "You're on the cusp of something big. You have a true star quality, I can feel it. You give off Norah Jones vibes."

She smiled. I suddenly felt really tired.

"What did you think of Hadi?" I asked. "He kind of kept me at arm's length all night. He was much nicer when he came to dinner with my grandparents the other day. It was weird."

"Honey, I think it's pretty clear he favored that waiter over either of us," she said as the train slowed to a stop and the doors split open. "To his credit, the waiter was cute."

Oh.

"Hey, it's my first weekend in Manhattan and I don't know anyone outside the students in my program," she went on. "How about coffee, maybe tomorrow or Sunday morning?"

I smiled and nodded. I ran through the evening with Hadi in my mind to understand how I had missed the signals. It all made sense now. Suddenly I liked him a lot better. Of course he was too shy to open up to me after my traditional grandparents had scouted him as a potential suitor for me. Phaedra and I took turns through the turnstile, ready to greet the cooler air as we climbed the steps up to the street.

"Listen, I would love to show you around," I said. "Maybe sweet-talk you into letting me write a story about you?"

"I'm starting to warm up to the idea," she said coyly, green eyes gleaming. "Ooh, my man is here. He told me he would come by after my show."

A man in a white hoodie walked up to us, nodding briefly in my direction before enveloping Phaedra in a bear hug. He was murmuring in her ear—I heard snippets about her sexy boots—so I quietly excused myself when we reached the front door of our building. She waved goodbye over his shoulder, promising to text me, while Hoodie Man kept his arms encircled around her waist, nuzzling her neck.

I had always assumed my grandparents had raised me like Arab girls "back home." But Phaedra seemed just like any other girl in Manhattan. Dating who she wanted. Kissing in public. Singing in bars. Freer, somehow, without the behavioral shackles I carried around. As I made my way to the basement in my dowdy clothes, I thought of Zeina and Richard in the alley. Of myself, so moved by Zeina's story that I got the extra push I maybe needed to finally kiss Jackson behind the comedy club. Girlfriend or no girlfriend. I had uncharacteristically acted on pure passion and emotion, abandoning reason.

I tried to picture myself locking lips with Jackson openly on the street, with people sidestepping around us. I shivered at the idea.

I tried to redirect my mind. My love life might be in shambles, but at least I had a solid potential story for work. Phaedra was truly talented and an exciting arrival to Manhattan's music scene. And tonight, before bed, despite my utter fatigue, I wanted to read the next entry of Teta's story. I had almost reached the end.

Back home, in bed, journal in one hand and my laptop nearby, I switched my phone back on. Jackson had emailed me from the "suggestion box" alias at work, telling me his office hours were now extended to midnight if I wanted to talk. I smiled.

Maybe I would write back.

CHAPTER
30

Zeina

Haytham Ramle's *bayara*, Jaffa, Palestine

April 1947

Zeina woke to soft light peeking in on her through the heavy curtains. For a second, she thought she was in her old room and that it was time for *Fajr* prayer, when she and her sister would grumble and follow their father to the living room at dawn. In the cooler months, she used to struggle to leave the warmth of her bed before the sun had risen to mumble the words. She already missed it desperately: her sister, Layla, standing and kneeling next to her, yawning her words while her mother turned her head ever so slightly in disapproval, followed by the luscious feeling of returning back to her bed for another hour or so of sleep.

Now it was late afternoon, her family was too far away to reach on foot, and she had an entire evening ahead of her of plastered-on smiles and empty words about her beauty from people she had never met. That was, apparently, the thing about her that people prized most. Her only measure of value.

Like a child running away from a mother's stern grasp, memories of Richard suddenly broke free in this foreign bedroom. She blinked soft afternoon light. Had she actually seen him earlier, or had her mind conjured a fantasy of him as one of the guards in the mansion?

Perhaps he was honoring his whimsical promise that they would one day visit the library in Jaffa together.

But I'm a married woman now, she thought, a mix of emotions rising up like bile.

She nestled back into her pillow, drawing the blanket up beneath her chin. What she wouldn't give to escape into a book, to another time and place. Her suitcases had been whisked away and unpacked earlier. Were the handful of books she had stowed away somewhere in this room? She looked around the unfamiliar space with clear eyes now adjusted to the dim light. There was a white dresser on one side that looked large enough for her to hide in. To the right, near the widest window in the room, stood a vanity with a mirror. Someone had placed fragrant fresh white flowers in a white vase on it. Right in front of her bed were two large doors with carved gold handles.

Do the doors lead to Abu Shanab's room? she wondered fearfully, still unable to shake off the silly nickname and call him by his real name: Haytham Ramle. The thought made her cover her entire head with the blanket.

She didn't know what time it was, whether she should get dressed, what to wear, and most important, where to get a little food ahead of the festivities. She had barely eaten today thanks to the knot of nerves in her stomach. The thought of waiting for a formal dinner, seated around strangers who would analyze her every bite, turned her stomach even more.

Like magic, Hiba appeared next to her. She had been sitting in a chair in the corner, sewing quietly and waiting for Zeina to awaken. After pouring her a glass of water, she gave her slippers that looked like moccasins but were made of the softest wool Zeina had ever felt. Hiba drew back the curtains, filling the room with silky afternoon light, then offered Zeina a fluffy white robe and led her to the double doors. Zeina placed a hand on Hiba's elbow.

"I would like to freshen up, perhaps use a bathroom, before we see Abu—I mean, Mr. Ramle," she said. "Would that be okay? And perhaps something small to eat?"

"Oh, that just leads to your private terrace, ma'am. Mr. Ramle asked me to help you get ready for dinner this evening and he will meet you there later, if that suits you," said Hiba, her face full of apologies for not explaining herself clearly earlier.

"Thank you. I just want to look my best, that's all," Zeina replied. "And please, no more of this 'ma'am' business. I think we are about the same age, right? Please call me Zeina."

"Thank you, ma'am, but Mr. Ramle asks the staff to address you properly, and Mrs. Ram—I mean, Mrs. Ismat . . . Mrs. Ismat, we have always called her 'ma'am.' I'm sorry, I didn't mean to bring her up, that was thoughtless of me today of all days." Hiba was trying to bury her words with the effort it took to unlock the heavy wooden doors and push them aside.

For a moment, Zeina forgot the conversation they were having. Behind the doors was indeed a private terrace, with two dainty white seats and a small table that barely fit a bowl of fresh fruit, slices of *manakish* bread with thyme and olive oil, and a pot of tea. She sat down, hungrily picking green grapes off the top, while Hiba poured her tea with fresh mint.

Zeina cast her eyes across an endless sea of greenery, ending with a horizon dotted with hundreds of olive trees. Branches reached up to greet the sky like dancer's arms. The air was fragrant with the scent of gardenia and jasmine flowers. Low manicured hedges formed a private enclave for her, and a big oak tree nearby provided shade. A yellow canary stood shyly on one of the hedges, eyeing the colorful plate of fruit. The scenery was beautiful.

Zeina took her first deep breath since arriving, and a real smile played on her lips as she leaned back in her seat.

A question nagged in her mind, though she hesitated to break the spell of beauty before her. But she had to know.

"Who is Mrs. Ismat?" she asked, plucking another grape. *And did she sleep in this room before me?* she wanted to ask but didn't.

"His first wife. She lives in another villa on the grounds now," Hiba said, preparing a plate for Zeina with banana and apple slices. "Her former room is on the other side of the house. A little bigger than this one, but Mr. Ramle thought you would enjoy this room more because of this private garden."

Hiba told her that Ismat was the woman in the dark red dress earlier that day. The staff had mostly been surprised to see her and her personal maid, Jumana, there. Hiba told her a little about Ismat and Haytham's four sons, before fetching another housemaid to refill the pot of tea.

Zeina felt an affection for this young woman, who could answer her questions without her having to voice them. Hiba came back and began to peel an orange.

"No oranges for me, thank you. And please, at least here in the privacy of this little haven, just call me Zeina. Can I invite you to sit with me and share this?" she said, squeezing Hiba's hand. "I–I need a friend. I have no one here."

Hiba smiled warmly. For weeks, staff had been worried about the new dynamic a beautiful young wife would bring to their household. Ismat had been kind and generous with the staff, but a formality always existed, even with the maids who had been present at the births of her sons and spoon-fed her soup when she was ill. It wasn't bad or good; it was just the way things were for decades, and the household ran smoothly. Ismat was closer in age to Mr. Ramle and had come from a very wealthy family. Her father had been a shipowner and had risen in power as Jaffa's port town grew more and more strategically important. She had grown up with servants in her household, someone always nearby to brush her hair or take away a crying child so she could rest. Zeina, on the other hand, had clearly come from a background similar to Hiba's own.

"Well, I would love to, but I don't want to lose my promotion as your personal maid on day one and go back to being a housemaid again . . . or worse, back to Ras El Ein to tend to my senile grandmother," said Hiba, picking off a grape and casting an eye to make sure nobody could see them. "She can't remember her own name or when she was born. I am sure she is at least a hundred years old, but she still orders us around like she is an army sergeant."

Zeina hadn't laughed unselfconsciously like this in such a long time. Then Hiba left her, closing the door to the private terrace, and Zeina tilted her head to let the sun warm her cheeks. She looked around at the field of trees and saw movement, a hand here, a pair of legs dangling beneath a canopy of leaves there.

Is Richard out there somewhere? she wondered. She stood up and shielded her eyes, taking in the scenery in front of her.

When she sat back down, she noticed a letter tucked beneath the plate of *manakish*. Olive oil stained the envelope. On the front was the letter *Z* in Richard's unmistakable handwriting.

> *Darling Zeina,*
>
> *It's all been so sudden. I thought I had offended you somehow. I kept revising our fleeting moments together in my mind, combing through memories*

trying to think of what I had done wrong. Seeing you drive off with your new husband was the single worst moment of my life.

I am not writing to burden you with the weight of my love, which I will carry with me forever. In the brush of every future woman's cheek, in the cry of any future baby, in the roses that line the path to any future house, there will be a shadow of you. I am just writing to let you know I understand. These are scary, trying times. When I heard you were marrying this powerful man, I discovered he regularly hires British officers to protect his land and I swapped with one of the lads to be here when you arrived.

I have received word that my deployment is officially ending. I will leave Palestine for good when the army sends me back home, or to another post, in a matter of days. There is nothing left here for me without you anyway. I will stay in this post for as long as I can just to drink you in for the last time before I go.

Can we say goodbye in person? If yes, just leave your terrace door unlocked tonight and switch the light on and off when you're alone. If not, keep it shut and dark. I promise I won't bother you ever again.

You are exquisite and I wish you every happiness. I will love you forever.

Yours,

R

Zeina's eyes brimmed with tears. She rubbed at them to keep the wetness from staining this beautiful letter. She felt relief, guilt, shock, and, mostly, a strange, bittersweet happiness at this desperate connection to her old life when so much was new.

Had Hiba carried the letter and hidden it where Zeina could find it? Did she know? Could she even read in English? Is that why she hadn't joined her?

Zeina looked out onto the horizon, wondering if Richard was watching her now, trying to anticipate her decision. She thought of him climbing into her bed, with its cloud-like blankets, and she blushed furiously.

"It's uncharacteristically warm, isn't it?" came Hiba's voice, as she opened the French doors a little. "I'll fetch you extra water."

A stretch of time passed, leaving Zeina alone with her thoughts for the first time in days.

"Hiba, tell me honestly, am I going to be okay here? Will I be happy?" asked Zeina, when the plate on the table was left with traces of thyme, crumbs, a banana peel, and the skeleton of a bunch of grapes. Reading Richard's letter, now safely hidden in the palm of her hand, had revived her appetite. She needed to distract herself by asking Hiba about something else; otherwise, there was no way she would be able to get through the evening.

"Happiness is up to you. Am I happy spending my life caring for others? I could feel sad that I don't have pretty clothes to wear to fancy parties like rich people do. Or I could be happy that I get to eat well and sleep in my own bed and not have to work in a field like some of my friends back home," said Hiba, glancing down at her hands, heavily lined from washing dishes and clothes. With a resolute smile, she began to pile the empty plates on top of one another, tendrils of her thick brown hair falling into her eyes.

Hiba told Zeina a story of how devastated her family had been when her baby sister had died at two years old of influenza. It shook the family, and her mother, in particular, never recovered. Eight years had passed since the incident, but the pain never really went away.

"We all still reel from it; it hits me every now and then when I see a little girl with dark curls like mine, but I realized I had a choice," said Hiba. "I could continue to drown in sadness forever or believe that life has set a new, different bar for me and I need to find ways of feeling okay again. The grief will always be there, like a scar, but I have to walk and jump and even dance again. So I find meaning in little things every day. Like now, I feel happy talking to you."

They smiled at each other. Zeina placed her hand over Hiba's in acknowledgment of her family's trauma. They stayed in companionable silence, gazing at the nature around them where trees rise and fall every year.

Growing up in Teenieh, Zeina had known everybody in the village, and they all knew her. Faces rarely changed. Richard's arrival had been one of the first times an outsider had been introduced to their family-like town, and even then, he would always be an outsider. She wondered if she and Hiba would become friendly enough for her to share the deepest of confidences . . . to talk about Richard.

Hiba cleared her throat and dusted the crumbs off the table.

"Anyway, speaking of pretty clothes and fancy parties, I have something to show you," she said. "Let's go back inside."

Zeina began to clear the dishes and stooped to pick up the tray.

"Please, please, leave them," said Hiba, and put an arm around Zeina's shoulders. As they walked back inside, two maids appeared to clear away the plates. They had already made her bed as well.

Back in the room, it took a moment for Zeina's eyes to grow accustomed to the lack of sunlight. Hiba went to the white dresser and gingerly pulled out a pale pink and white dress. She laid it out on the bed as Zeina stepped closer to examine it.

Layers of delicate pink and white silk folded over one another in the body of the dress like rose petals. The upper section was a white off-the-shoulder cut she had never seen before. Lifting the dress and placing it against her body, she realized it would show much more skin than she was used to. The idea of parading her bare shoulders around strangers so boldly made her smile unexpectedly. Zeina shimmied her hips a little and arched an eyebrow at Hiba, who rolled her eyes and laughed at her. She was imagining Richard's reaction at seeing her looking like a European lady, not Abu Shanab's, but Hiba didn't need to know that.

Hiba then took her to the vanity. There were pink flowers to be fastened to her hair and an assortment of rouge for her cheeks, kohl for her eyes, and French perfumes for her wrists.

Zeina slid Richard's letter, sweaty from her palm, into a drawer in the small desk.

"I'll show you how to apply all of this, don't worry. I'll go get your bath ready now," said Hiba with a squeeze of Zeina's shoulders. "Why don't you take a seat here and brush out your hair? Just give me a few minutes to fill the bathtub."

"Shall I help you fill the tub? Where do you keep the buckets?" Zeina asked.

Hiba smiled, then took her by the hand and showed her the faucet. With a nudge of a gilded lever, a steady stream of warm water spilled out into a stand-alone bathtub. The entire bathroom was like a private hammam, complete with a pink chaise longue to recline in while waiting for the tub to fill. To the right stood a sink large enough to wash a baby in. To the left was an entire wall of mirrors. Fresh flowers filled empty spaces. The bathroom was larger than Zeina's living room at home.

Well, her former home.

Despite the warm bath, complete with cucumber slices on her eyes, a yogurt honey mask for her face, and Hiba rubbing her shoulders for fifteen minutes, Zeina felt nervous about the evening ahead. Afterward, she sat in a fluffy white robe at her vanity while one housemaid massaged her feet and another her wrists. She sipped fresh sage tea, which she was pleased to discover helped keep her nausea at bay.

She closed her eyes while Hiba wrapped strands of her hair in rollers and then proceeded to line her eyes with black kohl. She added the lightest touch of rouge on her cheeks and colored her lips a rose red. Asking Zeina to keep her back to the mirror, Hiba then undid the curlers in her hair and began to fasten the flowers with bobby pins.

"I want you to see the full effect when I'm finished, so no peeking," said Hiba, bringing the dress to Zeina to pull over her head. Beads of sweat had formed at Hiba's temples from the effort.

"Okay. Now you can turn around," Hiba said as she stepped back to survey her work, her voice soft.

When Zeina opened her eyes, she could see Hiba and the two maids looking at her with a tenderness that usually belonged to family. Hiba was nodding in triumph, one of the maids was smiling with her hand on her chest, and the other actually started clapping. Feeling exhilarated, Zeina turned around to look in the mirror.

What she saw looked a little like her and a little like someone else. The new Zeina belonged more readily to her new surroundings somehow. The kohl and lipstick were sharp accents that made the green of her eyes jump out wherever they landed, like a cat from a tree. The colors, together with her virgin bared shoulders, enhanced the mischievous side of her personality. The dress looked like whipped meringue and felt like it was made of clouds.

She took a few paces, even walking differently, with her shoulders back and her chin held high, and began making regal gestures with her hands that made the other women laugh and curtsy.

A quick knock at the door broke the playfulness. A well-dressed woman with a tight bun walked in.

"Zeina, ma'am, you look radiant. Allow me to escort you into the banquet area. Your guests are ready," she said.

In an instant, Zeina cowered, remembering what lay ahead of her this evening. Walking out of this bedroom made everything too real. She turned with pleading eyes to Hiba, who came up to give her a hug.

"I'll be there, Zeina. I will quickly put on a dress and when you search the crowd for me, I'll be front and center," whispered Hiba in her ear.

"Please keep the terrace door open," Zeina said. "I want fresh air when I come back here later this evening. Please ask everyone to leave the room and lock the door behind us now. I am still getting used to all the household help . . ."

Her decision had been made. She wanted Richard to see her like this, in all her regal glory, perhaps for the last time. Hiba nodded and, as everyone scurried out behind Zeina, she locked the door and handed her the key to place in a small delicate purse.

Chin held up defiantly, Zeina walked behind the staff toward her wedding reception.

CHAPTER

31

My phone screen lit up. I jumped up with a start—I must have fallen asleep, the diary open on my lap. I rubbed my eyes and reached for my phone. More messages from Katie. And my follower count was growing out of control on Twitter. The thought of all those strange names liking my posts, leaving comments about the dreaded article or one of my shows, giving unsolicited opinions about the way I chose to live my life . . . It made me want to "accidentally" drop my phone in the toilet and never sign into any account ever again. I considered deactivating my account, but most of the comments were positive: supporting my comedy or minorities in the arts. Taking myself out of the conversation completely felt cowardly, not to mention the potential horror of reactivating the accounts weeks later to discover a hateful comment that should have been deleted. I decided to put my profile on "private" for now in order to deal with the deluge later.

How long could I realistically avoid the world, with its flashing notifications and its red-hot emotions? All I wanted was to sit back against my pillows with my laptop, my grandmother's journal, and a cup of tea. A Saturday morning holed up in my room. But the messages on my phone had grown insistent.

I scrolled through them without opening them. As expected, several were from Katie, which I didn't bother to read. I was still too upset to process anything she had to say right now. There was one from Jackson wishing me a good night around one a.m. and another from this morning, asking if he could see me today. I just wanted to hide in this room, under my duvet all day, until my fifteen minutes of fame blew over.

Most of all, I didn't know how to face Jeddo. Would he be as kind as Teta?

My stomach in knots, I considered a walk in the park to calm my nerves before talking to either of them. One of the best things about living on the Upper West Side is proximity to not one but two green spaces: Central Park and Riverside Park. Yet I never seemed to take advantage.

I laced my sneakers and took a hoodie with me to hedge against the crisp fall air. But when I got to the lobby, I kept climbing the stairs and found myself at Phaedra's door again. There was something about the breeziness and nonjudgmental attitude from a person with a similar background that I found reassuring.

I knocked, and she shouted out that her door was open. "I'm sorry, I don't know why I seem to come to you when I'm a mess," I said apologetically as I walked in. "My life is usually a lot more . . . vanilla than this. I didn't know who else to turn to, and I figured you might be home. Is that okay?"

I heard her laugh as I closed the door behind me, but I couldn't see her anywhere in the spacious living room. I looked closely and saw movement on the sofa, someone lying down. My heart raced: Was that her mystery man? I couldn't meet her lover wearing a hoodie that said *Fight Like a Girl*.

I walked toward the beige sofa. Someone was lying on it. I

hesitated, taking in long, strawlike platinum blond hair spilling over one arm of the sofa and the edge of a bright blue chiffon gown with tulle peeking over the other end. Stiletto-clad feet, with toes painted bright red, dangled down. A plume of smoke rose up from near the blond hair, obscuring the view of the Hudson River for a moment.

The blond woman sat up, and I saw Phaedra's familiar face. She was wearing a Madonna-inspired wig. Her heavily made-up eyes were framed by thick eyelash extensions. Her eyelids were covered in glittery blue eye shadow.

Phaedra cupped her face in her hands, arms resting on the sofa.

"What do you think?" she asked. "A designer sent over a complete costume kit, and I had to try it on. I think it would be really difficult to move around a stage in all this tulle, though."

From the kitchen, Hadi walked in holding steaming mugs.

"Oh, hi," he said, stopping briefly. "Good to see you again, Mia."

"No frilly costume for you?" I asked Hadi.

He broke into a smile, setting the mugs down on the coffee table and motioning with his hands for me to take a seat.

"Only if you don't scamper off and tell your grandparents now, you hear? Phaedra's is a safe space," he joked, taking his glasses off to wipe them before putting them back on.

We both looked at Phaedra in her over-the-top dress. She stood up and twirled for us, the blue gown rustling softly around her with each move. She pulled off her wig and sat down at the piano.

Hadi's smile faded, and he sank down onto the sofa. "Honestly, part of me wishes I could be so . . . free."

"Talk to us, Hadi," she said. "Mia and I get it. Tell us what's wrong."

His story came spilling out. Tired of fitting into a box, having mothers wave their eager daughters under his nose, Dr. Hadi had had an epiphany a few years ago. He didn't like women. But he also wasn't super interested in men.

"I totally thought you were into the waiter," Phaedra said.

He shrugged. He was ... ambivalent. Hadi was more into music, surgery, robotics, violin strings, the emotion behind art, and fashion as a confluence of history and design. His fascination with music therapy was as much about his patients as it was about himself.

"There's more to life than sex for me in a world that seems obsessed with it," he said simply, offering me a cigarette. "Especially Arab culture, my goodness."

As he and Phaedra talked about the sanctity of male virility in the Arab world, I sat back, my eyes ping-ponging between them. Women were asked to stay modest, chaste, look down, dress down ... but was an Arab man really a manly man if he wasn't a slave to his sexual urges?

"I'm just ... a music lover in a surgeon's scrubs. I don't fit into any box, and maybe that's okay," he said with a shrug. "People call me asexual. That feels a bit devoid of color, when it's clear I like all the extra color in life. I would wear dresses like that every day if I was a performer like you, Phaedra."

Phaedra stood up and gave an exaggerated curtsy. I completely understood how he felt, realizing his reservations about me were likely due to my traditional grandparents. I told him how much he and I were alike, and we exchanged sad smiles.

"You do you, honey," Phaedra told him, waving her cigarette in the air. "Because what I've learned is that people will talk no matter what, so you should enjoy your life your way. I'm not really feeling this dress, but maybe if I wear it with my black leather boots for a bit of an edge ..."

"It is a bit too Cinderella for your usual style," I said, thinking that her black leather boots would nonetheless elevate any outfit.

Phaedra put a hand to her lips.

"Pass. I'll have to return this dress to the designer; they wanted me to wear it in my next show," she said, and offered me one of the cups of tea on the table. "So, how are you, Mia? What's up?"

Phaedra reached over to pick up her phone from the coffee table as I spoke about my week, before squeezing between Hadi and me on the couch. Her blue dress spread out over our legs. She googled the article on her phone, alternately nodding as I spoke and glancing back down to read lines, all while daintily smoking her rolled cigarette. She was careful not to let any ash fall on her dress.

"You poor thing. This is what you were avoiding talking about yesterday, isn't it?" Phaedra said, her eyes moving back and forth, taking the article in.

"Oh, and . . . I still haven't spoken to Jackson about that kiss," I admitted to my shoes, pulling the hoodie over my face. "Maybe he regrets it."

"Gosh, you are too sweet," Hadi said, playing with the material on Phaedra's dress. "I almost don't want to tell you how I caught Phaedra this morning making out outside our building before sending her man home on a walk of shame."

Phaedra laughed and lightly swatted his arm. They snickered before turning back to me. I was subdued and worried on the sofa, my eyes on the article still open on Phaedra's phone.

"So, look, realistically, no immigration person is going to show up at your door with handcuffs because of a single article," said Phaedra practically. "It's unlikely your grandparents will get put on a plane and be deported an hour later. Usually, these things take time. It's not like you were caught robbing a bank."

"Want me to contact a family lawyer who can help?" asked Hadi.

I worried about bringing more people into this mess.

"I can put a feeler out for you as well," offered Phaedra.

I was starting to feel exhausted by the weight of these decisions. I had successfully performed in secret for years. Why did this have to blow up in my face right now? When my work situation was precarious? When I needed friends to lean on, rather than create more problems? I shrugged.

"I honestly don't know what to do," I said. "I'm hoping that my work will get a lawyer just in case we need damage control. If I had money, I would consider getting a lawyer to sue them if this gets out of hand."

"Don't worry until there's a real reason to do so," Hadi said soothingly. "Look, there's nothing here to explicitly indicate that they live in the United States illegally. I can't imagine those immigration people spending their time scanning *The Culturalist* for people gone rogue. I honestly think you will be okay."

Phaedra echoed his sentiment, wrapping her arm around me. I took a deep breath, feeling a little lighter.

"Maybe we can take the attention off this piece . . . with a profile about me?" she said. "I liked what you said, Hadi, about life being colorful. I'm going to steal that with pride. For the next time someone asks me where I'm from."

She stood up and grabbed the TV remote control, holding it like a microphone. Clearing her throat, she put one foot dramatically on the table, and began:

"'Nice name, Phaedra. Where are you from? You sound white. You look white.'

"Well, Nosy Person, the box I tick is 'Other.'

"I am *colorful*.

"My eyes are the shade of extra virgin olive oil when held up to the light.

"Sometimes my hair is made up of curly swirls of light chocolate mousse.

"Other times, it is blond and straightened. Especially at weddings. It depends who I'm going to see.

"I am a social chameleon.

"My breasts are like large Jaffa oranges—which aren't really all that large.

"The hills of my childbearing hips make up for them. They lead to the watermelons behind me.

"My lips are full, red, parted, inviting. But they are defined, outlined by boundaries. They have checkpoints called *Eib* and *Obalik*."

Hadi clapped at the Arabic words Phaedra had used for "shame" and "you're next," both phrases regularly thrown at marriage-age women. Particularly at weddings.

"I'm good at distracting you, aren't I?" Phaedra said, and winked at me. "You're going to be just fine. I can feel it. Hey, can we come to your next show?"

I smiled, grateful for my two new, dysfunctional Arab friends. At least I had found this amid the storm.

CHAPTER

32

Zeina

Haytham Ramle's *bayara*, Jaffa, Palestine

April 1947

Zeina walked behind the other woman, slightly unused to wearing shoes with a heel, back through corridor after corridor, until they reached two glass doors that led out to an airy, tree-lined courtyard. The sun was setting, and she could hear the strains of music and chatter through the glass. Lights were strung among the trees, and water bubbled in the fountain. Silhouettes stood in groups, holding glasses and shimmying their shoulders to the music. Men holding trays walked around serving food small enough to be held between thumb and forefinger. She squinted, trying to see more detail, when a large round figure blocked the entry and opened the doors, bringing with him a burst of outside noise.

She hadn't seen Abu Shanab since their car ride that

morning. While the trip had been pleasant enough, her time playing dress-up with Hiba and the maids had made her almost forget why she was really here. Her eyes darting back and forth, she began to shrink slightly as he walked up to her.

"Zeina," he said breathily when he reached her. She could smell mint on his breath, mingled with cigars and something else, something acidic. He caressed her cheek, kind brown eyes seeking hers. She wasn't sure whether it was her nerves or the effects of the sage tea wearing off, but the queasiness that had been her constant companion for the past few weeks reappeared like a loyal soldier.

"Before we enter together to greet our guests, I want to quickly show you something," he said.

They walked in silence a short way, around the corner from where they stood. Zeina tried to distract herself from her nausea by looking around, at the paintings on the wall of unfamiliar faces and women in fancy gowns, the vases filled with fresh roses, the gold-framed mirror that captured a snapshot of her red lips as she passed.

Finally, Abu Shanab opened a door that led to a room overlooking the courtyard. It was dark and smelled dusty. Through floor-to-ceiling glass doors, she could see women in brightly colored dresses outside talking and laughing with men in suits. She suddenly wished she were with them rather than with this strange man in this room. Alone with Abu Shanab in the dark, with no family, friend, or Hiba around. Could they see her, too, she wondered, or was it too dim in here?

"Do you like your room?" he asked, waiting for their eyes to adjust to the dark.

"It's beautiful. The terrace is heavenly, and Hiba is especially wonderful. Thank you so much for this dress, too, I've never seen anything like it," Zeina babbled, wrapping her arms around herself, attempting to cover her shoulders.

She knew that in order to maintain her family's reputation, relations must happen between them as soon as possible. Abu Shanab, and everyone else in her world, had to believe that the marriage was a success. How was she going to push her feelings of unease aside to accomplish this?

She shuddered.

"It is from Paris. I really hope to take you there someday soon," he said. "Perhaps for our honeymoon?"

Had she been looking at him, she would have caught a wink, but her eyes had now returned to the party outdoors, trained on the merrymaking like a soldier ready to fire a gun.

"Is—is tonight our wedding? Is this our wedding day?" she asked, part playful, part stalling. *Making tonight our wedding night?* she thought, her stomach dropping, thinking of seeing Richard in her private room after visiting Abu Shanab. She tried to picture him climbing into her empty bedroom before dawn.

"Normally, we would have a week of celebratory dinners and festivities. I just thought it distasteful to do that now, what with all the sadness, change, and loss of life sweeping the country at the moment . . . But I still wanted to celebrate you," he said. "Consider it a wedding party of sorts, and we will have a proper reception when the political situation improves. Hopefully very soon. Things have a way of changing drastically, overnight, and I remain optimistic. You look incredible, by the way. I can't take my eyes off you."

She smiled in response. He moved closer, and her heart began to hammer so loudly she was sure he could hear it above the din of the music. The band outside must have decided to take a short break right then, because in an instant the quiet in the room became as thick as molasses, punctuated only by Abu Shanab's heavy breathing. The dull chatter outside sounded as if it was underwater.

She asked about the room they were in, her soft voice tearing through the sudden silence between them. There was a large black object in one corner, and she could see that shelves lined every wall. Filled with books.

"Ah, yes. This is what I wanted to show you. Your grandfather is a poet, and some of his works are quite famous, you know," he said. "Can you read well?"

"Yes, and I am so happy you are familiar with his writing. I think I've read everything he has ever written," she said, happy to talk about a safe subject she knew well. "I even helped teach sometimes at my younger cousin's school, whenever a teacher was unable to conduct class. I would often refer to his poems."

"I wanted to bring you here to show you that a piece of your family history has always existed in my house. Your grandfather's works can be found on these shelves, as well as many other books you will probably enjoy. Feel free to spend as much time here as you like. I want you to be happy in my house," he said. "Our house now."

She was moved by his words, that he had bothered to learn about her and her family, her interests, beyond the veneer of perfect beauty, where people normally stopped. Her shoulders relaxed, and she voiced genuine gratitude.

"Thank you so much for every kindness. I—I hope I can make you happy as well," she said.

He lifted her hand and kissed it. His mustache scratched her as his kisses climbed higher and higher up her arm. Her heart began to pound again, and she kept a smile frozen on her face. His nose was now a finger's width apart from her own. He was close enough for her to see flecks of gray in his eyebrows and shades of caramel in his brown eyes.

"May I give those lips a kiss now, bride?" he asked, his voice gruff and his breathing growing louder.

She felt the weight of his belly on her.

"What's that over there?" she asked, her mind betraying her, scrambling for a distraction, her voice as loud and high as his was intimate and deep.

His body remained close to hers for another moment or two before pulling back. He looked in the direction of her shaking extended finger.

"I understand, *habibti*, my sweetheart, this must be intimidating for you. It must be the first time you have been alone with a man other than your father. I will be kind to you and you will find pleasure in this, I promise," he said, walking toward the black object.

Light from the party outside danced on the flat surface of the black wooden object. Going to one end of it, he gingerly lifted a lid, like lifting a skirt. His fingers landed on white and black keys. Sudden, loud notes burst into the room, and Zeina jumped as if people had walked in and interrupted an intimate moment.

"This is called a piano. A grand piano. It's the first of the few in Jaffa. Very popular in Europe," said Abu Shanab, patting it on the side like it was a loyal dog. "Are you interested in music?"

"I've always loved singing," she said, moving closer to run her hands across the keys, playing a note here and there, smiling up at him in surprise.

"I can bring a teacher to show you how to play. I've had this here for months and had no time to learn how to behave around it. I would love for you to bring music into this house," he said warmly. "Now, come on, bride, your guests await you. Are you ready to meet them?"

With a longing glance at this mysterious, sleek creature, Zeina reluctantly turned away and braced her shoulders. She had delayed his advances for a few hours, but she needed to get her mind around the fact that tonight she and this man might need to do what needs to be done between married couples. She shuddered again.

"With the escalating issues, I'm afraid that tonight will not be a true wedding night, but we have many nights ahead of us to make up for it together," she heard him say. "There are dignitaries here tonight whom I must attend to. Use tonight to rest and ease your nerves. My aim is happiness and pleasure, my dear. I can wait for you to feel ready."

He was granting her the night off. Zeina felt breathless, wondering if she was meant to protest and express desire but unable to contain her relief. Perhaps the stars had aligned for her to have one true night of passion—with Richard. Maybe her life hadn't all been decided for her by others after all.

She smiled demurely, her eyes on the floor, which Haytham Ramle found endearing.

Resolute and a little lightheaded, she boldly linked her arm with his, and they walked together toward the glass doors leading to the courtyard entrance.

The band started up again in anticipation of their entrance, led by a steady drumbeat. Guests turned to face the glass doors, throats clearing, eyes searching. Just as he was about to open the doors, Zeina tugged at his arm, pulling him back slightly.

"Thank you for everything," she said. "You have been so thoughtful. I hope you won't be disappointed if we wait, so I can be ready. It's . . . it's a delicate time."

Perhaps Abu Shanab thought she was mentioning women's troubles. It was his right to ravage his new wife immediately, and she shouldn't resist, but he had shown tremendous compassion.

The doors burst open to reveal Abu Shanab's hand on his new wife's cheek, planting a soft kiss on her lips. Most of the guests were household staff and longtime friends of his and his former wife's, people who for decades were used to seeing him with the red-haired Ismat. Elegant Ismat, who always acted appropriately, as if she was being watched at all times.

Abu Shanab's unexpected display of affection, coupled with the dazzling sight of Zeina in her daring dress as she held a hand shyly to her lips before smiling widely for the guests, was so overwhelming that silence engulfed the courtyard for a few seconds. Even the drummer stopped. Abu Shanab's lips were slightly red from Zeina's rouge. Then her mother's voice broke the silence, confident and full of joy.

"*Aweeeehaaaaa*, we are in the presence of true love, *aweeee-haaaaa*, and isn't it the most beautiful sight you've ever seen?"

This was followed by rounds and rounds of "*Yolololololeeeee*" ululations as people cheered the new Mr. and Mrs. Haytham Ramle. A group of men, all wearing black harem pants and red embroidered tops, started the drumming and singing of the traditional wedding *zaffeh*, bringing the party back to life.

Zeina scanned the crowd, seeking one of them.

Was Richard climbing through her new bedroom window right now?

CHAPTER
33

The longer you hide, the worse the problem gets. Phaedra's parting words rang in my ear.

I had spent the rest of Saturday afternoon at her place, playing dress-up and pretending like last night hadn't happened. Now I was standing in front of my door as if I were a stranger, my heart thudding in my ears. I could imagine my grandfather sitting in his leather armchair, trying to hold back his temper, his eyes trained on the door right this very second.

With sweaty, shaking hands, I turned the doorknob. I found Jeddo pacing. He stopped when he saw me, his dark eyes peering behind me, a sigh of relief as I shut the door and stood with my back against it.

All the speeches I had rehearsed in my mind abandoned me. Jeddo shook his head, and the crushing weight of his disappointment stole the air right out of my lungs. Time felt like it ground to a halt, respectfully standing aside until one of us called a ceasefire.

After what felt like hours but was most likely only a few minutes, I worked up the courage to speak.

"Teta told you?" I asked slowly, my voice breaking. "All I can say is I am sorry. I was careless and I will try to fix it."

"I am sorry," he said gruffly. "Everything we have done since your father left us too soon was to help you, and now it's all . . ."

He threw his hands up in the air and sank into his seat.

It was disconcerting to see my father figure, normally solid, always put together, rarely emotional, having a moment like this. I had no idea how to proceed.

I had pictured him shouting, the way he did when furious at a politician's inane comments on TV or a bad play in a soccer game, but I wasn't prepared to see his walls crumble. Watching my grandfather cry, a head full of heavy worry resting in his wrinkled hands, completely shook me. I went to him, kneeling before him, gently whispering apologies.

My grandmother stood with her arms crossed, leaning against the doorway leading to the kitchen.

"We knew a day like this would come," she said softly. "I told him we can't worry. It's out of our control. Maybe we will be lucky and nobody will notice. Just give him time."

I swallowed hard, thinking of the swelling number of text messages and missed calls as Katie's article gained more traction online. That familiar thudding returned to my ears as I wondered if I had made matters worse by talking to Phaedra and Hadi about it. The fewer people in the know, surely, the better. The apartment was quiet, too flooded with our deafening thoughts, with all the nervous, unanswered questions making the air thick. I could hear the kitchen fan in the distance whirring close and far and back again.

"Jeddo, please, I am so sorry," I said. "I didn't mean to hurt you."

My grandfather wouldn't meet my eye. My starkly different worlds had finally collided and brought our house down. Through my frivolous actions, I had ushered him right up to his greatest fear of being found out. I had prepared myself for a fight, for rapid gunfire shooting out of our mouths, or loud apologies. The silence in our tiny basement apartment was like a contained, rickety boat out at sea, our fears a thunderstorm above our heads.

My grandfather rubbed his sore knee.

"I will fix everything," I said with fresh resolve. "Leave it with me."

"I hope so," he said gruffly. "I just need to . . . rest now."

Teta placed a hot cup of tea by his side and patted my arm. She gave me a kiss on the cheek. I looked at Jeddo's pained expression, then went to my bedroom, eyeing the laptop on my bed, waiting for me like an obedient pet. A cold, half-drunk mug of tea sat on my nightstand.

Enough hiding. I needed to remedy the situation right now. Maybe I had to start by answering my messages.

My phone was still flashing with urgency. I half-heartedly went to it, the names Katie and even Isabel swimming among dozens of the usual press releases in my inbox.

And Jackson. Again.

Call me, read his message. *I think I found a solution. It's going to be okay.*

As I was mulling it over, my phone pinged with a second text from him.

Also, you can't just kiss me and disappear. It was too good.

In spite of myself, bubbles of relief rose up in me. I felt like I wasn't completely alone in this storm. And he had mentioned the kiss. Though I still felt burned by his decision to publish a video of me without my consent, a moment of calm spread through me at the sight of his name.

It was too good . . .

He's right, it was delicious, my heart confirmed. Little details flashed like snapshots: the look in his eyes as if he was really seeing me for the first time onstage; the subtle taste of banana gum, that brand that I recognized by the yellow wrappers on his desk at work; the way his mouth curved up in a semi-smile before our lips touched, just like it had when he broke the news that he had secured me a job at Vibe Media all those years ago. All the chocolates I kept in my drawer at work because I knew about his obsessive snacking habits.

I sank onto my bed, letting my mind wander to him freely. Thinking back on the texture of his coarse hair beneath my eager fingers, the fresh scent of a surprisingly fruity shampoo, the soft rain cooling my warm cheeks.

It was a big moment. And it was mine . . . and his. And it was real.

But it's so awkward now, my practical mind shouted. *What if he plans to see me behind Adriana's back? All I've shown him is that I'm afraid of being out in the open. What if this is going to cause real problems at work? Could me and Katie both be on our way out? What if Jackson can't do anything about it? Or won't . . . to save himself?*

As I sat there, anxiously considering my future, one shoe out of my sneakers and one in, my phone glowed to life.

Jackson calling . . .

Should I answer?

I watched it ring until it went to voicemail. I couldn't bear the thought of his voice, concerned and rich and wonderful, in my bedroom. I might crumble. My priority was to show Jeddo that I was doing something to make things better. Still, I sat on the bed and pressed play to listen to what he had to say in a voicemail.

"Me again. Starting to feel a little like a stalker. I'm truly sorry about what happened. Just a quick update: we've decided to take the story down and have contacted legal. Divya is on standby, ready to help. She has contacts in immigration law. Everyone's here to support you. Can you please call me to let me know you're okay? That you're not mumbling to yourself in a park somewhere?"

I shook my head again and texted him back: *Thank you. I'm just processing. Immigration hasn't knocked on our door yet. I should be back in the office on Monday morning.*

I'm with Michael at Madison Square Garden, he wrote. *Can we please, please talk later?*

He followed this up with a photo of the two of them with giant foam fingers that made my heart melt.

Yes, I'll call you tomorrow, I said. If nothing else, at least I could hear him out with regard to the immigration lawyer that Divya had lined up. Maybe a company-paid lawyer would offer Jeddo some measure of reassurance.

My eyes roamed over Katie's texts and missed calls. I felt a confusing mix of emotions. I was still angry that she had betrayed my trust, but she was normally the friend I turned to during moments of emotional turmoil. She had a natural knack for making heavy situations feel lighter, usually with snarky comments and a fresh bag of salt-and-vinegar chips. I missed her and was glad to see that she kept trying to reach me, but I just wasn't ready to talk yet.

Sunday morning, I woke up and stared at the ceiling, dreading what lay in store for me. A story about Phaedra in *The Culturalist* might help me secure the reporter job, but did I even want it now? Could I go back to work with Katie as my deskmate, sharing coffee like we used to every day? Could I forgive Jackson fully for recording and publishing a video of me online? Was I overreacting, or was I right to feel upset that neither of them had consulted me? Her behavior felt exploitative. She had used me.

Throwing my phone on my nightstand, I flipped Teta's journal open. I had used a movie ticket stub from a birthday trip to the cinema with Katie as a bookmark. I crumpled that up and rummaged around my nightstand drawer for a scrap of paper to use in its place instead. I went to the kitchen to make a fresh cup of tea, avoiding my grandparents, then softly closed the door and settled on my bed. I began to read.

CHAPTER

34

Haytham Ramle's *bayara*, Jaffa, Palestine
April 1947

Abu Shanab kept his arm linked through Zeina's as they walked out into the crowd. Amid endless new names and faces and well-wishes, she couldn't help but search for Richard's face in the crowd and in the dark gardens beyond. Was he here somewhere, waiting for her? Should she have disposed of his note? Her heart drummed with fear and adrenaline at the thought of a housemaid discovering his letter stashed in the drawer of her new vanity.

The wife of Abu Shanab's accountant was making polite conversation with her, telling her how much their husbands had enjoyed working together over the years. She spoke of how the powerful businessman had moved large sums of money to bank accounts abroad lately: to Beirut, Paris, London. Were these cities he and Zeina would visit together someday soon?

Then the accountant's wife launched into a long story about how her son loved Mr. Ramle's Jaffa oranges so much that he would hide several under his bed, thinking his mother would never find them.

Zeina listened, a soft smile on her lips to accompany nods of her head, but her eyes kept moving away from this woman, roving around the open space like a mosquito in search of one person.

She saw Hiba seated near a large olive tree along with several of the housemaids, their laughter filling the courtyard. Next to them, standing shyly to one side as if they were unfamiliar with the language spoken and the food being passed around on the trays, stood her mother, father, and sister. Though Layla was scowling, her eyes like two pieces of dark coal, Zeina had never been happier to see her.

She pointed them out animatedly to Abu Shanab, who immediately begged pardon from the accountant couple and guided her over to her family. When she was a few paces away, Zeina broke free of him and ran to hug her mother and sister, who patted her hair and her dress and cheeks, full of compliments. Hiba and several of the maids looked on warmly, remembering how special every reunion with family could be when they lived far away.

Tears of pride—and victory—shone in Fayza's eyes as Zeina spoke about her new home to them. Her mother had known Abu Shanab was wealthy, but not how to picture wealth exactly, aside from imagining more food and a larger house. This, however, this mansion, with its sand-colored stone and two stories, felt as big as their entire village back home. She looked at the party of infinite olive trees. She could hear the sound of the light breeze rustling through the branches in the distant darkness, above the conversations in the courtyard.

She couldn't believe how many guests—far outnumbering

the residents of Teenieh—there were to celebrate this union. Who were all these people? Fayza had never before been surrounded by so many faces she didn't recognize. She had left Teenieh with promises to Umm Mohamed and her neighbors to tell them everything she saw, but she didn't know the words to use to describe this bubbling fountain in the middle of the courtyard, which was the size of her living room, the diaphanous silks and chiffons of dresses worn by the elegant women here, how they made their cheeks and lips redder, how their hair was so tidy.

Fayza looked down at her dress, a blue one she wore at every important occasion, and noticed for the first time how the ends were frayed and that her shoes were scuffed. She fingered her earrings, the only gold she possessed, each a crescent shape the size of a fingernail. She looked around at the green, blue, and red gemstones that decorated the women like colorful birds in a garden. As the mother of the bride, Fayza greeted the rotations of people who came to congratulate her, and she discovered a shyness in her that she never knew existed. From the outside, this brought a humble warmth that Fayza would never have been able to fake, and people commented on how sweet Zeina's family seemed—especially her kind mother.

Suleiman, on the other hand, seemed right at home. Someone had handed him a cigar that fit his hand like an extra finger that had always been missing. He was smiling from ear to ear and nodding to people, shimmying his shoulders to the music, and sampling everything that passed by on a tray even if he wasn't sure what it was. At one point, he ate a flower that was meant to be a decorative garnish, but rather than feeling embarrassed, it resulted in an instant camaraderie with the waiter, who would bring new dishes out to him first to try.

Layla studied her younger sister, feeling like a black-and-white photo next to a colorful, moving picture. She was wearing one of Zeina's old dresses, a lovely bright pink one that brought out the wintery beauty of her fair skin and forest of dark curls, but she had to keep her back away from the crowd all night, because there were buttons missing from the dress.

She couldn't believe that Zeina, this ungrateful girl who had been given a bounty of beauty by sheer luck, who had snuck around with a foreign soldier, who pretended to well up from chopping onions so Layla would have to do it instead, had ended up with all this grandiosity.

What was the point of following rules if you were cast aside from the game? Or worse: Why did breaking the rules reap all the rewards? Why did Zeina literally get everything . . . while Layla's life remained exactly the same?

Zeina was like a queen, people continuously interrupting her conversations to compliment her on how stunning she looked tonight, to bless her new marriage. Hot tears sprang to Layla's eyes. She said she needed to find a restroom, and while everyone was still enraptured by Zeina describing her bathtub, she crossed the courtyard, slipped through the slightly open glass doors, and entered the house.

In the quiet, dark hall, with nobody else around, Layla breathed a sigh of relief and leaned her forehead against the cool stone wall. She took a few more deep breaths to center herself. She reminded herself that there were potential suitors, wealthy ones, at the party and that she should get back to it soon. First, though, she walked a few paces, exploring the dimly lit hallway, and ran into a housemaid.

"Are you lost, miss? Shall I help you find something or someone?" The maid had a pleasant voice and a wide, round face.

"I was just about to use the restroom, but no matter," Layla said shyly. "Hello, I am Zeina's sister."

"So lovely to meet you, and congratulations to you and

your family. *Obalik*—may you be next," she said. "May I ask if everything is all right? Shall I help you to the restroom or fetch you a glass of water?"

"I just can't believe Zeina has all this, that this is her new life," Layla admitted to the kind maid. "I mean, I am happy for her, but one minute we are making salad together and Zeina, of course, leaves midway through to take a nap while I finish everything, and next thing we know she is a princess in this castle. I'm still making salad."

"I wish you a wonderful husband ten times as rich," said the maid with a laugh.

"Thank you for saying that. Sometimes I wonder if it will ever happen for me," said Layla, looking at her shoes. "Sometimes I wish that I would get some of the stardust that naturally surrounds Zeina all the time."

Jumana listened to this young girl who was pouring her heart out to a stranger. After years of working as Ismat's personal housemaid, she wasn't used to someone from the family expressing such raw confusion and emotion like this.

Her madam, Ismat, always held herself together with grace, no matter the circumstances. Even now, at a time of great change for Ismat, moving to a new home and getting used to life as a second wife, she was handling everything elegantly. Jumana felt a warmth for this young girl, but she also saw opportunity.

"Come, come, child, don't fret. With that lovely buttery skin of yours and that thick, dark hair, I feel your time will come sooner than you think. Zeina is now committed and you should be happy for her. You are now the most beautiful, eligible young woman in that room. Go, enjoy, and I am sure that the next time I see you, I will be dancing at your wedding party," she said, patting Layla's shoulder.

Layla was so moved by this stranger's kind words—she

called her the most beautiful woman in the room!—that it gave her the confidence to return to the party with her shoulders back and a coquettish look in her eyes.

Jumana, though happy to have made the girl smile, was relieved not to have been asked why she wasn't at the party herself. Scurrying like a mouse, she ran through the dark corridors and out the back door into the night. She passed dozens of olive trees, a full moon lighting her dirt path, until she reached Ismat's small one-story villa. The fire was still roaring, and Jumana had gossip to share with her madam.

Meanwhile, a soldier leaned against the cold stone wall near Zeina's private terrace, waiting hopefully for a signal in the dark.

CHAPTER

35

I had spent all day in my room, bringing in food and tea. I blinked up at the window, noticing the golden light of evening. I hadn't realized that I had been holding my breath until I heard a knock at my bedroom door. Teta opened it a crack, and I sat upright in bed, trying to glean if there was anything to worry about from the look in her eyes.

"I came to check in on you," she said. "All okay? Do you need tea? Your friend is here. Waiting outside for you."

My heart thudded in my ears. I wondered immediately if Jackson had found me because I refused to answer his call. Could he have bribed HR to get my address? He could be standing at the front door right now. Or worse, he could be making small talk with Jeddo in the living room.

No. No, no, no. This can't be happening. I should have just answered his stupid call.

I debated changing into nicer clothes but began to worry that he might come into my bedroom in search of me if I took much longer. I glanced up at the Eddie Murphy poster on my wall and cringed. That was a thought I definitely couldn't handle right now.

I passed the kitchen, fragrant with the scent of fall spices, the table dusted with flour. Feeling like I was wading into deep, dark water, I walked with heavy legs into our dimly lit living room. Winter was coming, and the sun was setting earlier and earlier these days.

Jeddo sat in his leather armchair and didn't look up when I came in. He had a fresh cup of coffee on the side table next to him. The TV was muted. A rarity that meant it was best not to speak to him right now.

I opened the door to find not Jackson but Katie. Her black biker jacket was sprinkled with rain, wet at the shoulders. Her spiky pixie cut was limp and dewy. She licked her lips and began to speak, her hand reaching out to me.

I held both of mine up in protest.

"It's done—you did what you needed to do, and I don't feel like talking to you right now," I snapped, watching her brown eyes widen. "Respect that. You weren't really thinking of me when you did this, you were thinking of yourself."

She took a deep breath and said one word: "Stop."

The chartreuse-colored camisole beneath her jacket had dark patches on it from the rain. She repeated the word again, more softly this time: "Stop."

"I needed a story for the role, yes, but I honestly thought you would be happy," she said. "My aim wasn't to cross you to save my job at any expense. The best thing about working at Vibe is you."

"I don't believe that," I said, my voice dull like flat soda. I crossed my arms and leaned against the shut door behind me. "My grandparents both keep jumping up whenever there's a knock at the door. This didn't need to happen right now."

"This was always the case—they've been living this way for decades!" Katie burst out. "Writing about your success today doesn't necessarily mean they will get in trouble! For what it's worth, I think you are a fiercely talented comedian and you deserve support. And I hate that you don't believe that I would never intentionally hurt you. You're my friend."

She took a step toward me and lowered her voice.

"To prove my point, I've asked Jackson to take down the story, get Divya in legal on the case for you, and . . . I handed in my resignation," she said.

My eyes met hers to see if this was bait. She held my gaze, unblinking.

"I didn't ask you to resign. I just wanted to—"

"No, what you said really hit home," she said plainly, putting her handbag down on the floor. "I wasn't a good friend, and I was an even worse journalist. I got swept up in a good story. I'm sorry, and I genuinely want the best for you."

She pulled out a piece of paper from her back pocket. The top edges were wet and shriveled from the rain.

"I wasn't sure if you would agree to see me, so I printed this for you and was planning to slip it under your door," she said. "Read it and call me when you've . . . processed all this and . . . if you want to talk. I'm going to head out before someone steals my bike outside."

She handed me the paper, folded into quadrants. With a half smile and a wave, she walked back up the stairs toward the ground-floor lobby.

I took a deep breath and walked back through the living room. Jeddo was still watching the TV on mute. The coffee cup was half-full now. My grandmother was busying herself making date cakes, which I usually helped her sell at the farmer's market on the weekends. Teta looked up from the kitchen table as I walked to my room, her flour-dusted hands on the rolling pin moving back and forth. The air was scented with nutmeg, aniseed, and sugar.

Back in the sanctuary of my room, I unfolded Katie's note. It was an email sent to the editorial team at Vibe Media, flagged as an urgent request.

> *Dear Ms. Gromley,*
>
> *We are featuring a showcase of emerging talent in comedy and would love to include Mia. I have personally seen her perform in the West Village, and when I saw your recent article about her in The Culturalist, I immediately shared it with my team. We would love to meet her. We are constantly on the lookout for fresh comedy talent and believe she would add value to our upcoming show.*
>
> *Please let us know if you are able to put us in contact with Mia. We were not able to find her easily on social media. We have an available slot for a ten-minute audition at our studio on Monday morning at 7:30 a.m. sharp. Apologies for the short notice. We would really like to add her voice to our mix.*
>
> *Best,*
> *Conor Broderick*
> *Executive Producer*
> The Jordan B. Brown Show

CHAPTER
36

I reread the email three times. Rather than feeling a sense of clarity, random thoughts burst like popcorn in my mind. Was this a fake letter from Katie to encourage me to forgive her? Was this a real request, but a diversity play? Would I be a good addition to the mix only because I represented an ethnic minority? What should I wear on TV? Was the studio cold?

Is this the "dude in a suit" who handed Mr. Goatee a note for me after my show? I sat up with excitement, analyzing the email's reference to having seen me perform. *Conor Broderick.*

C.B.

And most important: If I managed to get away with keeping my grandparents under the radar despite Katie's article, was there any way to keep them safe *and* take my shot at stardom?

I thought of Jeddo in his leather armchair, shrouded in silence.

I couldn't see how I could do the audition and ever win my way back into his heart. Part of me wanted to run back upstairs, to lose myself in the laughter and smoke-filled, colorful haziness of Phaedra's penthouse. The other part of me wanted to take another nap to process everything.

Dazed, I sat on the bed, running through the options.

I admit that I felt a fizz of excitement at the validation. Katie's article was no longer online, but I remembered that she had included a few lines from my set.

I grabbed my phone and googled "Conor Broderick, Executive Producer on *The Jordan B. Brown Show.*" Images popped up of a man who looked to be maybe five years older than me, with wisps of dark hair and eyes the color of a pool. In several photos, he wore black-rimmed glasses and was looking off-camera, as if he had just burst into laughter at something funny. It made me smile. He had an impressive background, working his way up from being an intern at NBC, followed by a handful of years with Jon Stewart's team. His Twitter bio proclaimed his undying support of "rugby, because my Irish roots demand it," and "all things comedy, especially when it takes me by surprise."

I leaned my head back on my pillow, clutching the printed email to my chest as if it was a love letter. I ran through my set in my mind, imagining it through Conor's eyes. Was it the line about being engaged to an Arab doctor that had done it? The falafel infidel song? Or the passport control reference in my first set?

I really am good, I thought, feeling a warm glow. *Dad, you would have been so proud.*

I stared at the desk lamp, still angled at the brick wall behind me.

A difficult choice lay ahead of me. If I went to the audition, I still might not make it. I couldn't put my needs above my grandparents' needs, either. I wondered if the answer lay in my grandmother's blue journal. The final few pages waited patiently on my nightstand, ready to be translated. Did I take a risk or play it safe?

I want to save myself, I thought. *I did this. I need to undo it.*

Without Divya or Jackson or Katie. Without Phaedra or Hadi. Just me and my words.

I sat up resolutely, pulling black eyeliner from my bag, and began my transformation into my fiercely confident stage persona right at home. After locking my bedroom door and listening briefly to the quiet sounds on the other side, I propped my laptop up on my desk and stood with my back against the brick wall near my bed. I switched my faithful desk lamp on to create a spotlight. I faced my webcam and recorded a short set from my stand-up routine. Along with a special message.

Confidential: For the attention of Conor Broderick, read my email to him.

I sent Jackson a text telling him I had a plan. I even sent Katie a message to thank her for dropping by and asked her if we could speak in person at the office. Then I went into the quiet, empty kitchen, armed myself with snacks, nodded to my grandparents, and went back into my room.

I had a personal deadline and a new plan.

CHAPTER

37

Haytham Ramle's *bayara*, Jaffa, Palestine
April 1947

Zeina never expected she would be thankful that war was
brewing.

Within an hour, the initial merriment in the courtyard had
given way to clustered groups discussing the rising political
tensions. Zeina watched as men gathered in one area and
women sat near the fountain. Lately, it was all anyone could
talk about. When Abu Shanab thanked his guests for joining
them and said he understood if they had to leave to ensure
their safety, the crowd began to disperse. A handful of men
in suits, puffing at cigars and speaking in alternately hushed
tones and shouting voices, stood in one corner.

"I imagined spending our first night together calmly, lei-
surely, not like this," Abu Shanab said, rushing up to her and
kissing her hand. "There's talk that—Well, don't worry yourself

about it. Go get some sleep and we will celebrate our wedding night tomorrow. I must take care of a few very urgent matters that have been brought to my attention."

She released a big breath and reminded herself not to smile. She couldn't believe her luck as people began to scurry around her.

She would make it to Richard. Sooner than expected. Without planning it.

The thought of his lips against hers made her flush. She waved goodbye to the guests, who all remarked that marriage suited her and brought out her beauty in spades. Layla, eyeing her through dark lashes, even complimented her. She hugged her parents furiously, proud that Abu Shanab had arranged for them and Layla to spend the night in empty rooms in the main villa to avoid being driven back on unsafe roads at night.

Hiba touched her shoulder and began to guide her back to her terraced room. She made small talk about the party, but Zeina's mind was completely on Richard. As they walked in silence through the shadowy path of the olive grove leading to her private rooms, Zeina let her mind wander to their first kiss.

Her first kiss.

She hadn't allowed herself to think of that day in weeks. Her heart had pounded against her rib cage in protest, like a prisoner behind bars, whenever thoughts of that day seeped into her mind.

The day had started like every other, with Zeina singing at her seat by the window as she waited for Layla. They would then stop by Umm Mohamed's *dukkan* to pick up bread or oranges or milk. For years after she had finished her own schooling, she enjoyed the walk past Abla Nisreen's classroom, where boys and girls played together among the lemon trees during breaks. She relished the walk back home when the air was filled with the voices of mothers and children calling to one another in the street. The air was fragrant with the scent of figs, almonds, orange blossoms, and wild thyme, all mixed with the distant salty sea air. It was the most social time of the day for her.

Lately, a thick silence pervaded Zeina's neighborhood. Mothers kept their children indoors and men met less often after work to play *tawleh* or argue about politics in open-air cafés that lined the streets. At all hours, people kept their heads down as they walked, rather than risking eye contact with the British soldiers patrolling the streets or even friendly Jewish neighbors like Dr. Abraham. As trust and camaraderie were chased away, an impossible quietude swelled between the sounds of explosions and crackling radio broadcasts from Jaffa and her neighboring villages.

As Zeina walked back home that particular day, she smiled and waved to little Fawzi and his mother when she passed them. His mother had looked as though she was going to come talk to Zeina when she saw Richard walking toward them. Instead she turned back toward her stone house as Zeina hurried her steps. She had glanced up to see him tipping his hat to her, and right behind him, she caught sight of her father's friend, Zaki, raising his eyebrows at the interaction.

"*Sabah el-ward we el ful*," said the soldier to Zeina in heavily accented Arabic, using Egyptian phrases. Many of the British soldiers had come to Jaffa's villages from postings in Egypt and had picked up flowery, uncommon phrases just like this one—morning of roses and gardenias—by way of greeting. Such phrases would later make their way into the letters exchanged between them.

Zeina didn't answer him. She could see Umm Mohamed's *dukkan* nearby, marking the halfway point from her home. Zaki greeted her, asking after her father. A blush rising to her cheeks, Zeina answered him politely and made the briefest eye contact with Richard. He veered in another direction, and she breathed a sigh of relief. The last thing she needed was to cause a scandal, with Zaki assuming the role of her protector from the soldier's inappropriate advances.

The ones she had been fantasizing about for days.

She had quickly ducked into Umm Mohamed's *dukkan* and asked the old woman questions about oranges and neighborly gossip to buy time. Umm Mohamed's fourteen-year-old helper, Seif, offered Zeina a small piece of freshly baked *knafeh* to taste, and Umm Mohamed teased him about being infatuated until his cheeks flushed red.

"*Yeeee*, do you also daydream about our Zeina before you nap on your little mat outside?" said Umm Mohamed, and cackled, pinching Seif's cheek.

"Do you want sugar syrup with your *knafeh*, Anisa Zeina?" asked Seif, blinking rapidly, with his eyes trained on the ground.

"Naughty, naughty boy!" shouted Umm Mohamed as she pinched his cheek again, laughing to herself as Zeina politely accepted the pastry from Seif.

After about ten minutes of talk about weather and neighbors and *knafeh*, Umm Mohamed turned her attention to Mrs. Shawwi, who'd just walked in with fresh news about her daughter's latest suitor.

Zeina quickly paid and took the paper bag of oranges and milk from Seif. She walked outside and, not seeing Richard or Zaki, felt a twinge of disappointment. The small smiles between her and her British soldier gave each day some vibrant color. But the street was completely empty. She walked about five paces and let her shoulders drop as the sun warmed her cheeks.

She inhaled sharply as a hand clamped lightly around hers, tugging her into an alleyway between the shops.

"Shhhhhhh. . . ." Richard had breathed into her ear. He let

go of her hand and offered her a single white flower with the other. The brief, rough touch of his fingers and his audacity in pulling her into a quiet alley should have alarmed her, but she felt a buzz of pure excitement. Instead of walking away, as any proper girl would have done, she accepted the fragrant flower and used it to hide a small smile.

She had often fantasized about what it would be like to breathe the same air as Richard, smell his skin, touch his stubble. Now that he was here in the flesh, her senses felt like they were on fire trying to absorb every detail. Umm Mohamed's *dukkan* had a narrow, dark alley in the back where an oven crackled with fire. The air smelled sweetly of *knafeh* and sugar syrup, adding to the ever-present scent of orange blossoms in full bloom. Richard's hands found their way to her waist, and she breathed him in, a mixture of cigarettes and plain soap.

One hand grazed her cheek. He stooped down for a moment, using the other hand to take one of the oranges from the bag she had dropped on the ground. Slowly, without a word, he began to peel the orange, and the tangy scent filled the air. Zeina had looked around, terrified of getting caught but unwilling to move from the single most exciting incident of her life so far. Perhaps ever, if she was going to follow in the same steps as her mother, and her mother before her: marry a man of decent means, bear his children, tend to his house.

What was Richard going to do with the orange? Would he dare kiss her? Did he realize that by just being in this dark, secretive space with him, her entire reputation would be ruined if anyone found her? Was Seif lurking around back here, watching them?

The orange peel now lay on the floor, surrendered, spread apart. Richard stood up and pulled a single wedge from the round, naked fruit in his hand. He lifted it to his mouth, letting half the slice hang out, and leaned in toward Zeina.

Zeina didn't see it as a choice. His blue eyes drew her closer, and she felt her skin prickle in anticipation. She put her lips toward the exposed wedge, but before she could bite into it, he pulled it completely into his mouth. Her lips met his. He tasted of oranges, wet and sweet. Juice dribbled down her chin, and she laughed nervously. He put a finger to his lips, whispered her name into her ear, and trailed kisses up her neck until his mouth met hers again.

Now she stood at her bedroom door, hurriedly bidding Hiba good night and telling her she was capable of undressing herself. Alone in her room, she held her breath and waited for her eyes to adjust to the darkness. She locked the door with a loud *click*, then turned the key once more for safety. The door to her terrace was wide open, curtains moving gently with the breeze, as if taking deep breaths.

Quietly, she said his name, her voice barely above a whisper.

"Richard, are you there? Richard?" Her eyes roamed over her empty bed, the open terrace door. Then a figure materialized in front of her.

Even in the darkness, without seeing the sea blue of his eyes, she recognized his silhouette instantly. His slow, confident gait, the scent of cigarettes and soap, the short crop of his hair.

And when he kissed her, it tasted like oranges.

She heard booms in the distance, and Zeina faintly wondered whether it was Abu Shanab's car or a truck full of wooden crates of oranges . . . or something more sinister. The guests had all left by now, and her parents and sister were in rooms somewhere in the mansion. She didn't care about anything else at this moment. She didn't have any words, any thoughts. Richard brought her toward the bed, his mouth never leaving hers as they moved around the unfamiliar space together, smiling as

CHAPTER
38

It always took a minute or so to acclimatize to my own surroundings after diving into the world Teta described in her writing. I was surprised to find a tear trailing its way down my cheek. I blinked my eyes as if I had just woken up from a dream. I wiped my wet cheek, breathing in the scent of date cakes in the kitchen and listening to the soothing whirring of the fan.

The story had ended without an ending. Did Teta ever speak to Layla again? Her love for Richard, her willingness to take big risks in the name of passion, moved something in me. This was a defining, pivotal memory, the stuff of love songs and sweeping romantic movies, the meaning of life. Was that what Teta meant, that love is risky? That I was right to kiss Jackson, to play with the curls at the nape of his neck, to share his warm breath on a rainy night?

It was a quiet Monday morning. I knew I needed to get back to work, to face Katie and Jackson and life, but my real life seemed they knocked knees and then sank into the thick duvet. After string of stolen kisses in alleyways, a private room with a be was pure luxury.

Richard peeled the layers off Zeina until they found them selves skin to skin, as the rumbling noises outside grew more insistent. In another corner of the house, Haytham Ramle ran around, ordering staff to secure valuables and checking paper-work. They may have to leave sooner than expected if violence in the area continued to escalate.

He hadn't had the heart to tell his young bride that their days in this house were numbered. He'd initially thought he had a week or so to plan a safe escape. Or days . . . now maybe hours if they were lucky.

The journal ended there. The only way to find out what happened next was to talk to Teta. It was time.

to be unfolding right here at home. I needed to take another personal day.

I quietly opened the door a crack and walked toward the kitchen.

Instead of finding it empty, I found my grandmother in much the same position as last night: rolling pin moving rhythmically back and forth, surrounded by flour and aniseed at the kitchen table. A ray of early morning sunlight streamed through the window, a beam highlighting the quick movements of her hands. There were trays of date cakes cooling on the stove as she continued to make fresh ones.

"Are you trying to end world hunger?" I asked her softly.

"When I'm nervous, I bake," she replied in Arabic without breaking her rhythm with the rolling pin. "Nobody has come knocking on our door to kick us out over the weekend, but it may happen in the future. We need to really think about the way we are living our lives. Maybe move."

She had been saying this for years. The constant sense of instability seemed to lose its power when she uttered such phrases, so they almost became a comfort. Of course we wouldn't move. Of course Jeddo would keep maintaining this apartment building and she would keep cooking. Of course.

Right?

"Jeddo? Is he . . . ?" I looked toward the living room, his empty leather armchair.

"He's in one of the apartments working on a broken stove. Will take time. He's better today," she said. "He was just shocked."

I pulled out a chair and sat at the table. I took a date cake and breathed in its warm, sugary smell. Dawn was breaking, and more sunlight trickled in shyly, like it didn't want to intrude on our conversation.

"I finished," I said, dusting crumbs from my upper lip. "It's a beautiful, sad story. It sounds like you really loved him. Richard, I mean."

The rolling pin paused its back-and-forth motion. Teta's eyes darted up at mine and then returned to her activity. She cleared her throat.

"Yes," she said simply. "I did. Ah, Richard."

She said his name with a deep sigh. She looked up at me, her eyes unblinking. When Teta was full of emotion, she tried hard to put on a poker face. I'd seen her play this game before. Putting a hand over hers, I smiled and blew her a kiss.

"I just want to understand," I said. "No judgment."

She nodded.

She motioned to the right, where I realized she had made me a complete breakfast of mashed fava beans drizzled with olive oil. When I grabbed the tray, steam rose from the dish. The pita bread was still warm.

"Let me see the journal," she said. "It's been years. You eat and I will . . . look at . . . my past."

I brought the shoebox out and placed it on the table. It was dusty and gray, and I half expected her to remove it instantly and wipe the table down with lemon-scented Fairy liquid. Instead, she smiled, wrinkles forming near her green eyes. She shook her head, running her hands over the faded blue journal inside the box with tenderness.

"You really read it all?" she asked as I slowly began to eat, afraid to break her trance, worried that a wrong word would close her up again.

"But it ended with that night . . . with Richard," I said. "Are you ready to tell me how the story really ends?"

Tears in her eyes, she stood up and disappeared into her room. I pictured her throwing herself on the bed like Marcela from the telenovela, crying into the pillow, but that wasn't like her. Teta was too restrained. I finished eating and rinsed my plate, putting on the kettle for tea. I wondered if her love for tea—and its ability to solve all problems—came from British Richard.

"It's time for me to tell you the end. And there is one more thing for you to look at," she said, returning and placing the blue journal at the edge of the kitchen table. On top of the journal was a creased envelope tied with a white silk ribbon, the kind she used for her hair when it was her birthday or the rare occasion when she agreed to take a photo. "Let's sit and have a long, overdue chat. Your grandfather will be busy fixing the stove all day. It's acting up. Let's talk."

For the first time in a long time, despite a lack of resolution, I felt a little more in control. I had taken a personal day, needing absolute focus on this, not concerned with what Jackson or Katie or even Isabel might think. I was going to complete Teta's story and find our way back to some sort of a normal life.

CHAPTER
39

My grandmother had her back to me, steadying herself at the sink. I had finished my breakfast and was ready to listen. She cleared the table and placed a bowl in the center.

The sugary scents of baking—of nutmeg and aniseed and cinnamon—were replaced by the sharp smell of chopped onions in the bowl, mixed with uncooked rice, diced parsley, and tiny tomato cubes. She brought out a glass jar of California grapevine leaves, wrapped around each other in briny water, and placed it next to me.

"Have to keep my hands busy," she said, waving them in the air and taking a seat. "Otherwise, I fall down."

"Fall apart," I corrected.

"That happened already," she replied in Arabic, her voice dismissive. "Oof, many times."

I glanced curiously at the white envelope with the white ribbon, ready to tear it open but waiting for her instruction. I washed my hands and took my seat back at the table. I carefully peeled off a fragile, wet grapevine leaf from the jar, spreading it out on a clean tray until it looked like a flat green hand with veins running through it. With a teaspoon, I took a big scoop of the onion-rice-parsley-tomato mixture from the bowl and carefully placed it in the center. Then I wrapped the leaf around it, like a miniature burrito. I placed it next to Teta's perfect *wara enab* wrap in a big pot and moved on to the next one.

"I really did think it was love," she began, scooping the mixture onto her grapevine leaf. "Richard. He was exciting, different. I imagined a life outside Palestine, both of us traveling the world. I was young, sixteen or seventeen. Reckless."

"And that was the last time you saw him?" I asked, questions racing each other in my mind to be the first to escape my lips. "That, um, night?"

"It was," she said. "I was so oblivious to the tensions in Palestine, and how they would change our lives, honestly. Just cared about which dress to wear and how my hair looked. And Richard! Richard's cigarettes and his smiles and his notes. We had secret plans to keep sneaking around. Fools in love."

We wrapped the next few *wara enab* in silence. The pot was a quarter full of *wara enab*, stacked next to each other like fat fingers.

"Your sister is Layla, right?" I asked. My heart was thudding in my chest. The repetitive movements of wrapping the grapevine leaves felt so normal and therapeutic, but part of me wanted to run and get a voice recorder or a pen and paper to document every word that came out of Teta's lips.

"Ah, Layla," she said with a sigh, her hands pausing momentarily. "She was always angry at me, you know. She thought I was luckier because I was more beautiful. Look where beauty got me."

"Tell me about her," I prodded. "Have you reached out to her over the years?"

Teta kept rolling the grapevine leaves. I put a hand over hers, forcing her to stop rolling the *wara enab*, bending my head down until her eyes met mine. Hers were full of tears.

"That night with Richard was one of the most romantic nights of my entire life," she said defiantly in Arabic. "It was wrong, I know. I had just married someone else! But I wanted the right to love. To really *love*. And when he left my room before dawn broke, my paradise turned into hell."

She nodded at the blue journal and the white envelope on the edge of the table. With a quizzical look, I wiped my hands with tissue and pointed at the envelope.

"No, first, read these," she said.

Over the years, she had written dozens of "endings" and burned them, over and over, trying to find closure. She had kept a recent version that she now felt ready to share with me.

"This is the hardest part," she said, her voice barely above a whisper.

After washing and drying my hands, I placed the white envelope aside and picked up the blue journal. I discovered fresh loose pages tucked in the middle, written in her familiar script.

"Can you read it aloud to me and explain the words I don't understand?" I asked gently, worried that if I disappeared into my room with my laptop and Google Translate that I might lose the opportunity to talk to her.

"Bring me my glasses and hold it out to me," she said, not missing a beat while wrapping the *wara enab*. After placing her pink glasses gently on her nose, she cleared her throat and began to read aloud . . .

Haytham Ramle's *bayara*, Jaffa, Palestine
April 1947

The moonlight trickled into the room as the curtains billowed, the light breeze delicious on Zeina's bare skin. Her body hummed against Richard's touch, reveling in the heaviness of his legs intertwined with hers, the sheets twisted around their bodies. She had been taught to believe that lovemaking was a painful duty for women, an act that must take place to please a man and protect the sanctity of a union. But to her, after an initial sharp jolt of pain, it was utter bliss. So much so that they enjoyed two more rounds before falling into a dense, surrendered sleep.

Zeina woke to the sound of someone frantically trying to open her locked bedroom door. Kissing Richard hurriedly on the lips, she allowed him a few moments to locate his clothes and escape via the terrace. She put on the fluffy white robe as she watched his shadowy figure disappear into the olive grove. She missed his nearness already.

Dazed in the darkness of an unfamiliar room, she picked up discarded pillows and threw them back on the bed. Then she quickly took the key to the drawer in her vanity—the one that contained Richard's note—and placed it in the pocket of her robe. She went to unlock her bedroom door, alarmed that the handle was still moving up and down from the other side with such urgency. She finally opened it to find a breathless Hiba, along with Layla.

"It's happening," Hiba said, shaking her hands out nervously. "Mr. Ramle received word that Jaffa will be attacked in the morning. We must all leave at once to avoid any casualties. Oh, I wish I could go warn my family, but I think the smaller villages still have time. We must leave now, right now!"

"I don't understand. What's happening?" Zeina asked, peering out to find her parents standing behind Hiba. She knew that there was talk of Palestine's cities falling one by one, had deduced that the extra military presence was not a good thing, had heard of families being forced out of their homes in the dead of night and young men—barely teenagers—sent to prison. But she didn't fully understand why. The threats always seemed distant, like they were happening to other people in bigger cities. How could they be happening in her home, to her family, right now?

Zeina's father wanted to be driven back immediately to Teenieh, as the threats hadn't yet reached the smaller villages in that area, despite escalating risks. On principle, he refused to entertain the idea of ever being forced to leave Palestine.

"They can't stop me from going home," he declared. "It's been my family's house for generations. I'm not leaving it behind."

Zeina's mother was uncharacteristically quiet. This was not how her daughter's wedding night was supposed to unfold. She had assumed the rising troubles in Palestine were related to the big world war in Europe that had resulted in so much death and sadness. Why would the powers that be care about their sleepy, leafy little corner of the world? What could they possibly want here? How could the family still be unsafe in Abu Shanab's sprawling *bayara*, with its gates and its dozens of guards? Like her husband, Fayza just wanted to go home to familiar territory and hope that the problems wouldn't spread to the tiny town of Teenieh.

"Zeina, you stay with your husband. He will surely take good care of you," she said, patting her daughter's hand. "Take Layla with you. She can help you, and maybe Haytham Ramle will help her, too."

Zeina hugged her parents fiercely, unable to make quick decisions, wondering if she should insist that they stay, stop them from going, go with them . . . or wait for Richard. She must warn him to leave as well. Perhaps they could leave together?

Hiba began to throw clothes into a small bag for Zeina. Layla sat on her bed as Hiba went into the bathroom to gather a few toiletries. Sheer desperation rose up in Zeina at the thought of leaving the *bayara* without ever seeing Richard again. Would he think she had abandoned him after the intensity of the night before? What could she possibly do at this stage?

Zeina looked into her sister's dark eyes, the quiet confidence in her. Zeina knew Layla had taken a risk staying with her, headed toward an unknown future. Layla could have insisted on traveling back to the comforts of their village with their parents, but she hadn't.

"Hello? Get dressed," Layla said, throwing her hands up in frustration. "Or do you need Hiba to put your clothes on for you now, too?"

Zeina went to the large wooden wardrobe and picked out the same outfit she had worn yesterday when she arrived at the *bayara* as a new bride. Nothing in there looked familiar. Placing a light coat around her shoulders, she discreetly took the drawer key from the fluffy white robe and placed it in her coat pocket.

Layla, as usual, was watching her. They stood in silence, facing each other and breathing shallowly in the dark, listening to Hiba's frantic movements.

"I can't leave," Zeina whispered to her sister when she moved to stand next to her.

Her sister looked over at her. "What's gotten into you?"

"It's just that . . . I have to . . ." Zeina started, her hand clasping the key in her coat pocket.

"It's that soldier, isn't it?" Layla said, her voice low and stiff.

Zeina wondered how much she knew. For an irrational moment, she was terrified her sister had somehow seen him leave her room. She glanced at the bed, where his naked figure had lain intertwined with hers minutes ago. Could Layla smell his scent?

"You left him already, you fool," Layla said. "He's somewhere out there fighting in this madness. And we must leave right now to be safe. What are you thinking to do, go back to Teenieh with Mama and Baba?"

If Zeina did nothing, said nothing, she risked losing Richard—her everything. She could feel sheer desperation coursing through her veins. Checking quickly to ensure Hiba was not within earshot, she went up to Layla, held her by the shoulders, and lowered her voice.

"He's here," Zeina answered, her eyes cast down. "Richard is here. And I'm not leaving without him."

In whispered snatches of conversation, Zeina told her sister about seeing him at the front door when she arrived, about her burning love and worry for Richard. Layla recoiled and stepped away from her and from the bed when Zeina told her about what had taken place overnight.

"I knew about you two, your letters and your shenanigans behind the *dukkan*," Layla snapped, her voice a wagging finger. "You weren't so discreet, you know. But I just can't believe you would take it this far. Did you really spend the night with him?"

When Zeina nodded, Layla looked toward the bed again with a dark expression of disgust, bitterness, and shock.

"What an ill-fated, ridiculous charade of a wedding night," she said under her breath. "Were you thinking of Abu Shanab at all? Your husband?! Of the family and what marriage means to the community? Anybody else but yourself?"

The crumpled, bloodstained bedsheet was in a ball at the foot of the bed.

"You don't understand," Zeina said, walking up to her sister again, cupping Layla's face in her hands, and forcing her to look into her eyes. "I love Richard with every cell in my body. I think I might just die if I don't see him again. Please, help me. I'll do anything."

"So, what, you're planning to throw away a perfect life,

gifted to you, for the British soldier?" Layla asked, dark eyes wide and unblinking.

"For love," Zeina said feverishly. "I hope you will understand one day. For love. I want to be with him and only him. I'll do anything."

"Anything?" Layla said, her voice gaining strength. "Fine. Remember, this was your decision. Just go. Go find your lover. I'll take care of things here."

Zeina, tempted by freedom and love and willing to take a risk, didn't hesitate a moment longer. She hugged her sister, planting kisses on her dry cheeks. Layla stood still, her arms at her sides, staring off into the distance, not hugging her back.

Zeina ran blindly from her private terrace out into the field, in the direction she had seen Richard take less than an hour ago. She called out his name in loud whispers. She ran into Jumana, Ismat's maid, outside her terrace, as well as several field hands, but not her Richard. Her feet were cold from the damp earth and fallen olives. The booming sounds were distinctly closer than they had been hours ago, and she feared the shadows in the olive grove, imagining men with guns lurking in the dark of night. The sun was still half-hidden behind a distant hill. Her heart pulled her onward into the madness of recklessly searching for Richard.

To no avail. Desperate, tired, terrified of the dark, she stumbled back to the villa to find it eerily empty. The sense of abandonment and fear multiplied in her. What if armed men found her here alone, defenseless? What did it mean that Jaffa was going to be attacked by morning? Was the entire place going to be taken over, or bombed, or what?

Back in her bedroom as a last resort, hoping to catch her sister or Hiba or any of the dozens of maids, she found Richard waiting for her at last. They fell into each other, his arms wrapping around her waist, his hands then finding their way to her hair. Amid the chaos, this moment of pure unity validated her decision to choose a life with Richard.

He broke away from her for a moment, holding her face in his hands. He explained to her what he had heard from the other guards in their brief time apart. Jaffa was a strategic port town, and many believed it didn't belong to the Arabs, Jews, Muslims, and Christians who had lived there for centuries. Police and foreign army presence was going to increase, people were going to be forced to leave their homes, and anyone who resisted would be sent to prison . . . or worse.

"I'll spare you the details, darling, but we need to go and secure ourselves an escape. Now," he said, ushering her out of the room, walking in front of her to guide her to the front door. "I'll tell the guards I made a final sweep of the mansion and found you asleep, and that you must come in the van with us to the closest shore. Everyone else has already left."

Zeina and Richard held hands, climbing into a truck with a handful of British guards, who eyed them curiously. After a quick explanation, the focus moved to the safest route to the port. Zeina took a seat amid crates of oranges. She could smell the salt in the air as the van bounced along the road toward the seaside. The men didn't speak, and the van was moving so fast, they all kept jostling out of their seats and scrambling to get back in.

Zeina kept her eyes on Richard, who exuded a sense of calm and warmth. He had seen this before, he had seen worse, he would take care of her. Somewhere beneath the blind terror and sense of abandon, she felt a small thrill that her life was changing. She just needed to survive this escape, and perhaps divine providence had found a way for them to have an exciting life abroad together after all.

She tried to calm her mind, worried about her parents, wondering if her sister and Hiba were okay, wondering what would happen to the big mansion after they all left. Would someone else soon be sitting at that pretty vanity with the fresh flowers, brushing their hair in the morning? Wondering why the top drawer was locked?

She thought of Abu Shanab, wondering how he felt about leaving his home. Would he return to try to reclaim it? Had he kept the house key? Where was he now and was Layla with him? She felt a nervous flutter in her stomach, trying to imagine what his reaction had been when Layla and Hiba appeared without her. She felt a dull soreness between her legs, reminding her of the activities of the previous night.

How could life be the same for years and years and years, then bring so much sweeping change in a matter of hours?

She didn't have much time to dwell on her worry and guilt. She could hear voices rising outside as the army van slowed to a stop. The back doors exhaled open onto a sea of people, luggage, and crying children at the busy port. It seemed word had spread about the attack, and people were making quick escapes to family and friends in neighboring countries. Dawn was breaking, casting soft light on dozens of families trying to stay together and getting onto boats headed to Lebanon, Syria, and Egypt. It looked like the sea was on fire.

The guards were huddled together, discussing options to drive to Jordan or Syria instead, find a spot on a boat to Lebanon, or whether to stay and assist the army in case problems escalated further. There was no official mandate anymore. It was every man for himself.

"This is chaos," Zeina said, pulling on Richard's uniform. "Richard, what shall we do? Where do we go?"

Richard guided her toward a boat headed to Lebanon. It was the closest and most logical choice. He would be able to contact the British embassy or consulate more easily there. Richard had a former school friend, Simon, who had married a Lebanese woman and settled in Beirut. They'd traded occasional letters over the years, especially when both found themselves in the Middle East. Zeina liked the plan, knowing that her uncle also lived in Beirut, in case they needed to contact family. Hand in hand, they stood in the messy queue of refugees until it was their turn to board.

"Only women and children," shouted a steward. "You, you're British, you can go with the army or find help with your consulate. Only Arab women and children here."

Richard protested. Zeina felt sick to her stomach, clinging to his arm and attempting to speak to the steward in English. She even tried her best to put on a British accent, saying they were family and must not be separated. Richard echoed the sentiment, telling the steward that they were married and must not part.

It was no use. The steward didn't believe the lie.

"Don't worry, darling," Richard kept repeating, the color draining from his face, trying to stay calm for the sake of his love. "I promise I'll get on the next boat. When you get to Beirut, find a way to get to Café Fraise. Ask for Simon at Café Fraise, okay? I'll come find you."

Zeina couldn't process what was happening around her, wondering why Richard kept repeating Café Fraise. Why was he talking nonsense about strawberries and cafés right now? Too many threads were being pulled at once, and her heart was unraveling. The severity of what was happening to her came crashing down like an ocean wave. If she got on this boat, what were the chances she would ever see her family again? Her Richard? Her life as she knew it?

Did she have a choice?

"Get on the boat now, darling, and I'll come find you," Richard repeated, trailing kisses along her neck and face. Zeina didn't care who was watching anymore. A child wailed nearby when her toy bunny fell off the boat into the dark waters.

She got onto the boat and stood right next to the steward, her hand on the slippery rail. Salty sea spray kept hitting her cheeks. Her hands were shaking. Richard waded into the cold water and reached up to kiss her face, then her arms, then eventually her fingertips as the dinghy rocked gently away. She stared at his face until the horizon became blurry in the distance and dawn broke.

She never saw him again.

CHAPTER

40

"Never again," Teta repeated simply, her hands moving back to the *wara enab* rolls. Her heavy words hung in the air, her hands no longer moving to and fro. "It's not like today with the Googles and the Facebook, where you can find anybody. Back then, the way he traded places with another guard to be in Haytham's house . . . Mixed-up papers . . . I spent so long trying to find him. So long. Everyone was a mess, everything was a mess."

"I don't know what to say." I shook my head, a fiery lump forming in my throat. I still had another few pages to go, but Teta needed a break and I needed to process.

"Then, amid all the loss and shock, months later, I saw it," she continued.

"Saw what?" I said. I was hanging on every word, unable to distract myself with wrapping *wara enab* anymore. My Teta, who was always precise and neat and a homebody, had suddenly become a different person in my eyes. She nodded toward the envelope, which had fluttered to the floor.

I jumped up to wash my hands again, still shaking as I dried them and opened the creased envelope. Inside was a faded newspaper article with rough edges, as if it had been torn from the rest of the page. It was about the opening of a second jewelry store in the Gulf region, in the United Arab Emirates.

And there, in the center, was a photo of a large bald man with a mustache, holding a cane, standing with a petite brunette in a fur coat and a string of pearls. She had dark eyes, like a raven. They were both smiling at a ribbon-cutting ceremony. Even though it was a black-and-white photo, the woman looked like she was wearing dark lipstick. Her long, black hair was set in groomed waves.

Haytham Ramle inaugurates new Almas Jewelry store in honor of his wife, Zeina Almas, read the caption.

"And she looked exactly like that, in all her fur, pearls, and red lipstick, when I saw her for the last time," Teta said, nodding at the photo. "When she walked into Café Fraise, where I was working as a waitress. Let's finish the story. I'm ready."

I picked the pages back up, and Teta began to read.

Café Fraise in Beirut, Lebanon
August 1947

"Is that her? She's not even that beautiful. Look at the lines around her eyes and on her hands from washing dishes," said one woman, hovering near a table where the check had been paid, ready to sit as soon as the wooden chair was vacated.

"Simpleton refugee. I feel sorry for her actually," said another, shielding her expensive handbag as a couple squeezed past her in the busy café.

"I don't understand why we are here," said her friend, applying red lipstick that strayed onto her cheek when a waiter with a full tray bumped into her.

"Well, my brother's friend's cousin, who knows the owner's

wife's driver, said each of our husbands have come here in the evenings lately. This little siren is most likely the reason," said the one with the sharp eyes, lifting her shoe to see if some unsanitary substance in the café had made the sole sticky.

At that, they turned to look at a young woman—though they would all later say she looked haggard and at least twenty-five—with frizzy, dry, dark hair roughly tied in a bun with a rubber band. She wore the same red uniform with white polka dots as all the waitstaff at Café Fraise, with flat white shoes. She wiped a table with one hand and held a tray with empty tea glasses in the other, balanced on her hip. Someone heard she sold her hair for money. Another rumor had her pregnant with a driver's child. Nobody really knew, but everyone had a story.

"I just don't see it. She's so . . . average," said one of the women after a moment's thought, taking in the kitschy decor of the café. "I mean, I would never have noticed her. You're sure that's who they were talking about? Maybe the night-shift waitress is someone else, someone . . . worth looking at?"

When the waitress turned around to face the room, her chipped metallic name tag glinted in the sunlight for a split second: *Zeina*.

Zeina took the tray of glasses into the kitchen area, wiped her forehead, and made her way to the table of four women who had just settled down in the middle of the bustling café.

It was her third month on the job, and she was still getting used to being on her feet all day. She had had a lifetime of men sending her suggestive glances and women narrowing their eyes at her, but in this relatively new role as a waitress in Beirut, the comments she received on a daily basis were caustic and often downright mean. They made fun of her Palestinian accent, and at least once a day, someone pinched her bum. It was the laughter afterward, not the sting, that made her cheeks flame red.

Still, she reminded herself, she was making her own money.

When she first arrived, the guards at the port in Beirut had insisted she—a young woman, alone—be taken in by next of kin, so they contacted her uncle Saeed. Alarmed, he had taken pity on her when he found her in dirty clothes and with no luggage. He had tried, again and again, to convince his stubborn brother to join them in the relative safety of Lebanon, but Zeina's father insisted on staying in the family home. There was no safe way for Zeina to return to them, either. As she tried to find meaning in a temporary new life that she hadn't planned for in her initial few months in Lebanon, her uncle Saeed had shown her tremendous kindness.

Months passed. She still couldn't bear to think of Abu Shanab, of her family, of all the people who had lost everything when they fled Palestine, like her, like so many before her and so many after her.

Of Richard.

His contact at Café Fraise turned out to be a British journalist, Simon, whose Lebanese wife owned the little eatery in the heart of Beirut. When Zeina first arrived and found her way to Uncle Saeed, he was confused by her insistence on visiting the café right away. He had sent her cousin, Fadi, to chaperone her, but didn't protest when Zeina insisted on getting a job in the café to help make ends meet and gain independence.

What Uncle Saeed didn't know was that she was desperately trying to track down Richard, asking for help from Simon's contacts at his news agency, scouring the English newspapers for death notices, making official requests at the British consulate. All to no avail. She held on to the hope that he would walk into the café to surprise her one day, with a bouquet of red roses and a plane ticket back to the English countryside. Instead came Simon's crushing news one day that the unit Richard had served in had been called to Egypt.

What was worse? Holding on daily to fresh hope that her life would improve the moment she saw Richard again? Or the news that he was likely alive somewhere, knew where she was, but had not chosen to contact her or find her? Was Simon even telling her the full truth?

Then came a telegram:

Z—

Simon promised to look out for you. I am sorry that it can't be me. I am stationed in Egypt now. After these months apart, with the war still raging, I realized I couldn't give you the kind of life you deserve. I have seen so much ruin and feel this world has become hopeless. Where would you live? How would we exist together amid all this destruction? I am sorry. I really did love you. I loved the fantasy of us. It was a lighthouse for me. I will think of you always. Take care, my Zeina.

—RD

Zeina felt completely undone, like she couldn't trust anyone anymore. She felt physically sick to her stomach, felt like a vise was tightening around her temples.

She risked everything . . . for nothing.

Repeated telegrams sent in return went unanswered. A coldness settled in her, and she couldn't eat or sleep for weeks. Why did a broken heart feel like a broken body?

At the beginning, it was the slim chance of seeing Richard again one day that had kept her from drowning in depression. When that hope was finally extinguished, she felt pure anguish. Was this her punishment for the risks she had taken for a lover? Was God angry at her? Could salvation still walk through the door to save her from herself?

Her mind flitted to the decadent breakfast Hiba had prepared on that private terrace for her in Abu Shanab's house when she had arrived as a new bride. It felt like a lifetime ago. Or someone else's life entirely.

"Hello? Menus?" said the woman with the red lipstick, waving her hands at Zeina and whispering something to her seatmate. Both of them looked at each other, shook their heads, and looked back at Zeina.

"*Marhaba*, my name is Zeina. I'll be your waitress today at Café Fraise. I'll leave the menus here with you and can tell you the lunch specials if you like," Zeina said with a practiced smile that played only on her lips, not in her eyes.

"I don't know. Is the food here better than the service?" said the one with the sharp eyes, looking her up and down. "I'm losing hope."

Zeina squared her shoulders, ready to respond with a polite phrase. But when she looked up to see who had walked through the door, her legs almost gave way.

Layla stood at the entrance, wearing a coat made of exquisite brown mink fur, her black hair gleaming against it. She had a string of pearls like tiny moons around her neck. She wore a trendy hat like the ones Zeina had seen in the French magazines strewn around the café, along with high heels.

Maher, a fellow waiter, came up to her.

"Keeping the loveliest ladies in the room to yourself? Let me take over," he said gracefully. Zeina watched as the women smiled appreciatively, taking in Maher's honey eyes, thick dark hair, and crooked smile.

She looked back at her sister, confirming she wasn't a mirage or a ghost. Her eyes filled with tears, a burst of happiness popping in her chest. Layla looked well taken care of and put together.

And she had come to find her.

She walked quickly toward her sister, arms outstretched. Her walk slowed when she saw her sister's cold glare, the way she had moved to the side instead of forward.

"Layla, is it really you? I am so happy to see you," Zeina said, breathlessly walking up to her and looking her in the eyes. "Shall I—"

"I had to see it with my own eyes," Layla said, her voice as sharp and precise as an arrow. "You're a lowly waitress in this café in the middle of nowhere. Tell me, are you happy now that you threw away a lifetime with a good man? A kind man who didn't deserve to be cheated out of a faithful wife?"

Zeina was taken aback. In all the scenarios she had run through in her mind of reconnecting with her family, this was not what she had envisioned. A dull ache formed in her stomach.

"Layla, please, I acted with my heart," Zeina said, hands clasped to her chest. "I didn't intentionally mean to hurt anyone. I wanted to live my life and really love someone. I—"

The wooden door opened once again, bringing with it a gust of cold air and street sounds. Outside, Zeina recognized the slender older woman with the fiery red hair, the one who had worn a maroon *thob* and scowled at her the day she'd arrived to Abu Shanab's house.

"Ismat understands," Layla said plainly. "You never cared about anyone but yourself. We were both no match for your beauty, but together, we realized that we could show Haytham what real love is. Not those silly fantasies you had in your head that have led to . . . this."

With a face full of disgust, she swept an elegantly gloved hand around the room. People were starting to turn and stare.

"I am courteous to Ismat as Haytham's first wife, and she made room for me, too," she went on. "We have an agreement that works for us. You know, Haytham was so deeply embarrassed by what you did when we told him. He wouldn't eat for a week when we arrived at our villa by the sea on the French Riviera. We have about fifteen staff members—everyone was so worried about him. You did that."

What was Layla doing? Flaunting her wealth, when she could see Zeina's situation? Stepping all over Zeina's heart for sport? Was this a competition that Layla felt like she had won? Zeina's eyes brimmed with tears, and she couldn't bring herself to speak for a moment. Did this really make her feel good?

"And, what, you helped him feel happy again?" Zeina asked finally, her chest rising and falling with emotion. "Are you telling me you're really happy, doing this to me?"

"Well, in the chaos of war, nobody really knew who Zeina was . . . so I took over," Layla said. "I am Zeina now. The Zeina he deserved. I give him foot rubs, write the letters that he dictates to business partners late in the night, feed him grapes. He likes the fat green ones. I'm a better wife than you could have ever been to him."

Zeina looked across the street at Ismat. They locked eyes for a second, long enough for Zeina to see her shake her head, look her up and down, and look away.

"He was easy to convince after I showed him your bloody sheet," she said, inspecting a speck of dust on her leather handbag.

"How could you do this to me, Layla?" Zeina asked. "We are sisters. I thought you were helping me. I tried so hard to reach you over these last few months! Did you get my telegrams—"

"Don't ever try to contact any of us again," Layla said icily. "Him or me. Don't try to find any of us. Not Mama, not Baba, not even Umm Mohamed. The entire community is ashamed by your behavior. We all want nothing to do with you."

She placed a big wad of bills on the table.

"Some money for you, but that's all you'll ever get from me," she said.

"I don't want your money," Zeina said through clenched teeth, trying to keep her voice from rising. The patrons in the café were all looking at the well-dressed wealthy lady and the flushed cheeks of the green-eyed waitress. Whispers were starting to rise. Was she a prostitute? Had she slept with that rich lady's husband, who was now paying her off to stay quiet?

Layla shrugged and placed the money back in her leather handbag, pulling out a pair of chic sunglasses. After looking Zeina up and down, she slid them on and pursed her lips.

"The choices you make . . ." she tutted. "I just don't understand the way you think."

"Get out of here, Layla," Zeina said, her voice shaking.

"My name is Zeina," she said slowly, taking a step toward the door. She looked over her shoulder. "You're a nobody now. Just a common whore."

The door blew open again. Ismat stood dead center, completely ignoring Zeina. Her eyes were fixed on Layla, her voice even and calm.

"This place disgusts me," she said, her gloved hands clasped close to her chest as her eyes roamed over the peeling paint near the doorframe. "Haytham is craving seafood. What do you think? Oysters and grilled fish? Let's tell the staff to prepare the yacht for dinner. I am in the mood to celebrate."

Layla nodded and walked out behind Ismat, heels clacking, leaving behind the scent of expensive perfume. Zeina felt dizzy. She wanted to throw a chair through the window at her sister, call her to come back and embrace her in a hug that would change her attitude, tell her that Richard had let her down, ask her how their parents were because she missed them. At the same time, she felt immense shame at the way she had been treated. Tears streamed freely down her cheeks.

Was it possible to miss someone and hate them at the same time? Zeina had discovered a turbulent mix of emotions that left her shaking.

Maher came up to her with a glass of water, asking if she was okay.

"These rich people think they rule the world," he said quietly, walking her toward the back. "Keep it together here or you will lose your job. We can talk all about it later. I'll bring leftover chocolate cake from the café, the one you like."

"I don't care anymore," Zeina said, her voice wavering. "I've lost everything. Everything, Maher."

"I'm sure you still have something to live for, something to look forward to," he said kindly, bringing her a tissue. "What's meant for you will never pass you by. Good days are coming for you, I know it. You are good and sweet."

She looked up into Maher's warm eyes, noting the way he used his body to shield her from the prying eyes of onlookers in the café. His kind words felt like a balm on an open wound. Resigned and empty, she let him console her until her body stopped shaking and the tears stopped flowing. She took a few deep breaths, dabbing at her eyes, and told him she was a little better now.

The café was much emptier and quieter. The lunch crowd had thinned, and several waiters were smoking in the back.

"Why don't you go take a break?" he suggested, patting her shoulder. "Or you can play the piano, if you like? That always seems to calm you."

He knew her so well. Zeina managed a small smile, looking to the other end of the café, where the manager of the restaurant was waving her over. Like a magician, the chubby, grandfatherly man moved aside with one giant sidestep. He made a grand sweep with his arms toward the wooden upright piano that stood discreetly near the back wall. He pushed the microphone closer to it.

Color rushed to Zeina's face, and her eyes blazed with new energy as if she had been plugged into an electric socket. She glanced back outside to check that Layla and Ismat were no longer there, but she couldn't be sure. They had tried to kick her when she was down. She would not let them see her break down completely. Maybe later, in her own room, but not here. She wouldn't give them that satisfaction, at least.

Maher had given her the strength she desperately needed . . . and his words were true. After being enchanted by the grand piano in Abu Shanab's house, she had felt real delight for the first time since arriving in Lebanon when she discovered the upright piano in her new workplace. She had told Maher she loved to sing. When she discovered that he was a musician, she felt she had made her first real friend in a foreign place.

Over the course of these few months, Maher had taught her basic chord progressions and scales. She practiced in the early mornings and occasional late evenings in the empty café. After hours, she would listen to Maher play exquisite melodies, sometimes improvised jazz, sometimes classics she soon learned to recognize. Music had seen her through moments of loss and endlessly waiting for news. Music had saved her life in a way.

She gathered her hair into a tighter bun and ran a hand down her dress as she made her way toward the piano. She would show them all. She refused to become the focus of gossip in this town, too. Taking a seat and adjusting the microphone, she sang a simple song about lost love by a popular Lebanese vocalist. The chords she played were very basic, and her voice was airy and light, but it was the raw emotion that took over her body that captivated her audience. As she sang, all the thoughts she kept firmly bottled up in her mind for the sake of her sanity were allowed to roam free for a few minutes.

Her voice broke as she remembered Abu Shanab's grand

house in disarray. She recalled running in the dark through the maze of corridors with Richard that night, past the wedding cake that had fallen in half near the courtyard. Decorations and paintings had been torn off walls. Perhaps the accountant's wife had been trying to warn her earlier with her stories of Abu Shanab moving money. Perhaps Abu Shanab had kept up the pretense of preparing for a wedding to make their escape possible.

Zeina wept for her parents, her house, for Palestine, for her family, and mostly for Richard. Would she ever find closure? Would a part of her always hold on to flimsy hope that he would have a change of heart, that she would hear from him—a phone call, a letter, a surprise visit? How could one person suffer so much and be expected to carry on? To find light at the bottom of the ocean?

Questions swirled in her mind that she couldn't voice: Were other people living in the big house on the *bayara* now? Was someone else sleeping in the bed where she had become a woman and enjoyed long, luxurious kisses with Richard as if they had all the time in the world? Or would it remain a shrine to her old life, with a rotting wedding cake and broken lamps?

She brought the song to a quiet, thoughtful end as she reflected on what her life had become. She was better off than many Palestinian refugees, with food and shelter and a kind uncle who hadn't turned her away completely like the rest of her family. But her heart ached every day over her small life as a burden in her uncle's house, her changing figure, her uncertain path in life. The empty hole that her estranged family and Richard had left behind.

Her hands fell away from the piano keys, and she blinked a few times, bringing herself back to her surroundings.

The café was completely silent. Nobody was chewing food; the room had been robbed of the clink of knives on plates and laughter breaking out among the tables. Everyone wore a sober expression, completely spellbound by this young lady, her chest rising and falling with heavy breaths through strawberry-red lips, parted slightly. Her flashing green eyes handcuffed them to their seats.

"She's a witch," breathed one of the four women in the center in awe. "She's . . . she's ravishing."

Someone began to clap, which broke the spell and brought the café noises back into full swing. Zeina nodded in thanks, catching Maher's eye and smiling. He winked and punched the air in a show of camaraderie at the way she had pulled herself away from the brink. The manager patted her head kindly. Zeina was his little secret weapon who kept tables full day after day. As she stepped back into the crowd and began addressing each table's needs, she shrank back into her role as a waitress. Her frizzy hair and cheap clothes came back to the foreground. She had disappeared inside herself again.

Maher was right. She did have one thing left to live for.

And nobody else knew.

Her hand momentarily rested on her stomach before she jerked it away, awkwardly placing it on her hip. She tried to find anywhere else except for that part of her body to rest them, but her hands moved to the same spot without her thinking, like they answered to their own pull of gravity. She had only survived so far by pretending that her stomach was a completely separate entity—just like the alien she was now certain was growing inside of it.

Richard's child. Proof of love. Or lust.

The woman with the sharp eyes gathered her handbag, put on her sunglasses with shaky hands, and stalked out of the café. Zeina watched her walk away, heels clacking like sudden rainfall, as her hands found their way to her stomach again.

CHAPTER
41

"So she took my identity and played the role of his new wife without a backward glance," said Teta. "After all these years, it's still so hard to say out loud. Makes me feel like I can't breathe."

"But . . . how?" I asked. I was processing everything, trying to put my thoughts in order.

"Well, Abu Shanab took my travel documents when we married, right?" said Teta. "Layla finally got what she wanted: my life. And she didn't mind if mine was left in ruins."

"I just . . . I don't understand how she could do this to you," I admitted. "You really never spoke again? Not even to your parents?"

Teta shook her head sadly.

"Over the years, I kept writing her letters that I never mailed. I even started a new one when I gave you the journal . . . but even keeping it in the apartment was making me feel bad," she said. "One final letter. Telling her: 'Layla, I understand. When Mama and Baba went back to Teenieh, Haytham Ramle was all you had left. Layla, you were in survival mode, too. Layla . . . I forgive you.'"

Teta showed me the letter she'd written on a loose piece of paper. Unfinished, lines scratched out and rewritten.

"I don't *loathe* her," she said, using the strongest word for "hate" in Arabic. "There are so many conflicting emotions at play. She was cruel, she was selfish, she was unnecessarily competitive. But we are sisters. We are cut from the same cloth, we bleed the same way. I am her and she is me. So finding a way to forgive her means . . . forgiving myself. Somehow."

She stood up, switched on the stovetop, and watched the flicker of the blue flame. Then she burned the letter.

"Your past holds so much sadness and confusion, Teta. I'm so sorry," I said, holding back tears. "But you wrote about it so beautifully."

Teta had tried to reclaim her name by writing this story, seeing herself through the eyes of others. She wanted the real story of Zeina to live on in the blue journal.

Although Teta had changed her first name to Amal—meaning "hope" in Arabic—when she moved to America, she had kept her real last name: Almas. A part of her hoped her extended family or Richard might try to search for her, to forgive her, to look for her over time. For her part, Layla had kept the Almas surname. Teta assumed it was so Haytham Ramle could distribute large sums of his wealth through the jewelry business under the radar.

Layla and Teta's father would be so ashamed of how they had treated the Almas name.

I studied the flimsy newspaper clipping, looking into Layla's raven eyes. I stood up, letting it flutter to the ground, and I left it there. I reached out and embraced Teta, breathing in the comforting scent of her light jasmine perfume. I'm not sure how long we stood there, holding each other.

"How did you carry on?" I asked her incredulously.

"Maher, at first. He was so kind, so good to me. Then the baby, my Yousef," she said wistfully in Arabic. "And later, you. I don't think I would have survived otherwise. My life has been so full of hurt and darkness, but our little family ushered light in again."

We sat back down, and I asked her about Palestine. Did she ever miss her homeland?

"How do you process the loss of an entire nation?" she asked. "Even years, decades later, we all assumed things might return to normal. We never thought this would happen to so many of us. For families to experience rolling losses that don't seem to end. The only thing I had left of Palestine was the key to the drawer hiding the love letter . . . and I threw the key into the ocean at some point, so angry at Richard . . ."

"What brought you to America?" I asked, tears falling freely down my cheeks now. I could only understand how hard her life must have been, how much she had tried to protect me from. "I know you showed up to Ellis Island to start a new life. But you didn't do it alone, right?"

"Maher. We became very close friends, confidantes. I eventually told him my secret about the baby. He helped me, putting me in touch with other misfits like me: no papers, no hope, desperate for a better life," she went on. "He took me under his wing, protected me from advances, and made sure I was well fed. He gave me the coat off his back. He was like me, he understood me, he was there for me. He's the only one who never left me."

Maher was also a Palestinian refugee with no papers. Teta had initially been planning to escape to England, hoping that, once there, she could start afresh and live out the dreams she and Richard had shared. But could she really do it on her own?

Reeling from the loss of so much in her life and worn down by the constant hope that Richard would come back to her as she continued to search for him—all while pregnant—she fell into a depression. She stopped being able to take shifts at Café Fraise and cut ties with her uncle, who would be deeply ashamed when he discovered the truth. She would start to show within a matter of months. What options did she have left?

Without Maher, she might have fallen into deep trouble. Instead, he told her about America and a place called New York that was very welcoming of immigrants like them. No judgments, a fresh start. It felt like a new, lighter chapter. She could reinvent herself.

"Heavily pregnant, I worked for a few weeks washing dishes, hidden in a dirty kitchen of a restaurant, to save just enough money for a fake marriage certificate," she said. "Then, after your father, baby Yousef, was born, Maher and I got onto a boat headed to America," she said.

After the little family had arrived at Ellis Island with all the Irish and Italian immigrants, a guard there recognized their long journey and took pity on them. Young Teta had a wailing newborn and a still-big stomach. Maher told him he was a musician. The guard said he could make quick cash under the table as a superintendent in this building leased by Juilliard. Maher's skills in tuning pianos and guitars might come in handy, alongside the usual tasks of a superintendent. The guard's cousin worked there as an electrician.

"And that is how we became Maher, Amal, and Yousef of the Upper West Side," she said with a shrug. "In a building of musicians and pianos. Music saved me again. And Maher, your grandfather, showed me what true love really means."

Jeddo had taken care of a pregnant Teta, then raised Yousef and me as his own in a foreign land. He had provided for the family as best he could, breaking the law to stay in America for me. And he wasn't even my real grandfather.

I didn't even know his real last name.

As if he had heard his cue, the front door opened, and he shouted hello. A bundle of nerves formed in my stomach. We still hadn't spoken since our confrontation yesterday.

"It is really getting so cold outside," he said, taking off a heavy brown coat sprinkled with rain. "I had to check on the heater for the Dominicans next door. It wasn't working and their building doesn't have a superintendent like me. Their baby is little, only eighteen months old, *haram*. I could see my breath in the basement where they live. Did you burn something? Why does it smell like smoke in here?"

I rushed up to him and gave him a big hug. He stumbled backward in surprise.

"I don't tell you enough how much I love you," I whispered.

I felt his arms come around me. We held each other steady for a few beats, my tears staining his shoulder. I could feel his heart drumming in his chest. I pulled back and looked into his dark eyes, wet with emotion. He offered me a smile full of tenderness.

"So she told you," he said, his hands on my arms, his eyes trained on mine. "Finally."

And he didn't let go.

CHAPTER

42

After a while, I needed to get out of the apartment. It was evening now. I had meant to call Jackson that morning and hadn't responded to his latest messages. I felt fidgety, spent, now that I had finished Teta's story.

Jeddo was back at his usual post, watching the news with his glass of whiskey as a companion. Teta and I had filled the pot to the brim with *wara enab*, stacked like fat green fingers in concentric circles. It would take an hour or two, simmering on low heat, before the lemony meal was ready to eat.

I texted Phaedra, but she was in rehearsals at Juilliard and wouldn't be home for another hour at least. I laced my sneakers, took my phone, and bundled up in a fluffy, cream-colored coat. I welcomed the rush of cold air as soon as I stepped out of my building, pulling my hood over my hair and tightening the strings beneath my chin.

Hey . . . do you have ten minutes to talk? I texted Jackson as I walked up the stairs to the lobby of my building. I could hear strains of the cello from an apartment on the ground floor. It was time to face Jackson. I pushed open the heavy wooden front door and was surprised by the sharp chill in the air that greeted my face. I put my hands into my pockets for warmth. Jeddo was right. The evenings had been especially cold for late September.

I looked at my surroundings with fresh eyes. What must it have been like for a young Teta, a new mother, cut off from her family and the only life she knew, when she first arrived at this very spot here in Manhattan?

The Upper West Side is a nice place to settle, I thought, drinking in the quiet streets. *Calm, collegiate, cultured.*

I thought of summers, when the tenants of our building kept their windows wide open. Strains of cello music and elegant piano drills would fill the air. Now, as winter was getting closer and night was beginning to fall, it was quiet.

Yes! Give me two minutes and I'll call you, Jackson responded.

To the right, the street had a downward slope leading to Riverside Park, which I far preferred to Central Park. No camera crews filming TV shows at odd hours, no tour buses full of tourists with clunky cameras dangling from their necks. Riverside Park had the added bonus of overlooking the glistening Hudson River.

I walked there now, craving the peace of greenery and moving water nearby. When I caught sight of the river glittering in the moonlight, my eyes began to tear up again as I thought of Teta boarding a boat in Palestine, never to see Richard, her family, or her home again.

Is this part of why she sees sex as the ultimate sin? I wondered sadly, remembering her anxiety over the years every time a guy so much as looked in my direction. A note tucked in my lunchbox at school covered in crayon hearts, a boy's voice on our answering machine at home asking me to a school dance, lipstick and perfume found in my handbag . . . All had been met with nonnegotiable anger. A worry so serious that it would lead to irreparable damage.

My phone rang. Jackson's name flashed on the screen.

"Hey," I said. How original.

"I'm so glad you wanted to talk," he began. He sounded like he was walking, too. "I've been thinking about you. I get why you wanted to lay low. All okay?"

The sound of his voice raised so many mixed feelings in me. I softened at the thought of his voice murmuring in my ear when we kissed, steeled myself with the memory of the surprise in his eyes when I confronted him about the article.

"I think we're okay for now," I said. "I just . . . What were you guys thinking?"

He didn't speak for a beat. I had reached Riverside Park. It was windy, empty, and full of shadows, more like a setting for a murder mystery than a soothing place for me to come and find inner peace. It wasn't even that late—the sun had just set—but the recent shooting at the convenience store nearby came to mind. And wasn't there a man nicknamed the Riverside Reaper who'd been caught here a few years ago? I knew this was a relatively safe, calm area of Manhattan, but maybe walking alone in a park after dark wasn't my smartest idea. Instead of sitting on a bench like I had initially planned, I looped around and walked up the street back toward my building.

"I get it," he said. "I mean, it was . . . We honestly thought you would be happy. Katie and I care about you. But yes, I get you."

I nodded, though he couldn't see me. I wanted to talk to him openly, tell him about Teta's story, and work through my next steps with him. But I couldn't open up.

"Okay, well, I will see you in the office tomorrow, I guess," I said. "I'm working out a few—"

"Listen, Mia, we haven't had a chance to *talk* talk since that . . . kiss," he said. "You're always so reserved and it was amazing to see you come out of your shell like that. Was that, like, an impulse thing? Or . . . is there something there? Because, I've always, you know, kind of had a *thing* for you."

I couldn't help but smile. He was nervous. I had made him nervous! I reached my building and took a seat on the front steps, not ready to go back inside, too focused on the conversation to walk around aimlessly. I pulled my collar up to hide a smile. I pictured Jackson and me on those front steps, perhaps after a first real date, me holding a bouquet of fresh roses he had chosen for me, facing each other, nose to nose . . .

"Mia, are you still there?" came his voice. "Hello?"

"Yeah, sorry, I heard you," I said, clearing my throat. "We'll . . . talk. Because, yeah, you know, I always had a, uh, *thing* for you, too. But . . . work and . . . uh . . . expectations were in the way? I mean, you're seeing someone else now. Right? So there's that."

For two people who worked in media, we were having a hard time stringing together proper sentences. I held my breath, hoping he would tell me that she meant nothing, that I was everything. That he wouldn't let me down . . . the way Richard had never stepped up for Teta. The way Jeddo had always been there for Teta.

"There's . . . that," he repeated. My heart sank. Reading Teta's story had left my emotions brimming near the surface, and tears easily stung my eyes now. I blinked them away. At least we hadn't gone too far.

"Look, let's meet and talk it out," he suggested when I didn't respond. "Outside the office, a safe, neutral space. I'll explain. Maybe tomorrow right after work? I know you don't drink. Uh, chamomile tea, maybe?"

Was there a point? But maybe what I needed was closure. The kind that Teta never got. Maybe it would help me move on from this crush I'd carried around like a heavy stone in my bag. So, I agreed. We hung up.

I watched Phaedra walk up, chain necklaces jangling with each step, and stood to give her a hug. That's when I realized: Had Jackson finally asked me out?

CHAPTER

43

I sat on the creamy leather sofa in Phaedra's apartment, nursing a cup of peppermint tea. It was so much lovelier to admire the view of the Hudson River amid the soft glow of lamps in her penthouse than in the dark, empty park. She was sitting at the baby blue piano, trying to work out a melody.

I still couldn't get over the shock of Jeddo's role in my life.

"If Teta's story was a song, it would sound like this," she said after I had filled her in on the sad tale. She let her fingers run over a minor scale, playing a slow, haunting tune. I could feel a sense of loss and uncertainty, even in the rhythm.

"And if your budding romance with Jackson was a song, it would sound like this right now." She laughed, transitioning the song slowly to a bluesy major key, then letting her hands jump around with excitement.

"No, honestly, we're just meeting tomorrow to discuss what happened like two mature adults," I said. "He didn't say he's not with Adriana anymore. And I'm not going to be a side chick. So . . . we're just meeting to . . . stay friends?"

She shook her head and took a seat on the sofa next to me, legs curled beneath her.

"I don't buy it," she said in a singsong voice. "My takeaway of Teta's story is that love really does conquer all."

"What are you talking about?" I said, eyes wide. "Sleeping with Richard was the worst thing she could have done. She had one night of passion and it literally destroyed her life."

"No, it didn't. The war ripped them apart," Phaedra said, green eyes gleaming. "But I'm not talking about Richard. I'm talking about her true love: your Jeddo. He was there for her, he cared for her, he never left her. He waited until she was ready to love him back. God, it's so romantic."

I studied her wistful expression and then looked out the window. My eyes welled up again thinking of Jeddo's selfless kindness. Was that the moral of the story? That I shouldn't push so hard but let love wash over me with the right person? I thought of all those hours spent analyzing Jackson's social media posts, the way I wore red more often to the office because it was his favorite color, the chocolates I hid, hoping to see his crooked smile when he lingered near my desk with candy bars to add to my "goody drawer."

The churning in my stomach, just like indigestion, every time Adriana tagged him in a photo or her name came up.

Maybe I just needed to let go of hope and expectation . . . and just be open to what came next. Whether it was with Jackson or someone else. Maybe it was time to move on from Vibe Media. I wondered if Conor had opened my email. Would he respond right away? Or had I missed my shot with him? I breathed anxiously.

"Sorry I couldn't tell you more about the Almas lady in Dubai." Phaedra's voice brought me back to the conversation. "She's just known to be this sort of eccentric, wealthy patron of the arts who ran a theater at one point. Wears a lot of makeup. The Almas family owns a few jewelry stores, but I don't think she managed them herself."

I nodded, wondering about her life in Dubai. I had never even traveled out of the country, much less visited the Middle East. I had tried to google Layla and Zeina Almas, even Haytham Ramle, but couldn't find much about any of them online. Did they have children? Could I have cousins I didn't know about?

"Honestly, it's also the stuff about Teta's wedding night that was just . . . I'm still processing it all," I admitted, shifting gears, still thinking about Jackson with a ball of nerves in my stomach. "Do you think you could ever cheat on your partner? Or be with a married man?"

I thought of the man in the white hoodie who was too busy making out with Phaedra to introduce himself to me the night after her show at Smokey's. I wondered if she would open up to me, since I had shared so much of my strange family story with her.

"Define cheat," she said, mischievous eyes twinkling. "Honestly, I'm the jealous type. If my man so much as 'likes' another woman's photo on Facebook, I consider that a betrayal. So, no, I don't personally condone cheating, because then I would be the biggest hypocrite."

She was wearing a fuzzy lavender sweater that brought out the green in her eyes. Her black pleather leggings gave her look a trendy edge. I would never think to pair the two items of clothing together, I thought, glancing at my plain black top and jeans. She had an effortlessly stylish flair; even her tea cups were pink with gold trim.

"So what's the deal with that guy I saw you with?" I asked her. "You haven't mentioned much about him. Hoodie Man? You had said something about a woman not letting him out or something. Did I mishear that?"

Phaedra shook her head slowly.

"How rude of me—I didn't introduce you!" she said, putting her hands to her cheeks. "Joshua is the most talented music producer. Meeting him helped me evolve my musical style, you know, move away from the classical stuff and try to be a little edgy. We met at a concert when I visited New York months ago to get ready for my big move here, find an apartment. Instead, I found him."

"He seems to really like you," I said when she didn't elaborate on his secret family.

"And no, he's not married or anything. I wouldn't do that!" she said with a laugh, rolling another cigarette. "It took me years with one guy to lose my virginity. Clearly I don't get into relationships casually. The woman you heard me talking about was his mother."

"His mother?" I asked. "What's she got to do with it? He lives with his mom?"

I cocked my head to one side, wondering if she was dating a penniless artist who was after her money. I watched her light the cigarette and take a slow drag before setting it down on an ashtray on the wooden coffee table. Was Phaedra actually naive?

"So, here's the backstory: he produced a few tracks that went really big for Rihanna when she first started her career. Her team has been amazing with royalties," Phaedra said, piling her hair up into a topknot. "But Joshua's mom is losing her memory a little, acting out a lot. Doctors think it's early onset Alzheimer's. Stress from losing her husband, Joshua's father, a few years ago, maybe. Whatever it is, she is really demanding of his time. And money. He tried to get her the best doctors, but she's been going downhill."

She explained that Joshua had hired a private nurse to look after his mother, but she was always after him to do little things: fix the remote, put her feet up. She'd shout at him belligerently when she failed to read a clock or couldn't recognize the doorman they'd had for twenty years. As an only child, he felt it his complete duty to take care of her.

"He's truly wonderful with her, but . . . it's a lot. On him, on our relationship, on the future," she said. "Guess it makes it all that much sweeter when he can get away for some alone time with me. I don't want to complain. I imagine him taking care of me like that in my old age. I just miss him all the time."

Every person in my life seemed to be a walking Love Unfiltered column. I put my hand over hers and leaned over to give her a hug. She promised to share a song she and Joshua had written together with me, perhaps to include as an exclusive audio release along with my profile of her.

With an air-kiss goodbye, I got up to see if the *wara enab* was ready for me to devour. All these unfulfilled love stories were making me hungry.

CHAPTER

44

I felt wired as I walked into the office after a fitful night's sleep. Despite how delicious the stacked lemony *wara enab* rolls had tasted last night, I couldn't bring myself to eat a full dinner, and I had skipped breakfast this morning. My stomach always felt upset when I was stressed; some people ate junk food, but I just over-caffeinated. Now, with coffee pumping freely through my veins thanks to an extra espresso shot, I felt like I should have considered a morning run to diffuse some of my jittery energy.

I arrived early on purpose, hoping to avoid a scrum of concerned well-wishers like last time. Ivory was already at reception in a lime-green dress with matching eyeliner. She asked if I was feeling better and then motioned to my desk, where a small stack of letters lay waiting for me. Was this an influx of handwritten Love Unfiltered columns? Thanks to my newfound social media popularity, I had expected more interest than usual—but my desk was stacked with colorful envelopes.

And there were two chocolate bars waiting.

I sat down, looking at the empty seats around me and listening to the hum of a distant printer coming to life. The gray cubicles were overshadowed by colorful layouts of articles tacked onto the walls. The lights were still off in Jackson's and Davie's offices, but Isabel's monitor was on and I could see a red jacket slung on the back of her tan Herman Miller chair.

I switched on my computer, wondering how to approach my first postwar chat with Katie. We needed to talk about her resignation letter. She shouldn't lose a job she loved because of this mistake. Was the lesson here, perhaps, that I was the one in the wrong line of work if her career at Vibe meant enough to her to take it this far? To sacrifice our friendship?

"Mia, you're here," came Isabel's voice, full of warmth. "I heard about everything. I set up a meeting with legal for you. You've met Divya, right? How are you doing?"

I swiveled in my seat to face her, taking in her dark hair, which was in a tight, low bun. She had the straight-backed posture of a ballerina. She was wearing a navy blue pantsuit accented with gold bracelets and earrings. She moved the pile of letters aside with a perfectly manicured hand and leaned against my desk, clasping her hands and giving me her full attention.

"We're all okay," I said, nodding. "It's just this strange part of me that I always felt I needed to protect, to hide, to overcompensate for . . . I don't know. I didn't want to be judged. I mean, I'm American and I have rights, but my grandparents don't. So I just focused on keeping my head down, working hard, and being a perfectionist who doesn't . . . leave room for any mistakes."

She smiled and patted my shoulder.

"You can't control everything, Mia, much less people's reactions," she said softly. "And you're doing a great job. Just cut yourself some slack. Katie told me about that musician you were planning to profile for *The Culturalist*—that's exactly the type of content we need to elevate our online game. Keep it up and that new reporter opening could be yours."

After letting me know that her door was open if I ever wanted to talk, she knocked on my desk once, signaling the end of our conversation, and walked away. Rather than feeling elated, I felt a big responsibility to define the next steps of my career, potentially at the cost of Katie's. And face Divya in a stiff legal meeting later.

Avoiding the uncharacteristic flood of emails I'd found in my inbox, I took an envelope addressed to me from the top of the pile. I found a letter from a young girl in Brooklyn decorated with sparkly star stickers.

> *Dear Miss Mia Almas,*
>
> *I am thirteen. I hate it when my mom sends these really smelly kofta sandwiches in my lunch box to school. She says I should be happy I have food, but most days I just give it to the homeless man near my bus stop. He sleeps next to a vegan coffee shop and he is happy to eat these meat sandwiches, even in the morning. He says they are delicious.*
>
> *When I read about you in* The Culturalist, *it made me feel better. My mom said I should think about becoming a doctor or a banker when I grow up, but I like what you do better. I don't know what a banker does exactly, but my doctor definitely never laughs. I like that you make people laugh.*
>
> *I have boring brown hair and glasses, so I don't want to be an actress when I grow up, like Allyson in my class. She has the shiniest blond hair, like in a shampoo ad. But maybe I can be funny like you. Or work at a cool place like Vibe Media. Thanks to you, I am kind of proud of being the Arab girl in class with the smelly sandwiches. I ate it for the first time today at school and the homeless guy was right—it is delicious.*

Thank you for making me feel good. I hope you will be my friend.

Love,

Safa from Brooklyn via Syria

My eyes welled up. This young girl had gone out of her way to send a letter through the mail to my place of work, hoping it would reach me. I felt a warm glow, running my hand over the stack of about ten other envelopes. The next letter came from a PhD student working on a thesis about third-culture kids, while another was from a teacher inviting me to speak to her students. Several others were from comedy clubs inviting me to perform. In my fifteen minutes of fame, I had received fan mail!

People began to arrive at their desks, saying hello to me and chattering about the unexpectedly cold weather the night before. It felt good to have a normal morning. Now I just needed to survive my conversations with Katie and Jackson.

His name popped into my mind just as he walked in. His curls framed his lovely face; his eyelashes reached all the way up to his eyebrows. No suit and red tie today, just a casual blue sweater. His brown eyes lit up when they settled on me. My heart jumped into my throat, and I could feel my face start to flush.

"Welcome back, Mia. Great to see you. We're still on for later, yeah?" he asked as he walked past. "Right after work?"

I nodded, still feeling emotional from the letters and not trusting my voice. I breathed in the scent of his aftershave and felt the hairs on the nape of my neck rise as he patted my back.

"Good to have you back, Tina Fey," he said. "Isabel set up a meeting with Divya for you later. She's going to be a big help, I think."

Bubbles of nerves and excitement rose up in me at this new inside joke between us.

"Hey, uh, Jackson," I called out to him, rising out of my seat slightly. "Katie is coming in today, right? She told me she resigned, but we really need to talk about it."

"She should, yeah—she has a two-week notice period," he said, nodding slowly and looking at the floor. "Text her. She will be happy to hear from you."

It was time to make peace. I'd picked up my phone to text her when I saw an unknown number calling. I walked briskly into the conference room where I had had the confrontation with Katie and Jackson just days ago. It felt like a lifetime.

"Hello? This is Mia," I said.

"Hi, hello, Mia, good morning to you," came a rich, accented voice. "This is Conor Broderick. From Jordan B. Brown's team."

I listened to his mellifluous voice, telling me how much his team admired the quality of my jokes and my ambitions. Several had seen me perform in the West Village. He had the same accent as Patrick Ryan, an Irish lilt that made words dance as he spoke. I couldn't sit—I stood next to the window, looking out at New York City sprawling beneath me, wanting to shout with excitement.

"I watched your video and understand that you didn't make it to the audition. I shared the video with my team, and they are all dying to meet you," he said. "Are you free to come in later this afternoon?"

I confirmed that I could escape the office early to meet his team at four thirty and hung up, allowing myself a small victory dance before looking up to see if anyone had caught me.

This meant I had to slightly alter my after-work plans with Jackson.

I was floating toward the glass door of the conference room, ready to head to his office to explain, when I locked eyes with Katie.

CHAPTER

45

I motioned for Katie to come into the conference room. Another messy confrontation was unlikely, but the office was starting to fill up, and I could see Mail Room Andy making his rounds. He had emailed me the opening pages of his sitcom script, and I hadn't read it yet. In any case, I preferred to have this talk with Katie in a private area, without an audience.

She put one finger up, telling me she needed a minute. I watched her slowly remove her black biker jacket and place it on the back of her chair. She nodded hello to Beth and Natalia from ad sales, then switched on her monitor. She was avoiding eye contact with me, which told me she was nervous. I watched her take a deep breath, fluff up her hair, then walk toward the conference room.

She was wearing an olive-green long-sleeve top with tailored black pants, which looked beautiful on her petite silhouette. But it was an unusually tame outfit for her.

"No metal earrings? No pink eyeliner?" I asked her as she walked in. "You are not okay."

She broke into an awkward laugh. She sank into a chair and swiveled around, covering her face with her hands.

"My head's a mess. I need to look for a new job. And I hate that I hurt you," she said, peeking through her fingers to meet my eyes. "I really am sorry."

I pulled a hand away from her face and held it.

"Katie, what you did to me was not cool," I said. "And I'm trying hard to work things out, but I think your resignation was premature."

"So you're . . . You would be okay with us working together still?" she said, big brown eyes growing moist. "You don't hate me?"

"You'll have to earn back my friendship. I am easily bribed with chocolate or coffee," I said with a theatrical shrug. "But seriously, Katie, this shouldn't totally derail your career. It's a mistake. People make them. Even though you did totally throw me under the bus."

She looked down at her hands. When she spoke, her voice was small and soft.

"I had a niggling feeling that I should talk to you about the article before it went live," she said. "But my intentions were honestly good. I just wanted to give you some good press. You're a great comedian. Better than that Puerto Rican kid with the braces who went on before you. Better than most people I see on TV, actually. For real."

I smiled and asked her to come with me to talk to Jackson. We needed to sort out her notice period, and I needed to break it to him that I might be a little late to our meeting-slash-date. Perhaps it would be prudent to push my meeting with Divya the lawyer to tomorrow, as well. I had to focus all my efforts today on putting my game face on to dazzle Conor Broderick and his team of merry comedy writers.

CHAPTER

46

I stood in front of 30 Rockefeller Plaza, nervously zipping and unzipping my jacket. Up and down, up and down. I was fifteen minutes early. I never came to this part of the city in the afternoon, when midtown was flooded with tourists. I stared at the red-and-blue neon NBC Studios sign in front of the tall, gray building. I pictured David Letterman and other famous hosts striding in at dawn to get their makeup done and rehearse their opening monologues for their talk shows.

And here I was in plain jeans and a tight braid.

Around me, groups jostled one another along the sidewalk, moving in big waves, bumping into me regularly. I listened to snippets of conversations in at least four different languages. A smiley Chinese couple wanted me to take their photo. They posed in front of the famous building, both holding small cartons full of steaming seasoned rice and chicken from the Halal Guys food cart a few blocks down.

When I handed back the camera, they asked me if I was a

New Yorker. When I nodded yes, they asked if I had ever seen any celebrities standing in this very spot. Part of me wanted to run around the corner to Magnolia Bakery and hide in the line of tourists waiting an hour to order a pink cupcake exactly like the one Carrie Bradshaw had on *Sex and the City*.

Zipper. Up and down, up and down.

My phone vibrated in my pocket.

You got this, read a text from Katie. *Let me know how it goes.*

I identified myself to the security guard in front of the building, who took my ID and checked me in at the reception desk.

"Right this way, Miss Almas," he said, handing me a white badge. I pressed it against a glass barrier that parted ways to let me through. He pushed an elevator button for me and smiled.

You got this, I repeated to myself, glancing at a young woman who was in the elevator with me. She was holding two cups of coffee and muttering to herself about having forgotten the sugar packets again.

I arrived at another reception desk in a stark, white lobby. The receptionist took me to a conference room not unlike our own at Vibe. I wasn't sure what to expect at a fancy TV studio; perhaps receptionists who all dressed exactly alike in tailored black dresses, walking past flashing screens in every hallway.

This just looked like a normal office, except for the neon sign behind the reception desk that read: *The Jordan B. Brown Show*. I felt a nervous thrill as my eyes roamed over the bright letters, again and again. I chose a chair at the big table close to the door, drinking in the magnificent view of New York spread out before me. From this vantage point, I could see the greenery of Central Park stretching out beyond the tops of skyscrapers.

"Mia, welcome," Conor said as he opened the conference room door. He was taller than I'd expected. I stood up to shake his hand as he introduced me to seven other people who filed in one by one after him. Each one took a seat around the big table.

"Please don't quiz me on all your names," I said, clearing my throat. "Apparently, my nerves also make it harder for me to speak in English right now. Hi, nerves."

Chuckles rippled through the room.

"See, I told you she was funny," Conor said.

"I actually saw you perform at that little comedy club in the West Village years ago," said a woman with red lipstick and pigtails. "Knew you looked familiar when Conor showed us the video you sent in. Great work."

"It was the bomb," said a man with an orange-and-black New York Knicks cap, twirling a pen in his hands and appraising me. "You are hilarious. Good setups, spot-on delivery. We need that fresh vibe here, man. Some of Jordan's openers are feeling stale, a little too safe. And that's on us."

Conor explained that this was his team of writers who worked on comedy material for Jordan B. Brown, planning funny bits with celebrities and polishing his opening monologues. I felt my stomach fizz with excitement, taking in his big smile and black-rimmed glasses.

"We all know why you're here, but I'm going to just replay the final few minutes of your video for Nancy, who was on holiday up until five minutes ago," said Conor playfully, pressing a button that brought a TV screen on the wall to life.

An Asian American woman, presumably Nancy, started telling Conor off for "hating on" her while she was "sipping well-deserved cocktails in Mexico," but I couldn't focus on the conversation around me. My eyes were fixated on the TV screen, where my giant face smiled back at me.

Conor pressed play.

"So, that was a short example of the type of comedy I perform," Video Mia said, my voice sounding much more confident than I currently felt. "But the real reason I wanted to share this video is to tell you that a one-off gig would obviously be an amazing opportunity for me, but you should consider hiring me as a comedy writer on your team. I think I've seen every single episode of Jordan B. Brown's show—I watch it regularly on my subway commute. I'm a great team player, an Ivy League graduate who appreciates toilet humor, and I'm currently a fact-checker at Vibe Media. I'm a closeted comedian ready to come out."

The video version of me went on to describe how many companies talk about diversity, but real change only happens with actionable steps. Adding an Arab American, female voice to their mix would bring a cultural sensitivity check and a fresh perspective to their stellar team. I hid my face in my hands when I watched myself list a few times when Jordan B. Brown had said plainly inappropriate or inaccurate things on national television.

"Don't get me wrong, this kind of thing happens all the time when it comes to non-white communities," Confident Video Mia said as I cringed. "I focused my master's thesis at the Columbia Journalism School on this. If you hire me, I promise to make you laugh and make you proud."

The video ended with me smiling and giving a cheesy thumbs-up.

Conor started clapping.

What ensued was a forty-five-minute group interview, with each person around the table taking turns asking my opinion on comedy sketches they were currently working on, trends in media, the type of pieces I fact-checked at Vibe Media, and why I would consider leaving my job.

After nearly an hour, I found myself shaking hands with Conor.

"Our legal team will email you the contract," he said at the end. "You very obviously got the job. It's not all fun and games, but there is a lot of that. This is all conditional on you meeting Jordan, the man himself, next, but he went wild for your video, so I think you're good. Welcome to the team!"

The next few minutes were a blur, a medley of blushing and congratulations and pats on the back. I walked on air out of the conference room. I somehow coherently bid goodbye to the receptionist and made my way down the elevator like a normal person having a normal day. Once I got outside, back within the anonymous throng of the swelling crowd, I shrieked with delight and danced a little jig on the sidewalk. Nobody batted an eye.

After wringing my hands to work off some of the excess energy, I shakily pulled out my phone. I didn't know whom to call first: Teta, Katie, Phaedra, Jackson? I found an email from the Jordan B. Brown legal team with a contract already in my inbox.

I had done it.

CHAPTER
47

I floated along with the crowd, like a leaf carried by water, until I stumbled upon a café a block or so away. It was a perfectly neutral place to meet Jackson. Perhaps the tourists were too busy wading through the fancy retail stores on Fifth Avenue nearby, taking photos at Bergdorf's and that fountain in front of the Plaza Hotel that featured in every romantic comedy, to bother with this modest little spot today. It was deliciously empty.

After texting Jackson the exact address, I estimated I had about ten minutes to myself to absorb what had just happened. This was a life-changing career moment. I sank onto a hard wooden seat at the coffee bar facing the window, watching the faces come and go outside.

Dad, there's nothing more I want right now than to tell you all about this, I thought, looking up at the sky. I vowed to rewatch our favorite Eddie Murphy comedy special, *Delirious*, at home later that night in tribute.

My phone in my hands, I was tempted to text Phaedra and

Katie with the news. But I wanted to be alert when Jackson arrived. Then my eyes settled on a man with a familiar walk in the crowd outside. Jackson's curls came into view, his tall frame towering above a group of young Asian students wearing cat ears. He was wearing a dark brown coat that brought out the warm tones in his eyes. He smiled through the window when he caught my eye.

"Random cafe in midtown? Okay," he said, giving me a hug. "This is a strange choice. What are we doing here, Mia? Second-hand bookstore nearby?"

We made small talk, standing in line together to get the promised chamomile tea. I was consciously aware of our elbows bumping as we chatted. He threw a giant chocolate chip cookie in with our order at the last minute.

"It's no Caprice chocolate stick, but it will do," he said, carrying a tray back to our window seat. He cleared his throat, put a hand over mine, and gave me his "serious talk" face, which I had seen in countless editorial meetings.

"So, look, let me talk about work first, because—"

"Jackson, I'm quitting," I blurted. "Vibe, I mean. My job. I—"

"Mia, what now?" he said, pulling back. "Are you seriously leaving because of the article? Or because of me? I—"

I put a hand up to stop him. We were both talking over each other. An aimless jazz tune was playing softly in the background, and a man took a seat in a booth nearby, pulling out his laptop. I took a deep breath and started over.

"Jackson, I actually have to thank Katie for writing the article, because I was scouted by Jordan B. Brown's comedy writing team," I said, more slowly this time. "It's a dream job for me. I get to be funny every day and put my fact-checking expertise to good use."

I described to him the surreal meeting I had just come from. I told him about the video I had submitted that the team had played of me on a big screen in a conference room, about meeting

Conor and wondering if he was the one who'd sent me the note at the comedy club, about the expansive view of Central Park from their office in 30 Rock, about my father's love of comedy.

As I talked, he shook his head in disbelief, his hand covering his mouth. The chocolate chip cookie lay untouched on the red tray between us. I became increasingly aware of the clean scent of his aftershave, his knee grazing mine as we sat facing each other on stools, the perfect curl that fell above his right eye. I actively resisted leaning over and brushing it away. The thought of my fingertips tracing his face, his jawline, his lips, made me catch my breath. I stopped talking for a beat, my mind racing back to our kiss in the alley. I paused to gather my thoughts and let him absorb the new information.

"I'm babbling because I'm excited and I'm nervous that you're here," I admitted when he didn't speak, pulling the plastic lid off my cup of chamomile tea. Steam rose up between us.

His hand found its way to my knee. His other hand moved away from his mouth, revealing a flashy smile. Boss Man Jackson was softening.

"I'm so, so proud of you," he said. "And in awe of you. It's a smart move, if I'm honest. It's good timing with what's been going on at work."

He told me that Vibe was worried I would file a lawsuit; the company couldn't afford any scandals when it was desperately trying to stay afloat in the cutthroat digital landscape and attract fresh investment. In fact, Divya had been appointed to help me enlist an immigration lawyer to formally represent my grandparents—on the company dime. It was my turn to shake my head in disbelief.

"I mean, I honestly wouldn't know how to even go about suing a major company," I said. "But having a lawyer for my grandparents, that really could make a difference."

For Teta and Jeddo, it had been a lifetime of cash earned under the table, of sending me off to school with neighbors and never attending parent-teacher conferences growing up, of never leaving the country. The path to getting legal status was still opaque and difficult; even with all my fact-checking prowess. The lawyers who signed up to take cases on a pro bono basis had never lasted long enough to improve my grandparents' situation.

Jackson said Divya would explain everything. He admitted he had played a big role in securing her help. I listened to his rich voice, his eyes seeking reassurance in mine. He chewed on his bottom lip, waiting for my reaction.

So he does care. My heart soared.

We were both dancing around the subject of the kiss. We had talked about everything else: work, comedy, my grandparents, the weather. Were we going to address it? Should I take courage from Teta's story?

Love conquers all, I thought, giving myself a pep talk. *If it's meant to be, it will be. And if not . . . I'll find my way. Just like Teta and Jeddo.*

I watched him rub the back of his neck, his eyes growing a little hooded. I watched his face as I slowly undid my tight braid and ran a hand through my free curls.

"I'll miss having you around, though," he said, pulling on one of my curls like it was a spring. "No more rooftop heart-to-hearts."

"It really will be so weird not to see you every day," I blurted, trying to warm up to the subject of the kiss but realizing it sounded more romantic when I articulated this feeling out loud to him. My face growing warm, I took another sip of the chamomile tea, watching him through my eyelashes. He smiled and broke off a chunk of the chocolate chip cookie, bringing it to my lips. The chocolate was warm and sweet in my mouth.

"And look, I'm sorry about kissing you," I said finally. "Because I don't want to get in the way of you and Adriana if she makes you happy. It's not right."

"Adriana, right," he said. "She's a wonderful person. But . . . she's not you. I mean, look at me, Mia. I put chocolates every day on your damn desk for a year. I just never knew where you stood. Then Adriana came into the picture and she was so nice and so into me. It felt good, easy. We were both in the Big Brothers Big Sisters program. I tried it out. But I've had a thing for you for years, Mia. You must know that. That kiss was . . . everything."

I stared at him, unblinking. My heart began to thud.

"You just always seemed closed off somehow, and I knew that if something started between us, it had to be real, not like a fling, you know?" he said. "When you stopped answering my calls after our kiss, I felt like I had lost you, and it scared the hell out of me. I told Adriana that she and I are . . . over."

I nodded, holding my breath.

"Because you need time to figure out what you want?" I asked.

Because, despite the butterflies, I finally knew exactly what I wanted. I wanted to be open to whatever it was that felt like it was starting between us—even if I got hurt. I was done romanticizing other people's love stories. I was ready for my own to start.

"Well, I'm thinking, since we don't work together anymore and we're both available and really good-looking . . . does this mean I can finally ask you out on a proper date?" he said, his eyes teasing me. "Dinner, flowers, the Jackson special?"

I nodded, too afraid that any response I had would come across as cheesy or too eager or too dismissive. I had come here mentally prepared for an awkward hug and a formal handshake. Was this really happening?

"Yes," I said, suddenly feeling at peace. "Just, let's . . . take it slow. I might have worked on Love Unfiltered columns for years, but I want to get it right for myself."

Yes, Mia, you're going to be okay and you are worthy of love, my heart sang in cheesy affirmation.

"You've got cookie crumbs all over your mouth," he said, nodding and leaning in closer.

He put a hand up to my neck, his fingers reaching into my hair, and pulled my face so that it was inches away from his. With his thumb, he traced my lips in a slow circle. I held his gaze, scarcely remembering to breathe. Then, in front of all of Manhattan, in a public café, Jackson kissed me.

And I let him.

CHAPTER

48

Five months later
February 2012

The snowfall was silent but full of energy. Jackson and I had
arrived to Central Park early to set up a dozen white wooden
chairs. We took turns unfolding and nestling them in the crunchy
snow, six on one side and six on the other, creating an aisle down
the middle. I pulled my big beige coat tighter around me, lifting
my face up to the sky to greet a snowflake. It landed on my nose.

"Okay, check this out," said Jackson. I turned to face him, my
eyes lighting up in delight. He had strung up fairy lights above
the very spot that would serve as a makeshift altar in front of the
seats. I shook my head at the beauty of the scene before me: a wild
olive grove in the heart of snowy Central Park, all dressed up in
white and sparkling with light.

The fact-checker in me had gone to great lengths to find a single olive tree in a park in New York fit for a couple to exchange

vows. What I found, instead, was a grove of at least sixty olive trees in Manhattan's biggest park. No one was sure how they got there; a park ranger I spoke to suggested that a single tree was planted and birds then spread the olive pits in the surrounding area, to create this wild grove over the years. With a simple phone call and a twenty-five-dollar park permit purchased online, a ceremony could take place under the welcoming arms of the olive tree branches.

It was perfect.

My Love Unfiltered columns had secured in me a confidence that fairy tales did happen in real life sometimes—and these were the moments worth celebrating. The sun would set soon, but for now the brightness of the sunshine filtered through the snow-laden branches to create speckled fanfare all around us. I breathed in the cold air and went to stand near Jackson, who had an expensive-looking camera set up on a tripod near the altar.

"There's another one over there, to get another angle," he said excitedly, pointing to the back of the chairs. I watched plumes of his breath in the cold and wondered if we were crazy to host this ceremony outdoors.

Soon, guests arrived. The Dominicans who lived next door walked up, waving hello and holding a bouquet of flowers and their gurgling baby. They took a seat next to Ghada and two other women I recognized from Teta's book club. I watched them take their phones out to record videos of the dreamy scene around them. Divya was there with her wife, a beautiful, blue-eyed British woman named Allison who worked in book publishing. They all wore warm coats in white, off-white, and beige, as requested.

"Should we start?" Phaedra whispered to me. She was wearing opaque white tights with sparkles and a shiny white jacket that looked like a spacesuit. Her blond hair was in a tight, high chignon dusted with snowflakes. Heart thudding, I nodded, and she went to stand near Hadi.

Hadi picked up his violin and began to play a mellow tune.

Phaedra had invited several of her Juilliard students to accompany her today, and as Hadi's melody progressed, a bass, a small hand *tablah* drum, and an airy clarinet came to life in an upbeat song. The friends gathered in the audience began to clap to the beat.

A Pakistani imam I had found in a downtown mosque had agreed to conduct this unorthodox ceremony. Wearing a traditional hat and dressed in a heavy white coat, he took his spot at the altar and give me a thumbs-up. He opened the Quran and looked expectantly down the aisle.

There, in a beautiful white embroidered Palestinian *thob*, stood my grandmother. I had a feeling she couldn't feel the cold with all the adrenaline pulsing through her. The freshness of the snow around her gave her an angelic glow and added a rosy tint to her cheeks. Her olive-green eyes were moist as she took in the close friends who had gathered to celebrate her today, smiling at Divya with a deep, appreciative nod of her head.

Thanks to Divya's connections and persistence, Teta now had an official birth certificate and other necessary documents to begin the long, winding road to legal status along with my grandfather. Divya's research had also led to the discovery that Haytham Ramle had passed away years ago—meaning my grandmother could officially remarry.

Divya's discovery team also found a newspaper clipping of Tamer, Haytham Ramle's son, standing with his young bride and his mother, Ismat. Her fiery red hair matched a fiery smile in the color photo, the trio standing in front of an Almas store, one of many she personally managed. After Haytham Ramle's passing, his inheritance had gone mainly to his son, because he and Layla had had no children, putting Ismat back in power.

Rumor had it that Layla Almas was now a batty older woman who wore a dirty mink coat and a large pair of diamond studs. She was often seen talking to herself in the streets while without shoes, and lived in a small studio apartment on a meager stipend.

While the theater crowd knew her by her chosen stage name, Layla, legally she still went by the name Zeina.

Teta had to decide whether to sort out the identity issues with her sister while pursuing legal status in her home in New York. It wasn't going to be easy, and it would take time, but Divya's team had paved the way to allow for this moment to happen.

Teta took slow steps toward the altar in time with the music. She didn't seem nervous; in fact, she shook her shoulders every now and then to the beat and winked, beaming when she caught my eye.

She had initially resisted the idea of a wedding, but I could tell she was living out a fantasy. The heartbreak of never getting closure when Richard was sucked out of her life, the disappointment that her only wedding was a sham marriage to an older man, losing her only son in a horrific incident that left an entire nation in mourning . . . Again and again, Teta had been cheated out of a chance to celebrate love.

So, one Saturday morning, partly inspired by Marcela from our favorite telenovela, who had an extravagant wedding to her fourth husband (the leader of a drug cartel), Teta simply said she changed her mind.

And now here she was in a bridal white *thob*, walking down the aisle, ready to face Jeddo.

I looked at my grandfather, his eyes red-rimmed and brimming with tears. I had watched him change his shirt three times that morning, settling on his only light gray suit that he now wore beneath a beige coat. He stood with his hands clasped in front of his body, looking shyly at the people sitting before him, their eyes trailing Teta's walk as snow fell all around her.

When she took her place next to him beneath the canopy of olive branches strung with fairy lights, he took her hand in both of his and patted it. I could see they were both shaking a little. The music came to a graceful pause as the imam cleared his throat and began to recite the *Al-Fatiha* prayer.

"I wish Yousef was here to see this," I heard Teta whisper.

"Look around you," Jeddo said, his voice thick with emotion, pointing to the snowfall. "He's here."

My eyes filled with tears as I watched them cling to each other while the imam spoke words about a man honoring his wife. This couple before him had already practiced marriage for decades: he had taken care of her when she was pregnant and penniless; they had raised a child and then a grandchild together under the most trying of circumstances. This felt like a natural affirmation rather than a fresh start. And if anyone deserved a moment perfectly tied up in a ribbon, it was them.

A Love Unfiltered column brought to life.

I looked at Jackson, who shifted the angle on the main camera slightly to zoom in on Teta's and Jeddo's faces. I should have known that a man who loved chocolate as much as he did would turn out to be a hopeless romantic.

"That Arabic music is awesome. Will they play it again? And do you guys break glass or jump over a broom or anything?" he whispered to me. "I don't want to miss an important bit."

"You're the important bit," I said.

I gave him a soft kiss on the cheek and leaned my head against his shoulder. Then the imam pronounced Teta and Jeddo officially man and wife. For the first time, perhaps ever, I watched my grandfather hold my grandmother's face in his hands in a rush of affection. He took his time, his eyes searching hers, both in disbelief at the situation. Forehead to forehead, they whispered words to each other. It was almost as if they had forgotten the rest of us were there, shivering but warm inside. The band waited to play, Phaedra's eyes flicking to mine for a cue. Then, in front of family and friends and a party of olive trees, Jeddo gave Teta the softest of kisses on the lips as snow danced all around them.

And she let him.

EPILOGUE

After years of performing stand-up comedy, and now working in the industry as a comedy writer, I was surprised to feel a fresh flutter of nerves. I sat in a dark stairwell near the stage, listening to bursts of laughter from the audience watching the current performer. My heart pounded as I waited for my name to be called.

I avoided peeking through the curtain, knowing Jackson was sitting there in the front row. Katie planned to make an appearance, while Phaedra and Hadi had shifted their air-tight Juilliard schedules around just to watch me perform. Even Conor and a few people from my new job had promised to drop by to support me. Knowing that the crowd tonight was sprinkled with familiar faces somehow made the knot in my stomach tighter. It was much easier to be funny with a faceless crowd of strangers in the audience than to speak in front of people I cared about.

I took a deep, meditative breath—in through the nose and out through the mouth—to calm my mind. I ran a hand down my dark jeans, tucked into the over-the-knee black leather boots I had borrowed from Phaedra. I touched my curls, then checked to see that my hoop earrings were still fastened in place. I pressed my lips together a few times, tasting my red berry-flavored lipstick. It wasn't my favorite one, but it matched my red tank top.

There had been whispers backstage of someone famous being slated to perform at the end of the show. That made me feel even more terrified. Could Eddie Murphy himself be waiting in the wings, pacing somewhere in the dark like me? I shoved the thought out of my mind, standing up to do a slow jog in place to get rid of excess nervous energy. Breathing quietly in the dark wasn't working out for me.

"Next up, we have a fresh voice serving up some special charm," boomed the emcee. "Everyone, please welcome Mia Almas!"

I put on a wide smile, squared my shoulders, and walked sideways onto the bright stage. I greeted the audience while adjusting the microphone slightly lower.

"Was the person onstage before me standing on a stool?" I started, tightening the clasp on the stand. "I'm wearing my tallest boots and I still need to bring this thing down."

Chuckles broke out through the audience as I took a moment to recalibrate. My eyes hadn't adjusted to the glare of the spotlight yet, but when I glanced over my shoulder, I felt a rush of pride at the sign behind me. In colorful, funky block letters, *Comedy Cellar* was written in an illuminated stained-glass sign sign hanging on the redbrick wall.

We made it, Dad, I thought silently. I felt a sense of peace wash over me, like I was finally in the exact spot I was meant to be.

Clearing my throat, I began.

"So, I'm Palestinian American . . . which should be an oxymoron," I said, my eyes washing over the sea of faces in the underground space. "I always feel like I have a big . . . inner, uh, conflict."

A girl snickered in the back. A soft ripple of laughter began to spread through the room.

"It's complicated, it really is. But that's the beautiful thing about living in New York: I found a boy who is *even more* complicated than me. My boyfriend is a Black Jew. Yep. So now I seem 'normal' by comparison. He's actually got a Colombian dad, too, so he's half Latino, half Black. And one hundred percent sexy. We can be complicated together. God bless America."

I smiled at the catcalls, my eyebrows raised in appreciation at a particularly loud meow from someone in the back row.

"We're both misfits. I grew up on the Upper West Side. He grew up in this foreign, magical place called Jamaica . . . Queens. And together, we can tell you where New York's finest kosher spots are across all the five boroughs," I said. "It turns out, that's the one thing that unites Blacks, Jews, Arabs, and Latinos: good food. It unites all of us, right? We may not all eat pig, but we can definitely all eat *like* pigs."

Clapping and hooting erupted from different areas of the audience. Oinking sounds came from a group of men to my right with large, frozen beer mugs on their tables. If I kept this up, I would turn the Comedy Cellar into a barnyard and never be invited back.

"Honestly, have you been to an 'ethnically diverse' wedding buffet? The wedding event packages come with an Alka-Seltzer station and an ambulance on standby," I said, eyebrows raised, patting my stomach.

"Like, seriously, are you going to eat all that?" I asked a man in the front row who had a burger and a separate basket of French fries on his table. "Sharing is caring in every culture, you know."

He leaned forward to offer his basket, and I took two golden, crispy fries, still warm to the touch, and smiled appreciatively.

"My new best friend, ladies and gentleman," I said as the crowd clapped for French Fry Man. "See? We're all easily bought with good food. Hey, just imagine what I would do for a whole basket of fries."

I wiggled my eyebrows and did a little hip shake. I turned my back to the audience, took two steps, then glanced over my shoulder and held the microphone close to my lips.

"Come find me after the show," I whispered loudly, winking at French Fry Man. The crowd whooped loudly with pleasure.

I smiled, drinking it all in. I could see Jackson now, sitting at a small table right up front in the crowded, staggered room. He had thrown his head back in full-fledged laughter, banging one hand repeatedly on the table. He made me so happy that I was tempted to abandon my set and run off with him. If I stretched my leg out and crouched down a little, I could touch his nose with the tip of my boot.

"No, but seriously, I already have a wonderful, kosher Black boyfriend. And where else in the world could a love like ours flourish?" I went on, my voice softer. I wiped the salt on my fingers on my jeans as I spoke. "Here, I get to have my halal hot dog and eat it, too. Wait, that sounded much dirtier than intended."

Unrestrained laughter broke out in the room, and the hooting grew more energized. I wasn't used to performing the later evening slots and wondered whether my comedy was bolder or if the crowd was just drunker. Perhaps both.

"Okay, settle down, you animals," I said. "Let me make it PC, reel it back in for you. My boyfriend actually met my very traditional grandparents. And he was smart. He didn't bring a sad little orchid or chocolates. No bottle of wine. No. My man brought some halal steaks. By the end of the evening, he and my grandfather were sending each other memes."

Amid the laughter, happy memories surfaced of weekend barbecues on our building's rooftop. The first few meetings between Jackson and my grandparents were expectedly awkward and stiff, full of polite small talk and furtive glances. But the walls melted as they spent months getting to know each other, particularly after my grandparents' wedding ceremony in the snow. Soon, when spring brought sunny weather back, hazy afternoons became a regular fixture of our lives. A warm feeling rose up in me at the thought of Jackson and my grandfather standing side by side in badly fitting aprons, grilling meat skewers on crisp Sundays on the roof, looking out over the Hudson River. It had taken us months to get there, but we had made it.

And Jackson was happy to wait. He continued to wait for me to feel ready to take things to the next step. No push, no pull, our own pace, without judgment from anyone outside our happy little bubble.

"The key is how much we have in common. My man and I both have curly hair and we love chocolate," I went on. "If that's not a solid foundation for a major relationship, I don't know what is."

Someone in the crowd yelled out: "I want chocolate!"

I didn't react but plowed on with my set.

"I'm serious about the curly hair thing. Hands up if you have curly hair? It's like having a child, right? Got a mind of its own! Tantrums! Costs so much money!" I declared, smiling at the heads bobbing in agreement. "You have to ask it nicely to behave on important days, buy the expensive stuff from the drugstore to maintain it, watch online videos about how to manage freak-outs—and you still wake up looking like Krusty the Clown."

I waved my hands at my hair, fluffing it out, letting the curls fall over my face.

"You straight-haired people will never understand what we go through. Oh, hello, Gwyneth Paltrow," I said, waving to a blond woman in the crowd with stick-straight, gleaming golden hair. "Listen, having curly hair gives you grit. It prepares you for the hardness of life. I'm telling you, if you are looking to hire someone on your team and you're in between two great candidates, choose the one with the curly hair. They go to battle every single morning and still manage to make it to work on time. It takes strategic planning, added dedication, and application of hot oil. There are limited career options that use those skills."

My eyes roamed the faces in the crowd as fresh laughter rippled through the audience. I spotted Katie in one corner, sitting at a small table with Kevin the photographer. I smiled when I caught her eye.

She had a notebook and was scribbling notes with a fuzzy pink pen. She was here to write a follow-up piece about me for *The Culturalist*, this time with my blessing. After I had been hired by Jordan B. Brown's comedy writing team, I had connected her with Phaedra to do a profile. The piece she had written about Phaedra helped her land the coveted reporter job she'd so desperately wanted.

And she was great at it.

"I think my boyfriend and I could only survive together in cosmopolitan cities like New York. What do you all think of London or Dubai? Dubai looks wild—has anyone here ever been there? Show of hands?" I said, shading my eyes and looking out into the audience. "Apparently, I have family there, and I'm dying to visit. They have the tallest tower in the world, an indoor ski slope with real penguins in the desert, and gold bar ATMs. Seriously? Like, who has a gold bar emergency? 'Honey, I'm going yacht shopping, do you think five gold bars will be enough?'"

I had spent a lot of time daydreaming about traveling to the Middle East lately, exploring my roots, meeting other Arab third-culture kids like myself, but I was nervous. It felt overwhelming to figure out where to go and if I would be welcomed by my extended family, if at all. I had never been out of New York, let alone America. But a cosmopolitan Arab city like Dubai—with a Nobu—seemed like a good place to start.

"Everyone is asking me if I hope to make it big one day, maybe land my own TV show or something, but my ambitions are much more specific," I said. "I want to fly to Dubai in one of those insane first-class cabins, in a plane that has a shower. Listen, I'm not a materialistic person. I don't like fancy handbags and don't care if my boyfriend doesn't have a car, but the idea of showering at thirty-five thousand feet is the closest I can get to heaven by wash-ing away my sins."

Someone in the audience shouted out about it being better than the shower in his tiny apartment. I gave him a thumbs-up. I felt like I could stay here onstage, drinking in everyone's laughter and acceptance of me, for hours. But I knew that one of the first rules of comedy was to quit while ahead, leaving people wanting a little more.

I waved at the audience, my heart swelling with pride as the clapping refused to subside. Jackson shouted: "Go, Mia-aooww, go!"

"What a wonderful crowd you have been tonight. You came in for a comedy show and got valuable life lessons," I said, nodding exaggeratedly. "Be kind to people with curly hair, eat that choco-late, and love who you want to love. And remember, Arabs were the first to put showers in planes. So even if your thoughts are dirty, you can keep your body clean."

The applause sounded like horses hooves, thundering in the small space. I could see the manager in the back nodding his head in approval. Performing here had been a lifelong dream, and the reality was even sweeter than I could have imagined.

Dad, this one's for you, I thought, closing my eyes briefly to feel the applause deep in my core.

Leaning over for my final words, I smiled and said: "I'm Mia Almas, and that's my time!"

Mic drop.

ACKNOWLEDGMENTS

I'm here. I'm finally, finally here. Some people hold a shampoo bottle in the shower and pretend it's an Oscar or a Grammy award, but I always spent time fantasizing about writing my acknowledgments section. How delicious will it feel to thank people who championed me along the way? This book took ten years to see the light because I was working full-time, had kids, survived a pandemic. . . . This moment feels as all-encompassing as when I had my two children, holding their warm little bodies against my chest for the first time at the hospital after long, hard pregnancies. So, thank you, first, for reading my book and finding your way here, right now, with me. I also want to thank myself for not giving up and divine providence for creating miracles. This moment is an honor.

Authors usually save their thank-yous to loved ones for the end, but it all started with family for me. Thank you to my parents, Lubna and Nabil Hamdan, for being the most caring, kind-hearted mother and father in the world and always encouraging me to travel, empathize with everyone, and aim for the sun. Your love and strength inspire me. Jamil, my husband and soulmate, thank you for reading every word, sharpening the stand-up scenes because you're a comedy expert, bringing me tea, talking through character problems as if they were real people, and entertaining the kids "so Mommy can write, it's important to her." My beautiful children, Adam and Serene, the next generation of third-culture kids who deserve a happy world: you bring so much meaning into my life. My wonderful sister, Lulu, for reading every draft and living each rejection and triumph as her own, and her husband, Alberto, for his kind words. I love our family with every cell in my body.

My grandmother, Teta Rawda, whose stories of her childhood in Jaffa and Gaza in the 1940s inspired many village scenes in the novel. Thank you, Patricia, my Irish mother-in-law with a giant Palestinian heart, for reading my early chapters and raising a son who turned out to be a great husband and father. My mom's helper, Lina, and my nanny, Siti, for helping to manage my crazy household—you are the reason I am able to focus on work and words, and why I didn't totally lose it during the pandemic.

I would have stopped along the way if not for the support of some magicians. Ahlam Bolooki, I will never forget sitting in the audience, listening to you announce the First Chapter: Emirates Literature Foundation Seddiqi Writers Fellowship in Dubai for those who dream of their books making it on the global stage. I had two completed manuscripts gathering dust in my drawer when the stars aligned thanks to you. You have become a sister to me. Isobel Abulhoul, your vision for the literary landscape of the Emirates changed my life. I was an attendee of the first Emirates LitFest, then a moderator, then eventually a panelist and author in my own right. The day my name flashed up on the Expo Dome after winning the Netflix Award was the moment I felt I could call myself a writer for the first time, and it's thanks to the two of you.

Hind Seddiqi, thank you for being our patron and benefactor for this incredible fellowship. Ahlam, Hind, and Isobel: your warmth and foresight are paving the way for a new generation of writers from the Middle East to share our stories in the biggest possible way. Dubai, thank you for being a city that pushes us to dream big . . . and where they come true.

I cannot wait to see more books out in the world from the fellows in my cohort of the First Chapter Seddiqi Fellowship: Muna Al Ali, Kate Tindle, Mustafa Al Rawi, Yi-Hwa Hanna, Zana Bonafe, and Moxie Anderson. Sarah Abdalla, fellow and soul sister, thank you for your beautiful energy. You were the first person outside of my family who I told about the book deal, walking along the beach, squealing in delight down the phone at each other. I can't wait to do the same for you. Annabel Kantaria, thank you for those coffee dates by the sea reassuring me that one day I'd make it, despite rejections—and those late-night frantic messages helping me choose an agent when I suddenly had them fighting to represent me. A huge thank-you to Carmel Rosato, Flora Rees, Faber Academy, Blue Pencil Agency, and my fantastic mentor Yrsa Sigurðardóttir for helping to polish my manuscript. Yrsa, your dedication to the craft, structured approach, and dry humor were such a perfect fit—thank you for going through multiple drafts with me! Thank you, Annabelle Corton, Gene Smith, Dania Droubi, and the entire LitFest team. I heart you.

I have a smile on my face thinking of my agents. Meredith Miller, from the first email exchange and call, I knew you were the perfect person to champion my work and become a lifelong partner. Thank you for your sunny attitude, your powerhouse negotiation skills, and your eagle eye for detail. Sheila Crowley, our relationship had a chance to build from the first time we met, in February 2020, when I moderated a panel for you at the Emirates LitFest. I feel so proud that my agent has also become my friend. Thank you for the priceless editorial insight. I am so blessed to call you both my agents. Ethan Schlatter, thank you for your reassuring emails and your positive attitude. Thank you to J. Davis, paired with me as my mentor at my day job with ties to the literary world, for connecting me with Meredith! You are an example of a true miracle in my life. Thank you to the incredible people at United Talent Agency, including Addison Duffy, Orly Greenberg, Jessica Rios, Tiffany Wang, Melissa Chinchillo, and Yona Levin, and at Curtis Brown, including Kate Burton, for your work on the book.

Thank you to Shannon Criss and Amy Einhorn at Henry Holt at Macmillan for outbidding the other publishers at auction and giving me a splashy book deal. The money is nice, but it's really the value placed on a story I wrote (at my dining table with kids fighting around me) that had me in awe. Maya Ziv, thank you for your genuine interest in the book—I think we could have made magic together and hope our paths will cross in the future. The biggest thank-you of all to Micaela Carr, an angel of an editor who found the book land in her lap and gave it so much heart and attention. I am so grateful that you were there for me as an expert editor and a happy presence. I am so excited to work on my next book with you! Thank you to everyone at Henry Holt and Macmillan, including Hannah Campbell and Clarissa Long.

To my friends Lauren Browne, Nour Brair, Tala Al Ramahi, Rasha Al Duwaisan, Kat Hicker, Rupert Wright, Dean Sree, Anita Quade, and Mariam Danielyan—you believed I could do this before I did. My ultimate work wife, Nour: I remember coming back to Google after my second maternity leave, wondering if I would ever have time to write a novel, and you told me, "It's okay if you don't." This gave me the push I needed to make this a priority someway, somehow. Kat, our coffees by the beach have been pure therapy and the best kind of friendship, thank you for living through the ups and downs of the publishing journey with me. Rasha, fellow writer and mom buddy, every chat inspires me.

Lauren, my writing soulmate—I can't wait to read your novel on the bookshelves someday soon. Mariam Danielyan, my former college roommate and bestie, your love of stand-up comedy inspired many of Mia's character traits!

Thank you to Bea Carvalho of Waterstones and the folks at *The Evening Standard* and Netflix UK for giving me a writing award for a little short story that was an excerpt from this novel. That night in London in 2021, amid the darkness of the surrounding pandemic, launched my career as an author. Thank you, Rami Al Ali, for the stunning dress that made all the papers run my photo, even though I was only runner-up for the Netflix story award.

To Sarah Khan, Neeta Bushan, Eric Preven, Anton Brisinger, and Anamika Chatterjee, thank you for spreading news about the exciting publishing journey before the book was even out. Your incredible support gave me a boost of confidence and shows what kind, generous hearts you have.

To Hana Jabri, your story of being part of the DACA program as an undocumented immigrant and getting a Harvard degree inspired many of the feelings Mia had in the novel. To David Yates at Tamimi & Co, thank you for working on my book contract for many, many months!

A humanitarian catastrophe is unfolding in Palestine as I type these words, and my hope is for peace, for a final end to suffering and the need to be so resilient for seventy-five years. My wish is for my children to be able to live in a future where they can experience true peace, to continue to be as proud of their Palestinian roots as they are of their ties to Greece, Ireland, the UAE, the UK, and the US, and to always celebrate differences and similarities across cultures. Because we're all human . . . and I believe in love.

I'll end this where I began: thank you to my beautiful family. Thank you for making me laugh and being there when times were tough. It's all about you, for you, inspired by you. Thank you for teaching me what love can do.